BLACKTHORN

EMILY EVE

EMILY EVE

To my fellow fantasy lovers & book nerds — this one's for you.

To Luke — I love you!

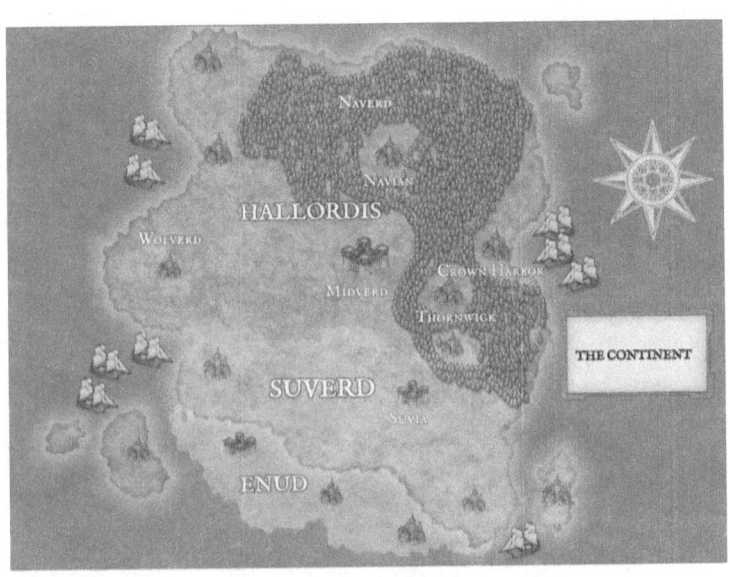

CHAPTER ONE

THE ASSASSIN WATCHED THE MAN BREATHE.

In, out. In, out.

It would be easy to kill him, she thought. *Too easy.*

He really should reevaluate the security in this place.

Her job tonight wasn't to kill him, though. In order to suffer, he needed to live.

As she took in Lord Frederick Stonewood's sleeping form, she thought he looked peaceful. Beautiful, even. Dark brown hair curled over his forehead, stirred by the gentle breeze coming from the open window. A cup of tea sat on the bedside table beside a large, leather-bound book.

Shifting his head on the pillow, he snored loudly. Very undignified, for a lord — especially for the son of the king's advisor.

Across the room, lurking in the shadows, the assassin wore a stolen servant's uniform. She tensed, hand reaching for the knife sheathed at her hip, and relaxed only when he settled down once more.

She shook her head to clear it of any wayward thoughts. She had a job to do.

1

Dodging several leaning book towers — some stacked as high as her waist — she crept towards the desk in the middle of the room. Her feet, clad in black silk slippers, made no sound on the plush carpet.

Papers covered almost every inch of the desk, the sort of things one would expect from a man known for his love of libraries and knowledge.

There was nothing unusual — for now.

The assassin removed the materials she'd hidden under her clothes. Leaflets from vocal citizens criticizing the king's unwarranted use of power. A small notebook written in an easily breakable cipher. A wanted poster for a member of the rebellion, complete with a scribbled note in its margin that looked suspiciously like the lord's handwriting. Several ledgers accounting for supplies not found within the castle walls. She tucked each of these in random spots.

Nothing too obvious — nothing that would stand out in the chaos on the desk. But if a letter arrived in the morning that claimed that the Lord of Navian was associated with the feared rebel group, the Amlucen . . .

Questions would be raised. Questions that the lord could not answer. Questions that might sow doubt among the king's inner circle, even if Lord Stonewood were to protest his innocence.

Doubt was a powerful weapon. Doubt could topple entire kingdoms.

Job done, she turned to make her escape. And stopped in her tracks.

Lord Stonewood wasn't sleeping anymore.

He stood in front of the door, dressed in a pair of loose-fitting nightclothes, hands in tight fists by his side.

"Who are you?" His voice came out in a low growl.

She cursed. How was he awake? His nightly tea should've

been laced with enough sleeping draught to knock him out for hours.

She weighed her options. She really, *really* didn't want to kill him — he was worth more alive. Killing him would complicate too much.

Maybe she could bluff her way out of it.

She gasped, raising a trembling hand to her heart. "I'm sorry, milord." She bobbed a curtsy, ever the flustered servant. "I didn't realize you were here — I don't see so well in the dark, milord, and I was supposed to come up to clean earlier, but Agnes in the kitchens needed help, so I was late coming in to clean —" She kept her head bowed, her gaze on the top of his bare feet.

"I don't recognize you. What's your name?"

She kept her head bowed. "Bonnie, milord. I'm new here. I'm so very sorry — this won't happen again, I swear, milord!"

Inwardly, she cursed again. She hadn't meant to use her real name, but she was flustered. She hoped her servant's uniform — all black — hid the outline of the knife sheathed at her hip.

"Get out." He moved to the side, leaving an open pathway to the door.

Bonnie schooled her face into a look of dismay, bobbing one more curtsy before making her way towards the exit. It took all of her willpower not to smile, annoyed as she was that things hadn't gone according to plan. At least she had planted the evidence needed to condemn him.

She reached out to turn the door handle.

"Wait."

Bonnie looked over her shoulder.

He stared at her, eyes narrowing. "I oversee staffing in the castle — we don't have a servant named Bonnie."

Damn it.

Lunging toward the door handle, she pulled it inward. She

heard his footsteps a moment later, saw his hand reach over her head to close the door.

Bonnie ducked out from under his arm, jumping to the side. She heard the deadbolt slide closed as she sprinted to the open window.

Boom!

She flew through the air, landing on the floor with a *thud*. She glanced back to see Lord Frederick stalking towards her, stepping over the pile of books she had tripped over.

Surging forward on her hands and knees, Bonnie tried to get to her feet. In her haste, she knocked into another one of those blasted book piles. She grabbed one as she jumped to her feet — it was *heavy* — and threw it at him. He let out a curse as the book hit him square on the chest.

Bonnie could feel the wind on her face as she neared the window. Only a few more steps to go . . . she bent her knees, prepared to jump. They were on the second floor of the castle — her landing would hurt like hell, but it wouldn't be fatal. She hoped.

As she bent her knees, she felt something grab the back of her shirt. A moment later she flew through the air once more, this time away from the window.

Pain flared — she hit another pile of books as she crashed to the floor.

Cursing, Bonnie stood and winced. She brushed her hair out of her face.

Lord Frederick had stopped by the window, hands on his knees, panting.

"Is this how you treat your servants?" she spat as she backed to the door. With every step she second guessed her decision not to kill him.

A grunt was his only reply. Then he glared at her. "Don't lie to me — you're no servant. Why are you here? Did Jasper send you?"

Bonnie paused. Why would his older brother send someone to his room? The spies in the castle had reported that Lord Jasper was visiting the king in Midverd.

Rumor had it there were problems between the two brothers, so close in age and yet so different. The Lord of Libraries and the Duke of Debauchery — it made sense that Lord Jasper would send someone to check in on his more ambitious younger brother.

"Yes," Bonnie lied. "Lord Jasper sent me. To check up on you, milord. I'm to report back to him in Midverd."

He blinked, eyes narrowing. "And what are you supposed to report back? Why were you looking at my desk?"

"To see if there was anything that may interest him, milord. Any reports you've been looking at, any letters you've received." She watched as he went to his desk, walking around it so he still faced her. Bonnie backed up another step when he looked down to study the papers littered there.

"You've got quite a big mouth for a spy."

"I'm no spy, milord. Just someone who needed a little extra coin to feed my family."

He sighed and massaged the spot in between his eyebrows with a finger. She resisted the urge to retreat another step.

"What do you plan on telling my brother?"

"I was going to tell him that there was nothing unusual to report, milord."

He shot her a look. "Oh?" He gestured to his desk. "Nothing at all?"

"Not that I saw, milord." Not that she could read, anyway.

He shifted a few pages before his fingers stilled. He looked at her, his gaze sharp. "You're a rebel," he breathed.

Damn it.

She launched herself across the room before he could say anything else, unsheathing the knife at her hip. She jumped on his desk, papers flying across the room, and landed a kick to his chest.

He stumbled backward with a groan, falling to the floor. Bonnie jumped off of the desk and landed on his chest. Her knife went to his throat.

"How did you know?" she asked. He couldn't live after this — not now that the plan had been so thoroughly destroyed. It wouldn't hurt to find out where she went wrong, though.

He froze, eyes wide. "My brother returned home this morning. He would *never* send someone to spy on me. And I know every single piece of paper that sits on my desk. You weren't here to spy for him. You *put* paper there, paper that I've never seen before. About the Amlucen."

"Smart boy," Bonnie purred. "It's a shame I have to kill you."

"No, you don't." He winced as she pressed her knife into his throat, leaving a thin line of blood in its wake.

"And why is that?"

"Because," he panted, the whites of his eyes showing. "I want to join you."

CHAPTER TWO

Twelve years earlier, when magic still existed within the borders of Hallordis, it would've taken a truth mage only seconds to determine whether Lord Stonewood was telling the truth.

Bonnie didn't have the luxury of letting someone else make the call. The only thing she had to rely on — that she *ever* had to rely on — was her gut.

And damn it, her gut was confused.

"What did you just say?" she said.

"You heard me," he said, a little louder. "I want to join you."

"*Liar.*"

There was no way they'd let him join; Lord Frederick stood for *everything* the Amlucen opposed. Surely he knew that.

"I swear it. Look in my desk drawer if you don't believe me."

Removing her knife, Bonnie got off his chest. But she kept it leveled at him as she stood. All it would take was a flick of her wrist and his blood would stain the lovely carpet.

It was tempting to do just that. The world would be a better place with one less loyal noble in it.

The papers littering the ground crunched under her feet as she backed toward his desk. "Where?"

"Top drawer. There's a false bottom."

"Sneaky, sneaky."

She took a moment to light the candle inside the brass lantern on the corner of the desk. Pulling open the heavy drawer, she grunted in surprise at the weight. A large, leather-bound book took up most of the space, along with some broken quills and an empty ink pot. It looked like a graveyard for old, broken things.

Bonnie set the book on the desk. Out of the corner of her eye, she saw him sit up. She tensed, glaring at him, but he held up his hands to show her that he was unarmed. She turned back to the drawer, and he watched in silence as she emptied the rest of the contents on the desk.

"In the back of the drawer, there's a —" He trailed off as she pulled on a brown velvet ribbon, the color a nearly identical shade to the inside of the drawer.

The bottom lifted, exposing the additional space beneath. There were dozens of papers stacked in a neat pile — everything from pamphlets to notebooks to drawings of different rebels. He had even got his hands on a detailed map of the country, complete with scribbled markings that circled different areas. It was concerning how close the markings were to a few of the actual hideout locations.

Looks like she didn't need to bring her own documents to plant on him after all. His personal collection was much more damning.

Leafing through everything, Bonnie tried to hide her surprise at the breadth of intel he'd collected. "How did you get these?"

"I told you already — I want to join your cause. But I needed to do my research first. Figure out what I was getting into."

Bonnie huffed a laugh. "Lord of Libraries, indeed."

He shot her a look.

"Who is your source?" she asked.

"I'm not going to tell *you*." She could feel his scorn from across the room.

"Why not?"

"I want to talk to someone in charge."

"How do you know *I'm* not in charge?"

He looked at her long enough that she felt self-conscious. Even from his position on the floor, he made her feel small.

Arrogant prick.

Bonnie's fingers stilled on a wanted poster of her adopted father. She frowned; it was an excellent likeness. She put that page on the bottom of the pile.

"Why join?" She used her knife to gesture around his bedchamber. "Why give all of this up?"

"I have my reasons."

Bonnie stabbed the knife in his direction. "Not good enough, *milord.*"

He swallowed, eyes following the blade. "Not everyone supports the king. My father lost *everything* when the king took over. He needs to pay. We have the same goal: remove him from power."

Bonnie chose not to point out that Lord Stonewood's father hardly lost everything, because what he said was true, in a fashion.

The tyrant known as King Rupert Aborn was the second-born son of the king and queen of Suverd, the largest country on the continent. Knowing that Thorstan, his elder brother, would become king upon his parent's abdication, Rupert had set his sights on creating a kingdom of his own.

And he did.

Over the course of a decade he had done the impossible: he united the small, warring countries north of Suverd and created a kingdom worth something. People watched as Hallordis, his new kingdom, became a powerhouse on the continent.

Slowly, over years, Aborn conquered the smaller, less powerful countries that bordered Hallordis in a never-ending quest to expand his borders.

The problem? He held onto his power through bloodshed, corruption, and an elite magical army. Thousands died under his rule, and with no checks to his power, he wasn't likely to be stopped. Power-hungry men like Lord Frederick's father kept him in power.

Duke Alistair Stonewood once ruled over the continent's northernmost country, Navian, but had been one of the few who allowed Aborn to take over without a power struggle. He and his sons — Jasper and Frederick — now ruled over northern Hallordis in Aborn's stead, with Duke Alistair also acting as the king's advisor.

And now it looked like the duke's son wanted to become the prince he would've been if his father hadn't given up his seat of power. Interesting.

She continued flipping through the papers, even as her mind raced. "And what exactly do we both want?"

"Freedom."

Bonnie narrowed her eyes. "You are a lord, born with a silver spoon in your mouth. Access to anything and everything you could ever need or want. What, pray tell, do you need to be free from?"

"Even those born in privilege can live in cages. It may look different from yours, but I am no more free than you."

If he was a liar, he was a good one. Every word that came out of his mouth seemed sincere. He sat tall, maintained eye contact, didn't fidget, showed no signs of deception.

"Why should we bother speaking with you?"

He shook his head. "I'll only share my information with Oll Blackthorn."

The nerve. Of *course* he'd assume that he'd get an audience with the leader of the rebellion. "What makes you think he'll deign to speak with you?"

"I'm the son of the king's advisor. He'll talk to me."

"You're pretty full of yourself, *milord*."

He shot her a look. Before he could reply, the sound of loud footsteps sounded from outside the room.

Bonnie ran behind where Lord Frederick still sat and crouched behind him. He hissed as her knife made contact with the tender spot on his throat.

"Freddieeee!" a male voice sang. "Freddieeee! Come plaaaaay!" The sound of uneven footsteps got louder, as if whoever approached wasn't steady on his feet.

"Who's that?" she whispered.

"Jasper."

"Say one word and you're dead."

"He'll try to come in if I don't say something," he hissed.

"I should just kill you now, *Freddie*."

A sharp intake of breath. "There's going to be a raid on a rebel hideout in one week's time. Take me to Oll Blackthorn and I'll tell him everything I know."

Her hand stilled, the knife still at his throat.

Shit. If he was right . . .

Bonnie lowered her knife. "Get rid of him."

Lord Stonewood stood with a wince and went to the door. Bonnie followed, pressing the knife into his lower back. She wasn't taking any chances.

Knock knock knock. Lord Jasper pounded on the door, shouting for his brother again.

Lord Frederick took a deep breath and opened the door. He stuck his head out. "What do you want, Jas? I'm trying to sleep."

Bonnie could smell the alcohol fumes emanating from the

elder Stonewood son from where she stood out of sight. It was like he'd bathed in beer. How was he functioning at this point? She wasn't sure if she was disgusted or impressed.

"Freddie!" he slurred. "Come and drink with me. I've missed you, brother."

"No, Jas — I need to sleep. I, uh, have a busy few weeks ahead."

She heard liquid sloshing around a bottle. Lord Jasper burped. "Whatcha doing? Why are you busy?"

"Err — I'm leaving for a few weeks."

"Why?"

Bonnie gripped her knife tighter, waiting for him to slip up. Was it a Stonewood family trait to ask so many bloody questions?

"An acquaintance of mine found a rare manuscript I've wanted to get my hands on. I'll drink with you when I'm back."

"You and your books! You're no fun." Another burp.

Lord Frederick forced a laugh. "That's nothing new, Jasper. Go get some sleep. I'll see you soon."

A pause. "You're not seeing *her*, are you?"

Lord Frederick went rigid beside Bonnie. "No. Go to sleep."

Interesting. Bonnie wondered who *she* was. She added it to a list of questions she wanted to ask dear old *Freddie*.

"Freddie. What happened to your neck?"

Tensing, Bonnie calculated how she could dispatch both brothers if she had to. She had forgotten the knife wound she had given him earlier. It luckily hadn't bled too much.

Lord Frederick lifted his hand to his throat and winced. "Oh, this? I cut myself shaving. Too distracted by a good book." Another forced laugh. "I'll see you soon. Go sober up."

Lord Jasper groaned. "Fine, fine." He sighed, rather melo-dramatically. "Goodnight, dear brother."

The sound of his retreating footsteps echoed along the stone hallway, but Bonnie didn't relax her grip on the knife until she was sure he was gone. Stepping back, she re-sheathed it.

Lord Frederick raised an eyebrow. "Trust me now?"

"No, I don't." But she couldn't threaten him at knifepoint every time they ran into someone. Because if he was right, and there *was* an attack planned against the Amlucen . . . Bonnie couldn't ignore that possibility.

"I've made my decision — you're coming with me. Just remember that I'll gut you in a heartbeat if I think you're lying to me."

He swallowed but said nothing.

"Who was he referring to?" she asked. "The woman he thought you were going to see?"

He frowned. "None of your business."

More secrets from the Lord of Libraries. He was turning out to be more interesting than she had expected.

"Pack clothes. And change what you're wearing. Wouldn't want you to be seen in your nightclothes, *milord*."

He muttered something under his breath before walking to his wardrobe. Bonnie watched as he started filling a leather satchel. He chose well — plain items, bare of adornment. While they were of fine make, he wouldn't stand out.

But who was he trying to fool? He would *always* stand out, no matter what he wore. Not only was he a head taller than most, there was something about the way he bore himself that marked him as different. Other. While his broad shoulders could pass as ones that worked hard harvesting wheat in the fields or cutting down timber, he didn't act defeated like the rest. He stood tall and proud, where others were stooped and weak.

Hardship and oppression did that to people. Bonnie doubted he had ever suffered a day in his life.

She went to his desk and stared at the map that had a few of the rebel hideouts circled in black ink. Was he telling the truth?

They had dozens of hideouts across the country. Which one was compromised?

How many more of her friends and family would die at the hand of the monster who ruled the country?

Bonnie noticed that he kept glancing at her. She raised an eyebrow. "What?"

He shook his head. "Nothing." He continued to stuff items into his satchel.

Bonnie gestured to herself. "Like what you see?"

The Amlucen had done their research. Or tried to, anyway. While Lord Jasper romanced just about anyone — blondes, brunettes, redheads, slim, curvy, male, female, you name it — Lord Frederick was more . . . *discreet* about his personal life.

He snorted. "No."

"Then why do you keep looking at me?" Maybe curvy, brunette women weren't his type after all. Didn't matter either way. She doubted Oll would let him live much longer. Not if killing him would make a bigger statement than using him for his intel.

"It's just . . . you look familiar."

"We haven't met before."

"No," he said, turning back to his wardrobe. "I would've remembered."

For a man at a disadvantage, he sure wasn't afraid of insulting her. The urge to threaten him with the knife at her hip grew stronger.

"Hurry up, *Freddie*," she snapped. "This is taking too long."

He shot her a look, his face set in a scowl. "Don't call me that."

Bonnie smirked. "Why not? Lord Jasper can call you Freddie, but I can't?"

"Jasper is my brother." He didn't need to remind her that Jasper was also his equal, something she would never be. He didn't have to say it; his disapproving tone said enough. "Is your real name even Bonnie?"

"Yes," she answered. Not a lie — not as far as she could remember, anyway.

In truth? She had no idea if Bonnie was her given name. She had no recollection of anything that had happened to her before the age of eight, thanks to the head wound that left her with a jagged scar that stretched from her temple to the top of her right ear.

Aborn's men had brutally murdered her parents twelve years ago. She only survived the massacre thanks to the quick thinking of a rebel named Gwyneth, who saved her life before raising her as her own.

The lasting damage of that night had left her with more than just memory loss and an ugly scar, but Lord Frederick certainly didn't need to know about that. She had taken pains to cover the scar with carefully braided hair, so even if they traveled together he wouldn't get close enough to see it.

"Fine." He shouldered his bag. "Should I leave a note?"

"Why?"

"In case someone wonders where I've disappeared to."

"You told your brother."

He scoffed. "You really think he'll remember anything about our conversation?"

Fair point. "Make it short."

He scribbled something on a piece of paper, the hand-writing unintelligible. He held it up to her to approve.

Bonnie stared at the note for a second, willing her brain to make sense of the writing. It looked like a jumble of random lines and symbols. She could recognize individual letters but had never been able to put them together in a way her mind could comprehend.

No matter how hard she tried, no matter how long she studied, Bonnie had never been able to read or write. After the attack it had taken months to relearn how to speak the common tongue, but the lasting trauma made it hard to do anything else.

Not that she didn't try. Or suffer the migraines that came when she forced herself to focus.

Bonnie glanced away. "It's fine," she lied. "Leave it on the desk."

He looked contemplative as he set the note down. "I'm ready."

"Let's go."

CHAPTER THREE

BONNIE TRIED NOT TO FIDGET AS THEY ENTERED THE CASTLE courtyard.

On her own she wouldn't warrant a second glance — just a lone servant, happy to go home for some well-earned rest.

But with the lord of the city trailing behind her like a lost child?

It was a wonder that she hadn't already been questioned by the nosy onlookers.

If Lord Jasper had been the one leaving the castle in the dead of night, it would be one thing — the patrons of the various local taverns wouldn't blink an eye if he strolled around with an unfamiliar woman.

But the respectable Lord of Libraries? Unheard of.

Bonnie cursed herself for not taking the time to disguise him, but she'd hoped that the castle grounds would be empty at this late hour. She wasn't sure changing his appearance would do anything, anyway — a man like him would always stand out among mere common folk.

The few guards and servants who were still awake bowed

when they approached. A few glanced at each other with raised eyebrows.

Bonnie turned to see Freddie following a few paces behind. The flickering light of the courtyard torches turned his face harsh, and he walked rigidly, hands balled into fists at his sides.

No wonder people were looking at them with surprise. He looked like he was walking to his own execution.

She surveyed the courtyard, fiddling with the end of her braid. One guard, standing by the castle gate — a handsome man with golden hair — perked up when he saw them. He nudged the guard next to him. Both men frowned, and the one with golden hair put his hand on the hilt of his sword.

Shit.

Forcing a sultry smile to her lips, Bonnie slowed until she was only a step in front of Lord Stonewood. She fluttered her lashes. "Smile at me," she ordered, low enough that no one else could hear.

"What?"

"Act like you like me. Smile a little. Blush. Do something that makes it look like we're going home together."

He looked flustered. "What? Me . . . with *you?*"

Rude. Bonnie swore to the gods that if he didn't follow her instructions she would stab him and run, raid or no raid.

"*Yes,*" she hissed. "People are looking. At us. Right now. We need to give them a reason why we're leaving the castle so late together."

"Wouldn't we have just stayed in the castle? Why go to your place?"

She faked a giggle, the sound shrill even to her own ears. "Who cares? Act like you're interested in me. *Now.*"

His hand tugged at her wrist a moment later.

She came to a stop. Gone was the broody, awkward man who had been trailing behind her. Bonnie didn't know if it was the smile that lit his face, the sultry look in his honey-colored eyes, or if she had sustained a head wound that she had forgotten about, but she almost stepped back in surprise. His large hand came up to cup her face, warm and comforting. The other hand came up to untie the string that held together the end of her braid. His fingers started stroking through the different strands, freeing them. She couldn't stop the shiver that raced through her as their eyes met.

A shiver of disgust, obviously.

"Like this?" His thumb stroked her cheek. She leaned into it, despite herself.

"Yes," Bonnie breathed.

He leaned forward, his gaze moving between her eyes and her lips. His free hand gently set her unbound hair behind her ear. She watched his eyes widen, just a fraction, as he felt what she had carefully hidden under her braid. His fingers stilled as he felt the raised ridge of her scar.

Bonnie froze. Made to pull back. She didn't need his judgment, or his pity. What was she even doing right now?

He tightened his grip on her chin, his eyes searching her green ones. He leaned forward. "How was that?" he whispered in her ear.

Bonnie swiveled her head, planting a kiss on his cheek before he could react. He froze, and she stepped back. "Good, milord. Very good."

She slipped her hand into his as they continued walking. She was relieved to see that his cheeks were as pink as hers felt. His hand was warm and solid, and it made her feel delicate and small.

Bonnie shook her head, even as she kept the dumb, love-struck smile on her face.

The servants had turned away, no doubt to start the gossip that would circulate as soon as the sun came up. Only the brown-haired guard remained at his station, the golden-haired one nowhere to be seen. He bowed as they approached, smirking as he glanced at their joined hands. Freddie nodded at him, a self-satisfied smirk lighting up his own face.

The smile dropped as soon as they made it through the castle gates.

Good. No more playing at romance.

She released his hand, and he wiped his palm on his dark breeches.

Rude.

He kept pace as they navigated through Navian's city streets. Freddie's father had turned the once-sparsely populated, rough northern territory into a bustling metropolis.

Sure, the city still had unsavory areas, where the destitute scraped by to live another day. It'd be hard to find a city that didn't have its fair share of problems, after all. But as far as cities went, this one wasn't too bad. Most of the homes and shops, all made of the pine trees that Navian exported to other territories, were in good repair, and the streets were clean. Despite herself — and she would never, *ever* let Freddie know this — she didn't mind when her assignments took her here.

They walked in silence down the cobblestone streets. Freddie fidgeted at her side.

"Where are we going?"

Bonnie figured the man wouldn't be able to keep quiet for long. "Hideout."

"But *where*?"

She glared at him. "You'll see soon enough, *Freddie*."

He stiffened, but fell quiet. She led him down a series of empty, nondescript streets, moving further away from the main road.

A few streets later, Bonnie turned into a random alleyway. Freddie stopped at the entrance, nose wrinkling.

"What?" she said, as she navigated past heaps of rotten trash. "Too smelly for your pretty little nose?"

He grumbled something under his breath in Naverian

before he followed, his long legs stepping over the putrid puddles easier than she could. He swallowed nervously when he saw the ramshackle door she held open.

He peered inside the darkened hole that sat beyond the door. "Is this where you're going to murder me?"

Bonnie snorted. "If I wanted to kill you — and believe me, milord, I'm tempted — you would already be dead. Get inside."

He was taller than the doorframe and had to crouch to enter. She closed the door behind her, first checking to see if they were followed. All was clear.

The room was dark, for not even the moonlight could penetrate the boards that covered the windows. Bonnie went to the small table set against the far wall and took a moment to light the lone wax candle that sat upon it. The flickering light made the shadows dance on the walls.

A long counter ran down one side of the room. Cabinets lined the other walls, filled with mismatched pottery and other kitchen wares. A cold stone hearth was in the corner, a few chairs scattered in front of it. There were two other doors leading into the rest of the hideout, but it was too dark to see into either of them.

"Why are we here?" he asked.

Bonnie ignored his question as she grabbed her satchel. She needed her supplies, and to change out of her stolen servant's uniform. Keeping her back to him, she quickly stripped off her clothes.

"Woah!" Freddie exclaimed. "Give a man some warning!"

Bonnie shot a wicked look over her shoulder. Freddie stood there, wide-eyed and pink-cheeked as he looked at her backside. At least she was wearing undergarments.

When he noticed her looking, he turned and faced the other wall. She sniggered as she dressed in a dark sweater and pair of warm breeches.

"Where are we going?" Freddie asked, his voice a little strained.

Bonnie's smile faded. "Crown Harbor."

She didn't relish the thought of riding hard to the port city, but time was of the essence. They would need to be quick, if his intel proved true. They needed time to warn the others, time to evacuate her people. Time to prepare a counterattack.

She reevaluated the contents of her satchel. Blanket, spare change of clothes, an apple, bread, cheese. Her cloak, a little worse for wear. A few coins. It would do until they could stop somewhere to replenish her items. She had planned on staying in Navian to see the outcome of her mission, and thought she had time to get supplies for the journey back. She didn't even have a horse.

Bonnie blew out the candle and made her way to the door, his soft footsteps following close behind.

She paused before opening the rickety wooden door. She couldn't put her finger on it, but something felt wrong. Off. She held up a hand to stop him, taking only a second to note how firm his chest felt under her hand.

"What is it?" He breathed into her ear.

She shook her head, concentrating. Leaning forward, she pressed her eye against the peephole.

"Shit." She drew her blade from its sheath.

"What is it?" he repeated.

"The golden-haired guard from the castle — the one who disappeared. Do you know him?"

"Yes. Simon." He sounded confused. "What about him?"

"He's snooping around outside." She moved behind and stuck her knife into the small of his back. He froze and sucked in a breath. "Did you communicate with him, *Freddie*? Tip him off?"

"Of course not," he snapped. "How could I?"

Bonnie dug the knife a little deeper and he let out a hiss. "I don't know, but I wouldn't put it past you. You're a sneaky bastard."

"I *didn't*. I swear it. He must've known something was wrong and followed us here."

Despite her misgivings, Bonnie believed him. She stepped away, withdrawing the knife. "Fine. No problem. I'll get rid of him." She put her hand on the doorknob.

"*No*," Freddie said, dragging her away from the door.

"Get your hands off me," she ordered, "or you will lose them." She waited until he let her go before continuing. "We need to leave. Now. He's in our way. It's not my fault he's a nosy bastard."

"Don't kill him," Freddie insisted. "He's a friend. Please."

"No." She turned back towards the door.

"Imagine how suspicious it would look if I disappeared *and* a dead guard was discovered. Think about how complicated that would make everything. We wouldn't make it to Crown Harbor before we were hunted down."

Bonnie paused, her hand on the doorknob.

Shit, she thought. *He's right. If only we weren't short on time . . .*

She turned back to him. "Fine — he lives. We need to find another way out of here."

CHAPTER FOUR

FREDDIE LOOKED AROUND THE RAMSHACKLE SPACE, SPYING THE two other doors. "Do those lead anywhere?"

Bonnie grabbed his hand, dragging him toward the one on the right. He jerked back, threatening to pull away, before grasping it and following behind.

"How big is this place?" he asked as she dragged him through a series of rooms, climbing up a staircase as they moved through the building. They weaved through discarded furniture, bed pallets, and other odds and ends that were stored haphazardly throughout the space.

Bonnie didn't answer. He didn't need to know that the Amlucen had purchased the entire block of neighboring houses and then knocked down the interior walls to make one giant building.

As with any good secret hideout, this house had several boltholes they could use to make their escape. But which one was best? A few had been closed off, either too risky or too rundown to use safely. There was a window ahead that led to a balcony, or there was a small bolthole that led into a secluded alleyway they could use.

A quick glance at Freddie had Bonnie shelving that idea immediately — his shoulders were far too broad. Balcony window escape was their only option.

She dragged him to the right, veering towards a tall wardrobe that sat along the far wall. He whistled appreciatively when she opened the wardrobe door and he saw another room beyond. Bonnie let go of his hand with a smirk before climbing inside.

"Shut the doors behind you," she told him as she continued on.

This room was empty, save for the lone window on the far wall.

"Where now?" Freddie asked. "We're at a dead end."

Bonnie jerked her head to the window. "This is where we exit."

His eyes widened.

Bonnie peered outside, keeping out of sight. The street was crowded with working-class people — drunkards singing bawdy songs as they stumbled down the street, working girls trying to sell their bodies to whoever was willing to pay their fee, little street urchins running around, hoping to find an easy mark.

And, most importantly, she did not see any nosy soldiers sniffing around, trying to ruin her night.

She stifled a gasp when a whisper sounded in her ear. "Are you sure this is the right way to go? It's busy out there."

Sneaky bastard; Bonnie hadn't heard him make his way behind her. Where did he learn to move so quietly? "Exactly," she whispered. "Less chance we'll be noticed."

"True." He still sounded doubtful.

Bonnie tugged the neckline down so that her sweater hung off her shoulder. She tousled her long, brown hair, now freed from its braid, and licked her lips. Before he could protest, she stood on her tiptoes and planted a more solid kiss on his cheek, making sure her red lipstick transferred to his cheek.

He reared his head back, pink coloring his cheeks. "What was that for?"

"Our cover," she said simply. She reached her hands up and tousled his hair for good measure. He glared at her.

Bonnie took another look outside. "Do you recognize anyone?"

He studied the people on the street for a moment before shaking his head.

"Good. When we reach the ground, act the same way we did at the castle. Hold my hand, flirt with me, things like that. Make it look convincing."

"Where are we going once we're down there?"

"We need to make it to the outskirts of the city."

It took a moment to raise the window and make it onto the balcony, Freddie following a step behind. He closed the window as Bonnie peered over the railing.

"Shit."

He was at her side a second later. "What is it? Another guard?"

Bonnie shook her head and pointed to the balcony.

The ladder was gone.

Or, most of it was gone — the last six feet were rotted. She judged the distance from the balcony and shook her head. Too far to jump. It wouldn't be a fatal plunge, but she didn't want to risk broken bones.

Twelve years ago, a broken bone would be nothing to worry about — a quick trip to a local healer would sort out any issues immediately.

Back then, people were blessed with a variety of magical powers. Those with healing powers were coveted, as well as those blessed in the fighting arts. Those with the ability of persuasion or mind reading were feared, even while being heavily sought after by the king.

Now? Magic was gone, at least in Hallordis. It still existed in other lands. No one knew why, although the Amlucen had their theories.

Vale Magicae, people called it. The day magic disappeared.

A broken bone was something to be feared now. One *could* see a physician, skilled in knowledge but with no magic to aid in healing. A sad excuse for the way things used to be.

At least that's what Bonnie had been told. She had no recollection of a time when magic existed.

"Shit," Bonnie repeated, biting her lip. They could go back in the house and try another exit, she supposed, but what if Simon had entered the hideout by now? How far would he go to find his wayward lord?

Freddie leaned over the balcony railing. "We could jump."

Bonnie shook her head. "Too far. We'd risk breaking a leg." Or worse.

He judged the distance again. "I'm taller than you — it'll be fine. I'll catch you."

She gestured to herself. "I'm too heavy."

He rolled his eyes. "I'll catch you."

Rocking back on her heels, Bonnie eyed him warily. He *looked* strong enough. And they were running out of options. She blew out a breath. "Fine." She gestured to the railing. "You first."

He shook the balcony railing to test its strength. Deeming it sturdy enough, he hopped over.

It was a testament to how rowdy the streets were that no one noticed when a large man dropped out of the sky and landed with a *thud* into their midst.

Bonnie could tell immediately that something was wrong. Freddie's shoulders caved inwards after he landed, his hands in tight fists. He didn't put any weight on his right ankle, instead dangling it a few inches above the ground.

It might've been a trick of the light, but he also *looked* paler, as if pain leeched all his color away.

He must've landed wrong. Bonnie *knew* this idea was stupid. What an idiot. And she was an idiot for agreeing to it.

Bonnie was about to tell him she would find some other way down when he turned to her, grimacing. He raised his hands towards her.

"You're injured," Bonnie called down.

He gestured impatiently. He looked better, even a few moments later — he stood solidly on both feet, and the color was returning to his face. No sign of clenched fists. Had she misread the signs?

"Jump," he told her, and she swore every ounce of his noble arrogance was shoved into that one syllable.

Fine. He wanted her to jump? She'd jump. Not her fault when she broke his body upon impact.

Still, she hesitated.

"Come on, sweetheart," he sang.

A few curious passersby looked her way. A drunk courtesan tittered merrily at her predicament, while a vagabond leered from his perch on a nearby stoop.

Oh, what a *bastard*. Now she had an audience.

"I'll catch you, my darling honeybum," he called up with a smirk. "Just jump!"

"Oi! Honeybum!" the drunkard jeered. "Jump!"

"Coming, my sweet love muffin," Bonnie called down through gritted teeth. Maybe she would stab him for this.

"Okay, Bonnie," she muttered to herself as she took a few deep breaths. "You can do this. Don't look down — or, wait, *do* look down — don't miss where he's standing or you'll break something . . ." Her heart raced, and she found it difficult to get in a deep breath. She took a step back, still holding the balcony railing in a white-knuckled grip.

"Trust me," he called, a little less loudly, but a little more sincere.

That was the thing, wasn't it? Bonnie wasn't sure if she *could* trust him.

But she didn't really have a choice.

Bonnie took one last breath before she launched herself over the railing.

Air whooshed by as she plunged toward the ground. As she opened her mouth to scream — her final one before her body became irreparably damaged, no doubt — everything stopped, her body coming to a standstill.

Opening her eyes, Bonnie met his honey-colored ones. *His eyelashes are unfairly long*, she thought in a daze. *Pretty eyes are wasted on him.*

"Hi," he said.

"Hi," she blinked back at him.

Someone whistled nearby, and Freddie's head whipped toward the sound. Shaking her head, she pushed against his chest. He lowered her to the ground.

Taking a moment to straighten her clothing, she surveyed her surroundings. While her descent had garnered some attention, most people had already grown bored and found other diversions.

Freddie took her hand and started leading her down the street. Bonnie followed behind blindly for a moment before coming to her senses. She tore her hand from his grasp.

"Where do you think you're going?" she hissed.

He raised an eyebrow. "I figured we needed to get a move on. We need to make sure that Simon doesn't follow us, right?"

"Yes. But we're going the wrong way."

He had the good sense to look sheepish as he scratched his neck, messing up his hair. "Oops. Lead the way then, my lady."

Bonnie took his arm, once again playing the part of interested lover. "Lady, huh? Don't let anyone else hear that kind of talk."

She steered them toward the outskirts of the city. They needed horses, and fast. The Amlucen had a stable full of them nearby, but the last thing she wanted was to show Freddie another valued secret.

Or worse — lead Simon to them. Bonnie didn't doubt he was still around somewhere, searching for the man who swaggered next to her.

"Sweetcheeks," Bonnie murmured. She felt him tense as he lowered his head to listen. "Do you have any money?"

"Some," he hedged. "How much do you need?"

"Enough for horses." She saw his eyes widen a fraction. "Or we could steal some. Or I could kill someone and we could take theirs." She couldn't help but enjoy herself as some of the color drained from his face.

"I might have enough," he finally replied. "We'll have to see how much they're charging."

Eventually, they stopped at a livery on the outskirts of the city. Freddie approached the pot bellied man who lurked under one of the few lanterns lit at this hour. It cast eerie shadows along the ground.

"We need to buy two horses," Freddie told him.

The man looked at the two of them shrewdly. He responded in Naverian. Freddie shook his head and responded in kind, frowning.

Bonnie scowled. She hated being left out of conversations. An occurrence that, unfortunately, was all too common thanks to the scar hidden by her hair.

Freddie turned to her, obviously aware she wasn't following the conversation. "Honeybum," he said, leaning close. "He's asking for two gold sovereigns."

"*Two gold sovereigns?* Who does he think we are? That's robbery!"

The man shrugged. The lamplight glinted off the top of his balding head as he said something to Freddie in Naverian.

Whatever he said had Freddie moving out of the glow of the lantern, his face now covered in shadow.

Freddie turned to Bonnie. "He told me I look familiar."

Bonnie grabbed Freddie's arm. "Not good. Let's go try a more *reasonable* place —"

Words died in her throat as she squinted down the street. Were her eyes deceiving her, or did she see a familiar golden-haired guard walking this way? She clutched Freddie's arm and felt him turn.

He swore in Naverian.

Luckily for them, Simon moved down an alleyway a moment later.

Freddie turned back to the stable master and held out one gold sovereign. The man eyed it greedily, and Freddie pulled it out of reach when he tried to take it. Freddie issued a list of demands — at least, that's what it sounded like to Bonnie's untrained ear. The man's expression soured, but he made his way inside.

Freddie took Bonnie's hand and led her into the stable. "One horse," he told her under his breath. "One horse, with all the equipment and food we need for a journey to Crown Harbor."

She followed as he went from stall to stall, looking over their options. The scent of fresh hay and manure made her nose tickle.

"Only one?" she whispered as he evaluated the horses in each stall, pausing only long enough to get a good look before dragging her onward. She gestured between the both of them with her free hand. "We're not small people. One horse won't be enough."

He stopped in front of the stall at the very end of the row. A horse that stood much taller than the others peered out of his stall. His brown coat looked in need of a brush, but he seemed healthy enough.

"Our size won't matter if we have a horse big enough," he said as he stared inside the stall.

Bonnie couldn't help but shiver. It seemed as if the beast was aware of what was going on as he looked between the two of them.

Then the horse looked over her shoulder and bared his teeth.

"Oh, I wouldn't choose *that* one, sir," the stable master said in heavily accented common tongue. He gave the horse a stern look as he took a step back. "Brute."

The horse snapped his teeth in his direction. Apparently there was no love lost between the two.

Freddie stared at the horse thoughtfully. "We'll take him. Get his tack and we'll be off."

The man bristled for a moment before dashing off again. He returned, throwing a heap of gear onto the ground.

Freddie bent over the pile, picking up a few pieces and inspecting them. Satisfied, he tossed him the gold coin. The man grabbed it, eyes flashing with greed, before he fled.

The horse seemed calmer now that the stable master had left, and he looked at Bonnie with large, baleful eyes.

"Easy there, lad," Freddie said as he approached, fishing a carrot out of the feed bag in front of the stall. The horse nipped at Freddie's hand gently before eating the treat, and Freddie began saddling him.

Bonnie approached, holding her hand up to his big nose. He blew hot air in her direction — sad that she didn't come bearing treats, but still happy to see her. He nuzzled her with his large velvet nose, and she gave him a cheeky pat.

They led him out of the stable and into the dark night

within minutes. There was no sign of their golden-haired stalker, but Bonnie knew better than to let her guard down. He was still out there — and more clever than he first appeared. How did he find them this close to the edge of the city? They were nowhere near the rebel hideout, nor the castle.

No time to speculate. Bonnie looked at the horse — he was *huge* — and tried to gauge whether she could mount on her own. She looked around for a mounting block when she felt a pair of powerful hands grip her sides.

She felt all the air leave her body as she was lifted into the saddle. Freddie ignored her glare, too busy eyeing the surrounding area.

"Ready?" he asked.

Bonnie shivered as his warm breath tickled the back of her neck. "Let's go."

CHAPTER FIVE

"STOP LOOKING BACK," BONNIE HISSED AS THEY EXITED THE CITY gates.

She could sense him turning around every few seconds. She kept her eyes on a constant rotation ahead of them, trying to see if she could spot anything in the dense forest they were approaching.

Bonnie felt him turn back to the front. "I want to make sure no one's following us."

"You're making us look suspicious. Keep your guard up, but face forward. We can look behind after we enter the forest."

He grumbled but stayed silent.

The land beyond the city gates was bare — no trees, no shrubbery, no rocks marred the barren landscape. A safety measure enacted to ensure that no one could sneak up to the city walls once they exited the expansive Golwich Forest.

They traveled over the bare land in silence until they came to the edge of the ancient pinewood forest. A shiver ran down Bonnie's spine at the sight of the towering trees that were still cast in nighttime darkness.

She had never gotten used to it, the feeling that seemed to

wash over her every time she traveled through Golwich. She doubted she ever would. People whispered about how magic still lingered here, twelve years after it disappeared from the rest of Hallordis. Others claimed Golwich was where magic originated eons ago, which is why its essence lingered long after all other magic had gone.

For good or ill, this place always left Bonnie feeling unsettled. Like she was constantly being watched. Spied on. As if the trees and the plants and the animals were all watching her. Not necessarily in a malicious or dangerous way, but still. She felt their presence.

Freddie shivered as they crossed the border and she knew he felt the same way.

They traveled in silence, their giant steed trudging along under them, and saw no one else on the packed dirt road. They pulled off into the trees as the sun started rising over the distant horizon. There had been no sign of the guard over the hours they traveled, and Bonnie didn't want to risk injury by pushing forward too hard; it was time to rest.

They stopped and dismounted a safe distance from the road. Bonnie led the horse to a nearby stream, letting him drink his fill, before settling him to graze by a patch of wild grass.

After patting him on the neck a few times, Bonnie turned to Freddie, stifling a yawn. "We should rest for a few hours. We'll be useless if we don't get some sleep."

The horse stepped to where Bonnie was standing and nuzzled her.

"He likes you," Freddie said as he took care of unsaddling the beast.

Bonnie shrugged. "Animals like me. Not sure why." With one last pat, she stood back and looked the horse over. "We need to name him." She frowned, recalling the words of the stablemaster. "Something better than Brute."

"Do you have one in mind?"

Now that she could see him better, Bonnie saw he was less of a dull brown color and more of a chestnut. He needed a brush, but he still shone in the weak morning light. There were white socks on three of his legs, along with a beautiful white star on his face.

Despite his beauty, she still couldn't get over how massive he was. "Big Boy. Giant Killer. Alternatively, Tiny."

He snorted. "While, er, *creative*, I don't think any of those suit him very well."

"Well, milord," she scoffed, "what did you have in mind?"

"What about . . . Captain?"

Bonnie held back her snort as she considered the suggestion. It wasn't the best name, sure, but . . . it was apt. He looked like the type of horse that someone in command would ride.

"Fine. I hereby dub thee Captain," Bonnie told the horse seriously. "Rest now, noble steed. We'll set out in a few hours."

Turning, Bonnie went over to where she left the bag of supplies she'd grabbed from the hideout. Taking out a slightly stale bit of crusty bread, she ripped it half and tossed a piece to Freddie. He caught it deftly, but made a face when he studied it further. As Bonnie turned back to her pack, she swore she caught him sniffing it.

Arrogant prick. He was in for a rude awakening if he was serious about joining the Amlucen. No fancy dinners among rebels, unfortunately.

Bonnie hid a smirk. Maybe she wouldn't have to work too hard to get him to give up his dream to become a rebel. As long as he gave her the intel she needed, he could go back to his life as a spoiled noble and she could save her family.

Unless, of course, Oll Blackthorn decided Freddie was too much of a liability. In which case, his life was forfeit.

Not her problem.

Taking a woolen blanket out of her satchel, Bonnie laid it

on the ground by the foot of a tree. She groaned as she sat, her entire body protesting at the motion. She would need a very long, very hot bath as soon as this nonsense was over.

Freddie ambled over, Captain now grazing under a nearby tree. He took a blanket out of his bag and laid it down a few feet from her. He grunted as he sat down.

"Sore?"

"Yes," he admitted, no shame whatsoever. "Don't pretend that you aren't. I heard you groan when you sat down."

Bonnie rolled her eyes but said nothing. Insufferable man. She jerked her head to his blanket. "You first. I'll wake you up in two hours."

"I don't mind taking the first watch —"

"No," she cut him off. "I'll wake you in two hours."

He looked like he was going to say something — complain, no doubt — but held his tongue.

No, she wouldn't let him keep the first watch. Not so close to Navian, and not so soon after leaving its walls. Maybe he could take watch in a few days, far away from the people his family ruled over. It was a miracle that no one on the street had recognized him — although altogether not surprising. Bonnie had found that people of his status rarely dealt with the common peasants.

She settled in against a tree. Freddie's deep, even breathing was the only sound in their little clearing, apart from the occasional movement from Captain as he found new grass to graze on. Birds chirped from the sky, and a chipmunk scurried down a nearby tree and settled in her lap. She stroked its soft fur as she surveyed the area.

It was peaceful, but Bonnie couldn't relax. Not when the safety of her friends depended on her.

The two hours passed quickly. Fighting a yawn, she bid goodbye to her animal friend and rose to wake Freddie. She nudged him with her foot. He startled awake, blinking rapidly. His honey-colored eyes were wide as they made eye contact.

"What is it?" His voice was hoarse.

"Time to go, sunshine."

He propped himself on one shoulder, fighting a yawn of his own. "What about you? You need to sleep too."

"I'll survive. We need to keep moving."

He looked like he was going to argue, but wisely kept his mouth shut. He stood slowly, stretching, and gathered the items he had scattered on the ground.

They set off, navigating Captain back onto the road. While keeping watch, Bonnie had debated the merits of staying off the road — who knew if Simon had followed them outside the city limits? Freddie didn't seem concerned about the possibility — he must've thought that the guard had given up and returned to the castle. Their need for speed trumped the need for secrecy, so the road was the best way forward. The further out from Navian they were, the better odds that no one would recognize the duke's youngest son.

Bonnie didn't know how much time had passed — an hour, maybe two — before a headache formed near her temple. She rubbed her scar to relieve the pressure, but it persisted despite her efforts.

"Does your head hurt?"

Oh, what a remarkable observationalist. "Yes," she said through gritted teeth.

"How did you get that scar?"

She didn't blame him for asking. Everyone did once they got over the initial shock of who she was. "My parents were murdered when I was eight. I almost died in the attack."

He was silent, perhaps too stunned to answer. It wasn't the type of confession that typically sparked a lively conversation.

"I'm sorry about your parents," he said after a lengthy pause. "Who killed them?"

"King Rupert Aborn."

She felt him stiffen behind her. "What?" she asked. "Not expecting that?"

"Are you saying that the king killed your parents?"

"Not him personally. But they were murdered on his orders. What — did you think your king is some sort of innocent angel?"

"Of course not — why do you think I want to join the rebellion? It's just hard to imagine the king ordering the slaughter of an innocent family."

Bonnie stiffened, hands tightening into fists at her sides. "My family wasn't the only one slaughtered by the king, *Lord Stonewood*. Half of the Amlucen is comprised of people like me. Do you think any of us deserved it? Did my family deserve to be slaughtered?"

"That's not —"

"My family were innocent victims in the king's bloodthirsty quest for power."

"Bonnie, I didn't mean —"

"Save it," she spat. "People like you would never understand."

"People like *me*?" His tone was icy. "What do you mean by that, exactly?"

"Your father is the advisor to the king," she shot back. "Sanctioning the murder of my parents was probably his idea."

No response. They continued on in silence.

After a mile, he cleared his throat. "What happened to you . . . after?"

"After your king and father murdered my family?"

He let out a frustrated sigh through his nose. "Yes."

Bonnie debated how much she should tell him before deciding on an abbreviated version. "A member of the Amlucen saved my life — saw there was still hope for me, even though my parents hadn't survived. She adopted me and raised me as her own."

"That's pretty incredible."

"I owe her my life."

"Are there any other side effects of your wound?"

"You're nosy, you know that? I still get headaches, especially when I'm tired." If he hadn't already figured out that she couldn't read or write, she wouldn't be the one to point it out.

"Couldn't a healer help you? Fix your head wound?"

She shook her head. "It happened on Vale Magicae."

He hissed through his teeth. "That's . . . unlucky."

Bonnie snorted. Getting severely injured the day that magic disappeared from Hallordis was unlucky indeed. "There's no use dwelling on it." She didn't want to keep talking about this. Not with *him*. How could he ever understand what she had gone through the day her life changed forever?

Instead, she feigned a yawn, which turned into a real one.

"Sleep now, if you're able. I'll wake you up if we encounter anything."

"I'm fine."

They rode on in silence, and she focused on the sound that Captain's hooves made on the firm forest floor. *Clop, clop, clop.* The sun felt warm on her face as they continued their steady pace. Despite the autumn chill, it was a beautiful day. She closed her eyes, listening once more to Captain's steady steps, and drifted off to sleep.

"Bonnie, wake up," Freddie whispered softly but with an underlying sense of urgency.

Bonnie opened her eyes, instantly alert. A quick glance at the sky told her she'd been asleep for at least a few hours. Freddie had slowed Captain down to an almost glacial pace.

"What is it?" she whispered.

"Movement up ahead."

Snapping her eyes forward, it took Bonnie a moment to figure out what he was looking at. Birds flew up from the bushes about half a mile ahead of them, and the bushes were shuddering unnaturally.

Shit.

"Either bandits or a wild animal." She wasn't sure which of the options would be preferable, not with their lack of weapons. It was too late to turn back now, and there was no faster route to Crown Harbor. "Do you have any weapons on you?"

"Two hunting knives," he answered. That made three, with the knife she had carried on her person since entering the castle yesterday morning. She had planned on purchasing more in the next town they entered.

"Get them ready, but leave them out of sight." She hoped they wouldn't need them.

Freddie twitched the reins and returned to a normal traveling speed. Bonnie wasn't sure how fast Captain could go, being the size he was, but hopefully he could outrun any danger if it came to it.

Any sounds they heard from a distance had ceased by the time they neared the bushes. Instead of feeling relieved, Bonnie felt more on edge.

Something was wrong.

A man dressed in tattered clothing stepped out from behind the bush. A woman followed moments later, her blue cotton dress covered in an assortment of dirty patchwork. She held one arm behind her back. Both were barefoot.

Freddie brought Captain to a halt. "Move."

The man took a step forward. "Sorry, mister and missus, but do you have any spare items for the needy? My wife an' I 'ere" — he motioned to the woman, who was eyeing their belongings with longing — "are hungry and in need of 'elp."

41

"No," Freddie answered. Bonnie kept her eye on the woman, even as the man took another step towards them. Captain took a step back and bared his teeth.

"Mighty fine 'orse you have there," the woman broke in. She cocked her head to the side, making her greasy hair sway as she did so. "Surely those with such a fine 'orse would 'av somethin' to spare to those in need?"

"We do not," Bonnie snapped. "Move."

The woman looked at her with evil in her eye. "Or what?"

"We'll run you over."

The man looked over at the woman, who glanced at him with a small smile that made the hair on the back of Bonnie's neck stand up.

"Go," she told Freddie. "*NOW.*"

The woman moved as soon as Freddie snapped the reins. It was now apparent why she'd been hiding her arm behind her back — she was armed. She nocked an arrow on her hidden bow and aimed it directly at Bonnie's chest, almost too fast to see. It wasn't a large bow — she wouldn't have been able to hide it, otherwise — but the iron arrowhead still looked lethal.

A sudden paralyzing fear overtook Bonnie, and she watched in horror as the woman fired. She tried to duck to the side, but was too late.

The woman's aim was spot on.

Freddie's hand tightened around Bonnie's waist, and suddenly she was falling to the ground.

A sharp pain burned in her left arm, and she landed on the ground with a *crash*. Her head hit the ground with a *thud*. Stars swam before her eyes.

The next few seconds came to Bonnie in fragments.

The loud sound of Captain neighing.

Freddie shouting her name.

The crunch of feet on the dry, brittle ground.

Breathe, Bonnie, she told herself, taking a few precious

seconds to make sure she was getting enough air. Gritting her teeth, she propped herself on her uninjured side to assess the damage.

Definite head injury; hopefully not a concussion. A slice through her upper arm, which was bleeding freely but didn't seem deep. The arrow must have skimmed it instead of lodging somewhere in her chest, where she knew it would've landed if Freddie hadn't shoved her off before the arrow struck.

Shit. Freddie.

Bonnie looked around, ignoring the flash of pain that reverberated through her skull.

Freddie was a short distance away. He stood in a fighter's pose, both knives drawn. The others flanked him, but the woman was bleeding. Her bow was on the ground nearby, broken in half.

"'ow are you still standin'?" the man asked Freddie incredulously, waving his knife in the air. "That arrow should've killed you."

What was he talking about? Freddie appeared uninjured, apart from a little blood that stained his shirt. He stood tall as he faced the others.

The vagrants paid Bonnie no attention, too busy trying to dispatch Freddie. She lurched to her feet, grabbing the knife strapped to her waist. Creeping silently behind the woman, Bonnie grabbed her shoulder with one hand, holding tight.

She slit her throat with her other hand.

The woman didn't have time to cry out before blood started gurgling from the fatal wound. She fell to her knees, clawing at her throat, before keeling over onto the ground.

The man spun to face Bonnie, fury twisting his features as he saw what had happened to his companion. He let out a wild yell and began charging, his knife held out in front of him.

Freddie sprinted after him but was too far away to intercept. Bonnie raised her knife, ready to dodge out of the way or stab him. Either option worked for her.

Bonnie saw a flash of something large out of the corner of her eye but didn't want to take her eye off of the angry man. That was, of course, until Captain appeared out of nowhere, charging over her attacker.

One second the man was yelling, hellbent on running her through. The next second he screamed as he flew through the air, hitting a towering pine before landing in a heap on the ground.

He did not move again.

"Bonnie!" Freddie shouted as he ran towards her.

Bonnie realized she was on her knees, though she didn't remember falling to the ground. Probably when Captain was saving her sorry ass. She watched, almost numbly, as Freddie approached.

He walked slowly, hands raised as if approaching a wounded animal. Which, Bonnie supposed, she was. At least to him. She lowered the knife and heard it hit the ground with a *thud*.

Bonnie jerked her head toward the man on the ground, and the movement caused a flash of pain to reverberate through her skull. "Check on him first."

Captain had done his job well. The man would not wake again.

Freddie approached her once more, eyes wide. Bonnie looked down and realized she was covered in blood. Luckily her dark clothing hid most of the gore.

"Are you okay?"

Was she? She took stock. Her head hurt, sure, but that was nothing new. Her body hurt from being shoved off of Captain, but she considered it an ache worth having, considering the alternative would've been death by arrow.

Bonnie's arm hurt something fierce, though, and a quick

glance showed her she was still bleeding. Her blood stained the forest floor.

"I'm fine," she said as she grabbed the hem of her shirt with her uninjured hand. She needed to bind the wound before she lost too much blood.

He saw what she was unsuccessfully doing and reached out, touching her hand in a signal to stop. Eyes narrowed, Bonnie watched as he tore a strip of his own shirt from the fabric at the bottom. She averted her gaze, but not before she saw a flash of tanned skin right above his waistline.

He handed her the piece of fabric. "Use this instead — you're covered in blood. This is probably a little cleaner."

She handed the strip back to him. "Thanks. Could you —?"

"Oh. Right. One second." He left, heading back to the road to retrieve their packs. Taking the water canteen from his satchel, he set it aside. He studied her torn sweater. "I'm going to have to cut off the sleeve to bandage your arm."

Nodding tersely, Bonnie held her breath as he used his knife to cut the fabric. Breathing through her nose helped her master some of the pain. She seemed to feel every hurt a little more acutely now that they weren't in the middle of an ambush. He used the water from his canteen to wash the area around the wound, and then quickly bandaged her arm.

"You'll be fine as long as you don't jostle it. You probably should get it looked at when we reach Crown Harbor."

Bonnie nodded and limped toward where Captain was grazing. Before mounting, she turned back to Freddie with a frown. "Hold on. That arrow was flying right toward me. How were you spared?" It may have happened fast, but she was sure there was no way that he could have avoided being hit. What had the vagrant said? *The arrow should've killed you.*

Freddie's hand flew up to rumple the back of his hair before he let out a long breath and shrugged. "I'm quicker than I look.

After I pushed you off — you're welcome, by the way — I almost fell off myself."

There was a small bloodstain on his shirt but he didn't seem hurt. It must be the blood from the wound on her arm. The vagrant was probably drunk, she decided. Or Bonnie's arm must've changed its trajectory enough for it to have missed Freddie completely.

"What happened next?" she asked. "After you pushed me off?"

"Jumped off. The woman tried to grab Captain's reins like a fool, so I broke her bow when I dismounted. Held the two of them off with my knives until you came to."

Hmph. She looked at Captain. "You're worth your weight in gold, my friend," she told him fondly as she pat him on the neck. He had more than earned any treats that came his way tonight.

Freddie picked up both of their packs from where they lay on the ground. "Now what?"

"Continue on to Crown Harbor."

He nodded before looking toward where the two prone bodies lay on the forest floor. "What about them?"

Bonnie glanced over, trying to make herself feel any sort of pity. But then she moved her arm and almost gasped at the pain of it. "Leave them."

They set off again, alert for any more trouble. Everything was now quiet in Golwich Forest.

CHAPTER SIX

It wasn't as if killing didn't bother Bonnie.

It did.

The issue was that she had killed so many over the years that taking a life wasn't something she thought about for long.

Freddie, however, wasn't used to the bloodshed. His hands clenched the reins tightly as he sat stiffly behind her. He said nothing, for once out of inane questions to ask her.

Bonnie was relieved. She didn't want to be distracted again.

She kept to herself, speaking seldom as Captain navigated the path through the ancient forest. Hours passed as they drew closer to Crown Harbor.

"What are you doing?" Bonnie asked, eyebrows raised. They had stopped for the night, choosing a spot off the road alongside one of the many small ponds within the forest. Captain was grazing nearby, content to rest after a long day of riding.

"Fishing," Freddie grunted. He had rolled up the bottom of

his pants and was now standing almost knee-deep in the little pond. He turned in small circles, keeping his eyes on the water.

He looks like a fool, Bonnie thought as she took a large, crunchy bite of an apple. She held her hands up when he glared at her.

"My apple isn't scaring away the fish," she said from her blanket underneath a large pine. "You are. You're moving around too much."

"I know what I'm doing," he said hotly, keeping his eyes on the water. But his feet stilled.

Bonnie heard a splash several minutes later. She looked over to the pond to see Freddie emerging from under the water, holding a large fish proudly in the air. A grin lit his face from ear to ear.

Bonnie had to turn away so he wouldn't see her answering smile. She still thought he looked like an idiot.

She didn't watch as he returned from the pond, and instead chose to use her knife to clean the dirt from under her nails. She heard him searching through his satchel before hearing the unmistakable sound of wet clothing hitting the hard-packed dirt. He came into view, now dressed in dry clothes.

"Can I start a fire?"

Bonnie narrowed her eyes, surprised he even asked. She nodded before turning back to her nails.

After searching the forest in search of kindling, he swore under his breath in Naverian when his clumsy attempts to light a fire only produced a few sparks.

Bonnie smirked. "Need help, milord?"

He sent her a look before shaking his head. He bent back over his small pile of stacked wood.

"I'll help you if you tell me the intel you're holding onto," she offered.

Freddie didn't bother to look up this time, but she swore he started striking the flint with increased vehemence.

Bonnie made the same offer thirty minutes later. He made a rude gesture towards her in response.

"Fine," she said as she fought a yawn, glad he was going to take the first watch. She *had* to sleep; she had no choice but to let him stand guard. "Enjoy eating raw fish."

Eyelids heavy, Bonnie was on the verge of falling asleep when Freddie exclaimed in joy. She bolted upright, any chance of falling asleep gone.

Several pieces of kindling had ignited, which Freddie now sheltered from any errant wind. He blew on the embers softly, trying to get more wood to catch. When some of the smaller branches caught, he added bigger pieces to keep it going.

Bonnie wanted to go over and blow it out, just to spite him. Instead, she laid back down, turning away from the spectacle.

Sleep evaded her, but she felt calm as she listened to the crackling wood. A large hare scampered over to her and settled into the curve of her body, while a baby opossum warmed the tops of her feet.

Freddie tended to the fire, murmuring what sounded like a Naverian lullaby under his breath as he did so. The smell of cooked fish drifted through the air, making Bonnie's stomach growl. Her dinner of hard bread and apple seemed positively barbaric in comparison.

Time passed, and Bonnie heard Freddie's footsteps nearing her. She didn't move, but knew that she only heard him approach because he wanted her to. He was as quiet as a mouse when he wanted to be.

A moment later his footsteps faded, and she heard him settle by his own tree. Lifting her head, she looked behind her.

He left her half of the cooked fish.

BONNIE COULDN'T TELL IF HER HEART WAS RACING BECAUSE SHE was excited to return to Crown Harbor or dreading it.

On one hand, it would be nice to be rid of Lord Stonewood. It was hard to look at him without feeling the ache of missing her true, biological family, taken so cruelly from her at the hands of the king and Freddie's father.

On the other hand, Bonnie didn't know what Oll Blackthorn would do to him once they made it to the headquarters.

She didn't revel in torture or misery like some of the others, though she had no qualms about killing. Although she resented being stuck with him, she didn't want to see him hurt. She just wanted him to share his information so they could go their separate ways.

But what if he didn't have the right intel, or what if they didn't deem it worthy information? Would they punish her for bringing him to headquarters?

She knew what Oll Blackthorn was capable of; had seen the danger he posed to others firsthand. Had her own scars to show for it, hidden where others couldn't see.

Not to mention that some of his right-hand people were just as sadistic as he was. There was a reason he had stayed at the top of the Amlucen power structure for so many years.

It was a risk Bonnie had to take.

Before she knew it, they were exiting the forest, and she steered Captain up the hill that lay directly outside Crown Harbor.

Bonnie's breath caught as they reached the summit.

Crown Harbor laid like a glittering jewel below. True to its name, the golden rooftops of the city reflected sunlight, making the harbor look as if it was made of gold. Hundreds of ships were docked or navigating the deep blue waters. If she squinted, Bonnie could make out the outlines of dockworkers and merchants running around like ants in an anthill.

A sea breeze hit Bonnie's nose and she couldn't help but smile, despite the danger lurking in the city streets. She loved it all — the sights and smells that came with living beside the ocean. Although she had been told she had grown up in Midverd, Crown Harbor would always feel like home.

"Done gawking?" Freddie asked with a smile. He nudged Captain forward to join the line of people waiting to enter the city gates below.

Dirty from travel, the pair blended in easily with the others in line. They joined families traveling with squabbling children, single men who looked as though they were on the search for a job, and wealthier folk dressed in finery who looked unaccustomed to being around such rabble.

"Slouch," Bonnie told Freddie quietly. "You sit like a noble."

He grunted but did as he was told.

They eventually made it to the front of the line, and Bonnie craned her neck to get a full view of the massive, ornate gates that separated them from the city. A fool's purchase, spending so much on golden gates and rooftops when people across the kingdom were starving.

At least it looked pretty.

The guards waved them through without question. As they entered the stone walls that surrounded Crown Harbor on three sides, Bonnie saw movement to her right.

An urchin boy, no older than ten, scurried down a deserted alleyway, unremarkable except for the feather tucked behind his ear. One of Gwyneth's little spies, off to report that Bonnie had returned. The rebellion often took in orphans and runaways and put them to work spying and delivering messages throughout the city in exchange for food and a warm bed.

Bonnie couldn't help but feel a pang whenever she saw one of them; so easily could she have been a member of their ranks.

"Tell me what you know about our power structure," she asked as Freddie led Captain down the main street. She cursed herself for not talking to him about this sooner; she had been too busy trying to ignore him during their journey that she hardly said two words to him.

"Oll Blackthorn leads the Amlucen," he whispered, mouth close to her ear. His breath stirred Bonnie's hair as they rode. "He and his wife, supposedly, although there isn't much known about her. Oll's brother, Oren, formed the rebellion fifteen years ago, but Oren died on Vale Magicae. Oll took over in his stead."

She nodded at him to continue.

"Under Oll's leadership, the Amlucen expanded to a large rebellion that is strategic in its initiatives to remove the king from power. They have rebel hideouts throughout this kingdom, and probably our neighboring kingdoms as well. Not much is known about them — which I suspect is deliberate. Their anonymity allows them to operate in the shadows."

"Good," Bonnie said, a bit hoarsely. He wasn't far off the mark.

She grabbed him, nails biting into his forearm. "Be careful with Oll Blackthorn," she warned, her voice as cold as she could make it. "You need to watch what you say and how you say it. Intel or not, he *will* kill you if he thinks you've disrespected him."

He yanked his arm out of her grip. "Noted. I didn't know you cared, sweet Bonnie."

She turned to glare and saw a glimmer of mischief in his honey-colored eyes. Scoffing, she turned back to face the road ahead. "I don't care about you, Freddie dear," she told him drily. "I would just hate for Oll to spill your blood on my nice cloak."

A moment later Bonnie heard a whistle — almost identical to a seagull, but with a higher pitch. She answered back with her own specific call.

"It's time," she said, turning to him. "Pull over there" — she pointed to a nearby fountain, which featured a life-size statue of a child holding a basket of fish — "and tie Captain to the horse hitch."

On the ground, Bonnie rubbed Captain's nose. "You're a good boy. I'll check on you soon, okay?" She wasn't sure if he understood, but he whinnied anyway.

"Will he be safe here?" Freddie asked, his eyes darting around. People of every class walked the cobblestone streets, from those who would not look out of place in the King's Court to those barely clinging to life.

"The scouts who saw us arrive know he's my horse — they'll treat him better than they'll treat you, that's for certain. He'll be perfectly fine in our stables."

Freddie shot her a look. "Why would they treat your horse differently than another member?" he asked, his tone wary. "And why would they be on the lookout for you?"

Bonnie winked. "I'm a big deal, milord."

Two burly men appeared before he could respond, grabbing his arms. Freddie had the good grace to remain silent, even as he tried to wrench his arms out of their grip.

"Now, now," chided Hugo, one of Oll's thugs. His dark brown hair was tied in a ponytail that swayed as he shifted his grip. "We don't want to cause a ruckus, do we?"

Bonnie plastered a smirk on her face.

The other man, Leon, who was just as big as his brother but completely bald, chuckled darkly. "Mistakes happen during a ruckus. Deadly mistakes."

Freddie stilled before nodding stiffly. They released him when they sensed he wouldn't put up a fight, but continued to stand close enough to be threatening.

Turning on her heel, Bonnie strode down the street with a swagger that she did not feel.

They took circuitous loops around the city, dodging in and out of alleyways, taking cut-through routes, and avoiding the infamous fishmongers as they traversed with their carts full of stinking fish. If Freddie survived meeting Oll, they'd teach him how to find the headquarters more easily. For now, he'd get a scenic view of Crown Harbor.

They stopped around the corner from the hideout entrance. The houses on the street were all nondescript; anyone who found themselves here would have no idea they just stumbled upon the rebellion's largest hideout.

Hugo slipped a hand into his pocket and fished out a piece of fabric. He held it in front of Freddie. "You are going to put this on without a fuss."

Freddie looked toward Bonnie, eyes wide, and she nodded. He turned toward Hugo and inclined his head.

Blindfold on, they led him to the entrance. Nobody else was around — hidden or no, the people of Crown Harbor knew to stay away from the comings and goings of this particular area. Maybe it was the feeling of being watched as they walked through the area, or the rumors that people who traveled this road sometimes never made it to the other side. Whatever it was, the locals knew to stay far away.

Bonnie went to the sun-and-salt stained black door, which was marked in the top right corner with a small star, two slashes crossing through it, conscious of the eyes she knew tracked every movement — both from within this building and the surrounding ones — and raised her fist.

Knock. Knock. Knock. Knock.

After the fourth knock she paused, and then knocked one final time. *Knock.* The door opened a moment later.

"Why hello, Bonnie dear," a familiar voice sounded through the crack in the door. "Have a good trip?"

Bonnie held back her sneer as she forced the door open. "We have a lot to talk about regarding my trip, don't we, Felix?"

She hadn't forgotten that her adopted brother had been the one responsible for the logistics of her trip to Navian. She hadn't forgotten the parts of the plan that had gone wrong.

He said nothing, but she noticed he clenched his jaw when he saw Freddie standing behind her.

"It appears so," is all he said before he opened the door, motioning for the group to enter.

If anyone were to enter the hideout they would find nothing of note. A nicely furnished sitting room, vacant. A kitchen, devoid of anyone.

She knew multiple sets of eyes watched their every move as they walked through, and that every movement would be reported. The thought made her shiver, even though she herself had watched others from behind the walls hundreds of times over the past twelve years.

"Is he here?" Bonnie asked in a low voice.

"Yes," he replied shortly, and she saw his jaw clench again.

Shit.

Part of her had hoped that Oll Blackthorn was traveling. Hopefully Freddie would heed her warning to tread carefully.

"Gwyneth?"

"No. Suverd."

Again? That was the second time in just as many months.

They did not speak again.

A bookcase stood at the end of the corridor, flanked by empty rooms on either side. The group stopped just short of the bookcase, Hugo with a large hand on Freddie's shoulder to keep him from bumping into it.

Felix reached out and pulled a red book towards him. The bookcase swung forward with a *hiss*, revealing the true headquarters of the rebel movement.

Bonnie knew Freddie would have a million questions if he could see what was going on. Unfortunately, Hugo and Leon looked as though they weren't keen on removing the blindfold until they reached their final destination.

She figured his other senses would pick up on everything his eyes couldn't. The footsteps of over a dozen rebels navigating the network of hallways that just opened up in front of them. The sound of whispering voices from conversations too quiet to overhear. The wails and laughter of the rebel children, the future of the Amlucen rebellion.

Freddie probably smelled the vat of beef stew and fresh bread being cooked in the kitchen, the aroma infiltrating each corner of the headquarters with its mouth watering scent. Or the fresh scent of the laundry as they passed by steaming cauldrons of washed clothes.

This is where Bonnie spent most of her childhood. To her, it smelled like home.

And home, although it had its comforts, had its issues. With every head turned hastily away, every pained smile, every averted eye contact, Bonnie felt smaller and smaller. Their avoidance left a sour taste in her mouth.

So she stood taller, shoulders back. Let them believe she didn't care how they treated her — with respect, yes, but also a heavy dose of fear. Why should she care what they thought?

After a few turns they stopped in front of a wooden door. It was no different from the other doors they passed — bedrooms, conference rooms, strategy rooms, things like that. But every nerve in Bonnie's body went on high alert at the sight of the familiar wooden frame.

At least her hand didn't shake as she reached out to knock.

"Come in," a deep voice answered.

Bonnie squared her shoulders, opened the door and strode inside. Hugo and Leon followed, pushing Freddie ahead.

Felix stayed behind, which Bonnie thought was unusual. The nosy little rat normally insisted on being where the drama was.

Oll's office was by far the nicest room in the entire compound. Red velvet hangings covered the walls, contrasted by the plush green rug on the hardwood floors. Knives, swords, and other weapons were scattered around like his own miniature armory.

The man himself lounged in an ornate wooden chair, one that Bonnie imagined a king would sit in. Papers littered the surface of his desk — one missive had been speared through with a knife that was covered in dried blood.

The leader of the Amlucen had combed his thinning blonde hair over his bald plate. "You can remove the blindfold," he told the brothers. Once that was done, Oll Blackthorn told Hugo and Leon to leave.

Freddie stood there, blinking rapidly to help his eyes adjust.

Oll didn't speak again until the door had closed with a soft *click*. Then he whistled loudly. "Well, well, well. Bonnie, my dear, look who you have brought to us. A deviation of the plan, I see. Pleasure to make your acquaintance, Lord Stonewood." Oll tipped his head toward Freddie in a mocking gesture.

Oll turned to her. "Now, now, my Bonnie girl." Oll stood and held his arms out to the side. "We haven't seen each other in weeks and this is how you greet me? No hug for your dear, beloved father?"

CHAPTER SEVEN

"FATHER?!" FREDDIE LOOKED AT BONNIE IN HORROR.

She'd bet anything that every interaction they had was running through his mind right now.

"*Adopted* father," Bonnie amended as she approached Oll's desk. She stopped herself from shuddering as she gave him an obligatory hug.

"I don't like when you use the term 'adopted,' Bon," Oll said, eyes on Freddie as she retreated to the other side of the desk. "I'm the only father you remember, at least."

While that may be true, Bonnie refused to accept it. She was no expert at father figures, but she knew that most didn't lock their children in their room for days at a time for small indiscretions. Or force their children to watch while he tortured others.

Or break their bones to teach them what it felt like to be injured by the enemy.

She kept her arms loose at her side, though her fingers itched to run over some of the various scars that her dear father had given her as punishments for perceived slights.

He was a monster, and no true father.

"How are you?" she asked, and hoped her revulsion didn't show.

"Fine," Oll said as he glared at Freddie. "What is he doing here?"

"Lord Stonewood has information," she said. "Intel about a raid on one of our hideouts."

"Is that so?" Oll's voice had gone dangerously quiet.

"Yes, sir," Freddie said.

Oll looked at him with renewed interest. "And when is this raid supposed to happen?"

"In two days."

Oll blasted out of his chair, as quick as an adder. "TWO DAYS?!" he bellowed. "Why is this the first time I'm hearing about this?" He swept a stack of papers off his desk. Bonnie kept her eye on the knife that was stabbed into the paper, but Oll didn't seem inclined to start stabbing people. Yet.

"We just arrived, Father. We traveled through Golwich as fast as our horse could carry us. "

Oll's eyes narrowed. His breathing, while still fast, slowed, which Bonnie took as a good sign. "Tell me about this raid. What do you know? How do you know this? Why should I believe you?"

The door opened behind her.

A blur of movement crossed Bonnie's vision, followed by the sight of a knife embedded in the doorframe, inches from her adopted mother.

The knife on the desk was gone.

He might be crazy, but Oll's reflexes were unmatched. Plenty of people had tried to take him down and failed.

The brains behind the rebellion looked at the knife and raised a scarred eyebrow at her husband, who had the grace to look sheepish. Then Gwyneth's vivid green eyes lit up when she saw her adopted daughter.

"You're home!" Gwyneth exclaimed as she walked over,

arms wide. One of her hands clutched a familiar blue bag, and Bonnie felt the weight of it hit her back as she hugged her mother. She felt the knot in her chest loosen at the contact.

Freddie stared at Gwyneth, a calculating look in his eyes.

Strange, she thought, *but not unexpected.*

Few people outside of the rebellion knew about Gwyneth's involvement, as Oll had been the poster child for over a decade. Gwyneth preferred to operate in the shadows, letting her husband take all the glory — and infamy. Bonnie hoped to follow in her footsteps.

Releasing Bonnie, Gwyneth put the bag inside her pocket before grabbing Bonnie's shoulders. She studied Bonnie at arm's length, and her smile twisted into a frown. Worry flashed over her ruined face.

"Hello Mother," Bonnie said. "You look good."

A lie, but one that came easily.

Gwyneth did not look good, not in the traditional sense. A series of scars and burns ruined her face, the result of time spent tortured by the king's men. Her keen green eyes were untouched, though, and were by far her most striking feature. While others often stared, unable to look past the unwieldy slashes and burn marks that spared very little of her face, all Bonnie saw was beauty.

Gwyneth was a survivor.

Of what, she told no one. Bonnie had asked once, right when they first met. All Gwyneth told her was that speaking about that period in her life was too painful.

Bonnie owed everything to Gwyneth, and while she corrected those who referred to her as Oll's daughter, she didn't mind when people thought Gwyneth was her birth mother.

It was too bad she married an unhinged psychopath.

Gwyneth stepped away and walked over to Oll. Bonnie

couldn't help but notice how tense Gwyneth seemed to be as she kissed him on the cheek.

Luckily, Oll was too busy glaring at Freddie to notice his wife's discomfort.

Gwyneth cleared her throat. "What is Lord Stonewood doing in your office?"

Bonnie snorted, and Oll sent a glare in her direction. Oll's temper didn't worry her as much now that Gwyneth was here.

Now she was safe.

"They were just about to tell me, actually," Oll said in a huff.

"Ah, well," Gwyneth said, "Good thing I returned in time. You'll only have to tell your story once." Then she turned to Freddie, although she diverted her gaze over his shoulder. "My name is Gwyneth Blackthorn. Please continue."

She acted as though this interaction was an everyday occurrence and not something completely nonsensical. It wasn't every day that a member of the king's inner circle landed in the hands of the rebellion, and Bonnie didn't understand why they were so calm about this.

Freddie cleared his throat. "Thornwick. The king is going to attack your base in Thornwick."

Sharp inhales all around. Oll and Gwyneth exchanged a look that Bonnie couldn't read. A frown crossed Gwyneth's face as she fidgeted with the golden ring she wore.

Thornwick was located at the base of a mountain known for its wealth of stone and minerals. While it was one of Hallordis's smaller cities, it was still within a day's ride of Crown Harbor, which made it an invaluable location for smuggling operations. Bonnie had been sent there on missions many times and had fallen in love with the charming mining city.

Many rebel families chose to raise their children there, away from the crowded port city of Crown Harbor. And now the king was threatening to ruin their safe haven.

Gwyneth studied her nails. "How do you know this?"

"I sit in on strategy meetings."

"You? You are not the firstborn."

She did not say it cruelly, but Bonnie saw Freddie's frown deepen, anyway.

"Jasper does not have a head for politics or the court," he replied flatly. "He'd rather spend our father's money on ale and in brothels. My father knows my interests are more closely aligned with his."

Oll stood, eyes bulging. "More closely aligned with *his* views, eh? More aligned with the views of the king's advisor?"

He pointed his finger at Bonnie. "*You*," he spat. "*You* brought this . . . this . . . king *sympathizer* here!"

Bonnie held up her hands. "I didn't want to bring him here. Trust me. He wouldn't divulge the location of the raids to anyone but you, Father."

Gwyneth put a hand on his arm. "Bonnie wouldn't have brought him here unless completely necessary, I'm sure."

She paused, directing a look at Freddie, before speaking to Oll in a different language.

If the blank look on Freddie's face was any indication, he didn't understand what they were saying either. At least Bonnie wasn't the only one being kept in the dark this time.

Most people in Hallordis only spoke the common tongue, which was widely known inside and outside the kingdom. Other lands — the ones who had yet to be conquered by power-hungry Aborn — kept their native tongues, even if they also spoke the common language. Oll and Gwyneth were currently speaking in Suverian, the language of Suverd. It sounded like a bunch of hissing and spitting to her.

She'd be lying if she said that her parent's frequent forays into different languages didn't bother her.

Of course it did.

It had been happening for years, and while she had learned to ignore it, it still stung. Even Felix joined in, smirking the entire conversation. Everyone knew that her head trauma meant she couldn't learn other languages, no matter how hard she tried.

Once, when she was about ten years old, Bonnie had struck up enough nerve to ask Oll why they did it. His response was a slap across the face. Even now, ten years later, she did not have the courage to ask again.

After finishing their conversation, Oll sat back down with a *thump*. Gwyneth motioned for Freddie to continue.

"I've been sympathetic to your cause for a while," Freddie said, as if there had been no interruption. "When I heard the plans to raid Thornwick, I knew I had to do something. I didn't know how to find you, though, or get in contact. As luck would have it, our plans aligned. A few days later, I caught Bonnie trying to plant evidence on me. We've been traveling here ever since."

Gwyneth turned her quiet focus on Bonnie, eying her sternly. "And how did Lord Stonewood catch you? We went through the plan many times — it was foolproof."

A flash of anger flooded Bonnie's senses. "It *would* have been foolproof, had the others done their damned jobs. As it was, Lord Jasper was *not* in Midverd as reported. The sleeping draught? Non-existent. Lord Stonewood caught me because *he was never drugged.*"

All eyes turned to Freddie.

He shrugged, even as he frowned at Bonnie. "This is the first time I'm hearing that you planned to drug me, but no. I would've known. My father trained me to recognize different poisons. There was nothing unusual in my tea."

"Interesting," Gwyneth said. "I hadn't heard they were training the nobility to recognize poisons."

"Just my father," Freddie said. "After what happened with the queen, he thought it was prudent —"

"Yes, of course," Oll broke in, flapping his hands. "Talk to me more about what's being planned for Thornwick. Do you have any more details?"

Bonnie's mind spun as Freddie dove into what he knew. She came up empty — what happened to the queen?

King Aborn ruled his bloody throne beside Queen Celeste, a beautiful red-haired woman who also hailed from Suverd. She'd given birth to two heirs — Rosamund and Jameson, both a few years younger than Bonnie. Queen Celeste hadn't been poisoned, though, not that she was aware of . . .

Hold on. Queen Celeste was the king's *second* wife. His first — Queen Annabelle? Annabeth? Something like that — had died on Vale Magicae. Was that who Freddie referred to?

She cursed the head wound that wiped her memory away. The details weren't important, she supposed, but the absence of knowledge reignited her hatred for the king. *And* her disdain for Freddie, and his father, and the others who had a hand in ruining her life.

Bonnie tried to refocus on the conversation at hand.

"You'll report what you know to the Council," Gwyneth was saying to Freddie. "We'll plan an attack strategy from there. It'll take a few hours to pull the right people together, but we should have a plan in place tonight. For now, stay with Bonnie. Don't leave her side."

"What?" she exclaimed.

No. No. No. No. No. No.

She'd done her job — she had brought him here, had suffered his presence. This was when he was supposed to be shackled to someone else. Someone who was not *her*.

Three sets of eyes turned to her.

"Excuse me?" Oll said, his eyes glittering. "You heard your mother."

Bonnie swallowed but looked at Gwyneth. "I thought it might be more . . . prudent . . . if Lord Stonewood accompanied someone else. Someone more important than me."

A lie — Bonnie was destined to lead the rebellion one day. Still.

Oll chuckled as he sat back down, his chair creaking underneath his weight. "You're my daughter. Who else is as important as you?"

Bonnie kept her mouth shut. It was a miracle that Freddie could leave with her at all. She had half expected him to be taken away for an interrogation.

But this had all gone down so . . . *civilized.* Especially for Oll. For one so volatile, he seemed to take the sudden appearance of a Hallordian lord — the son of the king's advisor, no less! — surprisingly well.

Too well.

What was she missing?

Oll addressed Gwyneth in Suverian again. Bonnie turned toward Freddie, moving quicker than she should have, and jostled her injured arm. She grimaced.

Gwyneth stood in front of her a moment later, worry lining the harsh panes of her face. "What's wrong? Are you injured?"

Bonnie held back a sigh. "An arrow grazed me."

Oll, true to his nature, jumped up from his chair once more. The few papers that had lingered on his desk now littered the floor. "Grazed by an arrow? Why didn't you say anything?"

"I'm *fine*. Two vagrants attacked us in Golwich, and one shot an arrow that grazed me. It wasn't serious."

She left out the part about the possible concussion. No need for them to worry unnecessarily. She resisted the urge to check that her braid was still in place.

"And the vagrants?" Gwyneth's tone raised the hair on Bonnie's arms.

Gwyneth Blackthorn was a kind woman to those she favored, but there was a darkness in her; a darkness that brought her and Oll together. A darkness that enabled her to lead a rebel force that was a serious threat to the monarchy. A darkness that made her dangerous. Lethal.

"Dead."

Gwyneth nodded and stroked the side of Bonnie's face with a steady hand. Bonnie closed her eyes as Gwyneth's fingertips brushed over the scar. She hated when anyone paid attention to it.

Gwyneth gave Bonnie's cheek one last pat and backed away, saying something else to Oll in Suverian.

"Take some time to settle in," Oll ordered. "And be discreet with Lord Stonewood, here. We'll send someone to fetch you soon. "

Bonnie nodded, recognizing the dismissal. Turning on her heel, she strode past Freddie and wrenched the door open.

"Oh! I forgot," Oll's voice called after her, "I had a new knife made for you, my darling girl. Fetch it from the armory."

"Thank you, Father," Bonnie said as she left the office.

And ran right into Felix, his lanky frame far too close to the door to be casually stopping by. He must've been eavesdropping, the sneak.

Bonnie curled her lip. "Get out of my way."

He only smirked, his greasy blonde hair flopping over his forehead. Memories of their childhood spent laughing together flashed through her mind, but she blinked them away. Willed her face into its normal mask of indifference toward her adopted brother.

Even if her heart did hurt a little bit every time she saw him.

Felix's eyes widened when he saw Freddie following behind her. The door closed with a soft *click*.

"What?" Bonnie snapped. "Surprised he's still alive? Surprised he isn't in one of your father's many torture chambers?"

"*Our* father, you mean. Right, dear sister?" His voice

dripped with disdain, even as he stepped aside. He made a mocking bow, but allowed the two of them to pass.

"Whatever," Bonnie said, pushing past him. Freddie followed, wisely keeping his mouth shut.

It was almost comical how fast those navigating the hideout corridors swerved out of her way. Faster than normal, anyway, even as they made sure to smile in her direction.

Could this day get any worse?

CHAPTER EIGHT

Bonnie couldn't relax.

Not with Freddie standing in her bedchamber, contaminating what little personal space she had.

Inside the small, square room was the standard rebel-issued bed, dresser, and desk. Oll had offered her a suite of rooms closer to the rest of the family, but she declined. As much as she wanted to be close to her mother, she valued any distance she could create between her and Oll.

The only upgrade Bonnie conceded to was the addition of her own private bathing chamber. Others had to use the communal washrooms and toilets. No privacy, not for anyone.

It was there that she fled to now. Closing the privacy curtain, Bonnie used a water jug to fill the washbowl. Splashing water on her face, she took a few deep breaths to calm her racing heart.

Bonnie thought she'd be done with Lord Stonewood. She had fully expected that he would be someone else's problem now so she could go back to her normal life. Help with the effort in Thornwick without him following around like a neglected puppy.

Didn't they understand how hard it was for her to be around the son of the man responsible for killing her family?

She shook her head, told herself to get a grip. She had a job to do.

Feeling only marginally better, she reentered her room. Freddie stood over her desk, obviously trying to see what he could learn.

The joke was on him. She had no messages since she couldn't read — any reports or summons were given verbally. Her room was sparsely furnished, out of an abundance of caution. She kept her personal possessions to a minimum so that others couldn't spy on her.

"Snooping?"

His head turned, but he didn't look guilty. His brows were furrowed, hands in tight fists.

No. He was *angry*.

"Bonnie *Blackthorn?*" he said, his voice full of scorn. "Bonnie *Blackthorn?*"

She crossed her arms. "You never asked for my family name," she said. "Why should I have told you?"

"You knew I was looking for Oll Blackthorn. You could have told me he was your father!"

"*Adopted* father," she corrected. "Why does it matter? You wanted to share your intel with Oll, not his daughter. Would it have changed anything?"

A pause. "No."

Bonnie sat on her bed, suddenly tired. "Great. Stop complaining. Don't waste your breath."

He looked as if he wanted to fight, but chose instead to sit. "Fine. How did you become Oll Blackthorn's daughter? *Adopted* daughter?" he amended, when she opened her mouth to correct him again.

"I told you — the king's men killed my parents on Vale Magicae, and I was left for dead. Gwyneth saved my life."

"Gwyneth," he said. His eyes narrowed. "Who is she, exactly? How did she become Oll's wife?"

Bonnie's scar twinged, and she took a second to massage it. She decided that she didn't care if Freddie thought her weak for it. "She was married to Oren Blackthorn," she told him. Oll's brother, founder of the Amlucen. "She married Oll after Oren was murdered. Thought the Amlucen would be stronger if she and Oll worked together."

"What happened to her?" He gestured to his face.

"No one knows. She only shared that the king was responsible." And even if Gwyneth had told her the entire story, Bonnie would never tell him. It wasn't her story to share.

"Did it happen on Vale Magicae?"

She shook her head. "No. She's had those scars longer." He still had the weird, contemplative look on his face. "What?"

He shook his head, as if to clear it. "Nothing. She just seems familiar."

"You said the same thing about me."

He nodded. "Yes. I still feel that way."

There was a knock at the door.

"Come in," she called wearily, not moving from her bed.

Felix opened it. Bonnie wasn't sure if her patience — already stretched thin after her meeting with Oll and Gwyneth — could stand a meeting with him. "What do you want now?"

"It's time to meet in the Map Room."

He looked her up and down, no doubt noticing how travel-worn she was. His eyes focused on a spot on her cloak, and something flashed in his eyes.

"Are you injured?" he asked.

"No." Bonnie would never willingly disclose any weakness — to him, or anyone else. "What the fuck happened in Navian, Felix?"

"What do you mean?"

"Lord Frederick was never sedated."

"What?"

"You heard me."

"Gwyneth said she'd —" He broke off and then swallowed. "I'm not sure what happened. I've been here."

He looked troubled, though. His eyes darted around the room, taking everything in. His fingers, clutching a book she could not read the title of, turned white as he gripped it.

Strange, Bonnie thought.

"That's why he's here." Bonnie looked at Freddie, who was staring at Felix. "I almost killed him. Lucky for him, he had information that saved his life."

"What information?"

"I'm sure you'll find out soon enough. Now leave."

Felix looked as though he wanted to say something more, but kept his mouth shut. He left, shooting Freddie a wary look on his way out.

Bonnie counted to twenty before following him out the door.

Freddie walked half a step behind her. "Oll is Felix's father, yes?"

"Yes."

"But Gwyneth is not his mother."

"No."

"I thought so. Felix addressed Gwyneth by her name earlier. And he doesn't look like her."

Bonnie wasn't sure how he could tell if Felix resembled Gwyneth — her face was so ruined it was hard to picture what she may have looked like before the attack. Felix's mother had died when he was a toddler, and although Oll told her that she died of natural causes, Bonnie wasn't sure she believed him. Gwyneth was the only mother Felix remembered.

The sound of shouting could be heard from down the corridor, and Bonnie made sure her knife was within reach as they reached the Map Room door. She hoped she wouldn't need to use it.

Taking a deep breath, she opened the door. The room went silent as they entered.

Freddie's mouth dropped open when he saw what covered the walls.

Maps of Hallordis, neighboring countries, cities, towns, buildings, and waterways covered every inch of wall space. Paper maps, maps on wax paper, maps scratched on fabric or other textiles. If there was ever a fire, this place would go up in a heartbeat.

Bonnie bet they had more intel on the ins and outs of the land than even the king himself. Dozens of rebels died to provide this trove of knowledge. Every time she entered the room, the sight of it took her breath away.

A long rectangular table sat directly in the middle of the room. Oll sat at the head, with Gwyneth taking a seat to his right. A furious Amlucen council filled the rest. Every member stared openly at her in disgust.

Or, more accurately, at Freddie. Judging by the uproar they interrupted, not everyone was as oddly relaxed as Oll had been about Lord Stonewood's arrival. While a few of them presented calm exteriors, most openly sneered.

The Amlucen Council was weak; it consisted of powerless rebels whose only role was to make it look as though Oll and Gwyneth didn't have absolute control. They liked to huff and puff and argue their points for hours, sure. But Oll and Gwyneth ultimately decided the direction of the rebellion.

"Ah, our honored guest," Oll said as he smirked from his chair. "Come in, come in."

Bonnie entered cautiously, Freddie a step behind. While a few of the members — the smarter ones — nodded to her as she passed, the others stared them down equally. As if she, too, was a member of the ruling class they despised so much.

Dangerous. Especially considering Bonnie was the favorite to take over if something were to happen to the two rebel leaders.

It wasn't something they openly spoke about; why invite trouble into your home? But Gwyneth had been training Bonnie to take over if the need arose. Felix was related by blood, but Bonnie was the one the others turned to in a crisis.

She'd rule quietly, of course. From the shadows. Bonnie would never become the face of the rebellion, like Oll. Just as Gwyneth ruled from behind the scenes, so too would Bonnie.

Foolish of the council to forget that.

She noted those who openly scorned her. Maybe a council shake up was in the rebellion's future.

Oll stood with a dramatic flourish, and the smirk on his face made Bonnie's stomach clench. Nothing good came from a smirk like that — not from Oll Blackthorn, at least.

He stepped aside and bowed low to Freddie, gesturing to his chair. "Only the finest seat for the most established among us," he said, rather loudly for someone who already had the attention of everyone in the room.

Freddie frowned. "You are the only leader I see here, Oll Blackthorn," he replied solemnly. "I do not wish to take your place."

Oll rose from his subservient position. "Nonsense," he said as he patted the back of his chair. "This is the finest seat in the entire room — nay, the entire hideout! A chair fit for a lord. Sit." His eyes glittered dangerously.

To decline once was to be polite; to do so again would be outright disrespectful. Freddie seemed to come to the same conclusion. He bowed his head, gave thanks, and sat in the proffered chair.

Oll remained silent, and Bonnie couldn't tell whether he

was delighted or disappointed that Freddie followed his orders. Everyone watched as he leaned over and kissed Freddie's cheek before he straightened and looked around the room.

Freddie clenched his jaw so hard that Bonnie thought his teeth would crack. A faint blush colored his cheeks, and his hands were in tight fists.

Oll rubbed his hands together. "As you can see, we have a visitor with us today. My daughter Bonnie" — at this Bonnie inclined her head in acknowledgement, ever the obedient daughter — "discovered through covert espionage that Lord Stonewood was interested in joining our merry group. She also discovered that he has valuable intel about an upcoming raid."

Bonnie held back a snort. At least his retelling pictured her in a favorable light. His words had accomplished their intended effect, however, as a few rebels were now looking at them with curiosity instead of outright hostility.

Not everyone was so easily convinced. Harwin Stoke, one of Oll's favorite minions, stared at them in contempt, his pudgy face mottled with red. "How do we know he's telling the truth and that he's not here on behalf of Aborn?"

Oll leaned toward where Harwin sat a few seats away. "I have my own sources in Navian that have confirmed his story," he said.

Bonnie blinked. What sources?

"But . . . But . . ." Harwin stuttered. "How do we know he isn't setting a trap?"

Oll's fingers twitched, and Bonnie knew from experience that he was trying to stop himself from grabbing his knife.

A wave of red crossed her vision, and she rapidly blinked away the memory of a hand covered in blood, pinned to the table by one of Oll's favorite knives.

It took weeks for her not to hear the poor rebel's cries of pain. To stop hearing the echo of Oll's laughter as he watched the rebel squirming against the tabletop.

It appeared her mother remembered as well, for Gwyneth stood a moment later. She placed both hands on the table, mimicking Oll's posture as she stared at Harwin. "Tell me if I'm understanding you correctly," she said, her tone even and unthreatening. "Are you telling me, Harwin Stoke, that you do not trust your leader? You do not trust the word of Oll Blackthorn?"

Bonnie had been wrong earlier to think that the room was completely silent. Because now, after Gwyneth had spoken, everything went still.

Harwin's face went from red to pink to white in a matter of seconds. Eyes wide, he set his gaze on the tabletop. "Forgive me, forgive me. I do not wish to convey that I did not trust you, Oll Blackthorn," he said in a rush. "Of course I trust your judgment. And—and that of your family. Forgive me."

Gwyneth stared him down for another few seconds before nodding. She sat and motioned for Oll to continue.

"Thank you, my dear," he said as he turned back to the table. He smirked at Harwin, whose gaze focused on the tabletop. "Anyone else want to voice any concerns?"

No one said anything. Bonnie doubted anyone even moved a muscle.

"Good. That's what I thought." Oll turned to Freddie. "Lord Stonewood. Please enlighten the rest of the Council about what you told me."

Freddie, still looking uncomfortable, cleared his throat. "The king is planning a raid on Thornwick. He means to strike in two days."

Silence.

And then a similar uproar to the one they walked in on exploded throughout the room. A few council members stood, shouting their outrage at each other. Others sat as still as statues, apparently too shocked to respond.

Oll clapped Freddie on the back as he watched the pandemonium begin. Gwyneth's eyes darted around the room, keeping track of each council member. Bonnie wondered what was going on in that head of hers.

Standing off to the side, Bonnie waited for Oll to bring the meeting to order. It took a while; he seemed to enjoy the chaos. Just when she thought about bringing the room to order herself, he slammed the table with his fist. *Bang. Bang. Bang. Bang.*

All chatter ceased. When every eye was upon him, Oll spoke. "I know how you are feeling. This news was shocking to me, too. But I am confident that we will pull together and persevere against the tyranny that is King Rupert Aborn. Now, ladies and gentlemen, we plan."

THE NEXT FEW HOURS PASSED QUICKLY.

Bonnie sat in the corner as the meeting progressed, watching silently as rebels came and went. Separate groups formed and disbanded, tasked with strategizing in different areas — who would be responsible for the attack against the soldiers, who would sneak rebels unable to fight to safety, who would launch a counterattack, things of that nature. Members of the feared Rebel Guard were summoned, and each one acknowledged Bonnie with a nod when they saw her.

Others were busy trying to familiarize themselves with the ins and outs of Thornwick, heavily scrutinizing every map and scrap of information they could get their hands on. Plans were drawn, discussed, and redrawn as the rebels worked together.

Oll and Freddie bounced from group to group. Any issues people had with Freddie seemed to be abandoned as he worked with them.

They didn't fool Bonnie, though — she saw a few glaring at Lord Stonewood when he wasn't looking. She didn't blame them.

Most of those who joined the rebellion were victims of crimes committed by the king and his loyal subjects. And as the king's advisor, Freddie's father was one of the most despised people in the country.

Bonnie stifled a yawn as she watched Gwyneth approach.

The older woman rubbed Bonnie's shoulder gently. "Why don't you get some sleep? You've had a long day."

"I'm fine." She jerked her head towards Freddie. "I have to stick with him, remember?"

Gwyneth cocked her head to the side as she studied him. "He's different from what I thought he'd be."

Bonnie raised her eyebrow. "How did you think he would be?" She hadn't thought of him at all until they were stuck together.

Gwyneth shrugged. "He's acting like he really wants to help. And even though I'm loath to believe him entirely, I want to take his word at face value. He seems like the opposite of his father. "

"You say that like you knew him," Bonnie probed. "The duke."

Gwyneth frowned.

Oll came over, stepping in between the two women. He slung an arm around both of their shoulders, and Bonnie had to stop herself from stiffening at his touch. After a moment, she stepped away to face the two of them.

"I think planning is going well," he said, oblivious to her discomfort. "I sent messengers to warn the Thornwick rebels and asked them to prepare for our arrival tomorrow. We might have a chance after all."

Gwyneth paused, glancing at Bonnie, before she switched to Suverian. He responded in kind, effectively shutting Bonnie out of the conversation.

Distracted by imagining what they were talking about — were they exchanging bread recipes? Conferring about the weather? — Bonnie didn't notice that Freddie had left the rebel planning and was now standing next to her.

"Everything okay?" he asked.

She nodded, even as she felt her cheeks flush. It was embarrassing, not being privy to conversation. Did he realize she didn't know what they were saying? That she was an outsider, even among those who raised her?

"How is planning going?" she asked.

"I think we have a shot," he said. "The resources here are far greater than I predicted. The rebels should have no problem."

Bonnie's shoulders curved in relief. She had done it — she had made sure that the rebels remained safe. They weren't too late.

She yawned, and he did as well. It was time to get some rest. It would take most of the day to reach Thornwick by the main roads. They would have a few hours to settle in before they started the rescue.

Oll and Gwyneth concluded their conversation, and Bonnie bid them goodnight.

The corridors were empty as they made their way back to her room.

"Do they do that a lot?" Freddie asked as they walked. "Switch languages?"

"Yes," Bonnie mumbled. *How embarrassing.*

"What did they say? I couldn't understand."

"I don't know." The words felt sour on her tongue.

"It's rude," he said. Bonnie looked at him in surprise and he shrugged. "I understand the need for secrecy, sure. But there are other ways to go about it that are less hurtful."

"Why does it matter to you?" she snapped, even as she felt a sudden lightness in her chest. Maybe he wasn't so bad after all.

He opened his mouth and then closed it, finally at a loss for words. He shook his head and looked away.

A cot had been set on the floor next to her bed, and she

mentally thanked whoever had thought of it. It may not have been a bed fit for a lord, but it was certainly better than the hard forest ground. *She* certainly wasn't giving up her bed for him.

She fell into bed, exhausted. She was asleep as soon as her head hit the pillow.

CHAPTER NINE

BONNIE RAN AS FAST AS SHE COULD.

Today's the day, *she thought.* I know where to find it.

She navigated the hideout corridors with ease, ignoring the confused expressions on the rebel faces she passed.

They didn't like her; they were jealous. The only person she wanted to impress was Felix, and this was the perfect way to do it.

Bonnie slowed as she approached her mother's office door. Gwyneth was in Suverd on another mission. There were no guards posted outside — no one was crazy enough to enter.

Except Bonnie.

The door was locked, but it took only a few tries with her lock pick to open it. She mentally thanked the member of the Rebel Guard who taught her this new skill. He probably didn't expect her to use it for this.

Bonnie closed the door behind her and scanned the room.

Where would Gwyneth hide it?

A strange feeling washed over her as she rifled through the room. A feeling of foreboding.

Something was wrong. Something was coming.

Bonnie pushed those feelings down — she couldn't waste this opportunity.

A few more minutes of searching. It wasn't in the desk drawers or in the wardrobe. Was there a secret floorboard, perhaps? Bonnie wouldn't put it past her.

Aha! There it was!

Heart lighter, she lifted it from its hiding place. It was heavy, and softer than she had imagined.

The door opened, and a firm hand gripped her shoulder.

Bonnie screamed.

BONNIE WOKE WITH A START, DISORIENTED.

It had been a while since a nightmare had plagued her. They had haunted her frequently after the attack, but had petered out over the years. She hadn't missed them.

She looked to the cot and hoped Freddie hadn't seen her startle.

His bed was empty, his blankets nicely folded. She would've thought he was in the bathing chamber, but his shoes were gone, too.

Fuck.

Bonnie cursed and rubbed her eyes in frustration. Where could the damned man be?

She dressed quickly, grumbling about wayward nobles. After making sure her crown braid fully covered her scar, she left her room.

Where could he have gone? Maybe he had gone to the Map Room to prepare for the raid.

Still yawning, she poked her head through the door. Only a handful of others were awake at this hour, discussing raid logistics. Freddie was nowhere to be seen.

Maybe he woke up and wanted to eat — she could feel the

sharp pains of hunger setting in herself. He may not have gotten a tour, but he was resourceful. He probably asked someone where to go. Or followed the smell of bacon that wafted down the corridor.

Bonnie turned toward the kitchens, but a familiar voice called her name.

Freddie.

He walked toward her, carrying a paper bag.

"Where did you go?"

"There's a bakery in Crown Harbor that I visit every time I'm in the city. I woke up early and couldn't resist."

A thousand questions raced through her mind. "How did you get in and out of the hideout?"

"I'm very persuasive," he said, and shoved the bag into her hands.

"I didn't know you've been to Crown Harbor before," she said as she took his offering with a glare. She looked inside and saw a freshly baked cinnamon bun.

Freddie shrugged. "You never asked." He watched as she took a bite. "Where to now, fearless leader?"

She narrowed her eyes. "Map Room."

"Ah, come on. Give me a tour? I wandered around like a fool earlier."

That's the point, Bonnie wanted to say. "No," she said instead, and turned toward the Map Room.

"Did you pick up the knife Oll made for you?"

Damn. Bonnie had completely forgotten. She had been too tired last night to fetch it from the armory.

"No. I'll get it later."

"Don't want to disappoint Oll, Bonnie. We have time."

She grunted her disapproval, annoyed at his insistence. But she didn't want to get on Oll's bad side, so she turned away from the Map Room and led him down the long corridor. It was early enough that they didn't run into anyone.

Freddie pointed to a series of brightly colored doors that branched off the main corridor. "What are those rooms for?"

Bonnie led him toward where he pointed. The sound of crying and laughing drifted through one of the open doors.

"The children's wing," she said, and motioned for him to look inside.

Cots filled with sleeping babies lined the wall. A toddler girl chased around a younger boy with a toy block — her brother, by the look of their identical reddish hair coloring. Their squeals of delight brought a smile to Bonnie's lips. A wet nurse fed her charge in a rocking chair while a younger rebel consoled a wailing child.

Bonnie would never admit it, but she loved spending time with the babies and children. She always felt calm when she spent time there.

No rebel politics. No scheming or violence. Just pure innocence. It was refreshing.

She led Freddie to the next room.

"No babies here?" he asked, taking in the room. Posters of Amlucen teachings lined the walls, while desks and tables took up most of the floor space.

Bonnie avoided looking at the posters; she got a headache when she studied them too closely. She rubbed at the scar on her temple subconsciously.

"This is a schoolroom for the older children," she told him. "Those that are too old for the toddler room come here to learn their letters and numbers." She watched as he looked around, taking everything in.

His eyes widened as he saw the giant depiction of the rebellion symbol on one of the walls. It was identical to the one the king used to mark Hallordian goods and services — a four pointed star that pointed in each direction — but the Amlucen star had two slashes crossing through it. Gwyneth's golden ring bore the same symbol.

He pivoted again, and pointed to one of the many posters. "'DOWN WITH THE CROWN'? 'SEIZE OUR STOLEN GOODS?' What does that mean?"

"Exactly what it says," Bonnie said, studying her nails. "We want to take the throne back. We don't recognize Aborn's rule as legitimate."

"How so?"

She cocked her head at him. "Strange question from one who claims to be a rebel sympathizer."

He had the audacity to roll his eyes. "I believe in the Amlucen mission, Bonnie. But I didn't grow up here — I learned the rebellion ideals on my own. Humor me."

"Fine. Before Aborn rose to power, the continent was made up of smaller, individual countries, right? Small territories. But there was no peace — every man wanted what his neighbor had. The constant fighting weakened them enough that Aborn was able to take control. He used magic to manipulate the landscape so his armies always won the battles."

For Aborn, the ambitious second-son, was blessed with the ability to control the land beneath his feet. A rare power no one had seen before or since.

"He assassinated the rightful rulers and inserted his own people. His reign of terror hasn't ended — just last week he took over one of the smaller islands on the western coast. He needs to be stopped, and that's why we've all vowed to remove the tyrant from his blood throne."

Freddie blinked a few times, his mouth opening wide.

"What?"

"I don't think I've ever heard you speak that much in one go before," he said, his mouth curling up in a smirk.

Her cheeks heated. "No more history lessons for you, *milord.*"

"No, please." He looked earnest. "This helps me a great deal. I promise I won't make fun."

She grumbled. "What else do you want to know?"

"What do the rebels think happened on Vale Magicae?"

Bonnie flinched and stopped herself from rubbing the scar on her temple. "They think Vale Magicae was the gods' way of punishing Aborn for amassing too much power. That's why magic only disappears within the borders of Hallordis." She shuddered. "I can't imagine what magic wielders feel when Aborn takes over and their access to magic is cut off."

Freddie shivered. "It's not pleasant. Or so I imagine." He coughed. "I've heard it described to me as if a limb is severed — there one moment, gone the next. Must feel horrible."

That was enough magic talk for Bonnie. Why dwell on something that's been gone for so long? "Let's go," she said and exited the classroom.

She gave him a lackluster tour as she navigated them towards the armory. A few rebels walked the corridors now, heads down in the early morning hour. Anyone who looked at her looked away, too afraid to make eye contact.

He dragged her into the library, ignoring her protests when she tried to walk past it. His eyes lit up at all the bookshelves, and he trailed a finger down the leather-bound volumes as he walked down a row.

"Marvelous," he murmured as he took a book down. He studied the writing on the spine, and then examined the ones on the shelf. "Hold on. These are all about King Aborn and his rule." He looked at Bonnie, eyebrow raised. "Why would you have books about him? I would've thought they were banned."

Bonnie shrugged, looking away. She hated coming here. "Know your enemy, I guess."

He flipped through the book. "Huh," he said, and frowned. His fingers traced the jagged edges of paper. "Someone ripped pages out. Look, see — I think this is where a portrait of the king's family should have been."

"That's on purpose. Portraits of the royal family are prohibited."

Freddie looked aghast. "Why?"

"Why would we want to look upon the man who killed our families?"

She didn't tell him she wouldn't be able to pick the king out in a crowd. When it came to Bonnie and King Aborn, Oll and Gwyneth were overprotective to an extreme. They were worried that Bonnie would suffer some sort of mental break-down if she even glimpsed his likeness.

Remembering her nightmare this morning, Bonnie thought they might have a point. She had enough trauma to process without putting a face to the monster who killed her family.

"That doesn't make sense, though —" he pushed.

Bonnie had enough. "Are you questioning the will of our lead-ers?" she snapped. "Oll and Gwyneth have reasons for what they do — reasons that you are not privy to. Stop questioning them."

Freddie still looked unsettled. Bonnie thought he forgot, sometimes, how much Aborn took from those who walked these halls. It didn't matter if he agreed with the rebel mission — he could never truly identify with the others.

"Fine," he said as he put the book back on the shelf.

"We don't have all day," she said as he lifted a hand to take down another one. "Let's go."

He followed her out with a grumble, and she sighed with relief when she crossed the threshold. There was always a good chance she would run into Felix in there, and she wasn't in the mood to deal with his smug arrogance right now.

They continued on. Freddie whistled when they walked through the armory door.

Bonnie smirked. It *was* a sight to behold.

The armory shared space with the exercise arena used by the Rebel Guard. To access it, one had to pass by three large training rings. The first one, filled with archery dummies and racks of bows and arrows, currently stood vacant. Bonnie knew it was only a matter of time before it filled with rebels looking for target practice.

The second ring was empty, although a few weight bags lay forgotten to one side. No weapons allowed in this one, only weights. Bonnie hated every minute she spent in this ring doing strengthening exercises.

The third ring was Bonnie's favorite, and the only one occupied. Freddie's mouth dropped open at the sight of two rebels, one tall and covered in tattoos, the other bald and stout, circling each other, knives out. Blunted, of course, but sharp enough to slice skin if the fighter applied enough pressure. A few onlookers jeered as the big one stepped menacingly toward the other one.

Racks of swords — short, long, wooden, steel, anything you could imagine — stood outside the ring. Shields, too, of all different sizes and weights.

Bonnie couldn't guess how many hours she had trained here over the years. Hundreds, at least, under the watchful eye of Benji Strongarm. Bonnie wasn't sure where the scarred weapons master was — probably getting things ready for the rescue efforts.

"Are all rebels trained here?" Freddie asked as they passed the training ring.

"No. Only members of the Rebel Guard."

His eyebrow quirked up, but a voice rang out in triumph before he could ask another question. They looked over to see the muscular rebel celebrate his victory.

"Who's next?" he crowed, grinning from ear to ear. Sweat ran down his powerful body in rivers. He must've noticed them because a moment later he laughed.

"Bonnie Blackthorn!" he called out. Everyone turned to face

her, and a hush fell over the crowd. "Fancy a turn in the ring? It's about time we faced each other again."

Bonnie grinned. "Not today, Jack," she called out. "Another time."

Jack nodded and turned back to the onlookers. Bonnie waved good-naturedly at the rebels who acknowledged her.

"Friend of yours?" Freddie asked. She couldn't read his expression.

Bonnie nodded. "Of a sort. We've trained together for years. He's wanted a rematch for ages."

His eyebrows rose. "You beat *him*?" He looked at the fighter, who was now drinking from a canteen. "How?"

"I'll try not to be offended, lordling," she responded. "I'm more than a pretty face." She didn't blame him for his skepticism, though. Jack was quite the specimen, both in the ring and out of it.

Freddie was quiet as they reached the armory. She nodded to the rebel posted in front of the door — someone guarded the room around the clock — and went inside.

"Oh my," Freddie said, voice hushed.

Weapons of all shapes and sizes lined three of the walls. Swords, crossbows, arrows, knives, axes — dozens of each of these, and more, hung from hooks set into the wall and in wooden barrels throughout the space.

In front of the fourth wall was a long counter, where two familiar faces were chatting quietly.

"Benji, Martin," Bonnie greeted both men with a nod.

Benji looked at her with no expression, which Bonnie expected. The weapons master rarely smiled. But Bonnie could sense from the twinkle in his eye that he was happy to see her.

Martin, the rebel in charge of the armory, only grimaced. She didn't blame him; she wasn't always the most pleasant customer. Growing up with a knife fanatic, Bonnie was picky about her weapons. The difference between a good weapon and a great weapon could mean life or death. "Oll told me he had a knife made for me. Is it ready?"

Martin nodded and turned to head into a separate back room.

Benji crossed his arms across his chest, staring at Freddie. "I hear you're to thank for the warning about Thornwick."

Freddie nodded, his face impassive.

Benji continued to stare at him, unblinking. The scar that stretched across the top of his forehead, courtesy of a member of the King's Guard, twitched as his mouth settled into a frown.

Bonnie studied her nails, in no mood to officiate this inane display of masculinity. At least *someone* voiced their concern about Freddie being allowed to wander the halls.

Freddie said nothing, only shifted his feet as he stared back at Benji.

Bonnie wondered what he thought of the weapon master. If he realized how much danger he was in, standing next to a man who could kill him in a heartbeat. She was sure that nothing would please Benji more than to do just that. He had dedicated his life to dismantling the king's regime of terror since the king's men murdered his wife and child twenty years before.

And Bonnie had become something of his protégé. He had taken a sad, scarred girl and transformed her into a warrior. Bonnie would be forever thankful to him for that.

But that didn't mean she had to put up with their posturing bullshit. As she opened her mouth to say something, Martin rushed back into the armory.

"Here," he said, handing her the knife. His abruptness didn't bother her, although she noticed Freddie frown at the perceived rudeness.

Bonnie looked at the knife and tried not to frown. She couldn't deny that it was a nice knife — the handle was made of supple leather, and it was balanced nicely. A quick run of her finger told her the blade was wickedly sharp. A keeper, for sure. She just didn't enjoy the feeling like she owed Oll something. If Gwyneth had given her the knife, maybe she'd feel different.

Bonnie nodded to Martin in thanks before she pocketed it. With a quick goodbye to both men, she left the room, Freddie following behind.

"Rebel Guard?" Freddie asked as soon as they had left the training arena. The corridors had filled with rebels during the time they spent in the armory.

She snorted; he probably wanted to ask about it the moment she brought it up. "Rebel Guard. Aborn has the King's Guard trained to shed blood and conquer all. We have our own rebel army to fight back. Benji is the weapons master."

"Ah."

He kept silent as they passed the others. While they stared at him, they never looked at Bonnie directly. If they made eye contact, though, they made sure to smile.

One rebel approached — a pimply teenager with unwashed hair. "Miss B-B-Blackthorn," she stuttered, staring at the floor.

"Yes?" Bonnie shifted, uncomfortable. Fear radiated off the girl in waves. And although Bonnie expected it, it didn't feel good.

Freddie looked between them with undisguised curiosity.

"I was sent to inform y-y-you that there's been a ch-ch-change of plans. All rebels are to re-re-report to the Grand Hall."

The Grand Hall? That room was one of the few places large enough to host all of the rebels. The Amlucen thrived on secrets — it wasn't often that everyone was addressed at once.

"Thank you," Bonnie said, trying to infuse warmth into those two words. It didn't matter; the girl fled as soon as she replied.

"She's afraid of you," Freddie said thoughtfully. "Why?"

"I'm an assassin, Lord Stonewood. Isn't that enough?"

Everyone in the Amlucen was cautious as a general rule — everyone treaded carefully in an environment where secrets meant life or death. The fact that she was Oll and Gwyneth's daughter meant the others were more afraid of her than most, lest she bring them to the attention of her parents. Although they made sure to be polite to her face, she knew they all feared her and her influence.

For while everyone believed in the leadership of the Blackthorns, there was a hefty dose of fear there, too.

"*I'm* not afraid of you."

"Maybe you should be."

He thought for a moment. "Do you have any friends? Anyone you can rely on?"

"No."

"Why not?"

"Assassins don't make the best of friends."

"I disagree. Who better to have on your side than someone who would kill for you?"

Bonnie had no reply to that. The entire conversation made her uncomfortable. And sad.

So she turned and made her way down the corridor, Freddie following silently. They were about to enter the Grand Hall when Bonnie heard a cough from a nearby alcove. Felix stood there, his form partially hidden by shadows.

"I'll meet you inside," she told Freddie, and watched as he entered the room.

"What do you want?" she asked Felix when she joined him.

"Did you enjoy your cinnamon bun?" His blonde hair flopped over his forehead.

Oh.

Oh.

"I take it you had him followed?"

He nodded. "I wanted to see where Lord Stonewood went

when you weren't dragging him all over the place. I trailed him myself."

"And?"

Felix blew out a breath. "Nothing. Kept to himself, didn't talk to anyone. Visited a pastry shop down by the wharf. The Crown's Cookery."

Bonnie snorted. Sounded like a place he would go. "Good call to follow him." It was the nicest thing she could think of to say to the man who had once been her best friend, her confidant. Before jealousy and pride took over.

She turned to leave, hoping to end the conversation without a confrontation.

"You don't trust him?"

Pausing, she considered. In all honesty, Bonnie didn't know how she felt. "I don't trust anyone."

CHAPTER TEN

It took Bonnie only a moment to find Freddie in the crowded Grand Hall.

He stood tall as he watched rebels move to sit on the benches that lined the room. His ability to ignore the pointed stares of those nearby impressed her.

"Why do you think we're here?" Freddie whispered when she joined him.

"Oll probably wants to make an announcement."

Whispers filled the room as rebels speculated about why they were summoned. Babies cried, mothers tried to settle them, and children laughed and played in the aisles. The door closed as the last of the rebels entered.

Just when Bonnie thought Oll had forgotten about the meeting, the door crashed open.

Her adopted father strode in, dressed in a supple fur coat. With matching boots.

Bold, she thought with a frown, *to be dressed as richly as the king himself.*

Gwyneth entered after him. She, at least, wore normal clothes — dark-colored pants and a simple green sweater.

The older woman glanced around the room until she locked eyes with Bonnie. Bonnie raised an eyebrow, staring pointedly at Oll. Gwyneth grimaced, shrugged, and took her place beside him on the dais at the front of the room.

Oll clapped his hands with glee as he looked at the assembled group. "I am glad to see everyone here, bright and early!" In an instant, he dropped the grin, switching instead to a far more somber look; even Bonnie blinked at his sudden change in emotion. "I have grave news to share with you. Our brethren in Thornwick are under threat by our so-called king."

A collective gasp sounded throughout the room. Bonnie watched as rebels turned to each other in panic. Several women gripped each other tight, while the men looked on with grim faces.

"Do not worry! I have brought together a contingent of our soldiers to save our Thornwick brothers and sisters before the crown plans to attack. Together, we will thwart the imposter king. He will not get away with the murder of our people while I have breath in my lungs!"

A roar of approval met his words.

"Time is of the essence — our brethren in Thornwick are awaiting our arrival. Those who are coming with us — we leave now! To the stables!"

As one, the rebels stood and started chanting, "Down with the crown! Down with the crown!"

Rebel soldiers streamed out the door, leaving the women, children, and elderly behind. Bonnie and Freddie were the last to leave and quickly made their way to the stables.

Freddie's eyes went wide at the sight, clearly not expecting such a place within the rebellion. Some architectural genius had gutted two of the larger houses, creating one giant room. The perimeter of the building had been converted into stalls and tack rooms, but a fenced-in meadow, complete with grass and flowers, filled the middle of the space. The roof had been removed to allow for air flow, and while it exposed the house to the elements, Bonnie knew that the opening could be covered with thin sheets of metal if the weather got too hostile.

Bonnie walked up to the fence that enclosed the meadow. She spotted Captain, and then Belle, a golden horse with a white tail, and called them to her.

The two ambled over, Captain going to greet Freddie while Belle nuzzled Bonnie's outstretched hand.

"Hello, beautiful," Bonnie whispered as she stroked her mane. "Ready to go for a ride?"

A SERIES OF LARGE BOULDERS MARKED THEIR DESTINATION.

Bonnie felt a tingling sensation when she crossed into Golwich. She bowed her head in thanks to whatever divine being ruled over the forest and asked for a safe passage through the trees.

Magic may have disappeared, but one could never know who — or what — still haunted the ancient forest.

They had traveled for hours on the well-worn highway that connected Crown Harbor and Thornwick, stopping only occasionally to let the horses rest. Now they navigated their mounts toward a large clearing filled with rebel soldiers.

Leaving the horses to graze under the watchful eye of a younger rebel, they joined the others. Newcomers weaved around the group, solemn faces that had not been at headquarters. Bonnie recognized a few. Rebels from Thornwick, preparing to defend the city that they loved.

It gave Bonnie hope. Oll and Gwyneth had sent out riders last night to prepare for the raid, but even with advanced notice, she knew it would be a challenge to hide all the families who called Thornwick home.

The remaining groups trickled in by the time the sun had set over the forest. Oll and Gwyneth arrived last, Oll still wearing his ridiculous fur coat. He made eye contact with each rebel as he made his way through the crowd, clasping hands with some and nodding to others. The light from the full moon shone on him like a beacon.

Gwyneth joined Bonnie and Freddie near the outer perimeter. Her shoulders were tense, her jaw clenched.

"What's wrong?" Bonnie asked with a nudge of her arm. "Everything okay?"

Gwyneth nodded, even as a muscle in her jaw twitched. "Everything is fine," the older woman said. She twisted the gold ring she wore around her finger. "Just a long day."

A day of traveling with Oll probably felt like a week's journey, Bonnie knew. No wonder Gwyneth looked exhausted.

"Thank you for coming," Oll addressed the crowd. "It is a great thing to see so many of our brethren gathered to save our brothers and sisters. We'll work through the night to save as many as we can from the king's clutches. Based on our intel —" next to Bonnie, Freddie shifted on his feet " — the king's minions plan to strike at dawn. With luck and skill on our side, our plan is to save every Amlucenite man, woman, and child. Now is the time to come together, to save our people. Down with the crown! Down with the crown!"

Things moved quickly after that. They armed recruits, handing out the knives, swords, and bows that rebels had secretly transported in traveling carts.

Freddie chose a knife and sword with care, testing several options before selecting ones that were of decent make. Bonnie had brought her own sword and set of knives, including the one Oll had given her; she hoped she wouldn't have to use them.

She claimed a spot under a nearby tree, using a free moment to sharpen her blades. The sound of one sliding against her whetstone was pleasing to her ears.

She watched rebels as they scurried around the clearing,

darting to and fro as they chose supplies that might mean the difference between life and death. Any words that were spoken were in hushed whispers, conversations too low for easy eavesdropping. Wide eyes set in gaunt faces darted around the space, and the smell of hot metal, smoke, and leather filled her nose. The soft snorting of the nearby horses and the crackling wood in the small campfires were the loudest noises in the clearing.

Freddie stood alone near a small fire, his hands hovering over the flames to keep warm. He kept looking at something off to the side before turning back to the flames.

Bonnie followed his gaze and saw that he was staring at Gwyneth.

She frowned. Gwyneth wasn't a spectacle to be gawked at. She was a survivor, and much more than the sum of her scars. Bonnie rubbed her own scar for a moment before turning back to her whetstone.

Screeeeeeech.

She sharpened her knife a little too hard. Freddie's head whipped toward her as she stared him down. She turned her head slowly to glance at her mother, Freddie following her gaze.

He shook his head, stuck his hands in his pockets, and walked over.

"Stop staring at her scars," Bonnie told him, her voice cold.

He reared his head back. "What? I wasn't looking at her scars."

"Why do you keep looking at her then?"

He opened his mouth, closed it, and then opened it again, as if unsure of what to say. Of course — how could he justify what he was doing? It was obvious. Judging others was second nature to him.

Bonnie opened her mouth to say something nasty when an owl hoot cut through the air. Everyone other than Freddie froze and waited with bated breath. Freddie stilled, too, once he realized what was going on.

Oll returned the owl call with one of his own.

Two more calls sounded, and Bonnie tried to clear her mind. She needed to focus.

It was time to save Thornwick.

CHAPTER ELEVEN

THEY ENTERED THORNWICK THROUGH A SECRET HOLE IN THE wall that circled the city. She wasn't sure if the king's men knew about the vulnerable spot or if they were too lazy to fix it. Either way, it was the main point of covert entry for the Amlucenites who now snuck inside the city.

Thornwick was unusually silent.

There were no children running through the streets, awake far past their bedtimes. No courtesans flouting their wares near their brothels. No drunkards, hobbling around with bottles in their hand and meanness in their hearts.

Tonight, there was nothing but silence. Not even a stray dog or cat to be seen.

Her eyes darted around the streets, looking for evidence of something — *anything* — that might explain why the streets were so quiet and empty. Ears strained, she heard nothing but her and Freddie's footsteps as they snuck through the streets. The hairs on the back of her neck rose as her confusion grew . . . what was going on? Where was everyone? Oll and Gwyneth had sent a messenger, sure, but there was no way the entire population — rebels and non-rebels alike — could've disappeared with little warning.

They paused in the alleyway, almost at the city center. Freddie turned to Bonnie. "We need to talk."

She raised her eyebrow, although she wasn't sure if he could see her face clearly. It was dark, and the nearest oil lantern was a half dozen yards away. "About what?"

"About why I was staring at Gwyneth."

"Later."

"Now. I don't know the next time we'll be alone. How much do you know about her? About who she is and where she came from?"

"What kind of question is that?" she hissed, her voice rising. "She's my godsdamn mother, for fuck's sake — I know her better than anyone!"

"Shhhh," he cautioned. "Do you remember that I told you she felt familiar to me?"

"Yes."

"I realized how I know her. This may sound crazy, but I think —"

His voice cut out as a loud *bang!* sounded from directly outside the alleyway.

"Shit." She laid a hand on his arm when he rose, stopping him.

He paused. "We should go see what that was."

"Something is wrong," she told him.

"What do you mean?"

She looked around. "I can't explain it. Something's wrong, I'm sure of it. This feels like a trap."

He looked out of the alley again, more slowly this time.

"Where is everyone?" she whispered. "Why does it feel like we're the only ones here?"

His eyes grew wide.

"We need to leave," Bonnie said as she stood from her crouched position. "Now."

They turned to backtrack, and stopped short.

Three soldiers stood at the end of the alleyway, swords drawn, watching them with wolfish grins on their faces.

Freddie swore in Naverian.

The guards, dressed in the king's colors of blue and gold, advanced. One of them giggled as he ran towards them.

Freddie grabbed Bonnie's hand and dragged her into the street.

Bonnie's mind spun as they ran. Freddie *seemed* surprised to find the King's Guard already in the city, but was he responsible for this trap? Did he give the rebellion incorrect information?

The silence of the city broke as they ran, feet pounding on the cobblestone streets. Anguished cries rang out from all directions.

A majority of the fighting seemed to come from the alleyways the rebels had been sneaking around in, but fights now spilled into the street. Freddie, hand gripped tight around Bonnie's smaller one, maneuvered around the fighting with ease as he raced towards the outer perimeter wall.

Bonnie warred with herself. While she was prepared to stand and fight, she also recognized an ambush when she saw one. Nothing went the way they planned. To stay and fight, with the odds against them, felt like a death wish.

Oof!

Freddie pulled Bonnie to the side. She would've tripped over the body in the street if he hadn't kept her upright. As she regained her footing, she lost her breath.

It was the girl from headquarters — the pimply, unwashed one that gave her the message hours ago. Bloody wounds crisscrossed the young girl's body, as if her murderer taunted her before killing her. Sightless eyes stared at the night sky.

Anguish turned to anger.

They were *monsters*.

Freddie's hand squeezed hers as he stared down. A muscle in his jaw ticked.

He looked behind them and swore. Bonnie turned and saw a lethal-looking soldier walking toward them from down the street. Tugging on her hand, Freddie weaved them in and out of streets so quickly that Bonnie couldn't keep track of where they were.

The soldier followed, running fast. Bonnie felled a few soldiers who got in her way, stabbing her knife quickly in and out as she passed. Blood covered her in hot droplets and the tang of metal filled her mouth.

Just as they lost the attention of that soldier they ran into an ongoing fight.

Literally.

"Shit!" Freddie yelled, freeing Bonnie's hand as he slammed into one of the king's men. Bonnie used her momentum to roll to the right, ending on her feet. She assessed the scene.

Two guards versus a bloodied rebel. The rebel spit blood onto the cobblestone street and held his arm gingerly in front of him.

Freddie dispatched the first guard with a fist to the face, knocking him unconscious. He swore in Naverian as he rubbed the knuckles on his now-bloodied hand.

The second guard leered at Bonnie. She could tell he thought she was the weak link — how could she not be, when Freddie just knocked out the other guard with a single punch?

As the guard walked toward her, the injured rebel saw his opportunity to flee and took it. He hobbled down the nearest alleyway as fast as his injured body could take him.

Perfect. He would've gotten in the way.

Bonnie assumed a defensive position. She palmed her knife

in a tight grip, waiting to see who would make the first move. Anger coursed through her, and she smiled wickedly.

She would enjoy this.

Everything faded into the background. She didn't have to wait long for him to strike; he almost looked bored as he slashed his sword in her direction. Bonnie only had to step once to the right to dodge it, so lame was the attempt.

The guard grunted and slashed again, this time with a little more force.

She dodged once more, this time with a smirk.

His eyebrows furrowed as he looked at her properly, his expression souring when he saw the look on her face.

Good. Fuck him.

He grunted and took a step forward, his sword extending to bridge the gap between them. She parried with her knife, hitting his sword with her knife once, twice, three times, just to piss him off. The sound of metal on metal rang out through the night.

And then she spun so quickly he didn't have time to move another step. Before he could blink, she stuck her knife into his throat.

His life's blood spurted in an arc when she removed her knife, and she stepped aside so the hot drops of red rain missed her. She watched, expressionless, as he sank to his knees, his sword clattering to the ground as both of his hands went to the fatal wound.

He was dead moments later.

She wiped her knife on his shirt before turning back to Freddie. She couldn't read his expression. Disappointment, probably. And revulsion. She shrugged it off; she didn't need his approval.

Bonnie looked around. The outer wall was near — only a block away. She nudged him, pointing to it, and he nodded. He took one last look at the dead guard and swallowed hard.

And then they ran.

They made it to the bolt hole, encountering no one else. Freddie entered first, sword at the ready. No more surprises.

He looked back and she saw his eyes widen in fear.

Bonnie turned and saw a man dressed in the king's colors. She could do nothing as his sword slashed in an arc towards her.

Freddie called her name, voice panicked.

That was the last thing she remembered before everything went black.

CHAPTER TWELVE

BONNIE WOKE IN TOTAL DARKNESS.

Her head throbbed. Nausea rose. She coughed weakly, but there was nothing in her stomach to throw up.

She tried to open her eyes but couldn't. Reaching up, she felt some sort of rough fabric covering the top half of her face.

Where was she? How long had she been here?

The last thing she remembered was Freddie shouting her name. She thought for sure she was dead.

She opened her mouth in a silent scream as a wave of pain washed over her. She imagined this is what it felt like to be struck by lightning.

If this wasn't hell, it was an excellent imitation of it.

She tried to get her bearings. Was she in the king's dungeon? Midverd was days away, but she didn't know how long she had been unconscious. She couldn't rule out the possibility. It smelled like hay, though, and stale manure. Not what she imagined the castle dungeons smelled like.

Bonnie groaned as a fresh wave of agony hit her, driving all other thoughts out of her mind. She couldn't stop a pitiful whimper from escaping her lips.

Through the pain, she heard the *snick* of a door opening. And then the sound of footsteps coming closer. The sound of muffled voices, one male and one female.

They were there to kill her, she was sure of it.

A bolt of fear raced through her as she felt a pair of hands grab her shoulders. The touch was gentle, if firm. Almost as if whoever it was just wanted her to calm down.

But all she knew was pain and fear.

She fought harder, and the movement made her head throb. She knew she was close to passing out from the pain.

The taste of a bitter liquid filled her mouth. She tried to spit it out but it was too late.

She lost consciousness.

BONNIE WASN'T SURE HOW MUCH TIME HAD PASSED BEFORE SHE woke to the sound of voices outside of her room.

She tried to control her breathing. In, out, in, out. She didn't want them to know she was awake.

She strained to hear the voices, but all it did was make her head throb. A whimper escaped as the pain shot through her skull.

The voices cut off. The door opened with a *click*, followed by approaching footsteps.

A second set of footsteps, much softer.

"Is she waking?" a feminine voice asked. Bonnie didn't recognize it.

"I think so," replied a low voice closer to the bed.

Bonnie's breathing hitched; her attempt to feign sleep had fooled no one. She felt the man's firm hands grasp her shoulders again. She fought to raise her hands, but found that they were bound to her sides.

"Please," Bonnie rasped. "Let me go."

"You're not ready yet," the woman's accented voice replied

from the end of the bed. Bonnie heard glass clinking together. "You were gravely wounded. You need time to heal."

Bitter liquid filled Bonnie's mouth, cutting off her chance to reply. She choked on it, tried to spit some out. "But I've already slept enough."

Before she succumbed to the sleeping draught, she felt the man's hands stiffen on her shoulders.

"I thought she didn't know how to speak our language?" the man said.

Bonnie didn't know what he was talking about. She fell asleep, and any further protests died on her lips.

THE NEXT FEW DAYS PASSED SLOWLY.

Bonnie's head throbbed less each time she woke. She felt no other pain or weakness.

Any conversation came to a halt when her captors sensed she was awake. While they refused to answer any of her questions, they reminded her regularly to stay still, don't fuss. She needed time to heal.

After a few days, they left her hands unbound. Once, when she was alone, she tried taking off her blindfold. No sooner had she lifted but the tiniest corner of the fabric when a sharp pain radiated throughout her skull. She pulled the blindfold back, tears streaming down her face.

Lesson learned.

They didn't seem to notice the mice that had taken residence underneath her blanket. Or if they did, they chose not to say anything. Her little friends were quiet, but their warmth as they snuggled into her side boosted her spirits more than she could say.

Her captors spoke with accents that Bonnie puzzled over. It wasn't the hissing and spitting she associated with Suverian, nor was it Naverian. She couldn't place where these two had come from, which made her unreasonably bitter. Add it to her list of shortcomings.

She wasn't sure how much time passed, but she felt her strength returning. The woman surprised her when she declared it was time to remove the blindfold.

Bonnie eagerly agreed, allowing the man to sit her up against the headboard. She kept her eyes firmly shut as one of them took off the blindfold.

She opened her eyes, just a crack.

No pain.

She opened them fully.

She was in a small room made of stone, on a bed that took up most of the space. There were no windows; the only light came from sputtering candles on a wooden nightstand. There was a table in the corner, various herbs and vials littering the surface.

She turned to face the two people who saved her life as they watched her from the side of the room. As grateful as she was to be alive, she didn't know who they were and what they wanted with her. Did they heal her to save her life, or heal her in order to torture her?

The woman was smaller than Bonnie had imagined. She was slight, with soft brown skin, and wore a plain blue dress that hugged her body. Her face framed by wavy honey-colored hair, and her dark brown eyes looked at Bonnie warmly. A soft smile graced her lips.

The man stood by the door with a frown, so tall his salt-and-pepper hair almost hit the top of the doorway. He wore a white shirt and patched pants, well-made but well-worn. He nodded to Bonnie, and she returned the gesture.

Bonnie turned back to the woman, who was settling a tray of food on her lap. Some sort of meat stew, by the smell of it, and a rind of crusty bread. Her mouth watered as she smelled the feast in front of her. The last time she ate something other than watery broth was before the failed rescue.

She eyed her stew warily, but ignored her lingering paranoia. They wouldn't nurse her back to health only to poison her now. She hoped.

Taking a bite, she moaned with pleasure. It was delicious.

Bonnie eyed them. Who did they work for, and why were they helping her?

"What's going on?" she asked. "Who are you?"

"We're part of the rebellion," the woman said. "My name is Claire, and my husband's name is Stefan. We live in Thornwick."

Well, *that* was news to Bonnie. And welcome, if it was true. But how could she trust them?

"If you go to the river, take a right at the fork. Is the fishing any good?"

Stefan eyed her. "Only on Tuesdays, and on Thursday when there's a full moon."

Okay, that was something. They knew one of the code phrases that identified other rebels — but that still didn't mean they were trustworthy. She relaxed her posture, though, and hoped they believed her.

Then she frowned. "What the hell happened?"

Claire's shoulders slumped, and Stefan sat down hard in the wooden chair next to Bonnie's bed.

"It was horrible," he said, staring at the opposite wall. Claire walked to him and laid a hand on his shoulder.

"What happened?"

Stefan met her gaze, eyes wide with wild despair. "The king killed them all."

CHAPTER THIRTEEN

BONNIE COULDN'T BREATHE.

She sat as still as a statue, her chest heaving as she fought to get air.

Stefan was wrong. Stefan was *lying*. She didn't want to consider the alternative.

She couldn't lose her family again.

"Not everyone," Claire said in a rush. "A few people got out. The lucky ones. We got out."

"Did Gwyneth survive? Did Oll?" Bonnie only added Oll as an afterthought — truth be told, the world would be a safer place if he were dead.

"Both alive and unhurt."

Bonnie released a breath and pried her fingers from where they gripped the edge of her bed. "What happened?"

"We were leaving the city when we saw them — the King's Guard. They were already positioned around Thornwick. No one could leave. A few hours later, they rounded up any known or suspected rebels. Anyone not suspected of rebel activity was told to stay inside or risk death."

That would explain why Bonnie hadn't seen anyone when

she and Freddie snuck through the streets. "How did you escape?"

"We came here," Claire said. "We're underground," she responded, to Bonnie's questioning look. "Underneath the stables, actually. The Thornwick rebels built a network of tunnels under the city as a precaution. There are only a few entrances, and their locations are a highly guarded secret. No one saw us enter."

"What happened to those that were taken? Are they dead?"

"Took them to the mines," Stefan answered. "It's easy for them to defend — there are only a few entrances."

Bonnie shuddered at the thought of being stuck inside the damp, dark mines. She had only entered them once, on a recon mission for Oll. There was no real purpose to it — he wanted Bonnie to sneak in, look around, and report back. It wasn't much, to Bonnie's disappointment. She brought back some samples of rock that they had been digging, but didn't know why he'd be interested. He never brought it up again.

Bonnie studied the tops of her hands while her mind processed everything. There were cuts crisscrossing her skin, all shallow, now healed. Probably from her flight across the city.

She snapped her head up and grimaced as it throbbed. "How did I get here? How did I survive?"

"One of the secret entrances is by the hole in the wall you tried to escape through. We heard Lord Stonewood say your name, realized who you were, and knew we had to save you. We killed the guard — he had knocked you unconscious with the hilt of his sword — and brought you here."

Bonnie stilled. "You recognized Lord Stonewood?"

The pair shared a look, one that made the hair on Bonnie's arms stand up. "Yes. We know who Lord Stonewood is."

Bonnie swallowed and tried to ignore the weird feeling that settled in her stomach. "Is he alive? Did you save him, too?"

She knew, in her heart, that a good number of rebels would've taken an opportunity to end the life of the nobleman. And at one time she would've, too, no question. It didn't matter that Freddie wasn't the one who hurt their loved ones. He was a symbol of everything that Aborn embodied.

She was afraid that these people, the ones who kept her away from death's door, wouldn't be as forgiving as she had come to be.

"He's alive," Stefan said, but something about his tone felt *off*. He said it almost smugly, as if Bonnie was missing something. An inside joke, one that Bonnie was not privy to.

And she hated that.

"He's alive," she repeated. "Where is he?"

"In safe hands," he said as he shifted in his seat.

Bonnie said nothing, but continued to stare him down. She had been told that her piercing green eyes gave her the ability to intimidate even the most stalwart of people. She had used this to her advantage effectively in the past.

Tonight was no different. After a few seconds, Stefan squirmed in his seat. Claire's eyes shifted around the room.

"Where is he?" Bonnie repeated.

One second passed, and then another. When it looked like they wouldn't answer — and Bonnie wasn't sure what she would do, considering she was as weak as a newborn baby — Claire opened her mouth.

"He was taken," the woman blurted.

Stefan turned to her, eyes flashing. Claire stopped talking.

Bonnie sat up. "Who took him? The King's Guard?"

"Oll Blackthorn and his men."

Shit.

This was infinitely worse.

If the king had him, Freddie's father could intervene on his son's behalf. Maybe chalk up Freddie's actions as temporary youthful insanity.

But with Oll at the helm?

Bonnie knew she'd be lucky to find pieces of him after Oll and his cronies were done with him.

She knew she should be happy — he was a member of Aborn's inner circle, after all.

But it wasn't *right*.

Although his father was responsible for atrocities that had been committed against the rebels, *Freddie* wasn't responsible for them. He was only a year or so older than she was — he would've been around ten years old on Vale Magicae. *He* hadn't killed her family, or any of the rebels who lost their lives that day. And as far as she could tell, he'd only wanted to help the rebels since then, not murder them.

That guilt lied with Aborn alone.

Claire and Stefan started arguing in low voices, speaking in an unfamiliar language. It wasn't Suverian, or Naverian. Wolverian, possibly? She had yet to travel to Wolverd, the westernmost territory, but she'd overheard conversations between Wolverian traders in markets before. The language was comprised of clicks and pauses — at least, that's what it sounded like to her inexperienced ears.

Bonnie bristled. How dare they switch languages? It was like spending time with her godsdamn family all over again. She didn't know a single word of Wolverian, but that didn't stop her from trying to eavesdrop.

She blinked.

What was happening?

No.

It's not possible. She shook her head, sure she was wrong.

Bonnie understood every word they were saying.

BONNIE BLINKED A FEW MORE TIMES.

It didn't make sense; she didn't know how to speak Wolverian.

Not only that, but she didn't know if they *were* speaking Wolverian. All she knew was what once sounded like clicks and pauses now sounded like actual speech.

"Our orders were to keep Lord Stonewood's captivity quiet," Stefan was saying in a low voice. His fingers clenched his knee tightly. "Now she knows too much."

Claire glared at him. "So what if she knows? This is great news for the rebel cause."

Stefan glanced at Bonnie, and she hoped the confusion on her face hid the fact she could follow their conversation.

"We don't know where her loyalties lie," he said, turning back to his wife. "We were told they traveled together before the raid. How do we know he hasn't twisted her mind?"

Bonnie kept her mouth shut, but on the inside she was seething. How *dare* they accuse her of becoming a traitor? It was true Freddie gave incorrect intel — and the rebels certainly needed to figure out what happened. But he seemed just as surprised as she was that the King's Guard had been in Thornwick early. There had to be a reason for the change of plans. Freddie was foolish, but he wouldn't risk his own life.

Claire's eyes opened wide. "She's Oll Blackthorn's daughter, Stefan. You really think she'd betray us?"

"People do funny things when they're in love."

Bonnie turned her snort of outrage into a hacking cough when they looked her way. The effort made her head ache, and she winced.

The idea of being in love with Freddie Stonewood was absolutely ludicrous. Is that what people thought?

Fools. She barely tolerated the man.

"Where did Oll take him? Lord Stonewood?" Bonnie asked in the common tongue, acting as though they hadn't switched to their native language.

Stefan threw a smug look at Claire. "He's safe. They took him to one of the lesser-known hideouts outside of Thornwick."

Bonnie wanted to stab him. Instead, she forced herself to nod. "Good. We don't want to risk anyone retrieving him. I've spent time with him — got to know him personally. He's had training to withstand interrogation, but I think I know what Oll needs to do in order to break him."

Stefan's smug look turned into one of doubt, and Bonnie had to stop herself from smirking.

She wasn't sure why she could suddenly understand their conversation, but didn't have time to question it. She could figure it out later.

"You're weak," Stefan said. "You can't leave."

"It's true, Miss Blackthorn," Claire said. "You've been in bed for days. Your body is still healing. You need to rest."

"I don't care — I'll crawl if I have to. I need to see with my own eyes that Oll and Gwyneth are alive."

Claire looked at her with sympathy, and Bonnie knew she was winning her over.

The woman turned to Stefan. "It's not far," Claire said in Wolverian. "We can help her travel there. Stefan, *think*," she said as he made to protest. "Can you imagine what will happen to us if Oll Blackthorn realizes we kept his daughter from him?"

Hell would break loose, Bonnie thought, even as she kept a look of confused annoyance on her face. "Can you stop doing that? It's rude," she interrupted in the common tongue.

In reality, she hoped they continued speaking freely. But she figured they'd get suspicious if she didn't complain at least once.

"Apologies," Stefan said, as he continued to stare at Claire. "Old habits."

"Where are you from?" Bonnie asked. "I don't recognize the language."

"Wolverd," Claire replied. She played with a silver ring on her finger.

"What's left of Wolverd, anyway," Stefan said bitterly.

Wolverd had a mild climate, and was where most of the continent's food was grown. It had been historically neutral in the chaotic political relations on the rest of the continent — no one wanted to risk their food supply, after all. But Aborn didn't seem to care. He took over Wolverd and commandeered all of its crops and food stores. Now everyone, friend to Hallordis or not, had to deal with him or risk starvation.

Bonnie knew that Aborn's takeover of Wolverd had been especially nasty. Not only had he sent assassins to dispose of the royal family, but he also razed several of their more prominent cities to the ground. His cruelty had displaced thousands of people. It didn't surprise Bonnie that an increased number of Wolverians had joined the rebellion since Aborn had set his sights on it.

The destruction of Wolverd's capital city never made complete sense to Bonnie, though. Aborn was greedy as well as bloodthirsty — why would he burn down the place responsible for most of the country's wealth?

Bonnie nodded. "I sympathize with the plight of the Wolverians. What Aborn did was an abomination. He needs to be stopped *before* his reach extends to the entire continent. Lord Stonewood may be the key to his downfall — I need to see him."

Claire nodded in affirmation, while a shadow of a doubt lingered in Stefan's eyes.

"We'll help you," she told Bonnie, ignoring a glare from her husband.

Bonnie smiled in relief, even as she kept a wary eye on him.

He still had a white-knuckled grip on his knee, and he looked half inclined to tie Bonnie to the bed.

He shook his head before standing. "I still think this is a bad idea," he said to Claire in Wolverian, "but I won't stand in your way."

Claire left the room and returned with plain clothes in dark shades. "These might be a little big on you," she told Bonnie as she handed them over, "but it'll be better than what you have on."

Stefan left the room as Claire helped Bonnie change. The clothes were big, but Bonnie didn't mind. She was fine with wearing anything as long as they brought her protection from the autumn chill.

Most of the outfit was hidden by Bonnie's cloak, which she was happy to see had survived the attack. She discreetly slid a hand into her inner pocket and was relieved to find the small knife she had stashed there. Not much, but still something. She slid it out of her cloak and into one of her boots when Claire went to get Stefan.

The two of them helped Bonnie get out of bed. They weren't lying — she *was* incredibly weak. Her legs felt as though they were made of pudding, and her head throbbed with the effort it took for her to stand up straight.

"Step by step," Claire told her gently. "There's no need to rush. Save your strength."

"Are you sure you still want to go?" Stefan asked as he held onto Bonnie's other arm. "You're better off staying in bed to recover your strength."

"No," Bonnie said through gritted teeth. "I've been in bed for too long." She wasn't sure if there would be anything left of Freddie if she waited any longer.

Stefan only huffed in reply.

Bonnie grew more confident as they made it out of the room and into a long, stone corridor. She had been expecting a damp, dark passageway, but was pleasantly surprised. The space was a little dusty, but overall clean and well-lit by oil lamps.

The smell of hay and horse dung was far stronger here. "You said that we're under the stable?" Bonnie asked. "Which one?"

"The one on the outskirts of the city," Claire replied. "Closest to where you were attacked."

"And these tunnels extend throughout the entire city?"

Claire nodded.

"Ingenious," Bonnie panted. She wondered if they could implement this type of system everywhere. "And no one has found them?"

"A few people have stumbled into them," Claire admitted. "Not many though."

"What happens to them?"

"They're dealt with," Stefan said.

They traveled the rest of the way in silence, stopping only when they reached a stone staircase at the end of the corridor.

She was covered in sweat by the time they made it up the last stair. At the top, where her head met the ceiling, was a wooden board that Stefan moved out of the way. He stuck his head through the opening and declared the way all clear.

He went first and Bonnie followed behind. Grabbing her arms, he helped her through the opening before planting her firmly on the ground.

The scent of freshly polished leather and saddle soap hit Bonnie's nose as she took in the space. Rows of saddles, bridles, and other tack lined the small room.

Stefan slid the wooden board back over the entrance once Claire joined them. The floorboard matched the surrounding flooring almost perfectly. It was impressive; Bonnie would never have found the entrance on her own. There was a little

Amlucen symbol etched into the corner, the only sign that the board differed from its neighbors.

Claire pressed her ear to the door that led out of the room. "I don't hear anyone," she said. "We should be clear to go."

"Are you sure?" Bonnie whispered. "What about the King's Guard?"

"Most are now guarding the captured rebels," Stefan said. "While some still patrol, others went back into the hole they crawled out of. We're the only ones in the stables right now."

Bonnie followed Claire out of the room. The only other occupants were the snoozing horses in their stalls. She felt a pang of longing for Belle and Captain — they had left them in Golwich with the other rebel horses. She hoped they were safe.

Claire started saddling two of the horses, while Stefan disappeared.

Bonnie sat on a nearby bench, too weak to assist — the stairs and the walk down the tunnel had taken more out of her than she cared to admit. She hated feeling weak. And hated being at the mercy of others more.

Stefan returned just as Claire was tightening the girth strap on the second horse, and he helped lead the horses out of their stalls.

"The way is clear — the guards are elsewhere. We need to go now."

He opened the stable doors and moonlight streamed in. It shone brightly overhead, illuminating the street, and Bonnie guessed it was only a little past midnight. The wall that circled Thornwick was just up ahead.

The streets were empty. Bonnie shivered, but knew it wasn't just from the cold. It felt eerily similar to the night she was attacked.

She glanced at Claire and Stefan, suddenly unsure. Was this another trap? She wouldn't survive another one. Not with her head injury.

Stefan noted her look. "There's a curfew now, per the king's orders. There are guards who patrol at night, but they are so few in number that we can slip past them."

Bonnie nodded. "Let's go."

Stefan helped her mount the smaller of the two horses, and Claire sat behind her. Bonnie didn't know what to think of it. She was perfectly capable of riding on her own.

"It's for your safety," the woman said as she took hold of the reins. "I don't want you to fall off."

Bonnie held in her scoff as she raised her hood to cover her hair, as much for secrecy as to ward off the crisp autumn air. Winter was fast approaching.

The two horses set off toward the outer perimeter wall. They passed through the same gap where she had entered, encountering no one. Stefan led them into Golwich.

Shivering after crossing the invisible line into the forest, Bonnie thanked the beings that allowed her and her party to travel safely within its borders.

"Where are we going again?" Stefan had mentioned something about one of the lesser-known hideouts outside of Thornwick, but she hoped he would be a little more specific.

"Stoneforge."

Stoneforge. She couldn't read the names of the hideouts on the resources in the Map Room, but she knew where each one was in a general sense. Based on their trajectory, they were heading toward one that was about ten or so miles southeast of the city.

The only sounds in the forest were the ones made by their horses. Even the small animals that lived there were tucked away, probably sleeping until the morning sun shone through the treetops. Normally Bonnie would've envied them, had her worry for Freddie not taken over her thoughts.

Bonnie had to get him out.

Somehow.

CHAPTER FOURTEEN

They traveled for hours.

Bonnie chafed at their pace, but knew their slow speed was for safety. The rebels didn't want to risk injuring the horses. Or re-injure Bonnie, for that matter.

Her head throbbed with each step. She shoved aside the pain, using breathing techniques to help manage it.

An owl hooted nearby. Stefan jumped and let out a curse in Wolverian.

Wolverian.

Why did Bonnie suddenly understand it? She had never traveled to Wolverd before, and had only heard the language in passing. Now she was fluent. How could that be?

A part of her wondered if some form of magic gave her this newfound ability. She hadn't possessed a magical gift prior to Vale Magicae, as far as she knew. Losing her ability to channel magic would be something she'd remember, right?

And was this miracle limited to Wolverian, or would she be able to speak Naverian or Suverian? There were a half-dozen languages spoken on the continent . . . how many more would she be able to understand?

Maybe Freddie would know.

He was the only person she trusted with this information, as strange as it was to admit. And as close as she was with Gwyneth, she wasn't sure if she wanted her mother to know about it just yet.

The Lord of Libraries would know. Or if he didn't, maybe he knew someone who did.

"Almost there," Stefan said to his wife in Wolverian. "I still think this is a mistake, but I'll stick to our decision."

"I don't know why bringing Oll Blackthorn's injured daughter to him would be a mistake," Claire replied evenly.

"Because we were told to keep her away."

Claire huffed but fell silent.

Bonnie clasped her fingers together, stopping herself from grabbing the knife hidden in her boot. The urge to use force to get them to talk was strong.

Who told them to keep her away? What was going on?

Stefan and Claire turned their horses off the path, plunging deeper into Golwich Forest. The trees were more densely packed here, and Bonnie felt the back of her neck prickle.

A bird call pierced the air. Stefan pulled his horse to a standstill, Claire stopping behind. Bonnie sat up straight.

That was no true bird call.

Stefan returned with a call of his own, a series of four distinct whistles. They waited for the answering call before moving forward again.

Two hooded men appeared and signaled for them to stop. One carried a lantern that cast long shadows on the ground.

"What a mighty fine day to go for a picnic," the man on the right said.

Bonnie relaxed a fraction — she recognized Hugo's distinct voice. Which meant the burly man standing next to him was his brother, Leon. And while Bonnie was relieved to see familiar faces, her heart sank. Hugo and Leon were almost as bloodthirsty as Oll was, if a little less creative in their torture administrations. If they were here, they were no doubt involved in whatever was happening to Freddie.

"We've brought meat sandwiches for everyone," Stefan answered, completing the ritual.

Both men relaxed.

"Business?" Hugo asked.

"My name is Stefan, my wife is Claire. We live in Thornwick. We have Bonnie Blackthorn with us."

"Bonnie Blackthorn?" Hugo looked at his brother and then back at Stefan. "Bonnie Blackthorn is dead. She was killed during the attack."

Oh, no.

Did everyone think she was dead?

And if everyone thought she was dead, who told Stefan and Claire to keep her away?

"The rumors are false," she said. "I'm alive."

Both men jumped. She lowered her hood, and their eyes widened. Bonnie would have laughed had the situation been remotely funny.

"Gods above," Leon whispered, and made the sign against evil over his chest. Hugo stood there with wide eyes.

"It seems we have a lot to catch up on," Bonnie said. "Let us enter."

Both men seemed to snap to their senses. Moving to either side, they waved the travel party through and followed behind.

The group traveled the moonlit path until they reached a rock formation so large that Bonnie had to crane her neck to see the top of it, and so wide she couldn't see the entirety of it at once. It was as if the side of a mountain had come to reside in the middle of Golwich Forest.

It was not natural; dozens of stones in different shapes and sizes had been melded together to form one large, smooth mass. It probably had been shaped by a stone mage before Vale Magicae.

Hugo and Leon stepped in front and told them to dismount. Hugo took the reins of both horses and led them back into the forest.

Leon faced the formation. He used his lantern to shine over the stone, and Bonnie marveled at the way the light made it shimmer faintly. It reminded her of the rock she had taken from the mine in Thornwick on that mission from Oll.

After a moment, she saw a small, vertical crack appear in the stone — the only blemish on the otherwise perfect face. Leon knocked four times in a distinct pattern, and Bonnie watched as the cracks in the stone spread upward and then over on both the top and the bottom, forming three sides of a large rectangle.

A door, Bonnie realized, as it swung forward on hidden hinges.

Light shone out, and she blinked rapidly to adjust her eyes.

"Who is it?" a familiar voice asked from the doorway.

Felix?

Her brother hadn't traveled to Thornwick with the others — he had opted to stay behind in Crown Harbor. What was he doing here?

"Amlucenites from Thornwick, here with Bonnie Blackthorn," Leon said.

Felix's eyes widened as he looked past Leon to find Bonnie, Stefan, and Claire.

"But — you were dead," Felix breathed as he looked over Bonnie from head to toe. "Someone saw a soldier strike you down. They couldn't find your body, but they said there was no way you could've survived . . ."

If Bonnie didn't know her brother, she would've sworn that something like relief flashed across his face at the sight of her alive, mixed with another emotion that she couldn't name. "It's your unlucky day, brother dear," Bonnie said drily. "I have an exceptionally hard head. You're not rid of me yet."

She heard Claire and Stefan's intakes of breath, but didn't care. She was tired, she was hurt, and she did not have enough patience to deal with him right now.

Bonnie had to take a moment to breathe after crossing the stone threshold. She was weaker than she thought.

She took in the space. Four doors led out of the small room, presumably leading further into the hideout. There was a rack along one wall, filled with an assortment of cloaks.

Felix had been sitting at a small table, reading a book of some sort. A lone candle provided light.

Claire tried to help her take off her cloak, but Bonnie shook her head; she didn't want to accept help in front of the others. She was Oll Blackthorn's daughter, damn it. She couldn't afford to appear weak.

"Where's Oll? Gwyneth? I need to see them."

"In their private chambers," Felix answered. "Presumably sleeping, considering the time."

"Take me to them."

"We'll take you," Hugo said as he entered the room. Bonnie noted which door he used — by the smell, she knew it led directly to the stables. Might be useful in case she had to make a quick exit.

"We can take her," Stefan said. Bonnie knew he wanted the credit for saving her life.

Leon cracked his neck as he joined his brother. "We'll take her," he said firmly. He stared at Stefan with enough menace to make the taller Wolverian bow his head.

"Thank you for helping me," Bonnie said to both of them. "I'll make sure Oll and Gwyneth know who to thank for saving my life."

Claire bowed her head with a smile, while Stefan nodded. A muscle in his jaw tensed as he glared at Hugo and Leon.

The burly brothers smiled back at him, rotted teeth on full display.

"Now, now, children," she admonished. "Take me to my parents."

With one last leer at Stefan, the brothers opened the door to the far right. Bonnie followed Hugo as he led her down a long stone corridor.

The corridor was perfectly square, with oil lamps spaced every few feet. There were no windows; just stone. The same strange mixture of rocks glittered in the flickering light.

Bonnie touched the wall in admiration. She guessed that stone mages had made this corridor by blasting directly through rock — it was too perfect, too precise to be made by hand.

"Have you been here since the attack?" Bonnie asked.

Hugo grunted in affirmation.

"What happened in Thornwick?"

Neither man said anything, although they exchanged a look that Bonnie couldn't read. "We're trying to figure that out," Leon said.

Bonnie's skin prickled — he sounded almost gleeful.

Each step was an effort. The food she had eaten felt like lead in her stomach, and seemed to grow heavier with each step. She kept her back straight and her head up, though.

No weakness allowed.

Bonnie studied the wooden doors as they passed. No sound came from the other side of them, although she supposed most people would be sleeping right now.

After a few more turns down different corridors — true to Amlucen fashion, this place was a frustrating maze — Hugo stopped. This wooden door looked no different from the others they had passed, but he stepped back with a smirk, safely out of the way.

Bonnie shot him a disgusted look before she knocked on

the door four times. She hoped Gwyneth was the one who answered. Oll loathed to be woken up by anyone, for any reason. Several messengers had lost their lives when they disturbed his sleep.

She waited with bated breath and shifted her foot to make sure she had access to her hidden knife. She didn't want to use it, but didn't want to be murdered by her adopted father, either.

Footsteps sounded on the other side of the door.

She couldn't stop herself from flexing the fingers of her right hand, ready to pull the knife out and use it if she had to.

The door swung open. Bonnie let out her breath in a *whoosh*.

Gwyneth.

Gwyneth's vibrant green eyes, her only claim to beauty in her mangled face, went from heavy with sleep to as wide as saucers in the space of a heartbeat. The older woman clutched her dressing gown to her chest.

"Bonnie?" she whispered.

Heavier footsteps sounded. Oll appeared in the doorway a moment later, his eyes wide — not in surprise or shock, but in anger. Bonnie stepped back when she saw the knife clutched in his fist.

"What is the meaning of this?" he demanded, his eyes traveling over Bonnie and focusing on Hugo and Leon. He stepped forward menacingly, and both brothers stepped back in alarm.

Gwyneth moved her arm and clutched the doorframe, blocking Oll's path forward. He shot a look of pure venom at his wife before following her gaze.

His eyes widened as he looked at his adopted daughter. "Bonnie?" he whispered. "But you . . . we were told you were . . . *How?*"

"Hello Father," Bonnie said, forcing a smile to her lips. She met Gwyneth's shocked stare. "Hello Mother."

CHAPTER FIFTEEN

Bonnie sipped peppermint tea from a heavy clay mug, glad to have something to do with her hands.

She looked around Oll and Gwyneth's room as she sat alone. The room was big enough to fit their bed, a pair of worn armchairs, and a table that was filled with Oll's usual assortment of papers and weapons. She sat in an armchair as she gazed into the flickering fire.

Oll and Gwyneth had moved past their surprise at seeing her rather quickly. After fussing over Bonnie for a few minutes, Gwyneth had turned back to Hugo and Leon. Bonnie's ears pricked when she realized she had switched to Suverian.

"How is this possible?" Gwyneth asked.

"She arrived with two rebels from Thornwick," said Leon. "Felix is with them now."

"She's injured," Oll said. "Did they say how?"

"No. We didn't ask — we knew you would want to speak with them."

Their voices trailed off as they moved further from the door.

Bonnie relaxed, mind racing. She had understood every

word. Apparently, she was now fluent in Wolverian *and* Suverian.

What kind of sorcery was this?

She dozed as she waited for them to return, and almost jumped out of the chair when the door opened. Her hand shot to her boot, but she stopped herself from grabbing her knife when she saw who it was.

"Are you alright?" she asked as Gwyneth settled into the other armchair.

Oll stood behind, his hands gripping the back of the chair. The flickering light cast shadows on their faces. Oll reached forward to put his hands on Gwyneth's shoulders, but she shook him off as she leaned towards Bonnie.

"Are *we* alright?" Gwyneth asked, incredulous. "How can you ask that? We thought you were dead!"

"So did I," Bonnie said as she held out her hands for Gwyneth to grasp. Gwyneth's hands, though smaller, were cold. "What happened at Thornwick?"

"We're figuring that out," Oll said. "We were beside ourselves with grief. Your mother has hardly been out of bed for days."

Bonnie squeezed Gwyneth's hands before letting go.

"What happened?" Gwyneth asked.

Bonnie told them what she remembered of the ambush, of fleeing toward the wall, of falling into darkness . . . "And then I woke up sometime later underneath the Thornwick stables. Stefan and Claire took care of me, and after a few days I was well enough to travel." It was more or less the truth. Minus her new ability to understand languages. "What happened to you two?"

"We escaped," Gwyneth said. "We were ambushed, like you. A few members of our party heard the commotion and led us to safety."

"But not before I got this," Oll said, holding his arm in front of him.

Peering closely, Bonnie saw a thin slice that was stitched from the crook of his elbow to his wrist. She winced as he drew back his arm, even as part of her wished the wound had been fatal. No such luck.

Gwyneth turned to Oll. "Do you believe her?"

Bonnie stilled, anger flashing through her.

But then she realized Gwyneth had spoken in Suverian.

"I don't know why she would lie," Oll replied in the same language. "Her story matches what the other rebels told us. She admitted she was with Lord Stonewood, and that he seemed surprised by what happened."

"She could be lying," Gwyneth countered. "Or deluded into thinking that Lord Stonewood is innocent. She was hit on the head — she said so herself. How do we know if she's remembering everything clearly?"

Bonnie felt a weird pain in her chest, and she rubbed it absentmindedly. It wasn't the pain of being excluded that pissed her off this time. It was the fact that the person questioning her integrity was Gwyneth.

And she never would have known had she not suddenly understood Suverian.

It would be one thing if Oll questioned her story — he was paranoid at the best of times.

But not Gwyneth.

"Her story matches with what Lord Stonewood told us," Oll said. "What he told us in relation to Bonnie, at least. He seemed devastated by her death."

The pain in her chest intensified, and she rubbed the spot harder. She hadn't thought about how news of her death may have affected him. Was he truly saddened by the loss? Or sad that he had lost his only ally?

"He's a born liar. I'm sure his father taught him everything he knows," Gwyneth spat.

"How many people did we lose?" Bonnie broke in, using the common tongue. As fascinating as the conversation was, she knew they would find it suspicious if she didn't say something.

Oll frowned. "Too many."

"Those who weren't killed outright were taken to the mines," Gwyneth said. "We've been working on freeing them."

"Your aid may come in handy there, Bonnie," said Oll. "You've been there. You could help us with planning. We need to get those people out."

Bonnie nodded, even though the thought of returning to those mines was the last thing she wanted to do. She'd agree to anything, though, if it meant Oll and Gwyneth would look upon her favorably. "Absolutely."

Bonnie sipped her tea, wondering how to bring Freddie into the conversation. She knew she had to tread carefully.

"Do we have any idea why the King's Guard was already at Thornwick?" she asked. "Why were we ambushed?"

Oll's eyes glittered in the fire's light. "We're getting to the bottom of that," he said.

His tone sent a shiver down Bonnie's spine, even as she knew it was the opening she needed.

"What does that mean?"

"Not important," Gwyneth cut in with a sharp look at Oll. He promptly shut his mouth. She turned to Bonnie. "You need to rest, darling."

Bonnie shook her head. "I've been lying around with nothing but my thoughts for days. I want to help you figure out what happened." To hell with subtlety, she decided. "Did Lord Stonewood survive?"

Bonnie didn't miss the look they exchanged.

"Yes," Oll said after a moment's hesitation. "He's alive."

He was alive — she wasn't too late. Her relief was short-lived, though. Was he in one piece, or tortured out of his mind? With Oll involved, Bonnie couldn't be sure.

"Where is he? I presume you've talked to him about the intel he provided?"

"We've had . . . discussions, yes," Oll hedged.

"And?"

"Lord Stonewood claims he doesn't know why the timing of the attack changed," Gwyneth said. "He was adamant that he played no part in the king's plan."

"Do you believe him?"

"We're not sure. Further . . . *discussions* . . . need to happen."

"I want to see him," Bonnie said, lowering her voice as she scowled. "I need him to look me in the eye and tell me he's not responsible. I've spent the most time with him — I know when he's lying. Let me talk to him."

Oll and Gwyneth exchanged another look, and Bonnie had the sudden urge to stab one of them.

"What do you think?" Oll asked Gwyneth in Suverian.

"Lord Stonewood hasn't changed his story," Gwyneth replied. "She could help us break him."

"How? She normally stays away from interrogations."

With good reason, Bonnie thought. She wasn't the sadist that Oll was, or as cold as Gwyneth. Bonnie may be trained to kill, but she was more human than the two in front of her.

Gwyneth shrugged. "There are many ways to break a man. She may be the missing piece we need."

The casual cruelty in her voice sent shivers down Bonnie's spine, and she had to stop herself from flinching when Gwyneth reached across the distance and took her hands once more.

"Are you sure you're up for it, honey? You don't have to speak with him. We'd understand if there was any hesitation. He betrayed us. Betrayed *you*. Are you sure you want to go down that path?"

"Yes." Her tone brooked no room for discussion.

Gwyneth stared into Bonnie's eyes, searching them — for what, Bonnie wasn't sure. But after a moment, Gwyneth broke eye contact and turned to face Oll. Bonnie had to stop herself from smiling as she saw Gwyneth give Oll a short, perfunctory nod.

She was in.

INHALE, EXHALE. INHALE, EXHALE.

A wave of dread washed over Bonnie as she contemplated what she was about to do. She forced air into her lungs as she grasped the doorknob hard enough to hurt.

Oll and Gwyneth had left moments ago. Oll wished her good luck before departing, and it increased her anxiety about how she was going to find Freddie.

Bonnie wasn't sure where they were going, but she knew she wasn't truly being left alone with him. She grew up in the Amlucen — she knew their ways. There were likely rebels in adjacent rooms, spying through strategically hidden peepholes.

Breathing sharply, she twisted the knob and pushed the door open. She glanced around the room. And gasped.

Freddie was dead.

CHAPTER SIXTEEN

No.

He must've died during the night. There was no way someone that still, that silent, was still alive. He was lying on his stomach, arms stretched out ahead of him, his feet in a jumble against the wall. One of his arms was raised over his face.

She raced across the room and crouched down, careful not to touch him. He was dressed in clothes that were not warm enough for how cold it was in here.

A new way to torture him, she supposed. Torture by frostbite.

And by knives. Bandages stained pink covered both of his forearms, and Bonnie swore in sympathy.

She tentatively reached out a hand. "Freddie?" His arm was warm to the touch.

And then he struck.

He launched himself at her, moving faster than Bonnie dreamed possible.

One second she was sure he was dead, the next second she was flying through the air. She landed in a heap by the far wall.

"It's me, it's me!" she cried as he surged toward her. "Freddie, it's me! Bonnie!"

His eyes were round and wild as he rushed forward, arms swinging. He didn't seem to recognize her.

His face was covered in dried blood and bruises, like the rest of him. His lip had been recently split, and a line of blood trailed down his face.

Bonnie rolled to the side and jumped to her feet, her weak muscles making her movements slow. Fatally slow.

An idea came to her. "Freddie, it's me," she said in Naverian, her voice low, always cognizant they were being watched. She marveled at the way the words rolled off her tongue in the same pleasing way it did when Freddie spoke it. "Bonnie Blackthorn. Your . . . friend. Calm down."

He stumbled. His honey-colored eyes were wide as he looked at her, *really* looked at her. He tried to stop, but his momentum carried him forward.

They collided.

Bonnie tried to use whatever strength she had left to keep him upright, but she was too weak, her legs useless, and they fell to the floor in a heap.

She sat up slowly.

"I'm mad," he mumbled in Naverian. "I've lost my mind."

She shook her head, and the movement caused a flash of pain. "I'm alive," she responded in the same language. "I'm here, with you. You're not crazy."

He pulled back, eyes flaring. "*Liar.* You don't know Naverian — I'm sure of it. Or you're one hell of a player."

Bonnie's head throbbed, and she rubbed at her temple scar. She scooted backwards until she felt the solid stone wall behind her.

She took a moment to survey the room. It was bare, apart from a chamber pot that sat in the corner. Oil lamps, shining brightly, were spaced evenly at the top of the walls, too high for anyone to reach.

There.

In the middle of the wall, underneath one of the lamps, was where the peephole would be. It was the same setup in every rebel hideout.

Part of her was offended that no one had stepped in to save her. They knew how weak she was. It wouldn't have taken much to kill her — a simple knock on the head would do the trick. Maybe they had more faith in her than she realized.

Or maybe they want you dead, a traitorous voice whispered inside her head. *Maybe they view you as a liability.*

Freddie looked as though he wasn't sure if he was hallucinating or not. He stared at her, doubt still lingering in his gaze. "How do you know Naverian? Were you lying to me the entire time?"

"Come here," she said, patting the ground next to her. "We need to talk."

He looked half inclined to attack, but crawled a few paces forward instead. He stopped far short of where she sat.

It was enough — he was close enough that they could speak in whispers. There was a chance the others could hear their conversation, but she knew from firsthand experience how hard it was to listen to soft-spoken conversations from behind a normal wall. They probably couldn't hear *anything* behind the stone wall she leaned against.

For once, she was thankful for the lack of magic. No one with magically enhanced hearing could eavesdrop on their conversation.

She switched back to the common tongue. "I'll explain how I know Naverian later — it's not important right now. How can I prove that it's really me? I'm real — I'm alive. I promise."

He thought for a moment. "What is the nickname I've been calling you since we fled Navian?"

"Are you referring to 'darling honeybum,' by chance? Or just your normal 'sweetheart' or 'sunshine'? Pretty sure you called me your 'fearless leader' once. I liked that one the best."

That, at least, got his lips to twitch. Not quite a smile — she was sure it would be a long time before he smiled again — but it was something. Some of the distrust faded from his eyes, at least.

Bonnie frowned as she tried to ignore the wounds she saw. Some looked days old and nearly healed, fading into yellow, while others looked very recent.

They must have been at him for days — maybe since the day of the attack.

"The last time I remember seeing you was in Thornwick — by the hole in the wall," she said. "We were attacked by a soldier, remember? You shouted my name to warn me. Then everything went black."

"They killed you," he said, his voice hoarse. "I saw it with my own eyes. He struck you on the head with the hilt of his sword. Your eyes rolled up, and you gasped, and then you stopped breathing, and . . . I still hear the noise you made as you took your last breath in my sleep. There was no way you survived."

"But I did," she insisted. "Two rebels from Thornwick were there, out of sight. They brought me to safety. Healed me. What happened to you?"

"I fled." He looked away in shame. "If I had known you were alive, I would've stayed. I promise you I would have."

She nodded — she knew that. He wouldn't have left her.

"I made it back through the wall and ran until I was in the clearing where we had gathered with the others. It was chaos. No one knew what had happened or where to go. I thought you had died, and didn't know if Oll or Gwyneth had survived. So I hid."

"Hid?"

"I'm not stupid, Bonnie. I wouldn't blame anyone if they took the chance to kill me in the chaos."

His words were harsh, but she could read the truth in his eyes. Bonnie couldn't say that he was wrong, either. The rebel who killed the son of the king's advisor, especially after what had happened, would be a hero. "So, what did you do?"

"Do you remember the boulder on the edge of Golwich? The one on the road where we pulled the horses off — there's an opening to a small cave there."

Bonnie's eyes widened. "I had no idea there was a cave there."

"It was small, but I fit."

"Why didn't you flee? You were right there, on the edge of the road . . ."

"I wanted to see what happened — people were constantly coming and going, speaking loudly. I needed to get my bearings before I decided where to go next."

"How long did you hide?"

He blinked. "They found me five days ago. They didn't tell you?"

Bonnie shook her head. She may have been the one with a severe head injury, but she knew his timeline was impossible. He was covered in bruises — some of them were faded with age. What once was black and blue was now a soft, sickly yellow.

There was no way he healed that much in five days.

She gestured to his face. "Freddie, that's not possible. Not with the way you're healing. You must've lost track of time."

He raised his hand, covered in thin slices, and rubbed the back of his head. His hair, much longer than when she first met him, now stuck up at odd angles. "Maybe," he said, staring at the wall behind her. "It's been hard to keep track of time."

With the sheer number of oil lamps burning brightly above their heads, she didn't doubt it. They probably kept the oil levels filled to the maximum level to make it hard for him to sleep.

Bonnie wanted to tell him everything, but stopped herself. First, she needed to figure out how much the spies could hear. "I need to leave, but I'll be back." She held her hands up when a flash of panic crossed his face. "I'm going to figure out how to get you out, but I need time."

"You can't — I can't — they'll *kill* me," he said, and the speed of his breathing grew faster.

"They want you to talk. To confess. They think you're responsible for what happened at Thornwick. They won't kill you."

He shook his head. "Bonnie, I don't know what happened. You have to know that."

She looked into his eyes and nodded. "I know."

His shoulders slumped in relief.

"I'll be back," she promised. "I need to learn more about what's going on."

"Wait," he said, and moved close enough she knew that no one could overhear. "I overheard them talking on the way here. Something big happened, Bonnie. Something scared them."

"Thornwick," she said. "What happened at Thornwick scared them."

He shook his head. "No. Something bigger."

BONNIE WAITED FOR OLL AND GWYNETH FOR HOURS.

Hugo and Leon had been outside of Freddie's door, waiting for her. They said nothing as they navigated the stone corridors back to her parent's room.

Collapsing into the armchair, Bonnie waited.

And waited.

And waited.

She thought about what Freddie said. Stefan and Claire

hadn't mentioned anything besides Thornwick, and neither had Oll nor Gwyneth. She didn't doubt him, though. Not on this point. Losing track of time was one thing — imagining conversations was another matter entirely.

Bonnie debated whether to ask Oll and Gwyneth outright, but hesitated. She wasn't sure if she could trust them, especially considering their lack of trust in her.

Actually . . . maybe she *would* ask them, if only to see if they said one thing in the common tongue and their actual thoughts in Suverian. Worth a shot.

In order to ask them questions, however, they had to be present.

Bonnie readjusted her position. Where were they? She closed her eyes, breathing deeply to help her calm down.

For the second time since she entered Stoneforge, Bonnie woke to the sound of a door opening. Jerking awake, she watched as Gwyneth approached her while Oll went to the table set against the wall.

"There you are," Gwyneth said, as she sat in the other armchair. "We weren't sure where you'd gone."

Lie. Bonnie knew one of the brothers would have reported her whereabouts the moment they left her in the room.

Bonnie plastered a smile on her face. "I fell asleep," she said. She raised her arms overhead in a stretch as she yawned. "Where have you been?"

"Dealing with things," Oll said rather cryptically. He took a knife out of his pocket and idly turned it over as he looked at the papers littering the table.

"Things?" Bonnie raised her eyebrow. "What things?"

"Leadership things —" Oll started.

"Nothing you need to worry about, dear —" Gwyneth said at the same time.

"What's going on?" She looked from one to the other. "What 'leadership things'? You've never kept me in the dark before."

A lie, she now knew.

"You don't need to know," Oll said. He was still staring at the papers on the table, but was now holding the knife in one hand instead of twirling it. Bonnie hoped it wasn't a sign he was feeling particularly violent.

She looked toward Gwyneth, her ally. Or, at least, she hoped Gwyneth was still her ally. "Have I done something to make you doubt me?"

Gwyneth looked at her as though she didn't recognize her own daughter.

"Mother?" Bonnie's voice came out a whisper, and she wasn't faking the emotion on her face. "Have I done something wrong?"

Gwyneth pursed her lips before shaking her head. "No," she said. "You have not. But there are —" she paused for a moment, as if weighing her words — "*concerns* about the relationship you've developed with Lord Stonewood."

Bonnie huffed a laugh, even as her heart started pounding. "Relationship? What relationship?"

"Members of the council worry you have gotten too close. We don't trust Lord Stonewood, for obvious reasons. Some of that doubt has now been placed on you."

"You two told me to stay with him once we reached Crown Harbor — of course it's going to look like we're close. I was only following your orders!"

Gwyneth's lip curled. "You've had the time you requested to speak with Lord Stonewood. Did you find out any information?"

Bonnie shook her head. "He attacked me when I first went in, thinking I was a ghost of some sort. He thought I died during the attack. I spent most of the time trying to convince him he wasn't hallucinating."

"Did he say anything about what happened at Thornwick?"

Bonnie shook her head. "I need time — *more* time. And we

need to stop torturing him," she said, with a pointed look at Oll's back. "You haven't gotten anything out of him, have you?" Gwyneth shook her head, and Oll flexed his fingers in agitation. "We knew he was probably trained to withstand torture. Most of Aborn's people are. Torture isn't the way to go."

Gwyneth shook her head. "No. He will break eventually."

"He's expecting it — he's probably been mentally preparing himself for the possibility from the day I showed up in his bedchamber. We need to try something else."

Oll turned and rushed toward Bonnie. He leveled the knife at her face, grip so tight that his knuckles were white. "Are you saying you're smarter than your mother?" he asked, his voice dangerously low.

Bonnie kept her eyes locked on the knife mere inches from her face. She didn't think Oll would cut her, but she also knew he wasn't in his right mind.

Slowly, so very slowly, she looked away from the knife and met Gwyneth's stare. "No. I would never claim to know more than you, Mother."

The seconds Gwyneth took to weigh Bonnie's words were some of the longest of her life.

Finally, Gwyneth nodded. "Enough, Oll," she said.

Bonnie waited until Oll had stepped away, knife now hanging loosely at his side, before relaxing into the armchair.

"What are you saying then, Bonnie?" Gwyneth asked, as if Oll's intrusion hadn't happened.

"Lord Stonewood is expecting to be tortured. He's heard the propaganda about us from Aborn — torture first, ask questions later, all of that. He would've mentally prepared himself. What he's not expecting, I would imagine, is a friendly face. Someone who vouches for him. Someone to get him clean clothes, medicine, better food. Use me. Use our so called 'relationship' to lure him into a false sense of security. Maybe he'll tell me things he'd never say under threat of torture."

Bonnie held her breath. She wasn't entirely sure how she would proceed if they shut her down — find some way to sneak him out undiscovered, she supposed. Which she had to do, eventually.

But he was weak. *She* was weak. She needed time to gather her strength and make a plan before they made their escape.

Oll turned to his wife. "What do you think?" he asked in Suverian.

"Her account of what happened with Lord Stonewood seems accurate," Gwyneth replied. "At least, according to Annie and Desmond. But they both admitted they couldn't hear everything."

A wave of relief washed over Bonnie, even as she took care not to change her expression.

It *worked*. She knew she couldn't rely on that tactic all the time; it wouldn't take long for others to wonder why they only spoke in hushed whispers.

"Do you think her plan could work?" Oll's tone conveyed a heavy dose of skepticism.

Bonnie wasn't surprised; he was a torturer at heart. It didn't matter that information given under torture wasn't always reliable. All that mattered to him was fueling his bloodlust.

"I don't think it hurts to try. If she fails, we can always go back to our old methods."

"Do we have time? We have to return to Crown Harbor to assess the damage."

"We'll give her one day. Two maximum. We can delay our departure for now. Breaking Lord Stonewood may be what we need to figure out what happened."

Bonnie perked up. What happened in Crown Harbor?

Oll's fingers gripped his knife tighter, but he nodded.

Gwyneth turned to Bonnie, her green eyes glowing in the fire's light. "You have twenty-four hours to try your way with him. Do not disappoint us."

CHAPTER SEVENTEEN

THE FIRST STEP IN PLANNING HER ESCAPE WAS FIGURING OUT where she was going.

It didn't help that she had more questions than ever. Unfortunately, there was only one person she could trust to answer honestly.

Too bad it was one of the people she took great pains to avoid.

Even so, she let out a sigh of relief when she saw Felix was where she had left him hours ago. Or was it a day ago? The lack of windows made it difficult to tell how much time had passed.

He sat at the same table in the entryway, the single candle still flickering. He looked at her with a raised eyebrow as he set down his book. "Yes?"

Bonnie froze as she stared at its spine.

The History of Hallordis.

Emotion threatened to overwhelm her as she fought to keep a straight face. The last thing she needed was for Felix to find out the impossible had occurred.

She could *read*.

Bonnie shook her head, trying to stop her tears. She'd

marvel at this new development later, in private. Far from her adopted brother, who now watched her with a curious expression.

It was an effort to take her eyes off of the book, off the symbols that she used to resent but now would cherish, but she somehow managed. She looked at Felix, who stood, a curious expression on his face. "I need your help."

He pretended to stumble backwards as he slapped his hand over his heart. "You, the formidable Bonnie Blackthorn, need *my* help? I never thought I'd see the day."

Bonnie rolled her eyes. "Yes, brother dear. I need your help. Teach me about this place so I can be of greater use to the cause."

THINGS HADN'T ALWAYS BEEN SO STRAINED WITH HIM.

They'd been attached at the hip growing up. He was the one who spent time with her when she was recovering after the attack, the one who showed her the ropes within the rebellion. The one who retaught her the common tongue and read stories to keep her entertained.

The two of them ran wild. Oll was busy with his casual cruelty while Gwyneth spent a lot of time in Suverd. The other rebels were too scared to rein in the children of the rebellion's leaders.

She wasn't sure when things changed.

Maybe it was when she was accepted into the Rebel Guard and he was denied, weapons master Benji claiming that Felix lacked the tenacity to become one of the elite members.

Maybe it was when Felix threw himself into his studies instead, retreating to the library. The one place Bonnie could never join him.

Eventually, Felix started speaking Suverian in front of her, excluding her from conversations. So Bonnie stopped reaching out to him when she had problems.

She learned to rely on herself. *Only* on herself. And she avoided him when she could.

But time was not on her side, and even Bonnie knew when she needed to ask for help.

Two hours later, she stood in front of Freddie's door with everything that she needed. Felix had gotten her everything she asked for, no questions asked. He also gave her a tour, and didn't even make fun of her for the slow pace. She stayed quiet as she committed every turn to memory.

He was quiet, too. And pale. His oily blonde hair was more disheveled than she had seen in a while. She prepared herself to tune out his snide remarks or dramatic statements, but today she didn't have to. Something was bothering him, she was sure of it. He kept looking at her out of the corner of his eye, almost as though he was studying her.

He probably was surprised that she survived another head injury. She was still surprised, too.

Normally she would've said something — teased him, maybe. But she kept quiet. She needed to focus on saving Freddie, not figure out what was wrong with Felix. She had too much to deal with as it was.

Bonnie took a deep breath, centering herself as she stared at the wooden door. She wished she could've gone to the room where the other rebels were watching through the peepholes, if only to get a lay of the land. Maybe Oll and Gwyneth would give her access to it if she played her cards right.

She balanced a tray of food in one hand while she shouldered the door open. She poked her head through, just enough to make sure he wasn't waiting on the other side, before entering.

Freddie was once more across the room, but this time he was awake. He hugged his arms around himself as he rocked back and forth. It looked like he was having trouble sitting up straight. New cuts and bruises covered his body.

Someone had visited him.

She approached slowly, holding up the tray of food as if it was a peace offering. He eyed her warily.

Bonnie debated asking him to sit by the door, but the way he curled into himself made her question whether he could move on his own. She wasn't sure he was strong enough to walk.

He was far enough from the peephole that she decided they could risk a private conversation.

"Can I sit across from you?" At his nod, she set down the tray and took a seat.

He raised an eyebrow, and Bonnie winced when she saw the fresh cut that sliced through it. He flinched as if he, too, only just remembered it was there.

"This is an improvement," he said, nodding toward the food.

"I convinced them you may respond better to kindness. They've given me twenty-four hours to test my theory." She nodded toward the food. "It's not poisoned. Eat up."

He picked up the spoon and started eating the hearty meat stew. "What, no knife or fork?"

Bonnie rolled her eyes. "I can't arm you."

"Fair. Shame, though."

"When the time comes, I'll get you more than a butter knife," she whispered.

He looked away, chewing slowly. "I've been thinking," he said after a long pause. "Why are you helping me? We're not friends. And you made it clear you wanted rid of me in Crown Harbor. I'm the son of the man who killed your parents, remember? Why are you trying to help me?"

"I don't know," she said, the only truthful answer she could give. "You are the physical embodiment of everything I've learned to hate over the past twelve years. I need information from you, and so does the rebel movement. I should be *thrilled* that you're in this position right now."

"But you're not?"

"I'm not," she whispered. "Damn it all to hell, but I'm not. You are not your father, just as I am not mine. You don't deserve to be tortured like some common criminal."

Emotions flitted across his face.

Shock. Relief. Maybe gratitude.

And as shocked as she was to say those words, she was equally surprised that she believed them herself.

"We need to play along or they won't let me in here again. They think I'm trying to break you — they want information. There's a peephole between the oil lamps, placed so they can watch you. I have no doubt someone is in there now, trying to listen to every word we say."

He nodded as he continued to shovel food into his mouth. "I understand."

Bonnie coughed loudly, as if clearing her throat. "I'm glad you appreciate the food," she said at a normal volume. "I know it's an improvement. Know that I can improve your time here if you agree to help. First: food. Next? I bet a bed roll would improve your sleeping situation. Or maybe a bath and clean clothes would be preferable."

"Yes," he said, much louder. "All of that — I'll do anything you want. Just tell me what you want to know."

THE ROOM LOOKED DRAMATICALLY DIFFERENT A FEW HOURS later.

There was now a bed roll, complete with a blanket and pillow, in the corner. He had a change of clothes, and was able to wash off some of the blood and grime.

A physician had even come in, his crinkled eyes wary as he

looked between the two of them. Bonnie glared long enough for the man to swallow nervously.

When the physician ordered Freddie to take off his shirt, she didn't look away in time. Her jaw dropped.

Bonnie didn't think a single inch of him was free of colorful bruises. Dark hues of black and blue spread across his body while yellow and green tones filled the spaces between. There were red, swollen areas that had to be painful, and Bonnie hoped they weren't infected. Delicate knife slashes trailed along his torso, scabbed in some areas while others still dribbled fresh blood. Whether from movement or a repeated blade, she wasn't sure, but both thoughts made her queasy.

He was a fucked up piece of artwork. The kind only a sadistic ruler would display for all to see.

"Who did that to you?" she whispered, appalled.

"A lot of people." His eyes were haunted.

"When?"

"Every few hours since I arrived."

The physician said nothing, only glanced at Freddie's face with a furrowed brow.

Bonnie had to look away. She had lived with pain for as long as she could remember — it was a rare day indeed when her head didn't flare with agony at some point or another.

Bonnie didn't have many qualms when it came to killing people for the rebellion. She tried to be quick and efficient in all of her kills; a swift throat slit here, a stab to the heart there.

What she did have a problem with was needlessly inflicting pain.

And what bothered her the most? They'd been taking it easy on him, probably in fear of retribution from Freddie's connections. Other captives experienced much, much worse. Immediate broken bones. Pulled fingernails. Oll had even burned the Amlucen symbol onto a few of them.

Even so, those bruises *hurt*.

"One broken rib," the physician said. "Possibly two. The bruises will heal with time, as will the ribs. All the cuts have healed, even the deeper ones that should've needed stitching." He turned to Freddie. "You heal remarkably fast."

Freddie shrugged, but couldn't hide his wince as he bent to retrieve his shirt off the floor.

The physician turned back to Bonnie. "Do you want me to give him something for the pain?"

Bonnie shook her head. "No. But I'll take the medicine. If he continues to behave, I'll give it to him." She slid the vial of the tonic he handed over into her pocket.

For every new piece of information Freddie supplied, his situation improved. Only Bonnie knew he only shared parts of a truth — almost half of the intel he was giving the rebellion was a complete fabrication. Freddie refused to take any sort of blame for what happened at Thornwick, and stuck to the same story he had been telling from the beginning.

"I don't claim responsibility for what happened," he told Bonnie, loud enough for the rebels in the other room to hear, "but I think they changed any plans they had regarding the raid *because* of me."

"Why?"

"When we left my bedchamber — the night you saw the intel I had on the rebellion — do you remember if we put any of it away?"

Bonnie's mouth dropped open. "No. We just . . ."

"Left it on the desk," Freddie finished. "We were so focused on leaving that we left it on the desk. For anyone to see."

"Right next to the letter that you wrote. The one that said you were leaving for a few weeks."

A nod was his only answer.

Bonnie put her head in her hands.

Shit.

It made sense. If anyone in Navian had seen those papers —

intel that no one else had outside the rebel movement, intel that Bonnie herself had planted — they would've figured out that Freddie was a rebel sympathizer.

What had she thought? That she hadn't needed to plant her own documents. His personal collection was much more damning.

The Amlucen plot to frame Freddie had worked, but in the worst possible way. They must've seen the paperwork on his desk and jumped to conclusions.

So what did the sneaky bastards do?

They moved up the raid.

Bonnie and Freddie had made it all the way to Crown Harbor with outdated intel and had no idea.

Bonnie swallowed. That meant what happened in Thornwick was *her* fault. The rebel's fates, their lives, their health, were forfeit because of her.

Freddie shook his head. "We fucked up," he said. "But what happened in Thornwick is not yours to shoulder alone. We had no idea this would happen."

She stood. "I need to think," she said. "I'll be right back."

Bonnie walked to the door and knocked four times, and the door swung open a moment later. She thanked the rebel who had been standing guard and then asked where she could find Oll and Gwyneth Blackthorn.

It was time to talk.

CHAPTER EIGHTEEN

Bonnie shifted in her seat. The old wooden chair wobbled with even the slightest movement.

She was lucky. Oll and Gwyneth had been in the room next to Freddie's, which gave her the perfect excuse to scope it out. It would be useful to see how much of his room was visible using the peepholes.

As much as Bonnie dreaded this conversation, they needed to talk. She and Freddie had found a plausible explanation for why everything went wrong; maybe they would stop torturing him when they realized he hadn't betrayed them. That's what she tried to tell herself, at least. She knew the chances of that happening were slim.

Oll fidgeted with a knife across the table from her, which Bonnie kept an eye on, while Gwyneth was reading a new missive that was just delivered.

Bonnie didn't recognize the messenger. The man tried to stand tall, but Bonnie could tell how exhausted he was. His dark skin shined with sweat and his plain clothing was covered in dirt and . . . were those blood stains by his ankles? His eyes were bloodshot, his eyelids rimmed with red. Which outpost did he belong to? He traveled hard and fast — and possibly far.

What was going on?

She hoped he wasn't a rebel from Thornwick. Guilt churned in her gut whenever she thought of them.

Fear, too. Would she be thrown into the same stone prison as Freddie? Or would they be kind enough to give her a cell of her own?

Gwyneth pocketed the message before nodding toward the rebel in dismissal.

Then she turned to Bonnie. With narrowed eyes, she raised an eyebrow; the movement contorted her scarred face.

Bonnie knew that look. It did not bode well for her.

She cleared her throat and tried to figure out where to start. "Did you hear what Lord Stonewood and I discussed?" She jerked her head toward the wall where two rebels stood on chairs, their eyes glued to the peepholes.

"No," Oll said as he leaned back in his chair. "We're dealing with more important issues. What happened?"

What were they dealing with that was bigger than the attack on Thornwick? And why weren't they telling her?

Maybe this was her opportunity to spin the narrative — she could frame it in a way that wasn't so damning. She wasn't keen on joining Freddie in his predicament.

"We think we know why King Aborn moved up the attack — why Lord Stonewood's intelligence was outdated."

Gwyneth leaned back in her chair, arms crossed. Her green eyes glinted. "Go on."

"I was in Navian to plant the evidence that he was a rebel sympathizer, right? We wanted them to think he was part of the rebellion in order to create chaos within the inner circle. Before everything went sideways, I planted the intel we wanted — the mission was successful. We didn't know he actually *was* a rebel sympathizer."

Oll was now using his knife to clean his fingernails. "Your point?"

Gwyneth shot him an annoyed look.

Bonnie cleared her throat and hoped she conveyed confidence she didn't feel. "What if, after Lord Stonewood mysteriously disappeared, his father — or Lord Jasper, or anyone who had access to his rooms — figured it out on their own? What if they saw the planted evidence, realized that Lord Stonewood had knowledge of the king's upcoming plans, and moved up the raid before we caught wind of it?"

Oll sat up in his chair. He pointed the knife at Bonnie. "Are you saying that *we* are to blame for what happened at Thornwick?" His eyes glittered at the perceived insult. His knuckles that gripped the knife turned white.

"No, Father," Bonnie said hastily. "What I'm saying is that the attack on Thornwick would've happened with or without the intel from Lord Stonewood. What we couldn't control was the change in timing. Were any rebels able to escape before the king sent his soldiers?"

Gwyneth nodded, and Bonnie breathed a little easier.

"Good. So even though things certainly did not go to plan, the rebels who escaped benefitted from Lord Stonewood's intel. I choose to believe him when he claims he didn't have any knowledge that his intel was outdated. Someone in that castle must've figured out where he was going and alerted the king's forces from there."

Bonnie avoided Oll's intense gaze, looking instead toward Gwyneth. She couldn't read anything that was happening behind her eyes, but almost slumped forward in relief when the older woman finally nodded.

"That makes a certain amount of sense. As much as I despise Duke Alistair, he certainly is one of the smarter minions that Aborn has under his control. I wouldn't put it past him to figure out what happened."

Bonnie nodded enthusiastically.

She had done it. She had told the truth in a way that wouldn't get them killed.

It didn't mean that Freddie was safe, though, and she knew it. He was still an enemy of the rebel movement. Still the son of the king's advisor. While he'd been strangely welcomed in Crown Harbor, she knew it had been his intel that Oll and Gwyneth had been after. What would they do to him now that the raid was over — a disastrous raid at that? Would they torture him to get intel about the Aborn's inner circle? Was he to be used as a bargaining chip against the king and Duke Stonewood?

If his father and the king knew that he had turned traitor, would they care he was being held by the Amlucen at all?

Bonnie knew the odds. Knew that the likelihood of him walking out of Stoneforge alive was just as likely as Aborn giving up his bloody reign of terror. She needed to get him — to get *both* of them — out of this situation alive.

Four knocks on the door. Everyone turned to see who entered next.

It was a different rebel messenger. As he walked toward their group, Bonnie saw he was limping. His clothing was just as sweat-and-blood stained as the previous messenger's had been.

The messenger hesitated when he saw Bonnie sitting at the table, and she frowned when Oll gave her a nod of dismissal. She was supposed to be the heir to the rebellion leadership, damn it. How could she take over one day if they didn't trust her?

At least this gave her the opening she was looking for. She stood and went to where the other rebels in the room were standing watch.

One of the rebels, a young woman, gave Bonnie a smile before turning back to the wall where a peephole to Freddie's room was located. The other rebel stood absolutely still as he kept watch from his.

Bonnie hoped the girl was friendly — at least friendly enough to speak with. Hopefully friendly enough to answer a few questions.

"Any update?" Bonnie asked, nodding toward the wall.

The girl shook her head, her red curls swaying as she did so. "Not since you left. He either paces the room or sits on his bedroll." The rebel yawned, hiding her mouth behind one of her hands.

"This job doesn't seem the most exciting," Bonnie said with a small smile.

The girl blushed. "I'm honored to have this job." Her tone was formal, and the girl looked sideways at the rebel to her right. He didn't react. The girl looked back at Bonnie and lowered her voice. "It gets a little boring at night, though, when Lord Stonewood is sleeping."

Bonnie huffed a laugh. "I imagine so. Don't you get sore? I'm sure it isn't comfortable standing tall enough to reach the peephole. You must have outstanding balance."

The girl shrugged, even as she winced. "It's not the best, no, but we take breaks sometimes —"

"*Annie*," the other rebel hissed, looking sideways. "That's enough."

Annie, her blush deepening, winced as she looked back at Bonnie. "Sorry," she mumbled as she turned back to the wall. Bonnie watched as she wobbled for a second on the rickety wooden chair.

"Keep up the good work."

Oll and Gwyneth were still absorbed in the conversation with the new messenger. Taking her chance, Bonnie walked nonchalantly to the table standing against the wall. She crossed her arms over her chest and leaned against the wall, hoping that she came across as an exhausted, bored rebel. When she was sure that no one was paying attention, she glanced at the table.

Dozens of Amlucen missives, some confidential, littered the table. Bonnie never understood Oll's habit of throwing them haphazardly on any nearby table surface — if the information was important, why didn't he treat them with more care?

That was before she could read. Now she felt a rush of gratitude for his poor organizational habits.

Oll's knives, as always, were scattered amongst the surface, just a fraction of the collection that Bonnie knew he traveled with. A few had been stabbed into the paper, while others lay flat on their sides. Two had dried blood on the blades.

Her eyes widened as she scanned the papers closest to her.

Thirteen Amlucenites left alive after the assault on Thornwick. Currently in the mines. Need extraction immediately.

Midverdian rebels are reporting strange activity near the palace, another read. Will report back.

Wolverd rebels need help ASAP. Send support.

One of them looked like it was written on noble stationary, so nice was the paper quality.

G — Aborn is asking questions. He has not forgotten. How do I proceed?

Bonnie raised an eyebrow. She knew the rebellion struggled to infiltrate the castle. The security around Aborn and the royal family was tighter than anywhere else in the country, and with good reason. His family had been murdered once; he obviously didn't want to go through that again.

She committed this note — all the notes, really — to

memory. She'd ask Freddie what he thought when she had a chance.

One missive stood out, even more so than the note from the castle. Oll's knife was driven into it pretty deeply, almost as if he stabbed it in a fit of extreme anger. The message was short, written on a scrap of paper with torn edges, smudged with dirty fingerprints, and marked with scattered blood drops. Part of one side was singed, and the handwriting was sloppy.

> *The King's Guard has infiltrated Crown Harbor. Many dead.*
> *We have lost control.*

CHAPTER NINETEEN

WITH SHAKING FINGERS, BONNIE REREAD THE MESSAGE.

And then she read it again.

And again.

She felt the blood drain from her face. She leaned forward and grabbed the table for support.

The King's Guard has infiltrated Crown Harbor.

No.

That couldn't be right.

Apart from the base in Midverd, Crown Harbor was the most secure hideout they had. Hundreds of rebels called it home. It was *her* home.

Their security safeguards couldn't have failed. It was impossible.

Her heart sank. The Map Room . . . The knowledge in the Map Room was irreplaceable. Rebels had died to provide the information that covered those walls.

Part of the paper was singed. Did they . . . did they burn it? The Map Room?

Many dead.

Bile rose in her throat. Most of those left in the hideout had been women and children. Not entirely defenseless, but . . .

We have lost control.

What did that mean? Did anyone make it out alive?

A hand grabbed her shoulder, startling her.

"Bonnie?" Gwyneth asked, her tone sharp, the nails digging into Bonnie's flesh even sharper. "Are you alright?"

Bonnie willed her hands to stop shaking. *Pull it together, Blackthorn,* she thought. *Breathe.*

In, out. In, out.

Plastering on a grimace that wasn't entirely faked, she turned to look at her mother. "Headache," she said, lifting a shaking hand to her temple. She felt the rough edges of her scar, followed it as it stretched from her temple to her ear, and breathed easier. "I think I've been overdoing it."

Gwyneth's eyes softened at Bonnie's confession. She reached out and cupped Bonnie's face. "I knew it. I can tell how tired you are, and I can't imagine how sore you must be. Go back to my room and rest."

Bonnie nodded. She looked over Gwyneth's shoulder to see Oll and the messenger still speaking, both highly agitated. After reading that note, Bonnie had a good idea what they were talking about.

She also had an inkling why the last two messengers had been covered in blood.

Gwyneth turned to go.

"Mother?" Bonnie asked, unable to help herself. She pointed to the damning missive. "Why did Oll stab this? There's blood on it."

Gwyneth looked over Bonnie's shoulder, and a tight look crossed her face. "Oh, it's nothing," she said. "Aborn intercepted a weapon shipment to our Wolverian rebels. It's a hard blow, but we'll get them what they need."

Bonnie closed the door to Oll and Gwyneth's room with a *bang*, no doubt startling Hugo and Leon. The brothers had followed her back to the room like the good little watchdogs they were. She heard their footsteps stomp away moments later.

It had taken all of her willpower to walk out of that room without stabbing someone. Instead, she plastered a frown on her face, sad but not devastated at Gwyneth's news.

Those poor, poor rebels, missing their weapons. Such a shame.

The *audacity* of Gwyneth to lie to her face like that . . .

White hot anger now coursed through her veins. How many times had her family switched to speaking in Suverian? Hundreds of times, easily. It had bothered her before; she hated feeling excluded.

But she never thought they were lying to her.

Bonnie shook her head, trying to regain some composure. Her time left unsupervised in this room was short. It was time to investigate.

The table against the wall looked almost identical to the one in the meeting room — unorganized and covered in paper and knives. Careful not to disturb anything, she read as fast as she could.

Shipment of food delivered to the Suverian rebels. They request additional weaponry. Please advise.

Duke Carrowers grows suspicious of his butler. Ideal time to send in a rebel replacement. Please advise.

Contingent from Enud wants to meet. Sources have confirmed the identities as being sympathetic to our cause.

Bonnie shook her head. While all of this was fascinating, it had nothing to do with the attack on Crown Harbor.

Think, Bonnie, think. Where would Gwyneth keep more personal letters?

The answer came to her immediately.

Her bag.

Gwyneth always traveled with a small bag, one that she took pains to keep hidden from prying eyes. Bonnie had always thought it was beautiful — made of blue fabric, it was cinched with a heavy gold rope that was just as strong as it was soft. She had always wondered what was in it.

She almost found out, once. The memory haunted her nightmares.

A decade ago, she and Felix — high on adrenaline and fueled by boredom — dared each other to find the bag first. Whoever looked at the contents before Gwyneth found out would be the undisputed heir to the rebellion.

She made it her mission to win. Not just for the fake title. Maybe if she won, the others would try to include her more — spend time with her instead of being politely distant.

Maybe Oll and Gwyneth would love her.

They spent days searching the Crown Harbor headquarters, turning over furniture and interrupting meetings. They didn't tell anyone else what they were looking for; to give away the game would be to risk someone else finding it before they did.

Bonnie had found it first, hidden in Gwyneth's office. It was heavier than she thought, though she couldn't tell what was inside from feel alone. She had just started to open it, her fingers working deftly on untying the golden knot that sealed it shut, when Gwyneth found her.

Bonnie had not known genuine fear until she felt Gwyneth's hand grip her shoulder. She let the bag go, eyes wide in terror. It hit the floor with a *thud*.

And then Gwyneth backhanded Bonnie so hard that the Amlucen ring she wore left an imprint of the rebellion symbol that lasted a week. As punishment for her insolence, she locked Bonnie in her bedroom and didn't feed her for three days.

She and Gwyneth never spoke of it again.

When Felix was allowed to see her, Bonnie refused to tell him anything. He already resented Gwyneth for marrying his father — why would Bonnie stir up more drama? She wanted to forget about the entire ordeal.

That was when things started to change. The moment a crack formed in the foundation of their friendship, one that only grew bigger.

Focus, Bonnie.

Gwyneth's bag. She knew that Gwyneth still carried it — her mother had it in Oll's office when Bonnie and Freddie were in Crown Harbor. But Bonnie hadn't seen it on her since.

This room was the safest place to store something valuable, Bonnie figured. No one sane would dare try to infiltrate Oll and Gwyneth's bedchamber.

Good thing Bonnie wasn't sane. But where would Gwyneth hide it?

She checked the obvious places first — under the mattress, under the bed itself, in the side tables. It wasn't in the attached bathing chamber, nor in the small chest at the end of the bed. She went through Gwyneth's travel bags, and then Oll's, trying to touch their stuff as little as possible.

Nothing suspicious. She sucked on a small cut on her

finger, courtesy of one of the many knives Oll had scattered through his belongings.

How much time had passed? She cursed the lack of windows in this place. How did anyone know the time?

Heart beating madly, she considered every alcove, every hiding spot. Where had she not looked?

Her gaze settled on the armchairs. Could it be somewhere so simple?

It wasn't in the chair Bonnie usually occupied — she would've felt it. But every time Gwyneth was in here, she sat in the other one.

The dark blue cushions were well-worn with age and use. Bonnie smiled when she lifted the cushion.

Found it.

She felt like she was transported back in time; the weight and feel were nearly identical to what she remembered. She traced the fabric and marveled at how soft it was.

Loud footsteps outside of the room made her jump. Multiple people, from the sound of it.

Shit.

Bonnie shoved the bag into her pocket and hoped it wasn't too noticeable. Hustling to the door, she pulled it open just as the sound of footsteps stopped.

"Oh!" she exclaimed when she came face to face with Oll, Hugo, and Leon. "I didn't know you were there." She forced a laugh.

"Feeling better, dear daughter?" Oll asked. Concern — as much as a sadist could muster, she supposed — flashed through his eyes. He clutched a knife in his hand with loose fingers.

"Much better, thank you. Where's mother?"

"She left Stoneforge for the night to deal with a rebel matter. She'll be back in the morning. Where are you going?"

Bonnie blinked. Could she be so lucky? She had planned to

sneak the bag back into the room after she looked through it; now she had much more time.

"I'm going to the kitchens to get food for Lord Stonewood. I thought it would be a good idea to feed him before starting my next round of questions."

Oll spat on the floor before pointing his knife at her. "I know you like your way of doing things, but there's nothing wrong with good old-fashioned torture. You waste less food."

She nodded, while keeping a wary eye on the knife. Hugo and Leon said nothing as they loomed behind their leader.

"Yes, Father, I know," she said. "If he stops being talkative, I can explore your . . . methods."

Oll nodded. "Good. Now, if you excuse us — a group of rebel fighters caught a member of the King's Guard. They've brought him here for questioning." He clapped his hands together, eyes lighting in glee at the chance to break someone. Hugo and Leon grinned.

Bunch of savages, the lot of them.

"Don't let me keep you. Good luck with your questioning." She inclined her head and shuffled out of the way to let them pass into the bedchamber.

"I don't need luck when I have this!" Oll exclaimed as he entered his bedroom. Bonnie looked over her shoulder to see him thrusting his knife into the air with a cackle.

Bonnie swallowed hard and then hurried through the maze of stone corridors.

Shit. Where was the supply room? Everything looked the same – she needed to grab things for their escape. She wanted to store supplies somewhere that she could grab them easily and run.

She turned the doorknob on one of the identical doors hoping it was the right one, and poked her head inside.

And froze.

The room, larger than most of the others, was filled with

people. Bunk beds lined three of the walls, while chairs and tables filled the rest of the space.

At least seven rebels stood there chattering in Suverian. Talked ceased when they noticed her, and they all turned to the door, blinking at her.

They were ghostly pale, all dressed in threadbare clothing. And the room was *cold*. Abnormally so. But the temperature wasn't the only thing that sent chills down Bonnie's arms.

It was the strange metal contraptions that were scattered throughout the room.

It was the feeling of *other* in the room. Something felt *off*.

It was the haunted look in their eyes. Their complete and utter silence.

"S-sorry," she stuttered, and shut the door.

And then she ran, as fast as she could.

She stopped a few corridors away, chest heaving as she leaned against the wall.

What the fuck was that?

It didn't feel like a prison room — they had amenities that Freddie didn't have. And they were dressed in the same clothing that other rebels wore. But something was *wrong*, even if they didn't appear to be under duress.

Bonnie didn't have time to figure out what was going on, but she filed away what she saw. Maybe Freddie would have an idea. She had to rescue him to ask him, though. That was her top priority.

She navigated more carefully through the corridors, finding the supply room she had been looking for. She grabbed items she hoped wouldn't be missed and divided them between two satchels that she hid under her cloak.

Then she made her way to the Stoneforge kitchens.

Stopping outside of the entrance, Bonnie took a moment to adjust her shirt, pulling it down to expose more skin. She pinched both of her cheeks, scrubbed her teeth with a fingertip, and made sure that her temple scar was carefully hidden by her hair. And then she plastered on a smile before entering the busy room.

The kitchen, although only a fraction of the size of the one at Crown Harbor, was still large. It was the only place she had seen that had windows, most likely to let out some of the hot air from the enormous fireplaces. A quick glance out told her that dusk was approaching, the sun casting long shadows on the towering pine trees.

The kitchens operated in a state of organized chaos. Bonnie watched as a handful of cooks carried trays of ingredients around the room, while younger rebels assisted where needed. The roaring fire in the far corner was home to a cauldron large enough to bathe in. Bonnie breathed in the smell of what would be dinner simmering quietly and felt her stomach grumble.

One of the younger cooks, probably one a year or so older than Bonnie, stopped in his tracks when he saw her lingering. A smile lit up his face. "Hello again," he said in the common tongue, with a hint of a Suverian accent. "How can we help you?"

Perfect.

Bonnie had been hoping he would be the one who noticed her — they had met when she toured the kitchens earlier. She had noticed that his eyes lingered on her then, and was pleased to see that they lingered on her still.

"Hi," she said, her tone breathless. "I'm looking for dinner for two for tonight. I'll also need extra food rations for travel." She held up the two satchels she had taken from the supply room. "Can you help me?"

AFTER SOME STRATEGIC BLUSHING, EYELASH BATTING, AND

gentle arm touches, Bonnie finally found herself back in front of Freddie's room.

No rebels stood outside this time, probably off guarding the poor soldier Oll was interrogating.

Good. Maybe luck would be in her favor tonight.

Shouldering her way into the room, Bonnie stopped inside the threshold, using her body to ensure the door stayed ajar. She set the tray on the floor, discreetly swiping a spoon off it. As she bent down, pretending to adjust her boot — she didn't want those guarding the peephole to see what she was about to do — she stuck the spoon in the crevice where the door met the wall. Holding her breath, she moved her body to let the door close fully.

The spoon held — the door remained open.

They wouldn't be locked in.

Breathing a sigh of relief, she picked up the tray. Freddie was sitting on his bedroll, watching her with a guarded expression. A quick scan of his face and arms told her he hadn't been visited since she had last left the room. Or if he had, they had beaten him only where she couldn't see.

Maybe they believed that Bonnie's method of getting answers from Lord Stonewood was more effective than Oll's. Probably not.

Bonnie carried over the tray of food, setting it on the ground before him. Then she sat down on the bedroll next to him.

She yawned widely, covering her mouth with one hand as she motioned to the tray of food. "Eat."

"Cold?" he asked as he pulled apart a piece of warm, crusty bread. His eyes darted to her cloak and then back to his food.

"It's freezing in here," Bonnie said, loud enough for their watchers to overhear. "I'm glad we're having stew tonight. Hopefully it'll help warm me up. I might get some tea later, too."

Freddie said nothing as he started digging into the soup. Bonnie followed suit, blowing on her spoonful before trying it.

"Three spoons?" he asked, so softly that she knew there was no chance anyone else could overhear.

Bonnie knew what he meant. "I needed to make sure we could leave this room if we needed to."

A low inhale before he whispered, "Tonight?"

"Tonight."

CHAPTER TWENTY

Bonnie's stomach flipped at the cautious hope that crossed Freddie's face.

She couldn't imagine how he was feeling, especially considering what he had endured at the hands of her adopted father.

Even if the evidence of Oll's administrations had all but disappeared. The yellow and green bruises were gone, replaced by healthy-looking skin. Even the worst of his bruises were now more yellow than green, which didn't make sense. Maybe the physician had used an ointment to speed the healing process.

He had questions — Bonnie could tell by the look on his face. When he opened his mouth, she put her finger to her lips and pointed above her, toward the peephole.

His eyes widened in understanding.

They ate in silence. Every so often Freddie would glance at her and then quickly away, as if waiting for a signal it was time to leave. His knee bounced in nervous anticipation.

Bonnie, for her part, used this time to think through her plan. It relied mostly on luck, something that she wasn't entirely comfortable with. And considering that the last two plans she was involved in went to shit, she wasn't too confident about this one.

She didn't want to trouble Freddie, though. He had too much to deal with already. And it would be too hard to explain by using code words. Not with the rebels listening to every word they said.

"I need you to tell me about the layout of the castle in Navian," she said, projecting her voice. "I want to confirm whether the maps we have are accurate."

Clearing his throat, he began. He knew as well as she did that this line of questioning was bullshit, but Bonnie didn't care. Spending too long in silence was a surefire way to arouse suspicion. She had been told to interrogate him — so here she was, interrogating him. It didn't matter if the information matched with what they had on file, or whether it was information that the Amlucen needed.

It was a way to kill time.

So Freddie walked her through the layout of the castle library and the castle conservatory. And then the castle kitchens, and the stables, too.

The sun surely set by now, Bonnie hoped. They needed to escape tonight, while Gwyneth was gone and Oll was distracted.

Finally, Bonnie couldn't take it anymore. "I'm still cold," she said loudly. "I'm going to get tea. When I return, I want to hear more about any specialized training you received from your father."

"I'll be here," he said, gesturing to his bedroll.

"I'll be back soon," she said under her breath. "Don't leave without me." She stared at him until he gave her a nod.

He knew the door was unlocked; she feared he would try to escape on his own. If he wanted to live, though, he needed to wait for her.

Bonnie knocked on the door four times. Normally it took

only seconds for a guard to open it, so when no one answered she pushed the door open herself.

"Thank you," Bonnie said to the empty hallway. She stepped outside and closed it, making sure not to disturb the spoon that kept the door from closing completely.

Then she ran.

It wasn't long before she arrived back at the meeting room. Still no guard at either door.

Perfect.

Juggling a tray of food in one hand, she knocked four times. Doubt crept in as she waited for someone to answer. Was Annie still there, or had the shift changed? Was she allowed to leave her post?

Then the door opened and Annie's face appeared in the gap. The younger girl gave Bonnie a wide smile, although Bonnie could read the confusion in her eyes.

"Miss Bonnie! How may I help you?"

Bonnie held up her tray. "Care for some tea? Snacks?"

Doubt flashed across Annie's face, and Bonnie held her breath. Her escape tonight relied on getting into that room. That, and many other factors that Bonnie had no control over.

One problem at a time.

Annie motioned for Bonnie to enter, and Bonnie was relieved to see that no one else was in the room except Annie's surly counterpart. Desmond, she remembered Gwyneth saying his name was.

Bonnie set the tray on the table. "How is everything going?" she asked nonchalantly, pouring three tea cups full of steaming peppermint tea.

"Quiet tonight," Annie said. She stood a few paces behind Bonnie, halfway to the chair she was supposed to be standing on. She fidgeted nervously, her hands occasionally reaching up to smooth her red curls. Every few seconds she looked at the rebel who had his back to the two women.

He would be the more difficult one to overcome, Bonnie knew. How he held himself, all stiff-armed and straight-backed, told Bonnie he was listening to every word.

"I know how dull this job must be for you," Bonnie said, as she grabbed two of the three cups. She brought one over to Annie, who looked hesitant to accept it. Bonnie pushed the cup into her hand with a warm smile. "I wanted to find some way to say thank you for doing your job so well."

Annie sniffed the tea and gave a little smile. "I love peppermint tea," she said.

Bonnie winked as she approached the other rebel. "It's my favorite." She stood next to his chair, holding the tea out as a peace offering. "Here you go," she said.

Standing next to him, looking up at his side profile, she was struck by his good looks. He had short-cropped brown hair that was a few shades darker than his skin, and a jawline that she knew attracted the attention of other men and women. It was a shame, really, to place such an attractive man in front of a wall.

He said nothing. He only shook his head as he continued to stare through the peephole.

"Are you sure? It's pretty delicious."

He shook his head once more.

Bonnie looked toward Annie, who grimaced. "Sorry," the girl mouthed with a sad shrug.

Shit. He needed to drink, and fast. But how to make him?

"What's your name, rebel?" Bonnie asked as she leaned against the wall.

He didn't answer, but she saw a muscle click in his jaw. He was getting angry.

Good. She could use that.

"Don't be rude, Desmond," Annie said.

Bonnie raised her eyebrows. "Wait — Desmond? *You're* Desmond?" She whistled appreciatively. "Oh, wow."

This, at last, got him to look at her. A flash of confusion crossed his face. "Yes, I'm Desmond," he said. His voice was deeper than she expected.

She shrugged. "I've heard about you, is all," she said. "I'm Bonnie Blackthorn. Oll and Gwyneth have spoken about your work for the rebellion."

Based on the degree to which Desmond had stuck to his duties, she bet he was someone who craved upward movement. Which was great, in theory — the rebellion would've failed a long time ago if they had subpar leadership. But the glint in his eyes and the puff of his chest created a suspicion she had about the type of person she was dealing with.

"Oh?" he said, jumping off his chair. He towered over Bonnie's shorter frame. "Were they discussing how I extracted information from the man from Thornwick? Or how I helped discover traitors here in Stoneforge?"

Ding ding ding. Bonnie's hunch was correct. This guy would fit right in with Oll's usual crowd of sadists.

She glanced at Annie, who rolled her eyes as she took her first sip. "This is good!" she said, raising her mug to Bonnie.

"I'm glad you like it," Bonnie said, lifting the mug she had brought over for Desmond. "It's Oll's favorite." She winked at him. "Secret family recipe."

His eyes grew wide, and he reached out a large hand to take the mug. Bonnie spotted the Amlucen symbol tattooed on his forearm and had to stop herself from rolling her eyes — there was a reason why rebels didn't tattoo the symbol on their bodies. It was almost as if he was asking to be interrogated by the King's Guard. Fool.

She watched with satisfaction as he downed the tea in one gulp.

Annie took a few more sips of tea before walking over to

her chair. "Thanks for this," she said with a smile. "We better get back to work, though."

Bonnie couldn't help but admire Annie's dedication to her job, as boring as it must be. She felt an uncomfortable pain in her chest.

Annie was *nice*. Kind. Not afraid of her, like so many others. Bonnie would regret what would happen to her once she left.

Would she regret what happened to Desmond? Not so much.

Bonnie walked over to the table, trying to kill time. She was about to pick up the tray, still laden with the biscuits that no one would eat and the cup of tea that Bonnie would not drink, when she heard twin *thuds* behind her.

She couldn't stop her smile.

Both rebels lay on the ground, motionless. Others might think they were dead — they were certainly still enough. But Bonnie saw both of their chests rise and fall, ever so slightly. They would wake after a few hours. Bonnie hoped she and Freddie were long gone before they did.

She had debated killing them — although messier, it was far quicker. But she didn't want to spill rebel blood, and figured she didn't need to give anyone more incentive to hunt them down.

Bonnie ran to the table against the wall. A quick scan of the papers littering the desk told her that nothing new had been reported — nothing written, at least.

Scanning the notes, she took the ones that looked intriguing and shoved them in the same pocket as Gwyneth's bag. The last one she took was the note announcing the attack on Crown Harbor.

The King's Guard has infiltrated Crown Harbor. Many dead. We have lost control.

She pocketed the knife, too, along with a few others that weren't covered in dried blood. Pockets significantly heavier, she left the room.

The corridor was still clear. Bonnie cracked Freddie's door open and poked her head inside.

He stood next to his bedroll, eyes wide. "Bonnie?"

She pushed the door open wide and made a mocking bow. "Come, milord," she said. "It's time to leave."

Freddie grinned. When he reached her, he bent down and kissed her cheek. "Thank you," he said, his voice husky.

She blinked foolishly before shaking her head to clear it. "Don't thank me," she said. "We're not out of here yet."

Taking a knife out of her pocket, she grabbed one of his arms with her free hand. "Come here," she said.

He backed up a step, breaking her hold. He looked at her with wild eyes. "What the hell, Bonnie?"

"We can't just walk out of here — we need to keep up the ruse. You're still the prisoner, and I'm the warden."

"Oh, right. Fine."

As she watched him take several deep breaths, rolling his shoulders, she realized that although the cuts on his arms might be gone soon, it would take longer for the mental scars to heal.

If they ever did.

He squared his shoulders. "You didn't need to go through all of this trouble to commandeer me, honeybum," he said with a wink as he walked back to her. "If you wanted to play power games, all you needed to do was ask."

"Oh, bite me," Bonnie muttered.

"With pleasure. Only if you put your knives away."

Bonnie narrowed her eyes and reconsidered her plan. Maybe she would be better off if she stabbed him and ran.

She reached into a pocket to find the short length of rope she had stowed there earlier, using it to bind his hands tight enough to look official, but loose enough that he could free himself if he needed to.

Grabbing him with one hand, she stood behind him and used the other to dig the knife into his back. He let out an exclamation, and she loosened her grip. "Play nice."

"Only if you will."

Bonnie held her breath as she led him through the stone corridors. She wasn't sure if it was luck or simply the late hour, but they made it all the way to the entrance room without seeing a single soul.

She should've known her luck would run out at some point.

As she opened the door, Freddie entering before her, she glimpsed a familiar face. Her heart almost stopped.

Felix.

Shit.

"What are you doing?" Felix's eyes were wide. He was still reading his copy of *The History of Hallordis*.

She knew how strange it must look to see his adopted sister escorting a lord of the realm at knifepoint.

With no bodyguards.

In the dead of night.

Freddie froze for a moment before bowing his head and staring at the floor. His shoulders tensed, and Bonnie could see a muscle tick in his jaw.

Bonnie had never appreciated, until that moment, just how much Felix looked like his father.

She dismissed the explanations that ran through her head. Felix wasn't a fool. They may not be on good terms, but he was one of the smartest people she knew.

"We're leaving," she told him. "Lord Stonewood is needed elsewhere."

Felix narrowed his eyes. "Right now? In the middle of the night?"

"Yes." She figured the less she spoke, the better. She pushed Freddie forward, her knife still at his back.

They almost made it to the door that led to the stables when Felix spoke again. "Do Father and Gwyneth know you're leaving?"

Bonnie turned back to look him in the eye. She saw, not the bitter man that he had become, but the young boy she grew up with. The young boy she had once loved.

And she decided not to lie. "No."

Freddie's head jerked toward hers. He kept silent, though, even as they reached the door. Bonnie turned the doorknob.

"I won't tell anyone," Felix said. "But Bonnie, we need to talk about —"

"Tell anyone what?" a familiar voice interrupted from the other side of the door.

Bonnie froze in fear.

Gwyneth.

CHAPTER TWENTY-ONE

FREDDIE CHARGED WITH A ROAR, KNOCKING GWYNETH OFF balance. He landed on top of her, and they both crashed to the floor.

He scrambled off, eyes wild.

Gwyneth lay there, stunned.

Freddie moved quickly, positioning himself behind her. It took only a moment for him to take off his wrist bindings and lay the thick rope across her throat.

Then he pulled tight.

Gwyneth's mangled face contorted in pain, her beautiful green eyes wide with fear. Her hands came up to grab the rope, trying futilely to lessen the pressure around her neck. The sound of her struggle filled the empty stable. As she twisted and turned, trying to get out from underneath the rope, Freddie pulled tighter.

Bonnie stood frozen.

This wasn't real.

It couldn't be.

Was she dreaming?

"Bonnie —" Gwyneth croaked. Her face turned red, and her

eyes locked onto Bonnie's as tears started streaming down her face. "Help — me —"

Freddie's face was twisted in a rage she hadn't known he was capable of. It made Bonnie wonder about his time spent in Stoneforge before she arrived. Before she convinced them to try her method of interrogation.

How involved had her mother been in Freddie's torture?

She wouldn't. Torture was Oll's domain . . . right?

Bonnie reached out a hand. "Freddie, stop!"

"No."

Gwyneth squirmed harder.

Bonnie ran behind him, holding her knife to his throat. "Freddie, stop! Now!"

He stilled as he felt the cold tip of the knife on his throat, but did not lessen his hold. "You don't know what she did to me."

Bonnie felt hot tears come to her eyes. "You're right — I don't. But she's my mother."

Freddie didn't lessen his grip. Gwyneth's struggles became weaker.

Bonnie's voice broke. *"Please."*

He inhaled sharply, the sound full of hurt and pain and anger. Then he loosened his hold on the rope.

Bonnie lowered her knife.

Gwyneth shuddered in a breath, the sound wet and raspy. As she continued to wheeze, Bonnie stepped back and looked around.

Felix stood in the doorway that led back to the hideout, eyes wide as he looked from Bonnie to Freddie to Gwyneth.

"Don't move," she ordered Freddie.

They couldn't afford much more of a delay — the last thing they needed right now was for Oll to show up and join the fray.

She went to the last stall. She had chosen the largest horse for their flight, a gray one who accepted her carrot with a soft whinny. He wasn't as big as Captain, but he would do.

Peeking her head into the stall, Bonnie saw the supplies she had stowed earlier. Leaning over, she grabbed a satchel and brought it to Freddie.

Gwyneth was lying on the floor, her hand massaging her throat. The sound of her labored breathing echoed throughout the space.

Freddie was on his knees, head bowed, staring at the floor. It was as if all the fight had gone out of him. Both hands were bloody, and the rope sat a few feet away, covered in his blood.

Bonnie kneeled next to him, ignoring Gwyneth. Reaching into the satchel, she took out a cloak and shoes. "We'll clean your hands later," she told him, gently but firmly. "We need to leave. Give me your feet — I brought you boots and a cloak."

He let her drape the cloak around his shoulders, but pulled himself together enough to shoo her away when she tried to put the worn leather boots on his feet. He hissed as he clumsily tried to tie his laces with injured hands.

Bonnie turned to her brother, who was still standing in the doorway.

"You need to leave," he said. "Get as far away as you can."

"What's going to happen to you?"

Felix swallowed hard. "I guess I'll find out, won't I?"

"Come with us." She didn't know why she said it, but she meant every word. He wouldn't be safe here. Not anymore.

He shook his head. "My place is with the Amlucen. I don't know why you're leaving with him — but I trust you. I'll take care of Gwyneth."

Bonnie blinked.

He . . . He *trusted* her? The last few years had been so tense — why was he offering to help? What changed?

"You're not supposed to be here right now," he said quietly. "Everyone thought you were dead."

"What?"

Did . . . did this mean what she thought it meant? Was he the one who told Claire and Stefan to keep her away?

He shook his head, and she knew she would get no more out of him.

Unease filled her, even though she didn't have time to question him. She turned back to Freddie, who was once again on his feet. He glared at Gwyneth before following behind her.

Freddie mounted as Bonnie went to the far wall. A faux wall had been constructed out of plants and trees to help camouflage the entrance of the stables, and she needed to move it out of the way.

A cry from behind. She turned, and time seemed to slow.

Felix, stumbling away from Gwyneth. Dark blood sprayed through the air from a slash on his arm.

Gwyneth, lunging toward him with a knife in her hand.

"TRAITOR!" she half-screamed, half-rasped as she plunged it in and out of her stepson.

"No!" Bonnie cried.

Felix ran until he reached the wall, hunched over in agony.

Gwyneth staggered to her feet, her mangled face contorted with fury. Her eyes were wide with anger and hatred.

"TRAITOR!" she screamed again, this time at Bonnie.

Gwyneth stumbled forward in Bonnie's direction, knife aloft, gaining momentum with each step.

"Bonnie, run!" Felix shouted, and slipped back into the entrance hall. Only a puddle of blood remained where he had been standing.

Bonnie sprinted toward Freddie, and she almost slammed into the faux wall, stopping just inches away. Grabbing it — up close, she saw it was a green net woven with different forest plants — she hauled it to the side enough that Freddie could lead the horse out.

Then she mounted and looked back. Gwyneth had stumbled halfway down the stable, still yelling with every step.

Freddie flicked the reins. The horse jolted forward, clearing the entrance with only inches to spare.

Bonnie had to stop herself from weeping with joy as the crisp night air hit her.

She had done it. She had gotten them both out of Stoneforge alive.

A moment later, Freddie fell forward, his body crushing her. He hissed.

Bonnie turned as much as she could while bearing his weight, and she gasped.

There was a knife sticking out of his back.

"TRAITOR!" Gwyneth yelled one final time as she stood in the opening, gasping for breath.

Bonnie felt Freddie shift in the saddle. He groaned.

She sat up as straight as she could, trying to use the saddle for leverage. "Hold on!" she cried as she urged the horse to go faster.

Luck had been on their side; the night skies were clear of clouds, and the full moon shone brightly on the path. The horse pushed forward, navigating the hard dirt path with nimble feet.

Bonnie fought the urge to assess the damage. Instead, she kept her eyes forward for any danger.

She didn't know where to go from here. All she knew was she needed to get as far away as she could. Who knew if Gwyneth would send others after them?

Knowing her adopted mother, Bonnie wouldn't doubt it. They had to hide.

Freddie's breathing was labored, and she wasn't sure how long he could stay on top of the horse.

Where had the knife hit? Was he bleeding out?

When they had long left Stoneforge behind, when the sun

crept through the towering pine trees, Bonnie stopped. She found a clearing with a small pond, and deemed it safe enough.

The dismount was tricky, with Freddie's body weight pinning her to the saddle. She slid underneath him, hoping that he would remain on without her support.

As soon as her feet touched the ground, he lurched forward with a groan. That meant he was alive, at least. And conscious.

Reaching up, she tried to steady him as best as she could. She knew enough to keep the knife in; it was the only thing keeping the blood in his body, like a cork in a wine bottle. If she removed it, he might bleed out.

"What do I do? What do I do?" she muttered in increasing panic as she supported his body. She had to stand on her toes to even reach that high — the gray horse was *tall*. Not Captain tall, but still taller than most horses.

The horse needed a rest — even now, it was drinking its fill from the pond. But they also needed to get to a physician, quick. Where to find one? Her original plan had been to bring Freddie to Crown Harbor to see what remained of the head-quarters. She had steered their horse in that direction.

Now, she wasn't so sure. Kill orders had likely been issued already.

That was a problem to deal with later. Right now she needed to focus on keeping him alive. But where could they go if Crown Harbor was off limits?

"Bronwyn," Freddie whispered, his head hanging low.

Oh, no. Was he hallucinating? "My name is Bonnie, Freddie. Not Bronwyn."

"I need Bronwyn."

Bonnie tried to keep her breathing even. "Bonnie. Not Bronwyn. *Bonnie.*"

"Please, Bonnie. Get me to Bronwyn."

"Who is Bronwyn? Where is she?"

"Healer," he said. "In Golwich, by Blackstall. Please."

Bonnie knew he was hallucinating; healers didn't exist in Hallordis anymore. Maybe this Bronwyn woman had been a healer before Vale Magicae.

Hopefully, she knew how to heal without magic.

She recognized the name Blackstall; it was on the border of the country, where Hallordis ended and Suverd began. Golwich Forest extended on both sides.

It would take at least a day of riding to make it there. Would Freddie survive that long?

And would the horse make it? Its sides were heavy with sweat, and it was panting hard. Neither Freddie nor Bonnie were slight people — would they be too much to carry all the way there?

She heard the sound of branches being broken, accompanied by loud whinnying. Bonnie whirled toward the noise; even Freddie tried to sit up in the saddle.

No no no no no. They've found us.

Reaching into her pockets, she took two of her knives and slid into a defensive stance.

The sound of broken sticks got louder. A different horse whinnied this time, the sound higher than the last one. The gray horse answered with one of his own.

Bonnie only clutched her knives tighter.

Two horses, then. Maybe she could fight her way out of this. If she was lucky.

But she was so, so tired.

Two horses broke through the trees. They bore no riders.

Bonnie dropped to her knees.

Captain and Belle.

Bonnie rose, a bit unsteadily. Was *she* the one hallucinating?

They appeared unhurt — only covered in dirt and sticks. Bonnie couldn't stop the tremble in her fingers as she stroked their soft, fuzzy noses.

"Where have you been?" she whispered. "I didn't think I'd ever see you again."

Bonnie looked over to see if Freddie was as excited as she was.

"No!" she yelled, running to him as he started sliding off the horse. She caught his shoulders before he hit the ground, lessening the impact. The force of his body weight brought her to her knees. His knees landed with a *thud* a moment later.

"Freddie?" she asked, maneuvering him onto his side.

She studied the knife sticking out of his back. It was in pretty deep, damn Gwyneth.

Bonnie wasn't an expert at anatomy, but knew enough to know it had missed most of his vital organs. He wasn't out of danger, not by a long shot — he had lost a lot of blood, and he could still die from shock or infection. But it was better than she had hoped for.

They needed to leave. This Bronwyn woman might be his only chance at staying alive.

Running over to the gray horse, she took a water canteen from one of the saddle bags and brought it over to Freddie. She put it to his lips, and he didn't fight as she poured a small amount down his throat.

That would have to do for now. When she tried to put the canteen back in her pocket, it knocked against something. She felt inside, and her hand closed around something smooth and round.

A vial full of clear liquid. The pain medicine from the Stoneforge physician.

She poured it down his throat. He fought this time, coughing and sputtering, but Bonnie refused to lose a single drop. It wouldn't be much relief, she knew, but hoped it was enough to get him through the next patch of riding.

The sound of footsteps behind her, crunching on the

forest's leafy carpet. Captain nudged her shoulder with his nose a moment later.

"We need to get Freddie on your back, Captain. Can you lay down for me?"

She must be going crazy — talking to a horse as if he understood her? Insane. But she always thought that Captain was smarter than the average horse. That's why it didn't completely surprise her when he kneeled a moment later.

Freddie let out a fresh groan. He opened his eyes, and Bonnie watched him blink a few times.

"Cap?" he asked, his voice hoarse. He blinked a few more times. "What are you doing here?"

"He and Belle are here," Bonnie said. "They're going to take us to Bronwyn."

"Yes. Bronwyn," Freddie said, closing his eyes again.

She moved behind him. "This is going to hurt. I'm going to try to lift you onto him. You may need to help."

Freddie didn't respond. She wasn't sure if he was unconscious again, but knew she would find out soon enough.

Crouching behind him, careful not to move the knife, she put her arms under his. And then she heaved with all her strength.

Freddie groaned, louder than ever, as half of his body settled on Captain. The wound on his back dribbled fresh blood.

Bonnie panted, paced around the clearing for a moment to gather her strength, and then lifted him onto Captain's back.

"Great," Bonnie huffed as she stepped back. Freddie, now mounted, was leaning so far forward that his nose almost touched the saddle. There was a real chance he would fall off as soon as Captain stood. And a fall from that height would kill him.

Bonnie searched through the supply packs she had brought. *There.* Extra rope.

It took a few minutes for her to bind Freddie's arms and legs to different parts of Captain. She ignored his mutterings of protest, telling him that the alternative was much worse than his pride being hurt. Stupid man.

She watched with bated breath as Captain rose, and breathed a sigh of relief when they were upright.

The gray horse had been munching on grass near the pond. She pat him on the nose gratefully as she fed him a carrot. "You're free now," she told him. "Stay here, or go back to the stables. Thank you for taking us this far."

The horse gently nipped her fingers before turning back to the lush grass. Bonnie would regret it if anything happened to it, but it made little sense to take three horses. Hopefully it would find its way back to the stables before a hungry predator found it.

She mounted Belle before grabbing Captain's reins.

It was time to go.

CHAPTER TWENTY-TWO

THEY RODE HARD.

Bonnie tried to keep their pace smooth, but Captain had other ideas. Every time she slowed, Captain shook his head and went faster. It felt as though he was leading her and not the other way around.

Freddie said nothing. The only sign he was conscious was his clenched grip on the pommel. Bonnie was glad for the ropes that tied him to Captain; without those, he would've fallen off long ago.

Bonnie gauged their direction by the sun. If her recollection was correct, she figured they would reach their destination by nightfall.

She hoped Freddie made it that long.

Bonnie spent the ride talking to him about whatever came to mind. Memories from her childhood growing up in the Amlucen. Stories about the missions Oll sent her on. What she learned in her training with the Rebel Guard.

Her relationship with Felix, and how close they'd been until everything went sour. How she missed him, despite their issues.

Oh, Felix.

Gwyneth had stabbed him more than once, but it didn't look as if she hit anything vital. Did he escape? Would he be locked in the same room she had broken Freddie out of, with no one to help him?

Her voice grew hoarse as she talked to him about everything and nothing. Back in his cell, she didn't have the time or nerve to tell him about stealing Gwyneth's bag. She told him now, and speculated what could be in it.

And then there was her most special secret — the one she was most excited to share. Her sudden fluency in other languages.

And the fact she could *read*. She knew this, out of anything, would be of the most interest to him. He wasn't called the Lord of Libraries for nothing.

She forced water down his throat during their brief breaks. He was pale, frightfully so, but still grabbed Bonnie's hand when she was near.

"Thank you," he whispered.

"Don't thank me yet," was her reply. She squeezed his hand before letting go.

HOURS PASSED. THE SHADOWS OF THE TREES GREW LONGER.

Freddie's breathing grew shallower. His grip on the pommel grew weaker.

He would not survive the night.

Just as Bonnie began to lose hope, Belle broke through the trees and into an open area. Captain carried an unconscious Freddie a step behind.

She almost sobbed in relief.

A picturesque brick cottage sat in the center of the clearing, smoke rising from a small chimney. Bonnie nudged Belle toward it and hoped this was the place she'd been looking for.

A strange tingling sensation came over her, but Bonnie shook off the feeling.

Loud cursing sounded through the clearing. Bonnie tensed as a small, wizened old woman ran out of the cottage, her flyaway white hair surrounding her like a halo. The wooden door closed behind her with a *thump*.

The woman's bright blue eyes were focused on the spot where Bonnie stopped Belle. She sucked in a breath, nostrils flaring, before a scowl crossed her wrinkly face.

"Frederick?" Her tone was sharp.

Freddie's head was bent over Captain's mane, and it was clear he only remained on the horse because of the ropes. The woman ran right to Captain, ignoring Bonnie completely. She rested her wrinkly hands on his arms, his legs, anywhere she could reach.

Freddie did not stir.

Then she whirled to Bonnie, the whites of her eyes showing as she focused on a spot over Bonnie's shoulder. The woman scowled. "What happened?" she barked. "Did you do this?"

Bonnie reared her head back as she dismounted. "Of course not. He wouldn't be alive right now if it weren't for me." She paused, swallowing hard. "Are you Bronwyn? He said you could help him. Can you?"

Underneath her bravado lay an undercurrent of fear. The woman's eyes widened as if she, too, picked up on Bonnie's nerves.

The old lady turned back to Freddie. "Yes. Get him down."

Bonnie led Captain over to the woman's doorstep before she cut the ropes binding Freddie to him. She positioned herself on Captain's side, arms outstretched, and tried to lessen the impact as Freddie fell off the horse.

Freddie let out a groan when he hit the ground, but otherwise remained silent. And although Bonnie was relieved he was alive, she knew things were critical.

It may not matter that they had made it here after all. It might already be too late.

"Get him inside," Bronwyn barked, striding through the open door.

Bonnie held back some choice words. The woman hadn't lifted a finger to help. And Freddie was *heavy*.

Wiping her brow, Bonnie half-dragged, half-carried Freddie inside, avoiding the knife still sticking out of his back. Bronwyn was putting a sheet over a mattress that sat close to the floor.

The woman gestured to it. "Put him here. Face down."

Bonnie did as she was told. By the time she got him settled, he had stopped responding entirely.

She stood back as Bronwyn leaned over him. Taking out a knife of her own, the old woman cut Freddie's clothes off, careful not to jostle the knife. The woman constantly trailed her fingers across his back, as if taking full measure of his ailments.

And there were many — not only the knife wound. His body was covered in black and blue bruises.

It was a miracle he was alive.

Bonnie went to the door, shedding her cloak in a heap. Then she glanced around the cottage, noting any exits in case she needed to bolt.

It was cozy. A small bed was in the corner, covered in an array of colorful blankets. The window above the bed was open to the night elements, and a soft breeze blew sheer window hangings inwards, bringing in the soft scent of lavender and other sweet florals. Dried herbs were strung up on the walls alongside a tapestry with an intricately woven design.

A fireplace was tucked in a corner, and a small fire crackled merrily under a large cauldron. There was a rocking chair, and a basket filled with yarn next to it. A wooden table with two chairs was against another wall. A basket of fresh vegetables lay on its surface, and Bonnie's stomach grumbled at the reminder that she hadn't eaten in a while.

A flare of light caught her attention. Bonnie turned, and her mouth dropped open.

Bronwyn's hands were *glowing*.

A soft light surrounded the area where her hands touched Freddie's bare skin.

Bonnie blinked once. Twice. And then a few more times.

It wasn't a trick of the light. She wasn't hallucinating. Where Bronwyn touched Freddie, the bruises started to fade.

Bronwyn was *healing* him.

"Impossible," Bonnie breathed.

Bronwyn wasn't a physician, incapable of using magic to help others. She was a *healer*, just like Freddie said. And she was healing him.

Eyes wide, Bonnie watched as Bronwyn took her hands off him. The old woman sighed before grasping the hilt of the knife with both hands.

"This is going to hurt," Bronwyn muttered before yanking up.

Freddie arched his back with a roar.

Blood spurted out of the wound, while rivers of it made trails down his back.

Bronwyn lunged forward, throwing the knife to the side, and placed both of her hands over the gushing wound.

Freddie stilled immediately. The white sheet was now stained red.

Bronwyn grit her teeth. The old woman swore under her breath, even as the blood flow slowed.

Bonnie stepped forward. "How can I help?"

"Hold him down," the woman panted. "There must have been . . . rust . . . or poison . . . on the blade. The wound is infected. I need to draw the . . . infection out."

Bonnie went to Freddie's head. His arms dangled over the

side of the bed, but his fists were clenched so tightly his knuckles were white.

Crouching down, she stared into his face. His eyes were closed, and his face was scrunched in pain.

Lifting a shaking hand to his hair, she stroked her fingers through the soft brown waves. He tensed for a moment before leaning into her touch.

"The crazy old lady tells me that things are about to start hurting," she told him.

"*Start* hurting?" he ground out, his voice cracking.

"I heard that," Bronwyn snapped at the same time.

Bonnie grinned as she ran her fingers through his hair one more time. "I'm going to hold on to both of your hands. Squeeze them if you need to." She had a thought. "Wait, hold on."

She ran to the cottage door. Opening it with a *bang*, she glanced around. Captain and Belle stood by a pond at the far end of the clearing. She ran over and slipped Belle's halter off.

"Once he's better, I'll take care of you both," she told the pair before dashing back inside.

Bonnie took the thickest part of the reins and crouched by Freddie's head once more. "Open up," she said, and slipped the reins in between his teeth. "Bite on that," she told him, before reaching to take both of his hands with hers.

Bronwyn nodded, and Bonnie swore she saw a flash of approval in the old woman's eyes.

And then it was time to heal him.

Bronwyn covered the wound with her hands, ignoring the blood still flowing out. The light around her hands grew so bright Bonnie had to turn away.

Freddie bit down hard on the leather, leaving deep imprints. But while his hands flexed against Bonnie's, he didn't hurt her.

"You can squeeze tighter if you need to," she told him. "I can take it."

He shook his head, teeth still bearing down. He let out an agonizing groan.

"The old bat can heal me if you do any damage," she said, half-jokingly. Although Bronwyn might need some time to recover herself, Bonnie thought. She could hear the woman panting.

"Almost . . . there . . ." Bronwyn ground out. The light flared even brighter.

"Done," she said with a weary sigh.

The light faded, and the room suddenly felt very dark. The leather rein slipped out of Freddie's mouth as he took his first deep breath in hours.

Bonnie looked up to see Bronwyn sway where she stood, her wrinkled hands still on Freddie's back.

Racing across the room, Bonnie grabbed one of the chairs that flanked the table. She got the chair underneath Bronwyn just before the woman collapsed.

The woman pat Bonnie's hand in thanks but shooed her away when Bonnie asked if she needed anything.

"Just rest," she said. "I'll be fine." She closed her eyes as she relaxed into the chair.

Bonnie studied Freddie. He looked peaceful now, a soft smile on his lips. His hands now hung loosely off the side of the bed, no longer white-knuckled fists. She put two trembling fingers to his neck and found that his pulse was strong.

Her fingers danced over the healthy pink skin of his back that only minutes ago was black and blue and green and yellow. They paused where the knife had been.

The only evidence of his injury was a small scar, a few inches from top to bottom. It wasn't even raised like some of her own scars were; it was flat, and white. As if it had healed years ago.

It was a miracle.

Bonnie shook her head, glancing at Bronwyn in awe. She had questions. A *lot* of questions. But for now, she was content to marvel at what just happened.

TRUE TO HER WORD, BONNIE LEFT THE QUIET COTTAGE IN search of the horses, who still lingered by the little pond. She brought a small lantern with her, setting it on a large tree stump. As tired as she was, she needed to make sure they were taken care of before retiring.

"I don't know how you found us," she said to Captain as she brushed his face, "or why you came to us when you did, but you two are the reason that Freddie is alive. Thank you."

Captain whinnied, nipping Bonnie gently with his front teeth before turning to graze near Belle.

Moving the lantern onto the grass, Bonnie sat on the tree stump. She needed time to think.

Magic.

Magic had saved Freddie's life. It was incredible; she'd seen nothing like it. It was an absolute miracle.

Her thoughts were interrupted by a soft squeak. A baby mouse bumped into her foot, almost hidden by the lush grass. Bonnie smiled as she picked it up. She cuddled it for a bit, grateful for some simple, sweet comfort.

Night had well and truly fallen when Bonnie went back inside. The others were asleep, Freddie in his bed and Bronwyn in the chair.

It was quiet. The silence was only broken by Freddie's soft breathing, Bronwyn's loud snores, and the crackling of the fire.

The healing must have taken a lot out of Bronwyn, for she did not stir when Bonnie picked her up and laid her on her bed. She covered the old woman with a blanket before turning back to Freddie. The cadence of his breathing didn't change when Bonnie rolled him on his side to remove his blood-covered sheet, replacing it with a clean one before covering him with a warm blanket of his own.

Bonnie crinkled her nose in disgust when she looked down at herself. The clothes she'd fled Stoneforge in were now covered in blood, sweat, and dirt. She cleaned herself as best as she could using the water basin in the corner and changed into clean clothes. A bath could wait until the morning.

Weary beyond belief, Bonnie sat in Bronwyn's vacant chair. Shifting in her seat, she leaned forward to rest her arms on Freddie's mattress, careful not to touch him. Resting her forehead on her arms, she gave a long, heavy sigh and promptly fell asleep.

CHAPTER TWENTY-THREE

BONNIE WOKE TO THE SOUND OF A WHISPERED CONVERSATION.

She kept her breathing deep and even, making sure she didn't so much as twitch a finger.

The voices traveled from across the room.

"You need to tell her, or I will," an irritated female voice said in Naverian.

Freddie answered in his native tongue. "I *want* to tell her, but give me time. It's not something I share with just anyone."

A thousand questions raced through Bonnie's mind, but she forced herself to keep still. She knew he was keeping secrets — she herself had plenty she had not shared.

She had told him *most* of her secrets, though, on the journey to the cottage. She doubted he heard much, if anything. He had been unconscious during most of it.

Bronwyn scoffed but said nothing. They descended into comfortable silence, and Bonnie wondered how they met, this spitfire of an old lady and the Lord of Libraries. What was the story there?

Bonnie was about to feign waking up when Bronwyn spoke.

"Did you send the bird?"

"Yes."

Another pause. "How much does she know?"

Silence.

"Bits and pieces," he finally said. "I think she knows more than she lets on. But whether she believes any of it is a different story." A pause. "We should probably stop talking about it, though." He switched to the common tongue. "Bonnie's awake, and she can understand every word we say."

Caught.

Bonnie sat up. "How do you know I can understand everything you say?"

Freddie sat at the table, while Bronwyn sat on her bed. "You told me." He raised a chipped clay mug to his mouth and took a sip. "Tea?"

Damn it. Apparently, he had been more lucid than she thought.

She stood slowly, keenly aware of how stiff she felt. Dragging the chair behind her, she sat across the table from him. "How much of that conversation do you remember?"

"Most of it. It helped me stay awake. It helped me stay alive." He pushed a steaming cup toward her.

Bonnie ignored the feeling of pleasure she felt at his words. She sniffed the cup and smiled. Peppermint tea, her favorite.

Turning to where Bronwyn sat on the bed, Bonnie gave her a nod. "Good morning," she said. "Thank you for saving Freddie."

The woman waved her hand in dismissal as she stared at a spot over Bonnie's shoulder. "I care for Frederick as if he were one of my own sons. Of course I saved him." She leaned toward Bonnie. "And who are you, exactly?"

"Bonnie Blackthorn."

Bronwyn waved a withered hand. "No, no. That's the name

they gave you. The sociopaths who run the rebellion. Who are you, really?"

Bonnie opened and closed her mouth a few times. "I-I'm not sure," she stammered. "I was attacked and lost all of my memory." She pointed to the scar that ran from the top of her hairline to her ear. "Oll and Gwyneth Blackthorn saved my life. They told me my name was Bonnie, and I never questioned it."

"But you don't know *who* you are, do you?"

A flash of annoyance washed over her. How many times did she have to say the same thing? "No. Do *you* know who I am?"

Bronwyn said nothing, only sat up straighter. "You seem familiar." She paused. "You know, Frederick was never involved in such horrible situations before you came along."

"Excuse me?" Bonnie's mouth dropped open. "I would've gotten rid of him immediately if he wasn't so damned stubborn."

"Ah," Freddie interjected, "but then you would've been denied the pleasure of my company." He winked.

"What did Frederick mean, exactly, when he said you could understand the private conversation we were having?" Bronwyn asked. "Do you not speak Naverian?"

Bonnie shook her head. "I lost all memory before the attack, including knowledge of languages. After, I could only learn the common tongue."

"Until now," Freddie said.

Bonnie nodded. "Until now."

Silence.

Bronwyn spoke. "'Until now' — what does that mean?"

"I don't know exactly how it happened." She turned to Freddie. "How much does she know?"

"The basics," he said. "That's all we've had time for."

Bonnie nodded, tempering her annoyance at the fact they had been talking about her without her knowledge. "Members of the King's Guard attacked us — Freddie escaped, but I was

injured. Two rebels saved me. I was in and out of consciousness for a while, but when I came to I found I was fluent in a
new language."

"What language?"

"Wolverian."

Bronwyn cocked her head to the side. "And you've never
understood Wolverian before?"

Bonnie shook her head. "Nothing but the common tongue.
And even that took a long time to relearn after Vale Magicae."

Bronwyn frowned at the mention of that fateful day. "You
were attacked on Vale Magicae?"

Bonnie nodded. Speaking of . . . "What you did last night for
Freddie . . . it was wondrous. But how could you do that when
magic is gone?"

Bronwyn grinned toothily. "Magic is gone, yes. In *Hallordis*.
But we're not in Hallordis, are we?"

"We're not?"

"We entered Suverd when we came into the clearing,"
Freddie explained. "She lives on the border of the two
countries."

"Half of this clearing is in Suverd, at least," Bronwyn
corrected. "The other half is in Hallordis."

That explained her ability to heal. "Does Aborn know you
live here, on the border? Or King Thorstan?" The King of
Suverd, King Aborn's older brother.

Bronwyn cackled as she stood and went to tend to the fire.
She walked slowly, carefully. "They both know, yes. And they
also know to keep well enough alone."

Bonnie looked at the bold old lady with renewed interest.
Bronwyn was small but not frail — old, but certainly lively
enough. Today she had tamed her flyaway white hair with a
blue scarf, the color of which brought out the vivid blue of her
eyes.

Something bothered Bonnie about her eyes. They were

strange — now in the daylight, and aided by the light that came from the fire, Bonnie saw they weren't as blue as they could've been. Or rather, as blue as they *should* have been. It was almost as if something was covering them, like clouds covering the sun on an overcast day. A white sheen, almost.

Bonnie watched as the old woman gingerly picked up a piece of firewood from the stack next to the fireplace and placed a log on the fire. Every movement was slow, measured. Careful. Precise.

Bonnie sucked in a breath when she realized.

Bronwyn, to her credit, only huffed as she walked to her rocking chair. "Say it," she barked.

"You're blind."

It explained why the older woman never met Bonnie's eyes when speaking to her.

Bronwyn smirked. "You caught on faster than most, girl. It took Frederick here almost two days to realize."

"Not fair, Bron," Freddie said. "I met you when I was little more than a child."

Bronwyn only scoffed before she turned to Bonnie. "What gave me away?"

"Lack of eye contact," Bonnie said. She took another sip of tea. "I'm not sure I would've noticed otherwise. Are you completely without sight?"

"Almost. I can see shapes and movement when it's light out — I'm almost completely useless in the dark. So while I know where your head is when I speak to you, I can only approximate where to look when I want to fake eye contact."

"Fascinating," Bonnie said, and meant it. "You're a healer, though. Why can't you heal your vision?"

Bronwyn scowled. "Even magic has its limits." A pause, and Bronwyn shuffled over to where Bonnie was sitting. "Speaking of magic — may I?" She held up her wrinkly hands.

"May you do what?"

"Examine you. Your old head wound in particular."

Bonnie glanced toward Freddie, who gave her an encouraging nod.

"It won't hurt," he said.

After what Bonnie had seen Bronwyn do the night before, Bonnie knew the woman was impressive. Healers weren't known for inflicting pain and misery. And Freddie trusted her, which meant something. Still . . .

"Are you going to heal me?"

Bronwyn pursed her lips. "It depends on what I find. If the wound is old, I won't be able to do much. Relieve some of the pressure, possibly. If I was at my full strength, I could probably do more. I will admit that healing young Frederick took a lot out of me. For now, I would just like to look, in a manner of speaking. With your permission."

"Okay. Sure. Do I just . . . sit here?"

Bronwyn shooed Freddie away and sat down in his seat.

Bonnie couldn't help but stare as he walked over to sit on the bed. No pain laced his steps, no wincing at every movement. His face, now devoid of bruises, was pink and glowing with health.

He was healed. It made her feel like crying.

She turned back to Bronwyn, and couldn't help but tense as the old woman reached out a wrinkly hand to touch Bonnie's head.

"Sit still. He already told you it wouldn't hurt."

Bonnie rolled her eyes but allowed Bronwyn's fingers to roam her face. Her touch didn't hurt, but it did tingle. Probably a result of Bronwyn's magic exploring Bonnie's body.

Something about it felt familiar to Bonnie, almost as if this wasn't the first healing she'd experienced. Maybe she had been healed in her earlier life. Before she was attacked. Before she lost all of her memories.

A pang rang through her chest. She rubbed the space over her heart absentmindedly.

"Everything alright?" Bronwyn asked, her fingers still roaming Bonnie's head.

"Yes." She took her hand off of her chest, settling them in her lap. "This — this healing. It feels . . . familiar. I think I must've been healed before."

Bronwyn nodded. "Probably so. Although healers were relatively rare, most people could see them to fix any serious problems." She paused. "Do you often get this feeling? That you've recovered some sort of lost memory?"

Bonnie shook her head. "No. This is the first time. It's unsettling."

Bronwyn said nothing, only clicked her tongue in agreement as her fingers continued to study Bonnie's head.

Closing her eyes, Bonnie tried to relax. Now that she was getting used to the strange sensation, it really was quite pleasant. Almost like a head massage.

When Bronwyn's fingers touched her scar, the healer inhaled sharply.

Bonnie stilled and tried not to flinch. While the tingling didn't hurt, it felt like it had intensified.

"What's wrong?" Freddie asked. "Is everything alright?" He directed the question at Bronwyn, but Bonnie saw he was looking at her with concern.

"It's a miracle you're alive," Bronwyn said to Bonnie. "This wound — it would've killed most people. It was done with malice. With hate."

"You can tell just by touching it with your magic?" Bonnie asked.

Bronwyn shook her head. "My magic doesn't tell me the intention of those who committed the violence, no. But someone tried very hard to kill you. This scar isn't the result of a one time hit, but of several targeted blows."

Bonnie shivered at her bluntness. She wasn't surprised; anyone who tried to kill an eight-year-old in cold blood had to be a different type of monster.

"I wish I remembered who did it. I wish I remembered anything about my life before the attack."

"Your memories may come back," Bronwyn mused. "Only time will tell."

The healer then spent a few minutes asking Bonnie about head traumas that had happened in the years since. There had been a few, Bonnie admitted. Freddie pointed out that she had hit her head after falling off of Captain during the attack in Golwich Forest.

Bronwyn listened with a healer's quiet calm before she tapped on Bonnie's scar with a gentle finger. "This is where you were hit in Thornwick, right? Where your scar is?"

"Yes."

"And right after the attack, when you grew conscious, that's when you discovered you knew how to speak Wolverian?"

"Yes."

Bronwyn spoke in a different language, this one sounding similar to how a snake hissed at prey. It differed from the hissing and spitting Bonnie associated with Suverian, though. Like it was related, but somehow still entirely separate. Even so, Bonnie understood Bronwyn when she asked, "What language am I speaking now?"

"Enudian." The language of Enud, the desert country south of Suverd.

"Fascinating," Freddie said. "What are your thoughts, Bron?"

"I think there are two possibilities," Bronwyn said as she removed her fingers and sat in the other chair.

"Go on."

"Magic," she said simply. "One possibility is magic. You were in Thornwick when you regained consciousness, though. So while that would be the simple explanation, I do not believe that is the reason you now understand these languages.

"I think the answer might be simpler — and more complex. Your first major head trauma happened and you lost all of your long-term memories. What if the second major head trauma reset everything? What if it restored what you knew prior to the attack?"

Bonnie blinked a few times as she tried to comprehend what Bronwyn was telling her.

Freddie understood more quickly. "You think she knew these languages before she was attacked? That it's knowledge she is only now able to access?"

Bronwyn nodded.

Bonnie shook her head. "How would I know all of those languages, though? It's unusual enough to find someone who speaks more than the common tongue and one other language. For me to know —" she cut off, counting the number of languages that she discovered she knew, " — four languages on top of the common tongue? At only eight years old? Impossible."

"*At least* four new languages," Freddie amended. "You could know more that we don't know about yet."

"It would be unusual, yes," Bronwyn said, "but I would classify it as 'improbable' instead of 'impossible'. There could be a few different reasons someone so young would know so many languages."

"Like?"

"Your parents could be scholars of some sort," Freddie said.

"Or traveling merchants," Bronwyn added.

Freddie said, "Scribes typically know more than one language."

"Or maybe you just enjoyed learning new languages," Bronwyn said. "It'll remain a mystery unless you suddenly remember the first eight years of your life."

Bonnie snorted. "I doubt that will happen," she said.

It didn't matter that she wished with every fiber of her being that she could somehow learn more about her past. Who she was before she joined the Amlucen. Who her parents were, and what they did to incur the wrath of Aborn.

Bonnie turned to Freddie. "How are you feeling?"

"Alive," he said, using his hand to cover a yawn. "Tired. And I feel like I was beaten by something hard and unpleasant. But I'm alive." He laid on his stomach and propped his head on his hands as he faced the women. Then he blinked slowly a few times, obviously exhausted.

"You *were* beat all over," Bronwyn reminded him, her tone sharp. She stared at Bonnie with thinly veiled contempt.

Bonnie held up her hands. "*I* didn't beat him — I tried to save him!"

"You, young lady, are part of the problem."

Bonnie reared her head back. "Part of the problem?" She narrowed her eyes. "Do you mean the Amlucen?"

Bronwyn scoffed. "Yes. You rebels are the *worst*. Ruining things for others. Causing issues where you don't belong."

Bonnie's mouth dropped open. "Aborn is what's wrong. He's been using his power to slaughter and destroy anyone that's gotten in his way!"

"Who has he slaughtered? What has he destroyed?"

"He's conquered almost every country on the continent and destroyed everything in his path. He's slaughtered thousands of people to keep control. How can you argue that *we* are the problem? We just want our lives back!"

"Have you ever thought that maybe he had to take over for a good reason? That maybe he's more fit to rule than the others?"

"That's bullshit. He had no right to take over other countries. He had no right to slaughter innocents."

"Who are these 'innocents' you speak of? Have you seen them? Laid eyes on any dead bodies?"

"No, but —"

Bronwyn pointed a finger in Bonnie's face. "How do you know innocent people died if you have not seen them with your own eyes? How do you know King Aborn is the monster you claim he is?"

"Because he murdered my parents!" Bonnie said, shaking in anger. She pointed to the scar that Bronwyn had just stopped examining. "His King's Guard murdered my parents and left me for dead. That's how I know!"

Bronwyn said nothing, but Bonnie saw her eyes widen in surprise.

Bonnie tried to look to Freddie for support — it had been a long time since she'd been forced to have a conversation with someone outside of the rebellion.

But Freddie was asleep, snoring on the bed.

CHAPTER TWENTY-FOUR

"We'll talk about this later," Bonnie said as she stood. "I need to tend to the horses."

Bronwyn snorted, as if sensing her lie, but said nothing as Bonnie made her way through the cottage.

Bonnie felt some of her anger lessen as she passed Freddie's sleeping form.

He looked so peaceful now. So quiet. So remarkably different from the past few days. She paused for a moment beside the bed, pulling his blanket over him. She grabbed her own, discarded on the floor, before marching outside.

Squinting in the sunlight, she estimated it was almost midday. The autumn chill was brisk, and she wrapped the blanket around herself, grateful for its warmth.

She looked around the entire clearing for the first time since they arrived. Dozens of beautiful, sweet-smelling flowers surrounded the cottage, and there was a small pile of firewood tucked under the roof's eaves. A wooden perch stood a few feet from the door, and birds chirped at her in greeting as they pecked from a bowl of birdseed. The horses stood by the pond in the corner, grazing contentedly.

Bonnie sat once more on the tree stump by the pond. She bent over, staring at the green carpet below her bare feet, and put her head in her hands.

The conversation with Bronwyn had been disastrous. As skilled as the healer may be, it was clear there was a lot she didn't know about the world she lived in — the *true* world. Bonnie's world. The old woman had been living in this clearing for years. She knew nothing of the way Aborn ruled the continent.

How could Freddie stand to be around someone so obtuse? He wanted to join the rebellion, for fuck's sake. Did she realize that his family had lost their seat of power because of the king? That he was a lord, when he should rightly be the Prince of Navian?

How could the two of them coexist?

Freddie *had* been trained at court, she supposed, so he was used to masking his own thoughts and feelings to play the game of courtly intrigue. It didn't mean that he agreed with the old bat's viewpoints.

Even so, a few of Bronwyn's comments made Bonnie pause. She couldn't help but connect what Bronwyn was telling her with the lies Gwyneth told her at Stoneforge.

Bonnie shook her head, shoving the thought away. The entire rebellion wasn't built on lies. She had questions for Gwyneth and Oll, sure, but there was no way they could've deceived the rebels who looked to them as leaders.

Bronwyn must be wrong.

Not that Bonnie could ever go back to Oll and Gwyneth and ask them, she thought bitterly. She had hoped that she'd be able to one day, even after breaking Freddie out of his prison.

But now? She couldn't get the sound of Gwyneth yelling "TRAITOR!" out of her head.

No. Bonnie could never go back to the Amlucen.

The thought sent a pang through her chest. They were the

only family she had ever known. The only family she remembered, anyway.

Now she was alone.

A wild rabbit crossed into her periphery, making her smile. It hopped next to her, taking a moment to nuzzle her foot gently before hopping away.

The only good thing to come out of this, she supposed, was that she no longer had to pretend to like Oll. His own wife barely tolerated him. The day that sadistic fiend was cut down was a day the continent could rejoice.

Bonnie didn't even want to think about what could be happening to Felix right now. She hoped he had managed to bind his wounds before he bled out. Would Gwyneth and Oll take it easy on him, considering he was Oll's own flesh and blood?

Felix didn't know why Bonnie and Freddie had left; he had only promised to keep their departure a secret. As complicated as their relationship was, she didn't want him hurt. In fact, she wanted to find him — help him, like he had helped her in Stoneforge. Maybe figure out how they could be siblings who enjoyed each other's company once more.

She shook her head, clearing it. She didn't want to dwell on such matters right now.

Sitting up, she looked around the clearing with fresh eyes. What had Bronwyn said — that her clearing was half in Hallordis and half in Suverd? Bonnie stood and walked towards the edge of the forest where they had entered the night before.

There.

A tingling sensation washed over her as she stepped over the invisible border. On one side, the Hallordis side, she felt the loss; the grass didn't look as green, the sky not as blue. When she stepped back toward the cottage, the sensation of magic washed over her again.

What an odd feeling. How did the old witch end up here?

She returned to her seat. Time passed. A friendly garter snake slithered by on its journey to the pond. A bold squirrel chittered merrily from a few feet away as it tried to crack open a nut. She didn't realize how long she was there until a tall shadow covered hers.

"Everything alright?" Freddie asked, his voice quiet and deep. He sat on the plush grass next to her and waved his hand when she tried to offer her stump to him.

"I should ask *you* that," she said. "How are you?"

"I'm good. Great. Almost as good as new. It's amazing what some healing and a good night's sleep can do."

Bonnie couldn't help but agree. His skin was pink, and the bags under his eyes were gone. But that wasn't what she meant.

"No, really. How are you *doing*?"

His mouth turned down as he stared at the pond. A muscle ticked in his jaw, and he smoothed his hand over it. "I — I . . . I don't know."

She waited.

He blew out a breath. "It's easier if I don't think about it. What they did to me — I don't know if I'll ever . . . It's going to take some time for me to process everything, I guess."

"Do you want to talk about it?"

He shook his head. "No. Not now — maybe never. But not right now."

The cowardly part of her was relieved. "What can I do to help?"

"Just be you, Bonnie Blackthorn. Just be you."

She swallowed and stared down at her hands. She didn't know what that meant anymore.

THEY SAT IN COMFORTABLE SILENCE.

Birds chirped overhead, and the horses munched happily, swishing their tails to ward off persistent flies.

The sound of Bronwyn moving loudly through the cottage reached them. Pots and pans were banged together with excessive force, and the sound of loud, off-key singing filled the clearing.

Bonnie rolled her eyes, and Freddie let out a low laugh. She turned to him. "How did you meet the old bat?"

He hesitated. "She's a . . . family friend," he settled on after a pause.

Bonnie knew he wasn't telling her the entire story, but decided not to press. She'd find out eventually. "She sure is . . . something."

Freddie shot her a look. "What did you two talk about while I was asleep?"

"What makes you think we talked about anything?"

"I overheard Bronwyn muttering about 'delusional, irrational rebels' and about how she 'couldn't believe sensible Frederick has gotten wrapped up in such a farce'. Among other choice words."

Bonnie snorted. "We *may* have had a disagreement. I'm thankful for her healing skills, but that doesn't change the fact she's a cranky old witch."

Freddie swallowed, but said nothing.

"I guess it's been a while since I was forced to sit down and have a conversation with someone who is loyal to *him*."

"Bronwyn may be a lot of things, but she's certainly very loyal," he conceded.

Bonnie watched as a frog jumped from one lily pad to another. The impact made a small ripple that fanned through the water.

Loyalty. The last topic Bonnie wanted to talk about, considering the events of the last two days.

She sighed and turned to him. "We need to talk."

He stared at her solemnly. "Are you breaking up with me?"

Her mouth dropped open. "What?"

He grinned. "Joking. I agree." He blew out a breath. "About a lot of things, I think. But what do you want to talk about first?"

Bonnie thought about the velvet bag in her cloak pocket. "Gwyneth," she said.

He nodded. "Yes. We need to talk about her." His eyes went distant. "On the way here, when you were trying to make sure I stayed conscious, you mentioned something about a . . . a bag of some sort? That you stole from her? Did I hear you correctly?"

Bonnie nodded. "It's her personal bag — she brought it everywhere with her. No one knows what's in it. I'm pretty sure even Oll didn't even know."

"And you stole it?"

She nodded.

He nudged her with his shoulder. "Nice work, Blackthorn. What's in it?"

"I was too busy trying to save your imprisoned ass," she retorted. "I didn't have time to look."

"Should we look now?"

She nodded, and he stood.

"You said earlier — back in Thornwick, I mean — that you think you recognized her. That she may not be who she says she is. What did you mean by that?"

He swallowed hard, even as he extended a hand to help her up. "Could we look inside her bag first? I'd like to have solid evidence to back up my suspicions."

She snorted as she took his hand. It was callused, but warm, in her smaller one. "Lord of Libraries, indeed," she said as she stood.

He rolled his eyes and let her hand go.

Bonnie walked inside the cottage warily, unsure of her reception. Bronwyn's symphony of loud noises and horrible singing had ceased some time ago. Bonnie found her by the fire, feeding it another log.

The old woman glared in Bonnie's general direction. "About time you two came in," she said. "I've made supper." She sat down in her rocking chair with a *thud*.

Bonnie held back her retort when she saw the spread of food. On the table was a crock of hearty stew, crusty bread, hard cheese, and ripe autumn fruit. It was a meal that was too tempting to pass up, even if it meant that she had to deal with Bronwyn's ire.

"Thanks, Bron," Freddie said as he stooped to kiss her old, wrinkled forehead. Bronwyn brushed him away, although Bonnie saw a pleased sort of smile cross her face.

Bonnie sat at the table, Freddie taking the chair next to her. While Freddie dove in enthusiastically, Bonnie paused, studying the bread critically. She moved the spoon around her bowl, looking to see any foreign objects. She sniffed it.

"You don't seriously think it's poisoned, do you?" Freddie asked, his tone tinged with a hint of anger.

"The old crone hates me," Bonnie said with a shrug, and deemed the food safe. She ate a spoonful of the stew and gave a small moan as the flavors washed over her tongue.

Freddie's eyebrows raised, his cheeks flushing a soft shade of pink. Bonnie didn't notice, too busy devouring every morsel.

"This is fantastic," Bonnie told Bronwyn. "Thank you. The seasoning is wonderful."

"That'll be the poison," Bronwyn replied with a wink.

Freddie coughed as he choked on a piece of bread. Bonnie smirked at the old woman before she thumped him on the back. He waved her off, his eyes streaming. Bronwyn cackled.

Finished, Bonnie sat back with a satisfied sigh. She rested her hands on her soft stomach, feeling full for the first time in weeks.

Freddie finished moments later. "Shall we?" he asked. He

cleared the table of food, making space for what they were going to do next.

Bonnie retrieved the velvet bag, weighing it in her hands. It was heavier than it looked. Returning to her spot at the table, she placed the blue bag on the table softly, almost as if in reverence.

And then she stared at it, unable to move.

Freddie glanced from Bonnie to the bag and then back again. "Do you want me to open it?"

Bonnie shook her head. "No. This is something I need to do myself."

She didn't know why she hesitated; it wasn't like Gwyneth was about to stop Bonnie from exposing the secrets she held so dear.

But to take this last step — to violate Gwyneth's trust in this way — it seemed final. The ultimate betrayal.

Bonnie shook her head. Enough of that. The ultimate betrayal was when Gwyneth threw a knife at Bonnie's back.

It took a few moments for Bonnie to untie the heavy gold rope that sealed the bag shut. Instead of pilfering through it — she still had cuts from when she went through Oll's belongings in Stoneforge — she dumped the contents on the table.

Freddie sucked in a breath. His eyes were wide as he took in Gwyneth's carefully guarded secrets. Even Bronwyn left her rocking chair to come over.

Bonnie couldn't say what she had expected to be in there, and she wasn't sure how to feel when she finally saw its contents. Some things she had expected, others she had not.

There were several bundles of personal letters, tied into packets by lengths of black silk ribbon. A quick glance showed each packet was written in a different language, by different people.

A heavy silver key with four prongs of various lengths, the opposite end shaped like a crown. Bonnie ran a finger over the surface, expecting it to feel coarse and uneven, but was surprised at how smooth parts were. As if Gwyneth held it in her hands often, smoothing out the surface.

An assortment of jewelry, predominantly in blue, gold, and silver. A few pretty bracelets, several sets of earrings and necklaces. All looked to be of extremely fine make. One piece alone could easily fetch a hefty sum at a more reputable trader. But the entire collection? It'd be enough to fund the rebellion for years, if they were careful.

Two small vials, both half-filled — one with a clear, viscous substance, and the other with what looked like blood. Bonnie touched neither of these.

A bejeweled dagger with dried blood on the tip. Bonnie also refused to touch this, although she guessed it was the reason the bag was heavier than it looked.

There was a sprig of some sort of dried plant, wrapped in a piece of silk cloth and tied together with a red ribbon. Freddie grabbed her hand when she reached out to touch it. He stared at it with a frown.

"Poisonous," he said, before he let her hand go.

Bonnie shivered, doubly glad she had dumped the bag's contents directly on the table.

There were a few other odds and ends — coins of different origins, a few scraps of paper with strange symbols that Bonnie could not read, a plain gold locket that neither of them could open.

"This is . . . a lot," she said, after several minutes of silence. Freddie nodded in silent agreement, his eyes still traveling over the items.

Bonnie sat with a sigh, unsure of how she felt. It made her question everything she had known about her adopted mother. The fine jewelry alone gave rise to a lot of questions — where had she gotten them? Were they stolen, or given willingly?

Whose blood was on the dagger? And why did Gwyneth have a poisonous plant? What was in those vials?

She wasn't sure she would ever get the answers, though she knew that Freddie and Bronwyn probably had their own ideas. He was currently telling Bronwyn what was in the bag, and the old woman's head was cocked to the side as she listened. She drummed her fingers on the table in an up-tempo beat.

There was one place Bonnie knew she could start her search — one of the few items she could touch without fear of losing life or limb.

Gwyneth's letters.

Bonnie picked up one packet and untied the black silk ribbon with trembling fingers. The ribbon fluttered through the air and landed on the table.

Then she lifted the heavy parchment and began to read.

CHAPTER TWENTY-FIVE

IT DIDN'T TAKE HER AND FREDDIE LONG TO DECODE EACH OF THE messages that littered the table.

They were all written in the same cipher, one that Gwyneth and Felix had tried to teach her years ago in Crown Harbor. To no avail, of course, as her brain had refused to make sense of the letters on the pages, no matter how slow the two of them went over them.

It didn't make sense back then, but it did now. And luckily, she still remembered the codes that they had so painstakingly tried to teach her. Now she went, letter by letter, and decoded each of the messages one by one.

She looked at the decoded message.

> *My dearest G —*
> *Our time spent apart is almost too much to bear. I miss your beautiful face and cannot wait until you are out of the castle so we can be together once more. Be brave, my beloved.*
>
> *- Yours, O.B.*

Bonnie crinkled her nose in disgust, even as something nagged at her.

Freddie read her sloppy handwriting over her shoulder. "A love note? Really? I can't picture Oll Blackthorn writing a love note. A directive on torture, maybe . . . " A muscle ticked in his jaw and he shook his head.

Bonnie narrowed her eyes at the words on the page, above her own scribbled notes. "It's not his handwriting."

And she would know. Even though she hadn't been able to read it, she had seen letters written by him hundreds of times — delivered missives to rebel members dozens of times. She would recognize his handwriting, she was sure of it.

She turned to the next letter.

My dearest G —

I caught a glimpse of you tonight. You looked splendid in your gold gown, even if you had to play the part of the simple sister. Your talents are wasted in the company of such fools. One day the royals shall get what's coming.

Oll has secured what we need for your escape. Soon we shall be together. Be brave, my beloved.

- Yours, O.B.

"Hold on," Freddie said.

"Yes," Bonnie breathed, her suspicions confirmed. "O.B. isn't Oll Blackthorn."

"Who is it?" Bronwyn asked from her other side. "What does it say? What are you reading?"

"Love letters from *Oren* Blackthorn," Bonnie replied. "Oll's brother. Which makes sense — he was Gwyneth's first husband."

"Founder of the Amlucen, Oren Blackthorn?" Bronwyn asked.

"Yes. He's the one who convinced Gwyneth to join. Oren and Oll had started their efforts a few years before. He was killed by a member of the King's Guard on Vale Magicae."

"Or so Gwyneth says," Bronwyn muttered under her breath.

Bonnie ignored her and pointed to the letter. "What does this part mean? About the royals. Did Gwyneth know Aborn, or Queen Celeste? This makes it sound as if she's one of them."

Freddie's gaze was on the letter. "Let's reason this out. If Oren Blackthorn wrote this, we know it's more than twelve years old, since he died on Vale Magicae. It's probably older, if he's still in the stages of wooing Gwyneth."

"In the first letter he talked about her beautiful face," Bonnie added. "I know she got the scars in an attack that happened a year before Vale Magicae."

Freddie nodded. "So, assuming that the letter is at least thirteen years old, that means King Aborn would've been married to his first wife, Queen Annabeth. Not Queen Celeste."

Bonnie cursed the head wound that had wiped all her memories.

"She was poisoned, wasn't she? Queen Annabeth?"

Freddie nodded. "On Vale Magicae. She was alive when the king found her, but magic had disappeared at that point. She couldn't be saved."

Poison. What a horrible way to go. "That's why your father trained you in the art of detecting poison."

He nodded.

Bronwyn said nothing, but her face had lost some of its color. And she seemed tense. Probably because she was being left out of the conversation, although it could be because she didn't want to get into another argument. Bonnie ignored her.

She looked at the letter again. "Okay. So. Looking at this, we can assume that it was written at least thirteen years ago by Oren Blackthorn. To Gwyneth, who apparently was in the king's inner circle? Unless he meant some other royalty. Was she associated with the royal family in Naverd, Suverd, or Wolverd, maybe?"

"I don't think so," Freddie said. "Not in Naverd at least." He tapped his finger on the bag, discarded on the table. And then his fingers moved over to the fine jewelry that had been inside.

All of which were gold and blue.

"The king's colors," Bonnie breathed.

How had she not made this connection before?

"But Gwyneth *hates* Aborn," Bonnie said, her mind refusing to accept it.

Freddie eyed her carefully, and Bonnie got the sense he already knew how the pieces fit together. He wanted her to figure it out on her own. Insufferable bastard.

"Let's keep reading," he said, shuffling the letter to the bottom. They decoded a few more, which looked to be nothing more than standard love notes.

"Hold on —" Bonnie said, reading the last note to make sure that she deciphered it correctly.

> *My dearest G —*
> *The time is almost upon us. I know what you are about to face will be incredibly painful — please know we have the rebellion's best healers on standby to care for you. We have placed an operative in the castle hospital wing to ease your discomfort and aid in the deception.*
> *Any pain will be worth it, if it means you can step away from the monster you call sister. I love you, my queen, no matter how you may look. Be strong, my beloved.*
>
> *- Yours, O.B.*

"Why would she need a healer?" Bonnie mused. "What deception?"

More importantly, who was the monster that Gwyneth called sister?

Aborn didn't have any sisters; just his brother, King Thorstan.

Bonnie looked at Freddie, her eyes narrowing. "Did Queen Annabeth have any sisters?"

"One," Bronwyn replied. Her voice was soft. Freddie stared at Bonnie, eyes searching her face. "One sister. Her name was Gwendolyn. Gwendolyn Hatherall."

Gwendolyn. Gwyneth. So close, so similar, and yet different. Different enough?

Or close enough to be a coincidence?

"Gwendolyn Hatherall," Bonnie repeated. "What happened to her?"

"She died," Freddie said. "About a year before her sister. Assassins tortured and left her for dead. Presumably for any intel she had on the royal family. The palace healers couldn't save her."

Bonnie's eyes widened in shock as everything fell into place.

No. No. No.

It couldn't be true, could it?

Could her adopted mother, the leader of the Amlucen, be the sister of the dead Queen Annabeth? King Aborn's sister-in-law?

Freddie still looked at her carefully, no doubt watching the different emotions cross her face.

Shock. Disbelief. Denial. Acceptance.

Because even though this was shocking, it somehow all made sense.

The velvet bag, made up in the king's colors.

The jewelry inside, fine enough for royalty.

The fact that Gwyneth volunteered nothing about her past,

especially about her disfigurement. She had said she was tortured . . .

Bonnie turned to Freddie, oddly numb. She felt cold. "How long have you known?"

"Right before Thornwick," he said, his eyes sad. "Something seemed *off*, but I couldn't figure out what. Remember when she spoke to Oll in Suverian when I first met her? What she said to him didn't make sense."

That's right, Bonnie thought, as she recalled that meeting. She had forgotten that Oll and Gwyneth had switched languages — it happened so frequently that she was used to it. She had been relieved to see that Freddie hadn't been able to understand them either, but apparently he could. Cunning little liar.

"What did she say?"

"They talked about me. About my father. About the risk of letting me wander around the hideout, given who I was —"

"I wondered why Oll was fine with letting you right through the front door," Bonnie interrupted.

Freddie snorted. "He wasn't. He told her he wanted to 'study' me before killing me. That's why he left me with you — he thought you'd kill me if you needed to. Gwyneth wasn't so sure."

Aw. Bonnie would've been touched at Oll's faith in her if she didn't hate the man with every fiber of her being.

Freddie cleared his throat. "Gwyneth also said that I reminded her of my father. She feared I might remember her."

"Remember her?"

Freddie nodded. "I had met Gwyneth — as Gwendolyn — when I was a child. She had come to Navian on behalf of the royal family. Went on a tour through some of our wood processing facilities. I didn't like her then, and I like her even less now."

Bonnie nodded dumbly as she processed what he was saying. "Why not?"

"She was cold. Distant. Even more so than is typical for nobility. It's hard to describe."

That's why he stared at her whenever they were together — not because he was rude. But because he was trying to figure out how he knew her.

Because he had met her.

Known her.

Spoken with her.

Spent time with her.

Before the attack that ruined her face and concealed her true identity.

An attack that appeared to be orchestrated by Gwyneth and her lover, not unknown assassins.

Before she became Gwyneth Blackthorn, leader of the Amlucen, she had been Gwendolyn Hatherall, sister to the queen.

"That's why portraits of the king's family were forbidden in the hideouts," she mused. "Why the pages were ripped out of those books. She didn't want people to make the connection between her and the dead queen."

Freddie nodded. "That makes sense."

Bonnie sat in silence, staring at Gwyneth's — no, *Gwendolyn's* personal items. Bronwyn patted her shoulder before walking away.

"I'm sorry," Freddie said, a while later.

"For what?"

He shrugged. "As . . . tenuous . . . as things were between you, especially recently, she was still your mother figure. Still the woman who raised you. I can't imagine how this must feel."

Bonnie smiled sadly as she fidgeted with her fingers. "My entire world has turned upside down. I don't know *how* I should feel right now."

A steaming cup of peppermint tea was placed in front of her, set down by a wrinkly old hand. "If I were you," Bronwyn said, "I would start by feeling angry. And turn that anger into curiosity. Maybe the rest of those letters will tell us why she did the things she did, or lead to new information."

Bonnie thanked her. After taking a sip, she nodded.

Bronwyn was right. There was more to discover in these pages.

CHAPTER TWENTY-SIX

They divided the remaining letters between them.

Bonnie took the ones written in the common tongue, while Freddie took the ones written in Naverian and Suverian. A few were written in a more complex cipher that Bonnie hadn't been able to figure out, and Freddie took those as well.

Bronwyn scowled and made them promise they would relay everything to her. Bonnie felt an odd kinship with her in that moment — for years she would've been in the same position.

"These look to be early logistics on the movements of the rebellion," Freddie said after some time. "Letters from rebels in different locations. There's a few about discoveries made in different parts of the continent, but no one elaborates on what was found. Not sure why she'd keep these."

Bonnie agreed. Her letters appeared to be the same and, while interesting, didn't hold the same level of excitement that the first packet brought. "I can see why she would keep letters from Oren from an emotional standpoint. But why these? Maybe we're missing something."

"Oh gods," Freddie broke in, his eyes scanning the missive he was reading. "No way."

Bonnie and Bronwyn both turned to him. "What?" they asked in unison.

Instead of trying to speak, he handed two missives to Bonnie. She read it out loud so Bronwyn could hear.

> B—
> THE PLAN IS SET. YOUR WAY INTO THE CASTLE IS CLEAR FOR MIDSUMMER'S DAY. USE THE DEATHBLOOM, BUT TAKE THE KNIFE AS A PRECAUTION. GOOD LUCK

It was unsigned, and Bonnie didn't recognize the hand-writing.

"Next one, next one!" Freddie said.

Bonnie hurriedly switched to the second one. This one was written in handwriting that Bonnie knew immediately.

> B —
> GOOD WORK ON DISPATCHING A.A. AND O.B. YOU WERE RIGHT — THE KINGDOM IS IN CHAOS. THE FACT THAT MAGIC DISAPPEARED WORKED FOR US. ALTHOUGH UNPLANNED, WE SHOULD PRESS OUR ADVANTAGE.
> TIME FOR US TO TAKE BACK WHAT IS OURS. OUR PEOPLE NEED A UNITED FRONT.
>
> — O.B.

Bonnie sat back, her eyes wide.

> GOOD WORK ON DISPATCHING A.A.

"Does this mean what I think it means?" Bonnie asked, her voice shaking.

Freddie looked off into the distance, eyes wide. "If you think it means that Gwyneth Blackthorn, formerly Gwendolyn Hatherall, killed her sister, Queen Annabeth Aborn of Hallordis, then yes. That's what I think it means, too."

Oh, gods.

"Why did she kill her sister?" Bonnie whispered. "Why did she hate her so much?"

Freddie stared into the distance, his mind no doubt racing. "King Aborn and Queen Annabeth were an arranged marriage," he said. "Before he established Hallordis, King Aborn made a deal with one of the landowners of a small territory that the king could take over his land if he married one of his daughters. I remember my father saying that everyone expected him to marry Gwendolyn because she was the eldest. Everyone was shocked when he married Annabeth instead."

"They were in love," Bronwyn said softly. "The king and queen. Anyone who saw them knew that."

Freddie nodded. "They seemed very much in love from what I remember."

"Maybe Gwendolyn resented that," Bonnie mused. "If her younger sister hadn't caught the king's eye then she would've been queen. He spurned her. Maybe that's why she wants to remove him from the throne."

Bonnie reread the letter once more. "Wait — it says 'Good work on dispatching A.A. *and* O.B.' Freddie — this is in Oll's handwriting, I'm sure of it." Bonnie looked at him in horror. "Did Gwyneth kill Oren, Freddie? Did she kill her own husband?"

Freddie nodded, speechless.

Oren, whose letters she kept bound in silk. Oren, who professed his love for her in every letter. Oren, who found a way for her to leave the royal family, even if it meant she was disfigured forever.

In one year — the time Gwyneth left the royal family to the

time she murdered her sister and her husband — what had gone wrong?

She looked at Bronwyn. The old woman looked as shocked as Bonnie felt. The color had drained from her face, and she gripped the table with fingers that trembled.

Bonnie looked at the table, her gaze snagging on the sprig of poison that lay bundled in silk. She jerked her gaze toward that. "Is that deathbloom? The poison mentioned in the unsigned letter?"

Freddie nodded, his lip curling in distaste. "Nasty way to go."

"That's what was on the blade that was embedded in you," Bronwyn said. "You're lucky you're alive, boy."

Bonnie's gaze turned to the bejeweled dagger. She reached out and thumbed the hilt, her fingers moving over the bumps of each jewel. All the precious stones were blue and gold. "I wonder if the dried blood on the blade is Oren's," she mused. "I wonder if she kept this as some sort of fucked up memento."

Freddie and Bronwyn said nothing.

Bonnie struggled to come to grips with the fact that the woman who saved her from death's door — the one who nursed her back to health, who gave her love, and shelter, and a family — was the same person who murdered two family members in cold blood. Who murdered the *queen*.

"Why?" Bonnie whispered. "Why did she save me on the same day that she killed them?" She looked to Freddie and then to Bronwyn, who looked just as lost as she felt.

"Guilt, maybe?" Freddie guessed. "Or maybe she knew your parents before the attack and wanted to save you. There were a few families who were slaughtered that night — you might belong to one of them."

Bonnie turned to the old woman. "Bronwyn. What happened on Vale Magicae, exactly?"

"Everyone knows what happened that night," Bronwyn answered softly. "Surely you know."

"I can't trust anything that I've learned over the past twelve years," Bonnie said. "Everything I know is a lie. What happened that night?"

"Tell us what they told you," Freddie said instead. "It would be helpful to figure out where the stories connect and diverge."

Bonnie took a deep breath. "Oll and Gwyneth taught us that Aborn chose midsummer's day to make an example of the rebellion because it was a day of celebration, and the rebels didn't deserve to celebrate or rejoice. They taught us that the king felt threatened and wanted to make a statement that he was in complete control.

"He sent the King's Guard to different hideouts throughout Midverd with the goal of complete extermination. But blood-lust overtook the guards, and they killed anyone they encountered, rebel or not." Like her parents, Bonnie thought. Or so she had been told. "They claimed magic fled because whatever divine beings control magic needed to punish Aborn for his cruelty. That because the ground of Hallordis was soaked in the blood of innocents, everyone within its borders needed to be punished."

Bronwyn and Freddie said nothing, and Bonnie couldn't tell what they were thinking.

"The Amlucen were always good at spinning a tale," Bronwyn said with a sigh.

"What is your truth?" Bonnie asked.

"They weren't lying about the date, at least," Bronwyn said. "Back then, Hallordis — and all the territories and countries on the continent, mind you — celebrated midsummer. It wasn't uncommon for the celebration to extend well into the night. When the sun set, laughter turned into screaming. People were trampled in the streets trying to escape." Her voice trailed off.

The sound of screaming echoed through Bonnie's mind, as

if Bronwyn's words conjured the sound. She shook her head to clear it. "Escape what?" she asked.

"An attack. The Amlucen used the cover of the celebrations to try to overthrow the government. Armed rebels stormed the castle while others wreaked havoc in the streets as a distraction. Hundreds were dead by the time the King's Guard took back control. Your parents were probably among those killed that night." Bronwyn had the good sense not to say which side — rebel or innocent bystander — she thought Bonnie's parents were on.

If what she said was true, then Bonnie had to admit that it painted the Amlucen in a terrible light. If Bronwyn was right, it meant the rebels were not innocent victims, but the perpetrators of the bloodiest attack in Hallordis' history.

Was the truth somewhere in the middle? After opening Gwyneth's bag, she didn't know what to believe anymore.

"And the attack was when Gwyneth killed Queen Annabeth? It was a diversion?" Bonnie asked.

Bronwyn nodded and swallowed hard. "Queen Annabeth and her daughter were among the slaughtered."

That's right, Bonnie thought numbly. She had forgotten about the daughter.

"Do people think the Amlucen's attack is why magic disappeared? Or did it disappear before the fighting began?"

"Every magic wielder in the country knew the moment magic left Hallordis," Freddie broke in. "It was during the attack. One moment everything was normal, and the next it felt as if a limb had been severed."

Bonnie narrowed her eyes at him. "You speak as though you know this from experience."

He met her gaze, his honey-colored eyes holding hers steady. "Because I do. I was a healer."

CHAPTER TWENTY-SEVEN

Bonnie's mouth dropped open. "What?"

No. It wasn't possible.

Even when magic existed healers were rare. Coveted. There was no way he could've been a healer. Surely she would have heard that the second son of Duke Stonewood was a healer.

Wouldn't she?

Was this why he and Bronwyn were so close? Was she his mentor?

Her mind sorted through their conversations about magic, through all the times where they talked specifically about healing.

"But . . . you couldn't heal me after the attack in Golwich," she argued. If he was a healer he could've helped her. Instead, he left her with the arrow wound.

"We were within the borders of Hallordis," he said, his voice a little strained. "My magic is dampened within the borders of the country."

"We're not in Hallordis right now, correct? We're in Suverd?"

He nodded.

Bonnie rose from her chair, walking over to where she had left her cloak. She fished one of her knives from its pockets before she walked back to the table.

Freddie looked at her, eyes wide as Bonnie advanced with a knife. Bronwyn, hovering nearby, said nothing, but Bonnie could tell she was curious.

She stopped in front of Freddie.

"What are you doing?" he asked.

Instead of answering, Bonnie held out her free hand, palm up, and sliced. She winced and grit her teeth through the sting of pain. Blood started pooling in her palm. "Heal me."

Bronwyn sniffed the air and muttered something about not getting blood on her floors before she walked toward the kitchen area.

Freddie wrinkled his nose before he grabbed her wrist. His other hand went over hers, hovering for a moment before he connected their palms.

Both sets of eyes were locked on their joined hands, waiting for something to happen.

Nothing did.

At least not at first. And then the cut on Bonnie's palm began to tingle, the same way it had when Bronwyn healed her. A soft light grew from their joined hands, and she lifted her eyes to Freddie's in awe.

Every ounce of his concentration was focused on healing her. A few moments later, he let go of her with a sigh, sitting back in the wooden chair with a groan.

Bronwyn was at Bonnie's side a moment later, holding a dark rag. She cleaned off the blood that was still pooled in Bonnie's palm.

Bonnie stared at her hand in wonder. All that remained was a thin, white scar. "Incredible," she murmured to herself.

She looked toward Freddie, who watched her reaction. He looked tired. "Are you okay?"

He nodded, but ran his hand through his hair. "Healing is tiring, and I'm out of practice. I haven't been able to train with Bronwyn for a while, unfortunately. Next time don't cut so deep, please."

"Oops," Bonnie said, eyes returning to the scar. She marveled at the lack of pain. "So when you're within the borders of Hallordis you can't heal others?"

He nodded. "I can heal myself to a certain extent, though."

Wait, hold on. "You can heal yourself?"

Freddie nodded, refusing to say more. As if the arrogant prick was waiting for her to puzzle it out. This was quite an annoying habit he had developed, she decided.

Bonnie thought back to all the times he was injured — or times she had thought he was injured, only to have been proven wrong.

Had he healed himself, all those times?

After jumping out of the Amlucen hideout window in Navian Bonnie had sworn he had rolled his ankle — she remembered his grimace and how the color had drained from his face. But moments later he'd been fine. She had convinced herself she must've misread the signs.

There had been a bloodstain on his shirt after the fight with the vagrants in Golwich Forest, too. She thought the arrow had hit him — the dead man certainly had thought so, too, she remembered. But he had brushed off that claim, saying he had dodged the arrow. Had the arrow actually struck him and he healed himself before the wound proved fatal?

Then there were his injuries in Stoneforge. He had seemed so certain he had only been captive for a few days before she arrived. Bonnie had dismissed those claims, knowing that there was no way that his yellow and green bruises had healed after such a short amount of time . . .

Even the physician had accused him of healing remarkably fast.

How had she not realized?

"Why couldn't you heal yourself after Gwyneth knifed you?" she finally asked.

This time Bronwyn answered. "I told you before — the blade was poisoned. In his weakened state, after being tortured . . . he didn't have enough magical reserve left to fight. Make no mistake — anyone else would've been killed long before you crossed the border into my clearing."

Bonnie nodded, considering. While shocking, at least it cleared up some questions she had. And it certainly wasn't the most upsetting thing she had learned today, that's for sure.

"Okay," she said simply. She looked at Freddie, who was still watching her warily.

He raised an eyebrow. "'*Okay*'? Is that it?"

"How do you want me to react?"

"I don't know," he said slowly. "Differently, I suppose? With anger maybe, or disbelief?"

She wagged a finger at him. "Lord Frederick Stonewood, son of the king's advisor, how dare you keep this incredibly secret knowledge from me, Bonnie Blackthorn, adopted daughter of Oll and Gwyneth Blackthorn, the leaders of the Amlucen rebellion? Shame on you." Wag, wag, wag.

Even Bronwyn huffed a laugh. Freddie's shoulders sagged in relief.

"I understand why you kept it from me," she told him softly. "And to be honest, if I had a second to think it through, I might have figured it out on my own." She let out a sigh and laid her head on the table. "I'm just tired of secrets, is all," she said. "It's exhausting."

Freddie only fidgeted a little. Bronwyn muttered something under her breath and turned away.

Bonnie kept her forehead on the edge of the table, her eyes staring blankly at the wooden floor. The contact helped her stay grounded as her mind went around in circles.

Freddie was a healer.

Gwyneth Blackthorn was actually Gwendolyn Hatherall. Sister of the former queen. Sister-in-law to King Aborn. Murderer of her sister. A traitor to the kingdom of Hallordis. And a godsdamned liar.

How would the members of the Amlucen feel if they knew that one half of their leadership was related to the monarchy they were trying to dismantle? And not only that, but had a direct hand in killing their beloved founder, Oren Blackthorn?

More importantly — did anyone else in the rebellion know the truth, apart from Oll?

And then there was Bronwyn's explanation about what happened on Vale Magicae. Bonnie couldn't stop thinking about it. She had always known that Oll and Gwyneth's explanation didn't add up — it never sat right with her that Aborn would use a day full of joy and happiness to exact revenge on the relatively small rebellion. But she had always accepted it as truth.

What else had they lied about?

THE SMELL OF BLOOD, SO FAMILIAR AND YET SO JARRING, FILLED HER nose.

Felix was across the room, covered in it. He grabbed his arm, his face contorted with pain.

Bonnie ran forward, reaching out a hand to stop Gwyneth from stabbing him again. And again. And again.

But no matter how far she ran, she never got closer.

She watched as her brother bled to death.

Everything turned black.

Bonnie wasn't sure what time the fighting had started; it could have been minutes. Could have been hours.

The worst part was the screaming.

The horrible sounds blended in almost seamlessly with the revelry down in the city streets. It had taken a while for the beautiful music to stop, for even the musicians hadn't realized what was happening.

Now all Bonnie heard was screaming.

BONNIE WOKE WITH A GASP. SWEAT COVERED HER BROW, AND HER legs were twisted in the blankets. Her head hurt, and she rubbed her scar with a gentle finger.

A startled yelp to her right, where Freddie slept on his bed. He started thrashing, twisted up in his sheets.

Looks like she wasn't the only one having nightmares tonight.

Shaking off the vestiges of her dream, Bonnie climbed off her mattress and crouched by Freddie's head. He was pale, sweat beading his brow, and a vein throbbed on his neck as he fought whatever demons plagued his nightmares. Bonnie had an idea what — or who — he might be battling.

"Freddie, wake up," she said. And then again, louder.

No response. If anything, his movements seemed more panicked.

She gently prodded his shoulder. "Freddie, you're dream —"

Freddie sat up with a lurch, and both hands grabbed her by the throat.

"Aghhh!" she wheezed as his hands squeezed. His eyes were wild — he was still deep in the throes of sleep.

Panic surged, and she tried to pry his fingers from her neck. She couldn't.

Black started creeping on the edge of her vision. Instead of trying to pry his fingers off, she did the only thing she could think of.

She drove her thumbs into his eyes.

His fists squeezed as he yelped. She used all her strength, unsure if she could fight him off.

Just when she felt like she was about to pass out, his grip

loosened enough for her to pry his hands off. She lurched to the side, hands bracing the bed for support as she fought to get air.

"What's going on?" Bronwyn shouted from her bed.

Freddie lurched toward her, tears streaming down his face as he tried to grab her. They tumbled off the bed, landing on the floor with a crash. Bonnie scrambled away from him.

"Frederick! Bonnie!" Bronwyn screamed.

Bonnie had enough of this. She punched him, feeling the crunch of bone under her fist. Blood poured down his nose and into his mouth. He fell back, but before his body hit the floor, she got on top of him, ready to strike again.

One second he was struggling to kill her, the next second he lay prone. He blinked a few times, wincing as he touched his nose gingerly, fingers now sticky with blood.

Bonnie didn't lower her fist.

Freddie's eyes widened, focusing on hers for the first time. "Bonnie?"

After a moment, when he didn't seem inclined to strangle her, she relaxed. And then grew mortified when she realized she was straddling him. She scrambled off, sitting on the floor next to the bed, and massaged her throat.

Freddie sat up. "What happened?"

Bronwyn said from across the room, "Nobody tells me anything! What is going on?"

"Nightmare," Bonnie rasped. By the gods, even breathing hurt. The pain seemed to intensify now that she wasn't fighting for her life.

Freddie, his movements slow, climbed out of his bed and sat next to her. He looked horrified.

"Did I —" he motioned to his neck, squeezing it gently.

Bonnie nodded and then winced.

He held out a hand. "Can I heal you?"

She eyed him warily, but nodded. She had almost forgotten

that healing was something they could do here. Something Freddie could do at a moment's notice.

Bonnie braced herself as his fingers touched her throat. Gently, this time. His eyes were sad as he stared at the damage he'd done. She shivered when the strange tingling sensation washed over her, localized in her throat. It felt as though she had swallowed a bug or something. She closed her eyes at the flash of light, but by the time it faded, her throat felt back to normal.

She swallowed a few times and was relieved when there was no pain.

"Are you okay?" she asked him.

His eyes widened. "Am *I* okay? When I just —" he cut off, at a loss.

Bonnie shrugged. "I know it wasn't personal. You were having a nightmare."

He swallowed and looked away. And then winced, reaching up to touch his nose. It was slightly crooked now, giving him a villainous look.

"Sorry," Bonnie said, even though she really wasn't. He probably would've killed her if she hadn't broken it. "Are you strong enough to heal yourself?"

He nodded and shut his eyes in concentration. Bonnie watched, fascinated, as the bones shifted back to where they belonged. The bruises that had already started to form turned back into healthy, pink skin.

Bonnie wasn't sure if she ever would get used to magic.

"What happened?" Bronwyn barked.

"Freddie had a nightmare. Everything is fine — we're both fine."

Bronwyn huffed and rose to prepare breakfast.

Weak sunlight filtered through the cottage windows. Freddie stared down at his hands, eyes unseeing.

Bonnie nudged him with her shoulder. "Are you okay, though? Seriously."

He sighed and rubbed his forehead. "Yes. No. I don't know. The things they did to me —" he broke off. "I relive it in my dreams. I'm not sure I'll ever be okay."

She leaned into him, savoring his warmth. It took some time, but she felt when the tension in his shoulders lessened and he sagged against her.

They would get through this, she thought. But would they learn to heal together, or on their own?

CHAPTER TWENTY-EIGHT

THE NEXT FEW DAYS WERE RELATIVELY BORING.

Bronwyn insisted Freddie take time to rest, which Bonnie wholeheartedly agreed with. Although no longer on death's door, he needed time to build up his energy levels. She had caught him dozing off in quiet moments more than once. Luckily his nightmares were becoming less frequent.

Bonnie's nightmares lingered.

It was always the same one — Felix's stabbing, and then the sound of screaming. If Bronwyn or Freddie knew she woke up every night in a silent scream, they didn't say. And she didn't tell them. They didn't need to see her weak, and she preferred to suffer in silence.

So they rested.

Bonnie listened to Bronwyn teach Freddie about the art of healing, still in awe they were in a place where magic existed.

They spent time outside with Bronwyn in her garden, tended the horses, took inventory of their gear.

"You're a lot nicer to me now," Freddie said one afternoon as the two of them took a break from chopping firewood. They wanted to build up Bronwyn's stockpile so she had enough for the long winter.

"Don't let it go to your head."

"Too late. We're friends. Admit it."

Friends.

She didn't have many friends. Human ones, at least. Almost everyone in the Amlucen was afraid of her, or too afraid of her adopted parents to try and befriend her, even if it would be advantageous for them. Benji, the weapons master, tolerated her, but everyone was afraid of him, too. She had Felix, she supposed, but was a brother the same thing as a friend?

Animal friends were different. The animals that visited her didn't care if she was a killer, or what family she belonged to. Animals didn't fear her the same way humans did.

"Fine. We're . . . friends."

But even as she said it, the words felt wrong. What they had gone through together felt more meaningful than simple friendship. They were connected now, but she didn't know what to call it. But she didn't want him to know that.

He only smiled, and they continued chopping wood.

The three of them ate quiet dinners in the cottage, telling each other stories to pass the time. They didn't talk about what they'd discovered in the bag, or about Gwyneth, or about the king and the rebellion, or the raid on Crown Harbor. Or any topic that would cause Bronwyn and Bonnie to fight again.

Even Bronwyn, who was still not a fan of Bonnie, took part in their lively discussions with a smile that softened her wrinkled face. Bonnie learned that the old woman had two children she was no longer in contact with. She refused to talk about them, but Bonnie learned that her husband had died years before, leaving her alone in the world. She had adopted Freddie as a grandson of sorts.

"Why aren't you in contact with your family anymore?" Bonnie asked once, feeling particularly nosy.

"Don't mind your pretty little face one bit. I'm not talking about them," the old woman grumbled.

"You're blind. How do you know I'm pretty?" Bonnie teased.

"Frederick told me."

"*BRONWYN*," Freddie admonished from across the room, a blush rising to his cheeks.

Bonnie felt the tips of her ears turn pink, even as she stuck her tongue out at the two of them. Bronwyn cackled at Freddie's distress.

And the old woman refused to say any more on the topic. Bonnie didn't push.

It was nice, she thought. Being here with the two of them. Peaceful, even. She didn't want to ruin things.

She should've known the peace wouldn't last.

BONNIE WOKE THE NEXT MORNING FEELING REFRESHED. SHE HAD slept soundly for the first time in a long time.

Sitting up with a yawn, she realized she was the first one awake. The other two were sleeping, Freddie's soft breathing overshadowed by Bronwyn's obnoxious snores.

Bonnie grinned as she got up, wrapping a blanket around her as she quietly left the cottage.

Winter was coming fast; there was a layer of frost on the ground, and Bonnie could see her breath when she exhaled. The horses were huddled together by the big tree in the corner of the clearing, bundled in makeshift horse blankets.

Sitting on her tree stump, she reveled in the silence. It seemed as if even the birds and the beasts were asleep, so still was the clearing.

She knew her time spent resting was almost over. She could linger a day more, maybe two, before she had to get back to her real life.

The only question was — what did that mean?

Bonnie could never go back to her old life. Not after what happened between her and Gwyneth — *Gwendolyn*, she silently amended. She knew that the chance of a bounty on her head was high.

Even if things hadn't gone so disastrously wrong, Bonnie still wouldn't go back. Not after she learned Gwendolyn's secrets.

Where would she go now? She could assume a new identity and start over somewhere new. Now that she could communicate in different languages she could find work as a scribe or translator.

Abandoning her friends and family didn't sit right with her, though. She still believed in the Amlucen mission. Aborn needed to be punished, and a new system of government needed to be put in place. She couldn't let her life's work go to waste.

Bonnie couldn't go back to the Amlucen, but Crown Harbor was still her home. She loved the seaport city, with all of its charms and hidden dangers. She loved the people who lived there, too, rebels or not. Maybe she'd travel there first to figure out what happened to the hideout — see if there was anything she could salvage from the wreckage. See how far word had spread of her betrayal before she made any rash decisions about what to do with the rest of her life.

But would she be alone?

There was no reason for her to travel with Freddie anymore. And although she had yearned to be rid of him, a pang went through her at the thought of once again being on her own.

She shook her head, dismissing the feeling. It wasn't that she'd miss him, exactly. But she was going to be alone — perhaps forever, now. It wouldn't be the worst thing in the world if he joined her in Crown Harbor for a bit, would it?

Before he went back to his life as a lord of Hallordis.

How would he explain his absence these past few weeks? Especially if his father discovered he was an Amlucen supporter — would he be imprisoned for being a traitor to the realm? Lose his title, his power?

Maybe he wouldn't be in a rush to return to his old life, either.

Bonnie didn't know how long she'd been lost in her thoughts, but she didn't turn when she heard the cottage door close behind her, focusing instead on the little pond.

"Mornin'," Freddie yawned as he sat next to her, his blanket wrapped around him. He handed her a mug of peppermint tea.

"Good morning, milord," she teased as she accepted the offering.

"You like it out here, don't you?" he said after a few minutes of comfortable silence. He raised his mug to gesture around Bronwyn's clearing. "You're out here more often than you're inside."

"It's peaceful here. Quiet. I've made some animal friends, you see. It's nice to sit out here and see them."

Freddie snorted before he took a sip from his own steaming mug. "I noticed how much the animals are drawn to you."

Bonnie smiled into her cup.

Freddie blew out a breath. "As much as I'd like to, I don't think we can stay here forever." Bonnie couldn't help but feel a rush of hope that he had used the word *we*. "But where to next?"

"I was thinking Crown —" Bonnie began, but cut off when a shout rang through the air.

"Frederick! Come inside. I need help moving the cauldron."

They turned and saw Bronwyn standing in the doorway, her white, frizzy hair in a disheveled state. She waved Freddie urgently inside, and the cold air made her breath float up around her head like a fire breathing dragon. Freddie rolled his eyes good-naturedly and went inside.

The animals were waking up — Bonnie could hear the soft chittering of birds as they left their nests. She took another sip of her tea, content.

Two whinnies sounded, followed by hoofbeats. Bonnie turned, wondering what had spooked Captain and Belle. They ran her way, reaching her in seconds. They flanked each side, chests heaving as they stared at the forest border. She stood.

Birds shot into the sky. Bonnie's squirrel friend ran down his tree on the edge of the clearing, chittering angrily. His cheeks were still full of the nut he had been eating for breakfast.

Something was wrong.

Something was coming.

Bonnie slid into a fighting stance. She debated running to the cottage — not to hide, but to grab a weapon — but didn't want to turn her back on whatever was quickly approaching.

Through the chaos of the birdcalls, she could hear horses — two, if she wasn't mistaken. Riding hard and fast for the clearing.

She looked around for something to defend herself with. The days spent peacefully in the clearing had made her lazy about carrying weapons. How could she have been so foolish?

Tossing the tea onto the grass, she brought her mug down on the side of the tree stump. A loud crack filled the air as half the cup broke off, leaving her with the handle and jagged remains. Not perfect, but it would do.

Who could it be? A contingent of rebels hunting her down on Oll and Gwyneth's orders?

Seconds passed. More birds took flight. Bonnie bounced on her feet, waiting for the intruders to show themselves. Captain and Belle stood silently next to her.

The sound of hooves over the dirt terrain grew louder. Two people on horseback appeared through the gaps in the trees seconds before they entered the clearing.

Bonnie blinked. And then blinked again. She wasn't sure who she was expecting to enter her peaceful haven, but it sure wasn't these two.

Lord Jasper Stonewood and Simon, the golden-haired guard who had hunted them in Navian.

They found Freddie at last.

BOTH MEN STOPPED SHORT AT THE SIGHT OF BONNIE HOLDING her makeshift weapon.

In the back of her mind she knew she looked crazy standing there, flanked by two horses, hair unbrushed, a blanket wrapped around her with a piece of shattered pottery in her fist. She didn't care if it meant they kept their distance because of it.

"*You,*" Simon spat when he laid eyes on her.

Lord Jasper hadn't seen her that night in Navian, but Simon had. He hadn't been fooled by their romantic lover's façade.

How did they find them? She hadn't seen a hint of either since leaving Navian.

Bonnie stood there in her fighting stance, holding her makeshift weapon. She said nothing as she tried to calculate how to dispatch them before escaping with Freddie.

The cottage door crashed open, the sound of footsteps echoing through the now-silent clearing.

"Jasper, Simon," Freddie breathed from behind her.

Bonnie didn't dare take her eyes off the two men, although she wished she could see the look on Freddie's face. She imagined he looked as shocked as she felt.

Maybe she could communicate with him silently. Tell him to take Captain and run. Simon and Jasper's horses would be tired after making the journey here — Captain and Belle could outlast them, she was sure of it. And if it came to a fight, she could hold her own.

"Hello, brother," Jasper said from atop of his horse. The elder Stonewood son's face broke into a wide smile. "It's good to see you." He looked at Bonnie and his smile dimmed. "And you must be Bonnie Blackthorn. Charmed, I'm sure."

Simon glared at Bonnie. A muscle ticked in his jaw, and he rested one hand on the hilt of his sword.

Bonnie only bared her teeth.

"Hello, Jas," Freddie responded. "Thank you for coming so quickly."

Wait . . . what?

Bonnie whipped her head towards Freddie. He stood next to her, hands loose at his side, and smiled widely at the two intruders.

"Did you . . . did you send for them?"

"Oh, did he not tell you?" Jasper drawled. "Dear me, Freddie's been caught keeping secrets."

Freddie turned to her, his smile fading. A look of shame and regret crossed his face as he studied her. And then he nodded. "I can explain."

Bonnie heard the door to the cottage open. Bronwyn exited, a smirk on her face. "About time you got here," she barked as she ambled toward them. "Took you long enough."

Bonnie's eyes landed on the wooden perch next to the cottage door. The one that housed the birds.

Messenger birds.

In the excitement of the last few days, she had forgotten the first early-morning conversation she overheard between Bronwyn and Freddie — the one in which Bronwyn had asked Freddie if he had sent the bird.

This must've been what she meant, Bonnie realized.

"What are they doing here?" Bonnie asked.

Had he been lying to her the entire time?

"I can explain," Freddie repeated, keeping his voice low and gentle. As if she was some wild animal that needed to be coddled. "Can we go inside and speak, please?"

If anything, his tone had the opposite effect. She felt blood rush to her face as anger took over.

"What are they doing here?" she repeated, her voice stronger this time.

"Freddie boy, are you going to tell her, or do I need to?" Jasper said. He dismounted.

"Tell me what?" Bonnie said sharply. She didn't care which brother told her, as long as she got some godsdamned answers.

"Jasper, leave it —" Freddie started.

"Tell you about the king's successful raid on Crown Harbor, of course!" Jasper continued, straightening his travel-worn tunic. "We wouldn't have been able to do it without you, dear brother."

No. No. No. NO.

Time seemed to pause as Bonnie turned to face Freddie. Her heart broke at the look of utter devastation on his face.

He wasn't devastated at what he had done to the Amlucen — it didn't matter to him that years of rebellion work went up in flames, or that dozens of people were killed.

He was devastated that he had gotten caught.

Freddie's reluctance to talk to her about the raid now made much more sense — of *course* he didn't want to talk about it.

He was the reason it had happened.

"I *trusted* you," Bonnie's voice broke. She felt a stabbing pain in her chest.

He stepped toward her, hand outstretched. She took a step back, bumping into Belle, who still stood stoically by her side.

"I can explain," he repeated for a third time. He still held out a hand towards her, as if physical contact could somehow repair the damage that had been done.

Belle — sweet, gentle Belle — snapped her teeth and lunged. She would've broken skin if he hadn't pulled his hand away in time.

Bonnie shook her head wordlessly. Throwing down the broken mug, she stormed toward the cottage. No one, not even Bronwyn, said anything as she slammed the door shut behind her.

She grabbed her cloak and satchel off the hook next to the door, and spent the next minute running around, stuffing things inside the bag. She grabbed Gwyneth's bag, stuffing it in her cloak pocket.

The sound of angry voices floated in through one of the windows, but Bonnie ignored it. She raided Bronwyn's pantry, taking food that would travel well.

Bonnie didn't care if Freddie thought he had a good explanation for doing the things he did. She didn't even care to find out how he had helped facilitate the raid.

She just needed to get away from him, and fast. Or she would kill him.

The thought of ending his life *had* crossed her mind. But she was already being hunted by the Amlucen. She didn't need to be hunted by the king's men, too.

The sound of heavy footsteps sounded outside of the cottage and the door creaked open a moment later. Freddie entered, holding his hands up in a gesture of peace.

Bonnie almost snorted. The last thing she was feeling right now was peaceful. Especially towards him.

She scanned the room one last time before deciding there was nothing left that she wanted to take. As she stepped toward the door, Freddie used his body to block the exit.

"Hear me out," he said. "I can explain."

"Move," she said.

He flinched at her tone but held his ground. "Bonnie, please —"

"*Move*," she repeated, this time taking a knife out of her pocket. She held it in front of her as she took a step forward. "I don't think you want to test me right now. I will kill you so fast that magic won't save you."

Freddie's eyes focused on the tip of the knife as she moved closer. A look of despair crossed his face as he stepped aside.

She didn't look back as she exited the cottage.

He didn't follow.

Belle stood outside the door, as if she knew it was time to leave. Smart horse. Bonnie saddled her for the first time in what felt like ages. She debated slashing Captain's tack to prevent Freddie from following, but decided against it.

It wasn't Captain's fault that his rider was a lying, traitorous piece of filth.

Simon and Jasper had moved no closer, although Bronwyn now joined their little group. Simon's hand still rested on the hilt of his sword. The three of them were whispering, probably about her. Simon's eyes followed every move that Bonnie made.

Bonnie mounted, facing the three of them, unconcerned about Freddie. He could rot for all she cared. She made a vulgar gesture in their direction as she steered Belle towards the forest border. Simon's frown deepened, while a grin lit up Jasper's face as he returned the gesture with one of his own.

Nudging Belle's sides, they sprinted out of the clearing.

CHAPTER TWENTY-NINE

BONNIE'S SKIN TINGLED WHEN SHE AND BELLE CROSSED THE invisible border from Suverd into Hallordis. She shivered, but not from the morning cold. She felt emptier now.

Now that she was alone.

As dramatic as their exit was, Bonnie made sure not to push Belle too hard as they put miles between them and the cottage. The worst thing that could happen was an injured horse, too far away from civilization to get aid. So they rode slowly, sticking to the more well-worn paths within Golwich, stopping every so often for Belle to rest and graze and drink water.

It was during those down times, when Bonnie wasn't focused on the path ahead, or the direction they were traveling, or on Belle's health, that her mind wandered.

Freddie was a liar.

A liar who had the blood of all the slain rebels in Crown Harbor and Thornwick on his hands. He'd probably been lying from the moment they met.

She cursed herself for believing in him.

Believing in their friendship.

For deceiving herself. Because the entire time a part of her had known their friendship was based on lies.

She ran her fingers over the teeth marks that forever marred Belle's reins, courtesy of the first night spent in Bronwyn's cottage.

A flash of pain reverberated through her head and she rubbed her scar.

When would he have had time to sneak messages to his brother? Lord Jasper had said the raid on Crown Harbor wouldn't have been successful without the intel Freddie had given them . . . but when did he have time to relay messages? She was with him from the moment they had left his bedchamber in Navian.

Not every moment.

Bonnie slapped her forehead and groaned loudly enough that the nearby birds resting in their nests took flight.

The last morning in Crown Harbor she had woken up alone.

The bastard had left her room and went into the city before Bonnie had woken up. He'd arrived back to the Map Room with peppermint tea. Felix had trailed him to the small bakery by the wharf . . . what had it been called? The Crown's Cookery.

Felix said that Freddie hadn't met with anyone, or deviated from the normal route to the bakery. But it only would've taken him a moment to bump into someone, only a second to pass a note. Freddie didn't need to speak with anyone to help ruin the rebellion.

Gods above. How could she have been so stupid?

She cursed herself. For as long as she could remember, she had made it a point not to let her emotions rule her life. A necessity when living in the Amlucen, especially considering who her adoptive parents were. But all it took was kindness from a handsome stranger for her to turn her back on those who saved her life.

Even if those people turned out to be liars and murderers, too.

It took all of her willpower not to curl up against a towering pine and give up. Maybe there would be no shame in going to a new country and trying to live as a normal member of society.

But while the thought was tempting, Bonnie kept Belle steered towards Crown Harbor. They would head there until she decided otherwise. At least the city was big enough that she could easily hide.

It was quiet in the forest as they made their way to the seaside city.

That night, when she lit a small fire to keep warm, Bonnie never felt more alone.

A FEW DAYS LATER, ON THE CREST OF THE HILL OVERLOOKING Crown Harbor, Bonnie frowned. Even the sight of the glittering golden rooftops failed to bring a smile to her face.

She had taken pains to avoid the more commonly traveled paths through Golwich. Even now, as she spurred Belle towards the towering city gates, she chose a side entrance that was not heavily monitored.

Last night she took a knife to her long hair. The shorter style, which left her hair grazing her shoulders, was impractical. It was almost too short to pull away from her face, never mind style it in her usual braid. She made sure it was long enough to hide the scar on her temple, though. She didn't need anyone to take notice of it.

It had been a while since she had braided her hair across her crown, she realized. She had fallen out of the habit while in the clearing. Bonnie hadn't felt the need to hide it from Freddie, who had already seen it. Or Bronwyn, who couldn't see anything. She thrust the thought of them from her mind.

She didn't want to risk anything happening to Gwyneth's bag, so she hid it in the hollow of a tree and camouflaged it with a layer of leaves and sticks.

The guards let her through the city gates with hardly a glance, assuming that a young woman posed no threat to the safety of the kingdom.

Fools.

If only they knew who they were letting into their city.

Head down, she made her way through the streets, busy with people in the brisk chill of the morning. She dodged carts being pulled by horses and donkeys, navigated around sleepy sailors making their way to the port, and stuck to the outer edges of the streets.

After stabling Belle in one of the better liveries and paying for lodging for a month — she wouldn't risk anything happening to the beautiful mare, cost be damned — she started her recon. If anyone were to take notice of her, all they would see was someone wandering listlessly around the city. Someone lost, perhaps, or a newcomer who wanted to get a feel for Crown Harbor.

A few blocks from headquarters she slipped into an alley filled with rubbish and broken things. Derelict brick buildings surrounded her as she creeped through the debris, careful not to step into any disgusting puddles.

She ducked behind a towering pile of broken wooden crates and made sure she was hidden from sight. She crouched there, unmoving, and after several minutes she knew she hadn't been followed.

Bonnie used her foot to clear away the stack of wooden slats that had taken up permanent residence next to the crumbling brick wall. Gritting her teeth — the slats had been there for a long time and they were stuck — she eventually moved them enough to reveal a metal grate underneath.

Perfect.

Lifting with both hands, Bonnie moved it to the side, placing it gingerly on the ground. She peered down, swallowing her nerves as she looked into the hole.

Bonnie took a deep breath, steeling herself for what was next. Sitting down, she swung her legs into the opening before lowering herself into the darkness.

THE INSIDE OF THE CROWN HARBOR REBEL HEADQUARTERS WAS pure chaos.

That's what it seemed like from Bonnie's limited vantage point, at least.

Looking through a peephole, she couldn't help but admire the organization that thread itself into the madness. Dozens of the king's men navigated the twisting corridors, carrying boxes filled with who-knows-what, calling out orders, and speaking over each other. The confidence in which they systematically dismantled Bonnie's childhood home showed her that this wasn't the first time they had performed such a task.

It made her sick.

She crept over to the next peephole, stepping cautiously even though she knew no one could hear her over the noise. She'd taken a gamble that they wouldn't have found the hidden passageways that lined almost the entire hideout, and was happy to be proven right.

Bonnie had spent most of her childhood exploring in here, taking time each night to update Oll and Gwyneth on any interesting gossip she had overheard in her adventures.

The time Cecily admitted to her best friend that she cheated on her husband? Reported to her parents.

The time Reed was doubting his commitment to the cause? Reported to her parents.

The time Silas accidentally killed a soldier in a drunken fight and then hid the evidence? Reported to her parents.

She felt no guilt about relaying her observations — it wasn't *her* fault that people were so loose lipped. Oll and Gwyneth had always made time to listen to her reports, even the silly ones. But now that she thought about it, some of the rebels she spied on rose through the ranks, while others were never seen again.

Bonnie had never thought about what might have happened to the rebels she'd never seen again; she stopped thinking about them as soon as she relayed the information.

Now she fought feelings of guilt. But how could she have known what they would do with the information she gave? She just wanted to earn her keep. She just wanted to be a part of their family.

Bonnie chose a new peephole. The hallway near the main entryway was the same organized chaos. The king's men had figured out how to enter the rest of the hideout through the secret entrance — although, by the look of the splintered, battered bookcase, they had used force to gain entry instead of figuring out which book operated as the key. Brutes.

The main entrance door closed shut behind another group of soldiers. As they hustled through the space, she noticed two burly guards remained, whispering to each other.

Perfect.

Bonnie crept down the narrow passageway, shoulders brushing both walls. She doubted anyone would notice that each room was smaller than it should've been. She knew she couldn't rely on them being ignorant about the design of the hideout forever, though, so she wanted to learn as much as she could as quickly as possible.

The peephole closest to the door was at eye level. Despite

the noise in the hallway, she could hear the whispered conversation as easily as if she was standing right next to them.

The guard closest to her was tall with broad shoulders, his dark brown hair cropped close to his head. His voice was deep, with a rasp underlying his words. "Think we'll be out of this hellhole soon?"

The other guard, equally broad but a few inches shorter, shook his head. "Doubt it. Based on what I've heard, the king wants to keep this as a permanent base."

Bonnie's heart sank. Although she knew the Amlucen could never use this base again, it felt wrong for the king to use the same space.

"Godsdamned rebels," the taller guard muttered, before coughing loudly. When he didn't stop, the sound echoing as he fought to breathe, the other guard thumped him on the back.

"Smoke too much?"

Tears streaming down his face, the taller guard shook his head and took a sip from a canteen. "Still dealing with the smoke damage from the fire in that room."

"Still? That happened weeks ago. Did you ever figure out what they burned?"

"No — I only saw that the walls were covered in paper. The place went up faster than if I poured oil on it myself."

"Strange, these rebels," the shorter guard commented. "I wonder what they were trying to hide."

Oh, no. The Map Room.

Although losing such a valuable resource was devastating, the threat of the king's cronies finding all that information would have been much worse. Still, Bonnie swallowed a lump in her throat. That had been her favorite room.

Freddie had been with her the last time she stepped foot in there. She grit her teeth as a rush of anger coursed through her. Everything that was happening here, while she hid in the walls like a rat, was his fault.

. . .

BONNIE SPENT HOURS SPYING THROUGHOUT THE HIDEOUT BUT overheard nothing of note. She retraced her steps, leaving the same way she entered — through Oll and Gwyneth's own personal bolthole.

After making her way across the city, she ducked into a bustling tavern and chose a table in the back corner. Taking the only seat, she positioned herself so that she could view the rest of the establishment with ease. Waving the barmaid over, she ordered herself a hot meal, her mind spinning.

The damage from the fire had been limited to the Map Room and a few of the surrounding rooms, including Oll's office. Besides that, the damage to the hideout was minimal. There were no signs of a struggle — no sword marks to any of the interior walls, or telltale splashes of blood, which confused her. It didn't make sense that the rebels would give up their home without a fight.

Where were they? It was like they disappeared without a trace.

As she watched the other patrons laughing and joking with each other, Bonnie wished she had someone to talk to.

She used to have Freddie.

Her mother.

Even Felix, in the rare moments they weren't at each other's throats.

Now she had no one.

BONNIE SPENT THE NEXT WEEK LIVING INSIDE THE WALLS OF THE headquarters. During the day, at least.

Every night she rented a room in a different inn to avoid being seen in the same area repeatedly. She never traveled to her destination the same way twice, using different routes to avoid being followed. Her future in the Amlucen might be uncertain, but her training with the Rebel Guard and spymasters held firm. Sloppiness could get you killed.

One thing that she *couldn't* change was her entryway into the hideout.

Bonnie dropped into the hole in the alleyway each day before the sun was up. She followed the dirt tunnel in a crouch until she reached a ladder that led to the bolthole door. Listening carefully, ear pressed to the door, she waited until she was sure no one was in the bedchamber before sneaking in.

The bolthole door, its outline disguised by colorfully distracting wallpaper, was located directly to the right of a plush armchair Bonnie had spent many youthful evenings lounging on. Even though the rest of the room was in complete disarray — clothes strewn about, bedding destroyed, books ripped open — the chair remained unmoved from its location.

She wasn't sure if the King's Guard had found anything of note in their bedchamber; she didn't know exactly what Oll and Gwyneth kept in there. But she was grateful that the soldiers hadn't looked around the room too hard.

Because a few feet away, disguised by the same distracting wallpaper, was a hidden door that led into hideout passageways.

Bonnie had asked Oll once, when she was very young, why there was a bolthole *and* an entrance to the secret passage in the same spot — couldn't a rebel use the passageway to spy on him and Gwyneth in their bedchamber?

His response? No one within the Amlucen would dare spy on the two of them. He was *that* convinced of his complete control over the rebels.

Even at a young age Bonnie thought he was a fool. At least now she could take advantage of that foolishness.

She spent her first day studying the guard rotations to figure out their social hierarchy. The soldiers, just like rebels, had their share of leaders, followers, and those who *thought* they were leaders but who actually did more harm than good. Once she figured out the weak links, she could figure out a plan to aid the Amlucen.

Whatever that meant. She tried not to think about where she fit into the rebellion now.

Then she tried to salvage whatever she could from the greedy hands of the soldiers. Quick on her feet, she snuck in and out of the passageways whenever she saw an opportunity, hiding boxes of intel or books or whatever she could carry in the passageways with her.

The missing valuables sparked arguments amongst the guards, to her delight. Fights broke out when things went missing. She laid off the thievery when the guards became more vigilant, opting to collect spoken intel instead.

Tonight she had spent a few hours listening to two of the chattier guards, who seemed to spend more time running their mouths than sorting through the bedroom they were in.

These guards spoke so loudly she didn't need to press her ear against the wall to hear them gossip in their native Naverian. She shoved aside unwanted thoughts of Freddie as she listened to their conversation.

"Did you hear the news that just came in? Things are happening in Midverd."

"What do you mean? This better not be one of your stories."

"It's not, I swear! Ambrose was telling me about it earlier. You'll never guess who requested a meeting with King Aborn."

A loud sigh. "Don't make me work for it, Snell. Just tell me."

"Oll Blackthorn."

Behind the wall, Bonnie sat up in a lurch. Rising quietly, she put her eye to the peephole. The guards were standing where she had last seen them, lounging against the wall.

The taller guard, a handsome black man with a shaved head, whistled. "No shit."

Snell, a shorter, hook-nosed man, smirked. "C'mon, Clarke. Would I lie to you? Ambrose didn't know much more than that, though. Although he did say that this wasn't the first time they've met."

Bonnie felt as though her heart was going to burst out of her chest.

"And how did Ambrose know about it in the first place? That man is almost as useless as you are."

"Har har. He was in the detail that brought in the latest group of rebels. One of them must be important because by the time they made it to Midverd, Blackthorn had already requested to meet with the king."

"Wonder why, though? Surely no one is important enough for Blackthorn to put himself in such a situation. The man is a mass-murdering lunatic."

Snell laughed. "Truer words have never been spoken."

Bonnie sat against the wall as the conversation turned to gossip about their personal lives.

In her twelve years as a rebel, Bonnie had never once heard of Oll trying to meet with the king. And — according to this guard — this wasn't the first meeting between the two.

Something wasn't right. If the guards spoke true, why was Oll trying to meet with the king he so openly despised?

Bonnie listened for a few more minutes but for once the two soldiers were quiet as they did their jobs. She didn't think she had any capacity for more surprises tonight, anyway.

She made her way toward Oll and Gwyneth's bedchamber a few rooms over. Her stomach grumbled, and she looked forward to whatever the tavern had on special tonight.

Bonnie paused at the door, listening for sounds on the other side. Hearing nothing, she opened it, and aimed for the bolthole next to the armchair.

Something grabbed her shoulder.

Stumbling, she fell forward. She was saved from crashing to the floor when the force tightened, heaving her upwards.

Bonnie turned her head to the side, eyes widening when she realized that there was a large hand grasping her shoulder.

It was Clarke. He stared at her, mouth open.

Bonnie dropped to the floor so quickly that he let go, unprepared for the sudden deadweight.

She scrambled forward and sprinted as fast as she could toward the open doorway. She didn't look back as she crossed the threshold, but heard the soldier curse as he tripped over something.

She grabbed the door frame as she crossed, swinging herself around to keep her momentum going. Mentally calculating the best possible exit, she cursed herself for not taking more time to check that the room was clear before leaving the passageway.

Stupid rookie mistake. One that meant that her time in headquarters had come to an abrupt end.

Bonnie made it to the end of the corridor and was about to round the corner when she hit the wall with an *oomph*.

She fell to the floor, all the breath knocked out of her. Confusion washed over her as she lay there, stunned — she knew the layout of the headquarters better than anyone. Walls did not appear out of nowhere.

Bonnie looked up and felt her heart stutter.

Snell glared at her, his thin lip curled.

Damn it, Blackthorn, she cursed.

She'd forgotten about the second guard.

CHAPTER THIRTY

BONNIE HISSED AS HER TOE CONNECTED WITH THE WALL.

Add a bruised toe to her list of ailments — it would make a delightful addition to her bloody knuckles and newly swollen eye.

And her nose. Bonnie was pretty sure it wasn't broken, but the fact she couldn't breathe out of it didn't make the pain any less. She couldn't blame Snell for punching her in the face, though. She broke his nose first.

Before she could move he had overcome his shock, but hadn't been able to stop her from lashing out. Clarke had caught up by then, though, and it had been game over.

She had been roughly searched for weapons before being thrown into an empty room. One without windows and, to her chagrin, without boltholes or passageway entrances to aid in her escape.

That had been hours ago.

She resisted the urge to scream. She knew it wouldn't get her anywhere, even if it would feel good to direct her anger at someone other than herself.

Instead, Bonnie sat against the wall in the corner, as far

away from the door as she could. If someone were to enter, this position would give her time to figure out what to do.

Someone would enter at some point, she was sure. Surely they wouldn't let her rot in here . . . right?

Before sitting down, she took time to inspect every inch of the room for anything she might use. This room, if she remembered correctly, belonged to an older bachelor who was often away on reconnaissance missions across Hallordis.

Whoever he was, she silently sent up a word of thanks when she found several sewing needles and pieces of string that had been overlooked. It wasn't much, but it was something. She stored them in the lining of her breast band, hoping no one would think to search her again. The only other thing in the room was an unused chamber pot, which she supposed she should be thankful for.

She drummed her fingers on the worn wooden floor. Why had nobody come to speak with her yet?

They were likely exploring the passageways now that she alerted them to their presence. They could be watching her right now, through the peephole she knew was located halfway up the wall she was leaning against. Another reason she positioned herself in this corner — they would have a hard time seeing her unless they looked directly down.

Thud, thud, thud.

Bonnie straightened at the sound of footsteps outside of her doorway.

Two sets.

She stood, crouching low enough that she could launch herself at whoever entered. She held two sewing needles in her fist, just in case.

The door opened only for a few moments, just long enough for a tray of food to be shoved inside. She heard the same *thud, thud, thud* of footsteps marching away. The sound disappeared.

Bonnie studied the tray. It looked like crusty bread, a few

pieces of meat, and hard cheese was to be her dinner. And a small canteen, which, after a quick sniff, proved to be water.

Interesting. She didn't think the King's Guard would be courteous enough to feed her. Torture her, yes. But not feed her.

She eyed the food critically, unsure if she should eat it. It was likely unaltered, considering they hadn't interrogated her yet. Why kill her before getting any information? But that didn't mean the food was safe. She herself had used poison to incapacitate others without killing them.

Bonnie suddenly wished Freddie was here. He was trained in the art of poison; he would know if the food was clean.

She shut that line of thought down quickly. She wouldn't be here right now if it weren't for him.

Hours passed. Eventually hunger won out, and she nibbled on small sections of each food. When nothing adverse happened, she ate the entirety of her meal as quickly as she could. Bonnie had heard of prisoners going on hunger strikes in an effort to persuade their captors to free them — had over-heard Gwyneth and Oll discussing the merits of doing such a thing if they were ever captured. Bonnie never saw the sense in it; she'd rather be at full strength when the time for interroga-tions came.

More time passed, and Bonnie grew bored. She must have dozed off; she startled awake at the sound of the heavy wooden door closing with a *BANG*.

She jumped to her feet, fists out, ready to attack.

The two guards from earlier stood there.

The taller one, Clarke, had a somewhat bored look on his face as he looked at her. Almost as if he didn't want her to know how interesting she was to him.

The other guard, Snell — his nose inflamed and still crusted with dried blood — glared at Bonnie with undisguised hostility.

Bonnie rocked back on her heels in preparation, wondering which one would make the first move. She had been in uneven fights before; she could handle them with ease.

Clarke cleared his throat. "We don't want to fight," he said, his accent thick.

He was speaking in Naverian. Bonnie kept her face blank, unwilling to show that she understood him.

He repeated the phrase again in Suverian, and then in Wolverian. After she didn't respond to either of those, he finally switched to the common tongue.

Bonnie scoffed. "You grabbed me first, *guard*, and then threw me in this room. Excuse me if I don't believe your peaceful intentions."

Let them think she was some lowly, hatred-filled rebel. She wanted them to underestimate her.

They exchanged a look. "Stoobid rebel," Snell said in Naverian, spitting a wad of bloody phlegm on the ground. "I bed she's useless."

"How do you figure?" Clarke replied, as he eyed Bonnie.

"Dey wouldn't dell someone so hodheaded and stoobid anyding."

"We still need to question her," Clarke said. He took a step toward Bonnie, who was now backed against the wall.

Clarke paused and held up his hands. "We need to talk to you," he said. "We have questions."

"I don't know anything."

Snell snorted and then winced in pain. He touched his nose.

Clarke looked to the ceiling as if asking for patience. "Let's start with a basic question. Who are you?"

Bonnie stared at him with contempt.

The guard tried again. "How long have you been in the walls, watching us?"

No answer.

"How did you get in the hideout?"

No answer.

Snell had enough. Fumbling at his waist, he grabbed his knife and advanced toward her. She held her ground, but prepared to dodge out of the way.

"Stop it Snell," Clarke snapped. He grabbed the back of Snell's jacket before he reached Bonnie, and then pulled him to the other side of the room.

Bonnie spat at him. Intimidation would not work on her. It made her nose throb, but the look on Snell's face was worth every bit of pain.

After a hushed discussion — which Bonnie couldn't over-hear, despite her blatant attempt to eavesdrop — Snell nodded, a sour look on his face. With one last glare he left the room.

Which left Bonnie with taller, uninjured Clarke.

Though he seemed less inclined to violence, she couldn't let her guard down. If anything, being alone with him was worse. Snell's anger was justified; her torn knuckles were testament to that. But what was Clarke's angle? Why was he being so civilized? As part of the rebellion for as long as she could remember — literally, in her case — she didn't believe in his charity one bit. She was far too jaded for that.

"I'm not going to hurt you," he said, as soon as the door closed. "The King's Guard isn't in the business of hurting defenseless civilians."

Bonnie raised her eyebrows at the boldness of his lie.

He narrowed his dark eyes in response. "Yes, I meant what I said. We don't hurt the defenseless. Even if they're rebel scum."

Bonnie snorted. Her nose throbbed.

"Believe what you want, rebel. Now, I need you to answer some questions."

"Say I answer your questions," Bonnie said, forcing herself to relax. She leaned against the wall, arms across her chest, the very picture of nonchalance. "What then? You'll just let me go?"

The guard shrugged. "That could be a possibility. It's not up to me."

"Who's it up to?"

"Others," he said shortly, and Bonnie knew he wouldn't say more.

She wouldn't say anything either, if the roles were reversed. She also wouldn't have promised that no harm would come her way, though. Bonnie had been on the other side of interrogations. She knew how these things worked.

"Fine. Just so you know — I don't know anything. So ask all the questions you like. Just prepare to be disappointed."

Clarke blew air out and muttered what sounded to be like a plea in Naverian. "What is your role within the Amlucen?"

"Role?" she repeated, pondering her answer. "Foot soldier. We didn't have roles."

"How long have you been in the hideout?"

"What do you mean? This place is my home. I've lived here for years."

"Not what I meant. How long were you in the walls, spying on us?"

"A day or so. Not very long."

He didn't look as though he believed her, and for the first time she regretted stealing the contraband they had seized. Clarke seemed like a smart enough man; surely he realized she was the reason the boxes and valuables went missing.

She kept her face impassive, though, hoping he didn't see through her lie too easily.

"What do you know about Oll Blackthorn?"

Bonnie jerked, startled at the change of topic. "Oll Blackthorn? What do you want to know about him?"

He eyed her warily. "What do you know about him?"

"He leads us. Gives us work, puts a roof over our heads. That sort of stuff."

"How well do you know him?"

"Someone like me doesn't have a lot to do with Oll Blackthorn."

"Surely you've overheard plans. You must know where he wants to lead the rebellion."

"Even if I knew what his plans were," she said hotly, "why would I share them with you? I'm loyal to the Amlucen."

"I could free you," he told her, his gaze even and unwavering. "It depends on what you tell me, though. I won't be able to help you if you lie to me."

Bonnie stared at him, unnerved. He spoke as though he was telling the truth.

He kept pressing. "What do you know of Oll's wife?"

She cocked her head to the side. "Oll's wife? What about her?"

"What do you know about her?"

"What do *you* know about her?" she asked.

He declined to respond. "Why does Oll Blackthorn want to meet with the king?"

Well *there* was a question that she wanted answered herself. She played dumb, though, and shook her head. "He wouldn't want to meet with the king. Why would he?"

He said nothing, only rocked back on his heels.

A loud knock on the wooden door behind him, and Bonnie jumped. The door opened a fraction.

"We're not done here," Clarke said, before leaving the room.

Unable to help herself, Bonnie sprinted across the room, hoping to reach it before it closed. Her fingers clawed the edge of the door as it shut with a *click*. She hit her hand against it before retreating against the far wall. She sat with a *thud*.

Why was he so interested in learning more about Oll? Maybe it had something to do with the fact that he had requested an audience with the king. Bonnie just wished she wasn't as clueless as she had pretended to be.

And then there were his questions about Gwyneth.

The Amlucen had taken pains to keep Gwyneth's role in the organization a secret — and even though her self-imposed disfigurement meant that no one would recognize her, people who had known her in her former life could still identify her. Freddie had figured it out — surely others who had known her would, too.

She suddenly wondered if the reason Gwyneth frequently journeyed into Suverd was to hide from those who could recognize her. Why else would she visit the southern country on an almost monthly basis?

Bonnie hoped Clarke had bought her act as a lowly foot soldier. And also wondered how much further she could push her luck. He hadn't seemed inclined to violence, but that didn't mean the next guard would have the same scruples.

And gods help her if Snell was the one who came in here next.

Bonnie waited for Clarke to return, ready to answer some questions. She calculated what she could share with him. Innocent Amlucen lives were at stake, even if her own role in the organization was uncertain. She didn't want to say too much.

She had to share something, though. She didn't want to be locked in this room forever.

HOURS PASSED, MAYBE DAYS.

Food was shoved in at random intervals, and she soon lost track of time.

She tried calling out to those who delivered the food but no one ever responded.

Clarke didn't show up again. Snell didn't either, a small mercy. But Bonnie would've welcomed the sight of the angry, injured guard over the deep silence.

So she rotated her time between pacing the room, shouting for aid, and sitting in the corner. Push-ups and sit-ups helped keep her mind off of things for a while, and she did those until her arms trembled and sweat dripped down her face.

Still, nothing.

She took a couple of brief naps, too short to feel restorative. She was too anxious to let her guard down, anyway — the last thing she wanted was to wake up and find unwanted visitors in the room.

A wanted visitor *did* visit her, though, for which she was grateful. A little mouse, light brown in color, entered through a small hole in the wall. When she first felt its wet little nose against her hand, she feared retaliation from her captors — would they kill it for keeping her company? She eventually relaxed when no one came in to exterminate her little friend.

She smiled for the first time in days as she pet its silky hair. Gwyneth had hated when animal friends found her, and threatened to kill any non-human creature she came across.

Her threats didn't work. It just made Bonnie work harder to keep them safe. Her own little rebellion within the rebellion, she supposed.

But even her new little friend wasn't enough to distract her from the situation.

Just when Bonnie felt as if she was going to go mad, the door opened.

She didn't bother moving from her spot on the floor — all her other attempts at escape had been futile. She looked at the door when she realized that no tray of food had appeared.

Her mouth dropped open.

Freddie and Simon stood there, staring at her.

CHAPTER THIRTY-ONE

Bonnie shook her head, sure she was imagining things.

Isolation did that to people, right? She was hallucinating.

They looked so *real*, though.

Simon's mouth was set in the frown she had come to associate with him. His golden hair was wet, as was the rest of his standard issue guard uniform.

Bonnie only spared him a quick glance, though. She was too busy staring at Lord Stonewood.

Freddie stared at her, his face a mask of calm. His clothes were clean, though his cloak looked travel-worn. It was wet, like his hair. And although he frowned, Bonnie recognized the playful glint dancing in his eyes.

They might have ended things poorly, but her heart still leapt at the sight of them. But were they here as friends, or foe? It pained her to admit that it could be either.

She schooled her face to a mask of indifference. "What do you want?" She swept her arms to the side, the picture of a queen showing off her court. Her little mouse friend jumped off her lap, bolting to its hole. "I'm very busy."

Simon's frown deepened, while Freddie's mouth twitched at the corners.

"We're here to escort you to Midverd," Freddie said, and his deep voice — more than the message — made her shiver. "By order of the king."

Bonnie blinked. "What?"

"You heard him," Simon said, his voice cold. "Get up."

Bonnie shook her head, even as she stood. She backed against the wall. "Why?"

Simon didn't answer, but strode forward. Bonnie tensed when he reached into the pocket of his cloak. A lifetime of dealing with Oll's proclivity for knives was heavily ingrained in her. She relaxed when he took out a length of rope, although she still didn't like the sight of him with it.

She was sliding into her fighting stance when she saw Freddie shake his head, his eyes lifting to a spot on the wall over her head.

To where the peephole was located.

That gesture, made by anyone else, would have gone unnoticed. But this was Freddie; she was in tune with his every move. Of course she knew what he was trying to convey.

And as mad as she was, she trusted him. Damn it.

She blinked in acknowledgement and looked to Simon. And then she winked.

"Don't touch me!" she yelled, her movements loose and sloppy. "I'm not going anywhere with you!"

Simon advanced with a scowl, one hand stretched out towards her while the other clutched the rope. Bonnie lunged to the left at the same time he reached for her, managing two steps to the side before he grabbed her.

Bonnie made a halfhearted attempt at wrenching her arm away, but he didn't budge. She curved her shoulders inward, the very picture of defeat, as he tied her wrists together loosely behind her back.

Simon pushed her toward the door. "Move."

Bonnie jerked away, but did as she was told. Gods, he may be helping her, but she still didn't like the man.

She avoided making eye contact with Freddie. She didn't know whether to hug him or punch him right now.

Simon took her arm as they exited. He didn't grab too tight, but she still pulled away out of habit. He said nothing, only held on tighter as they navigated the hideout.

The corridors were filled with soldiers, more than she had seen during her week of spying. Probably an increased number now they knew about the secret passageways.

Former secret passageways, she supposed. She tried not to feel guilty — they would've discovered them eventually.

Whispers followed them. Bonnie glared at the guards as they passed, often receiving smirks in return. Nobody said anything, but she noticed that many of them bowed their heads when their group passed by. After a moment of confusion, she realized they were bowing in deference to Lord Stonewood as he trailed behind.

It was disconcerting — to her, he was just *Freddie*, not a lord of Hallordis.

It was a good reminder. She would not forget that again.

Simon led her to the stables. It was as lively and chaotic as usual, even with members of the King's Guard sullying the place. The awning had been drawn over the opening in the roof to shield the horses from the elements. The sound of heavy raindrops hitting the metal brought a sense of calmness over the bustling space.

The sound of whinnying intensified as Bonnie walked past the fenced-in meadow. Half a dozen horses broke off from a small herd and made their way to her, and she smiled, wishing her hands were free to greet them properly.

It was odd — she was used to this type of behavior from the

rebel's horses; she had known them for years. These horses were unfamiliar to her, and yet they behaved the same way.

Bonnie saw two soldiers approaching, and she averted her gaze. One guard, in his haste to reach the horses, bumped into her.

And then she was falling forward, free of Simon's grip. She screwed her eyes shut, unable to use her hands to stop her fall as the floor rose to meet her —

A hand gripped the back of her shirt. She flew up, her back slamming into something solid. Turning her head, heart beating wildly, she saw that Freddie was holding her against his body.

"Careful," he whispered, and set her down. The feel of his breath on her neck sent goosebumps down her arms, and she swallowed hard.

Bonnie shook herself out of his grip before glaring at Simon for putting her in this position. He and Freddie were exchanging a loaded look, one that Bonnie didn't know how to interpret. Ignoring her ire, Simon grabbed her arm and led her to two stalls at the end of the row.

She gasped.

Captain stood there, staring directly at her. The giant chestnut nuzzled her gently, and she kissed his face, wishing she could hug him.

"Hi, handsome," she murmured. He huffed at her in response.

Bonnie tensed when she felt someone behind her. A moment later there was a tug on the rope securing her wrists, and then her hands were free. She dropped them to her sides, but knew better than to make a big deal of her newfound freedom, even though she longed to rub the tender skin on her wrists.

And punch Freddie. Not necessarily in that order.

A tap on her shoulder had her turning around. Freddie stood close — *too* close. Only inches separated them.

She took a step back, bumping into Captain's stall.

Freddie looked at her with a sad smile and gestured with the rope in his hands.

She stood tall, holding her wrists in front of her. "No horse for me, *milord?*" she bit out as he tied her hands together. The knot securing it looked tight, but she could undo it with no problem.

A bit of good will, perhaps, from the person who destroyed her life.

It didn't matter that they had been friends, she decided. Or that she found him attractive. It didn't matter that he was supposedly rescuing her right now.

He was still the reason everything went to hell in the first place.

"No," he said. His voice was husky, and she felt a stirring in her lower stomach. "Too suspicious."

Bonnie turned to face Captain. She needed to distance herself from Freddie before she found some way to stab him.

Simon came over with a familiar cloak a few moments later.

"Time to go," he said, as he draped it over her shoulders. She didn't move as he fastened it under her chin, but couldn't stop her sigh as she felt its comforting warmth envelop her.

She hadn't realized how cold she had been until that moment.

They led the horses out of their stalls. Simon's horse, the large black one she'd seen in Bronwyn's clearing, regarded her with calm eyes.

"Get on," Simon ordered as he mounted. He jerked his chin toward Captain.

Bonnie shook her head. "I want to ride with you."

"No. Get up."

The last thing she wanted was to ride with Freddie.

"Wouldn't it be unwise to let a rebel assassin ride with your lord? You're the soldier. It would make more sense if I rode with you." She hated how desperate she sounded but couldn't help it. She really did *not* want to ride with him.

Simon shook his head, though he looked like he agreed. "Get on the damn horse, rebel."

Bonnie glared as she held up her bound hands. "Hard to mount with these, *guard*."

"I've got you," Freddie said.

Bonnie felt his powerful hands at her waist a moment later, and then he lifted her into the air. She had enough sense to brace herself for impact as he set her atop of Captain's wide back. Lurching forward, she grabbed the saddle as best she could and tried not to fall off when Freddie mounted behind her. She ignored the pleasant feel of his body heat and tried not to flinch when he reached around to grab Captain's reins.

"Everything okay?" he said, his voice low. "I've been worried about you."

Bonnie didn't trust herself to say anything.

Freddie nudged Captain to follow behind Simon. After a brief salute to the soldiers at the exit, they were out. Even the weather couldn't dampen her spirits as she raised her eyes to the dark sky.

She was free.

Bonnie felt a tug, and a moment later her hood was placed on her head, saving her from the fat raindrops that fell down in sheets. She grunted her thanks.

Captain followed Simon down the empty cobblestone street. He was leading them toward the main city gates, Bonnie realized, which would put them on the most direct path to Midverd.

She stilled. She thought they had been lying when they said they were taking her to the capital city . . . but was it the truth?

If so, she had to find a good place to escape. She couldn't go back there — she'd avoided the capital city since the attack twelve years before.

And if the rumors were true, and both Oll and Gwyneth were there? She couldn't be in the same city. Running into them, or any member of the Amlucen, was the equivalent of signing her own death warrant.

Freddie must have sensed her discomfort, for he leaned forward a moment later. "We'll talk after we leave the city."

"I have to get Belle," she said. There was no way she was going to leave her behind. Especially in Crown Harbor, where other rebels might recognize her.

"I have operatives in the city," he reassured her. "They'll get her and meet us on the way to Midverd."

Bonnie stiffened. "Operatives? Who *are* you?"

The Freddie she had known didn't have *operatives*.

He chuckled. The sound grated on her nerves. "You'll see."

Bonnie rolled her eyes and said nothing more. While on the surface she appeared calm — as calm as a prisoner could be, anyway — inside she warred with herself.

On one hand, Freddie and Simon had rescued her. Using their help to escape made sense; who knows what would've happened if she had refused to go with them? The thought of spending more time in that windowless room awaiting a visit from Snell . . .

No. She did not feel bad about using the two of them to escape.

But did that mean that she would go along with whatever plan they had come up with?

Also no. It was their fault she was in this mess. It was their fault that the only home she had ever known was now over-taken by her enemy.

She kept quiet as they continued at a brisk walk. The rain, though it presented its own problems, at least cleared the city streets. It felt as though they were the only ones in the city.

Bonnie decided she would escape once they reached Golwich Forest. Once she got Belle back she would take off and ride as far and as fast as she could.

She had started her life completely over once. She could do it again.

They approached the city gates. Even in the rain, the massive gates looked majestic. Their little group passed through with hardly a second glance, the guards more focused on who they were letting into the city than who was leaving it. Even Bonnie's bound hands hardly caused any reaction, not when she was accompanied by a guard in uniform.

Fools.

And just like that, Bonnie was once again on the other side of the Crown Harbor walls, facing the border of Golwich Forest.

Free, but more entangled than she had ever been.

CHAPTER THIRTY-TWO

They traveled without speaking. The sound of the rain filled the silence.

Bonnie kept vigilant, watching for the operatives Freddie claimed he had. The only sign of life was the movement of small animals and birds as they tried to take shelter from the storm.

After stopping at the tree where she hid Gwyneth's bag — she wouldn't risk leaving it there, even if she didn't trust her travel companions — they entered Golwich. Bonnie sent up her usual prayer to the beings who governed the forest, thanking them for safe and swift passage through the trees.

The tall pines sheltered them from the bulk of the rain, and it was a relief to get a respite from the heavy drops. Bonnie liked rain well enough, but only when she was curled up on a chair, eyes closed, listening to it under a warm blanket. She had a feeling that she wouldn't have an opportunity to do that again for a while.

Captain was a steady presence under her, plodding calmly behind Simon. They walked for about a half an hour, putting a good distance between them and Crown Harbor, before Simon pulled off the path. When he disappeared between two trees, Freddie nudged Captain to follow.

Simon eventually stopped and dismounted in a quick, simple motion. Bonnie lurched forward when Captain stopped, and felt a distinct lack of warmth when Freddie dismounted a moment later.

Freddie reached up and grabbed her waist before settling her on the ground with ease. She was impressed despite herself; she was not a small woman.

She kept scowling, though. He didn't need an ego boost.

Bonnie held her bound hands in front of her. "Take it off."

"Not until you hear what we have to say," Simon said from his spot under a tree.

"That doesn't foster goodwill," Bonnie muttered.

It didn't matter, though. Freddie had tied the ropes loosely enough that she could take them off if she needed to. For now it might be advantageous to let them think she was incapacitated. Lull them into a false sense of security. They wouldn't expect her to fight back if things turned bad.

"The lady has a point," Freddie said with a smile.

Bonnie frowned and looked away. She plod through the wet ground, sidestepping a puddle as she made her way to Simon. He felt like the safer option. She kept a healthy distance away from him, though, ready to bolt. She didn't trust him. And she knew he disliked her.

For good reason, sure. But still.

"Where are we going?" she asked. It was much drier here under the eaves, and the sound of the rain faded into the background. A bold squirrel ran down from its hiding spot and nuzzled her foot before dashing away.

Freddie shook his head and droplets flew off, reminding Bonnie of the way wet street dogs shook off water. "We told you. Midverd."

"I thought you said that just to get me out of there."

"No."

"I can't go there. I haven't been back . . . " She didn't need to finish her sentence for understanding to flash in Freddie's eyes.

"Been back since what?" Simon asked.

Freddie looked at Bonnie, as if asking for guidance. She didn't feel the need to lie, but also didn't feel the need to explain her history, either. She ignored Simon's question. "Is there an important reason we need to go there? Why *I* need to go there?"

"They have Felix."

Bonnie stilled. "What? Who? Why didn't you tell me before?"

Memories of the last meeting with her brother flashed before her eyes.

Helping her get the knowledge and materials she needed to flee Stoneforge.

His pledge to keep her secrets.

Gwyneth stabbing him repeatedly. The blood that flew through the air as their adopted mother slashed at him over and over and over again.

She relived these moments in her dreams. Her nightmares.

"When would we have had time to tell you?" Freddie asked, his tone patient; Bonnie hated him for it. "The Crown has him in custody. Felix was found in Thornwick — someone recognized him and alerted the King's Guard."

"What are they going to do with him?" She heard stories of what Aborn and his men did to captured rebel soldiers. No one ever survived.

"We're not sure," Simon said, and Bonnie couldn't tell whether he had any sympathy for Felix's fate. Simon could be drinking buddies with Aborn for all she knew. "Question him, at the very least."

"Is that why Oll's meeting with the king? To bargain for Felix's life?"

Simon shot her a look. "How do you know about that?"

Bonnie glared at him, waiting for an answer. She didn't need to explain her sources. Not to him. Not to Freddie, either. Not anymore.

Freddie said, "We're not entirely sure why your father —"

"*Adopted* father," Bonnie cut in, out of habit.

Freddie rolled his eyes. "We're not sure why he's trying to meet with the king. Or why the meeting is being publicized."

"Publicized?"

Freddie nodded. "Jasper found out a few weeks ago that Oll set up a meeting with the king. The knowledge was top secret, though. After the attack in the Crown Harbor, word spread."

"How did Jasper find out if it was top secret?" She thought back to the drunk, bumbling lord from all those weeks ago. Surely *he* wasn't one of the king's top advisors.

He had just returned from a trip to Midverd that day, Bonnie remembered. He must've found out about it during that trip.

"Accidentally," Freddie said. "The king gave Jasper several missives to give to our father upon his return to Navian. Father opened it while the two of them were debriefing Jasper's trip, and he asked Jasper if the king had mentioned anything about it."

Interesting. That meant, if Jasper had known about this meeting weeks ago, that it wasn't scheduled in response to the attack on Thornwick, the attack on Crown Harbor, *or* in response to Felix's capture.

When Bonnie said as much, Freddie nodded. "The entire thing is suspicious."

"It's not my problem anymore. I'm not going back to the Amlucen. I'm leaving Hallordis."

Freddie's eyes widened. "But . . . What are you going to do instead? You can't leave."

She narrowed her eyes. "Why not? I'm going to be hunted

for my part in freeing you. I'm going to start a new life some-where new."

A look of guilt crossed his face but Bonnie didn't care. It was true.

"What about Felix? Come to Midverd with us. We'll help you free him." He looked so eager that Bonnie felt some of her iciness thaw a bit.

She shook her head. "He got himself into this mess. It's not my job to help him." But she hated the way the words tasted in her mouth.

Freddie cocked his head to the side as he regarded her, and she swore he looked disappointed. "I know you've had your problems with him, but he helped us in Stoneforge. Are you really going to let him rot? Let him hang?"

Damn him.

Simon turned to Freddie, ignoring Bonnie completely. "Why bother? Let her go — you don't need to help her just so you can assuage your misplaced guilt. We need to leave. With or without her."

A pained look crossed Freddie's face, echoing the feeling Bonnie felt in her chest. But before Bonnie could respond, a nearby branch snapped with a *crack*.

Everyone stiffened before moving into action; the men reached for their swords, while Bonnie worked at undoing the rope that held her wrists together. It fell to the ground and she slid into a fighting stance.

A three note whistle cut though the air, and the men relaxed. Freddie sounded a reply.

A friend, then. Maybe Freddie's operatives. While it compli-cated things, she was glad — it would be easier to escape from these fools on horseback.

Lord Jasper Stonewood rode into the clearing atop his horse, grinning wickedly as he surveyed their little group. Belle followed closely behind.

Bonnie couldn't stop her smile. Belle's white hair was braided and her golden coat was gleaming. Stabling her with that livery had been worth every coin.

The mare walked right up to Bonnie, ignoring the muttered curses of her rider to stop, and nuzzled her velvet nose into Bonnie.

Bonnie stroked her face, making good use of her freed hands. The length of rope that had bound them together was stuffed into her cloak pocket.

"Hello, old friend," she whispered. Belle blew into Bonnie's face.

Bonnie's mouth dropped open when she saw who rode her. "Bronwyn? What are you doing here? You haven't left your clearing in . . ."

"Twelve years," the old woman muttered as she tried to dismount. Simon strode over to help. The old woman straightened up with her typical scowl, her white hair tamed by a colorful fabric headband. "For good reason. I don't like to involve myself in the drama of the continent. I feel itchy without the full use of my magic."

And you're blind, Bonnie wanted to point out. She couldn't imagine how Bronwyn was feeling, away from the comfort of her cottage. Things must be pretty dire if the men had convinced the old witch to leave her sanctuary.

Bronwyn slowly made her way to stand under the tree near Bonnie. Jasper, uncharacteristically quiet, stood outside of the clearing in a heated discussion with his brother.

Freddie, scowling, gestured wildly. Bonnie was too far away to hear anything, and watched as the two brothers made their way back to the group.

Jasper only gave her a perfunctory nod before glancing away.

Odd. That was an unusual greeting from the normally animated brother.

Bronwyn clapped her hands. "What are we waiting for? Is it time to leave?"

"Bonnie hasn't decided if she's coming," Freddie said.

"What?" Bronwyn barked. She turned in Bonnie's general direction. "Why wouldn't you come?"

Anger coursed through her. "I'm *done*," Bonnie hissed. "I'm going to be hunted for the rest of my miserable existence. I'm exhausted. I'm angry. My entire life is in shambles. I don't need to go to Midverd to save the life of a man who has spent most of his life hating me. I don't need to risk being seen by anyone in the rebellion. I. Am. Done."

"Oh, stop being dramatic," Bronwyn snapped, flapping a wrinkly hand at her. "You've heard what the boys have to say. I don't know how you could be on the fence about coming to Midverd, considering what we found."

"What are you talking about?"

"We haven't had time to tell her," Freddie said.

"Well, what were you doing while Jasper and I were getting the nag? Braiding each other's hair?"

"What am I missing?" Bonnie asked, deliberately calm. If someone didn't tell her what was going on in the next ten seconds she would stab someone. Her fingers twitched in anticipation.

Bronwyn looked towards Freddie. "Tell her."

Freddie frowned as he turned to Bonnie. "Gwendolyn killed your mother."

Bonnie took a step back. "*What?*"

That was the last thing she expected him to say.

Freddie reached into his pocket and took out a piece of parchment. "This was one of the letters that was written in the more complex cipher. I decoded it after you left."

She took it with trembling fingers. Sheltering the paper

from the few errant raindrops that broke through the boughs above her, she read the new missive.

The top, written in cipher, was in Oll's handwriting. Freddie scrawled the translation underneath.

G.,

THE GIRL SURVIVED. SHE REMEMBERS NOTHING — WE WON'T HAVE TO KILL HER. WE CAN WAIT TO USE HER TO OUR ADVANTAGE. SHOULD BE EASY, CONSIDERING SHE DOESN'T REMEMBER YOU KILLED HER MOTHER. I RENAMED HER "BONNIE" IN HONOR OF YOUR OLD NURSEMAID.

— O.

Bonnie read the missive once, then again.

And then a third time.

She looked at Freddie with tear-filled eyes.

"I'm sorry," he said. He took a step forward, looking as though he wanted to reach out and comfort her, but stopped when she shook her head.

She turned to face outside of the clearing and tried to gather her thoughts.

Gwyneth — no, *Gwendolyn*, she corrected, for no longer would she ever refer to that hateful woman by her false name — had done some pretty horrible things. Bonnie *knew* that. She knew the messed up shit she had done before taking Bonnie in, and more recently, too.

But this? This was something else entirely.

This was personal.

Gwendolyn had lied to Bonnie for *years*. Poisoned her against the king. Fed her lie after lie about how Aborn murdered Bonnie's family.

Was any part of the last twelve years true? Was the king even a fraction as evil as Gwendolyn Hatherall proved to be?

A sharp pain. Her hand was clenched so tightly that her fingernails broke skin. Dark blood welled up in four crescent-shaped arcs, and she watched the blood pool before it rolled off her hand and fell to the forest floor.

Drop, drop, drop, drop.

She wasn't worried about coming face to face with Gwendolyn anymore. Oll, either.

No.

She *wanted* to see them.

She *wanted* to see the light leave their eyes as she shoved her blade into their twisted hearts.

And she knew where Oll was, thank the gods. After ending his miserable life she would hunt Gwendolyn down — she was probably in Suverd, like always. Bonnie would take her sweet time killing her.

She rejoined the circle, shoulders bowed with the weight of this new knowledge. Bronwyn was speaking quietly with Jasper off to the side, while Simon checked on the horses. Freddie watched her, expression wary. She gave him a perfunctory nod, the only acknowledgement she would give him right now.

"I'm sorry that you had to find out this way," he said, his voice gentle.

Bonnie had to look away or risk breaking down. What he had done paled in comparison to what she just learned. But she was still mad at him. And she still didn't understand *why* he did what he did.

The others rejoined them, and Bronwyn cleared her throat. "Well?"

"I want to free Felix. And if I run into either of my dear, sweet parents," she bared her teeth in a violent smile, "I'm going to kill them."

CHAPTER THIRTY-THREE

THE GROUP MADE GOOD PROGRESS THROUGH THE ANCIENT forest. The rain had finally let up, although Bonnie's clothing was soaked.

She didn't feel the cold. White hot anger fueled her now.

Jasper led the group, followed by Freddie and Bronwyn on Captain. Simon followed behind Bonnie, and she had the sense that he put himself there to watch over her. She didn't care; his dedication was flattering.

Jasper led them to a small clearing. "We'll camp here for the night," he said.

It was the first time Bonnie had heard him speak since he had joined the group hours before. Part of her wondered why he'd been so quiet. It certainly was a marked change from their previous interactions.

A bigger part of her didn't care; she was focused on revenge.

Bonnie pulled Belle to the outskirts of the clearing. She wiped her down as best as she could with the damp clothes she had, promising a night in a cozy stable sometime soon.

She felt a warm presence behind her and knew without

looking who it was. She kept quiet, though, not in a mood to talk. Freddie respected her wish and said nothing while he tended to Captain.

A few squirrel friends chose that moment to greet her. Belle stood calmly as they scurried up her tail, and the sight of the two tree rats holding pine nut offerings made Bonnie smile. She thanked them profusely, sticking the seeds in her pocket, and watched them scamper back into the trees.

Turning, Bonnie froze when she saw Freddie looking at her with a smile; she had forgotten he was there. Any happiness she felt disappeared almost as quickly as it had arrived. Turning away, she made her way towards the fire that Simon was trying to start.

But not before she saw the flash of hurt that crossed his face.

She ignored it. It wasn't her job to placate his ego, and she still wasn't ready to forgive him.

It didn't matter that the rebellion was based on lies, and that he proved her adopted parents were murderous psychopaths. He broke her trust and fucked over the Crown Harbor rebels. She may not believe in Oll and Gwendolyn anymore — she hadn't for a while, to be fair — but that didn't mean that she owed him anything.

Simon didn't glance up when she walked by, too busy trying to coax a fire from the wet wood. Bronwyn muttered to herself as she felt through the many bags she brought, while Jasper stared at her sullenly from his seat on a nearby tree stump.

His annoyed look was enough to break Bonnie out of her reverie. "What is your problem?" she snapped.

His lip curled.

She stopped, crossing her arms over her chest as she stared down at him.

He stood, his dark eyes flashing. "Stay away from him," he said, his voice a low growl.

Bonnie feigned stupidity, even as her heart started racing. "Simon hates me," she told him crossly. "You don't have to worry about me getting close to him."

Unless she was getting close enough to stab him, she supposed. And she had been sorely tempted during the short time she'd spent with him.

"That's not who I meant and you know it."

"I have no interest in forgiving your brother."

"Good. The sooner you leave our lives, the better."

"Hold on. Do you think everything that happened here is *my* fault?"

"Yes."

Bonnie's mouth dropped open. "How do you figure that? Your brother is just as much at fault as I am."

Jasper's face turned an interesting shade of red. "You involved us in your rebel drama the moment you set foot in his bedchamber. If you hadn't shown up, none of this would've happened."

"You don't get to blame this all on me. Freddie could've stayed in his room. But *no*. He insisted on withholding information. He forced me to bring him to Crown Harbor."

Freddie walked over and stood between the two of them. "What's going on?"

"Your brother is blaming me for everything," Bonnie said.

"Nothing," Jasper said at the same time.

Freddie only raised his eyebrows as he looked between them.

"None of this would've happened if she hadn't targeted you," Jasper finally said.

"That's a lie," Bonnie said with a sneer. "Stop acting like it was a personal attack. Targeting your family was a matter of politics. We wanted to shake up the kingdom to make Aborn look weak. It wasn't personal."

"You made it personal!"

"How did I make it personal? Freddie's the one who decided to travel with me. I'm not the only reason we're sitting here in the middle of this godsforsaken forest!"

The trees, which had been swaying gently in the night breeze, suddenly rained pine needles. Bonnie muttered an apology to those who watched over Golwich.

"Why do you even care? You got valuable intel from Freddie's little adventure," she said. Freddie flinched. "Not only were you able to attack in Thornwick, but you also captured the headquarters in Crown Harbor, too. Two birds, one stone. The rebellion is in chaos, thanks to you two. Isn't that what you wanted?"

"Not at the expense of my brother," Jasper said, chest heaving.

"Jas —" Freddie broke in.

"You almost killed him, didn't you?" Jasper continued. "When he caught you in his room?"

"Yes," Bonnie said, spreading her arms wide. "Is that what you want me to admit? Fine. I thought about killing him, yes. It was lucky he convinced me otherwise." Anger flashed through her when a look of triumph crossed over his face, as though he won a secret battle she hadn't been aware she was fighting. "You could've stopped it, you know. You showed up at his room right before I had to make that decision. Do you remember? Or were you too drunk to recall anything that happened that night?" Something like loathing flashed through Jasper's eyes, but Bonnie didn't care. "If you want to blame anyone, blame yourself for not seeing what was going on in front of you."

The color drained from Jasper's face. "Do you think I don't know that?" His voice broke on the last word, and he looked away.

Oh.

Oh.

Jasper wasn't angry at Bonnie about what happened that night. He was angry at himself.

And with that realization, all the fight left her once more.

"It wasn't personal," she told him again. "Believe me when I say that if I could go back and change what happened, I would. I regret meeting any of you."

"Bonnie," Freddie breathed, but she couldn't look at him.

She walked to the far side of the clearing, past Simon and Bronwyn, who looked in her direction. For once the old woman kept her mouth shut.

Bonnie sat at the base of one of the tall pine trees and stared into the fire.

Part of her wanted to leave the group and make her way to Midverd on her own. But as much as she disliked the man, Jasper's love for Freddie sent a pang through her. She understood why he hated her, even if some of his anger was misdirected.

His love for his brother made her think of the man she considered her own brother.

Bonnie couldn't leave Felix behind. He would try to save her if their roles were reversed, she was sure of it. He had saved her before, in more ways than one. He was her brother — not by blood, but in all the ways that counted. It was time to return the favor.

That meant the best course of action would be for her to stay with the group. She hadn't been to Midverd since Vale Magicae — it would be foolish to go back there without a plan.

Not only that, but they had connections that might prove useful. The Amlucen were surely hunting her, and she knew she couldn't count on their help to free Felix. The rebels on the ground weren't aware that Bonnie's adopted parents were lying assholes. That knowledge, unfortunately, was known only to a select few.

The others kept a wide berth. Freddie kept stealing glances

at her, and more than once Bonnie caught Simon shaking his head at him.

Good. She wasn't in the mood to speak to anyone tonight.

Bonnie didn't offer to take a watch, and no one approached her about taking one, either. They probably didn't trust her enough to warn them of danger, she thought.

And with good reason. She was just rebel scum in the midst of royalty. An assassin raised by murderers.

She was no one.

Nothing.

Curled in her cloak, she lay her head down on the damp ground and somehow fell asleep.

BONNIE WOKE TO THE FEELING OF SOMETHING MOVING IN HER hair.

She didn't startle; it was small, whatever it was. Probably not dangerous. She opened her eyes to see weak sunlight filtering through the trees.

The creature in her hair squirmed, pulling out a few strands of hair in its struggle.

"Stop it," she chided sleepily, reaching up to untangle it. She felt soft feathers, thin legs, and a hard beak that gently nipped her fingers. Chuckling, she freed the little bird and set it on the ground. It chirped once in thanks before taking off into the trees.

Bonnie blinked a few times, willing the sleepiness away. She slept surprisingly well, considering the ground was hard and the company not ideal. And although her cloak was still damp, she felt warm.

Odd.

Propping herself on an elbow, she looked around.

Two rabbits were curled together in the crook of her belly, sound asleep. A small skunk slept on its back behind her knees, and Bonnie swore she could hear it snore. A fox had draped itself over her legs, its reddish orange coat a stark contrast to the dark color of her cloak.

It was perfect.

Something moved nearby, breaking Bonnie out of her reverie. Freddie strode into the clearing from the direction of the horses. He rubbed his hands together, and plumes of smoke rose where his breath met the wintry morning air.

They locked eyes, and Bonnie felt a pang in her chest. She hated how complicated things had gotten between them and longed for the time they had spent in this forest weeks ago. Before her life had gone to shit.

His expression turned soft as he noticed the sleeping animals. It had always amused him to see her little friends.

Bonnie looked away, even as her lips twitched.

He made his way over, careful not to wake the others. No one stirred. He sat a cautious distance apart, and Bonnie had the feeling he was trying to judge how violent she was feeling today.

She honestly wasn't sure herself.

"Sleep well?"

Bonnie grunted. She reached over and softly stroked a bunny with a finger.

He let out a deep breath. "Look . . . I'm sorry, Bonnie. I'm sorry you were hurt, and that so many horrible things happened to you. I'm sorry that I didn't talk to you sooner about what was going on. I'm sorry about a lot of things."

Bonnie looked up from the sleeping bunny. "You never wanted to be a rebel, did you?"

She didn't know why this question, out of all of them, was the one she wanted him to answer first. But it bothered her, damn it. The only thing she had to rely on was her gut feeling, and when she first met him, her gut had been confused. And when she began to trust him, she ignored the misgivings she had about trusting a lord of Hallordis. He tricked her, and now she doubted herself.

"No, I didn't. But I didn't want to die. You saw my desk — I was looking for information to help *dismantle* the rebellion. I thought telling you I wanted to join was the only way you'd let me walk out of there alive."

She'd come dangerously close to ending his life that night.

And what a shame that would have been.

"So, what? You passed information along to Jasper and Simon the entire time?"

"Not exactly. I didn't want to risk speaking to them in Navian — you were watching me too closely. It was pure luck they tracked us to Crown Harbor. I left headquarters before you woke up the first morning, and I was surprised at how easy it was to get a message out. No one stopped me when I tried to leave."

"Felix trailed you," she admitted.

Freddie smirked. "I figured someone would, which is why I made sure the handoff in the bakery was discreet. I'm honored that your brother deemed me enough of a threat to trail me personally."

He stayed quiet, letting her think. The fox that was keeping her feet warm got up and nuzzled her leg before scampering off, while the skunk rolled to its feet, chirped a few times, and wandered in the opposite direction. The bunnies stayed put, and Bonnie stroked their soft fur gently.

A part of her hated how comfortable she still felt with him, even though he had lied to her from the moment they met. It felt different, somehow, from the lies told by the people she thought were family. His lies were to ensure his own survival; she couldn't fault him for that.

The lies they told? There wasn't a punishment harsh enough for them.

"I know now that the rebellion was founded on lies," she

said. It was a morning of sharing information; she figured it was time to share her thoughts. "But I still find myself hesitant to accept that Aborn is as great as you all seem to believe."

If Freddie was surprised at the change in topic, he didn't show it. "I learned a lot about the way the Amlucen operated while I spent time with you. Saw their teachings." He paused, and a muscle in his jaw twitched. "Almost everything they've taught you is a lie."

"Like what?"

"The king doesn't go out and murder rebels for sport. Or for any reason, really. You were taught that the rebels who were caught by the King's Guard were murdered in cold blood, right?"

Bonnie nodded.

"That's a lie that Oll and Gwendolyn spun, then," he said. "Are rebels killed in battle? Sure. But contrary to what you've been told, the king doesn't round them up and kill them."

"What happens to them? I know at least a dozen rebels who've disappeared over the years. Everyone told me that the king had taken them."

"There's a settlement up north where the Crown sends rebels. They have to work to earn their keep, but they're not tortured or killed."

"What's it called?"

"Treehaven."

Bonnie hadn't heard of it, which she thought was odd. Surely Oll and Gwendolyn knew about its existence. "Are the rebels allowed to leave?"

"Eventually."

"So it's a glorified prison, then. A labor camp."

Freddie sighed. "What would you have him do? The rebels want to take over the country, through death or other means. Would you rather he kill them? Torture them? Imprison them? They have to work, yes — but they have warm beds and good food and comfortable clothing. Many have stayed, even after being released."

Interesting. Bonnie supposed he had a point. The king couldn't just release the rebels — what would stop them from trying to overthrow him again? Putting them in the settlement and making them work off their anger seemed like a decent compromise.

Better than death.

"Do you think that's where the king will send Felix?" she asked.

"No. Your brother is too important to send back into the arms of the other rebels. I imagine the king would worry that Felix would use his connections to promote an uprising." He swallowed. "They might decide to make an example of him."

Damn it.

"I'll take you there one day, if you want," Freddie said. "To Treehaven — it's north of Navian. My father oversees it."

Bonnie nodded. It would be good to verify this newfound information with her own eyes. She would have a hard time trusting anyone after all of this was said and done.

If she survived the next few days.

"Why does Aborn keep conquering other countries? Most of the continent has fallen to him now. Why won't he stop?"

Freddie's mouth tightened, and he looked as though he was trying to figure out how to respond. "It's complicated," he finally settled on. "I don't know all the reasons. Bronwyn mentioned information in passing, though. According to her, there's something . . . *off* about the monarchs in other countries. Something is wrong. Whenever I've asked her to elaborate, she changes the subject."

"But how would she know anything? She speaks as though she knows him. Knows the court. She lives in her little clearing — how would she know any of this?"

Freddie laughed. "She's old, our Bronwyn. And she *does* know the king."

"How?"

He looked over to where the old woman slept. "That's for her to share," he said softly. "It's not my place."

Bonnie followed his gaze, and saw that while Bronwyn still slept, both Jasper and Simon showed signs of waking. Their time to chat privately was over.

There was more they needed to talk about, Bonnie knew. Hurts that needed to be aired. But the tightness that lived in her chest had loosened somewhat. He had been open and honest with her, and she had a feeling that he was finally telling her the full truth. For the first time, she saw a path forward.

"Come on," she said, getting up. "I need to go to Midverd so I can kill my father."

"*Adopted* father," Freddie amended.

Bonnie smiled.

CHAPTER THIRTY-FOUR

The smell of blood, so familiar and yet so jarring, filled her nose.

Felix was across the room, covered in it. He grabbed his arm, his face contorted with pain.

Bonnie ran forward, reaching out a hand to stop Gwyneth from stabbing him again. And again. And again.

But no matter how far she ran, she never got closer.

She watched as her brother bled to death.

Everything turned black.

Bonnie wasn't sure what time the fighting had started; it could have been minutes. Could have been hours.

The worst part was the screaming.

The horrible sounds blended in almost seamlessly with the revelry down in the city streets. It had taken a while for the beautiful music to stop, for even the musicians hadn't realized what was happening.

Now all Bonnie heard was screaming.

Bonnie's mother — her kind, gentle, fierce mother — dragged Bonnie to the bedroom door. Cracking it open, she checked that the corridor was clear before pulling Bonnie close.

"Sweetheart, you need to hide. Do you remember the secret room we showed you?"

Bonnie nodded, though she had hated the small, cramped room that housed her family's unused trinkets. The dust always made her sneeze.

"You need to go there. Now."

"But I don't want to leave you," eight-year-old Bonnie whined. "Let me stay. I promise I won't get in the way."

"I'll join you soon, my love," her mother said, before she pulled her daughter into a bone-crushing hug. "Your father and I will join you as soon as we can."

Bonnie nodded, frowning. She was used to being told what to do, what to wear, who to be. She would obey her mother's wishes, even though she wanted to stay with her.

The screaming had gotten louder, though, and Bonnie did not want to be alone.

Her mother cracked open the door. "I love you, my princess. Now go, as quick as you can."

Hiking up the hem of her blue dressing gown, Bonnie fled. The corridor where her bedroom was located was empty, but she heard loud sounds up ahead.

More screaming. More crying.

She stopped before she reached the first crossroads. The torches on the wall flickered, casting long shadows on the floor. She heard nothing, saw no one. She continued on.

Sounds of movement again, just around the corner. Bonnie slowed her pace, slippered feet silent on the stone floor.

She heard one soft cry before she heard heavy footsteps running in the opposite direction. She crept forward, peering around the corner.

There was a dead body lying on the floor.

The woman, a servant, stared sightlessly at the ceiling. Blood sluggishly trickled out of the jagged knife wound that almost decapitated her.

Stumbling away, Bonnie made it a few steps before bile rose in her

throat. She threw up, tears streaming down her face, and hoped she
wouldn't be next.

The same heavy footsteps sounded down the corridor, closer than
they had been.

Turning, she ran back to her bedchamber as fast as she could.

She almost cried in relief when she neared the door, opened wide.
It was her haven, her safe space; no harm would come to her there.

She didn't even pause to think about why *her door was wide open.*

Bonnie crossed the threshold, looking for her mother. She paused
when she saw a cloaked figure standing there, back to the door.
Strange markings covered the floor, written in dark red ink.

The stranger must have heard her gasp, for they started to turn . .
.

"You need to relax," Bronwyn hissed. "Stop drawing
attention to us."

"Shut it," Bonnie whispered. She paused. "How would you
—?"

Freddie chuckled in her ear, while Bronwyn frowned. "I can
feel the tension radiating off you from over here, girl."

Bonnie didn't know how the two of them could be so cava-
lier at a time like this. The meeting between the king and Oll
was *today* for fuck's sake. Even riding as hard as they could,
they only arrived just in time. She was pissed off, and it made
everything worse.

Plus, she was exhausted. Her nightmare had returned last
night, and it was worse than before.

She wanted to ride straight to the castle gates and demand
entry but was outvoted. They were filthy; they needed a quick
bath and a change of clothes before going anywhere near the
castle. So off to the Stonewood's city residence they went.

Bonnie now sat on Captain in front of Freddie, while
Bronwyn rode Belle by their side, a lead rope connecting the

two horses. Jasper and Simon, on their own mounts, brought up the rear.

She wasn't entirely sure she bought the excuse that she and Bronwyn had to switch horses because the old woman was sore from riding Captain. It was more likely they had to switch because Freddie was afraid she'd run off.

Bonnie straightened in the saddle, distracted by the solid, warm presence behind her. She tugged the end of her shortened hair, still surprised at how much lighter it felt.

Her heart thumped wildly as she looked at the gold-covered gates that came closer with every step. They towered impressively, over twenty feet tall.

Shaking her head, Bonnie willed herself into her killing calm. She had a part to play; she needed to focus. Softening her posture, she melted into Freddie's hard chest. His arms tightened around her for a moment, maybe in surprise, before relaxing once more. She stayed in that position, unmoving, as they approached the city gates.

"Business here?" a burly guard asked when they reached the front of the line.

"Returning home," Freddie said in a clipped manner, playing the part of the haughty lord.

The guard straightened in response to the command in Freddie's tone. With a harsh face and shaved head, he looked to be a seasoned member of the King's Guard. He peered at Freddie's face more closely. "Excuse me, Lord Stonewood; I did not recognize you. Of course you and your —" he hesitated, trying to find the correct word to describe Bonnie, who was still melting into him, "*companion* may enter."

Freddie nodded. "My grandmother is on the golden mare, and my brother and his guard are behind her."

The guard nodded as he looked down the line. He waved them through. "All cleared to enter. Have a good day, milord. Welcome back to Midverd."

Bonnie held back her snort until they were out of earshot. When she woke up this morning, she thought they'd have to sneak her through the front gates. "I guess it pays to be a lord of the realm, then."

He huffed a laugh. "It has its uses."

The group set off, and Bonnie's mouth dropped open as she took in the capital city. If she thought the golden rooftops of Crown Harbor were a lesson in opulence, it was nothing compared to the wealth of the capital city, Midverd.

The buildings were made of an impressive white stone that gleamed beautifully in the morning sun. The streets, crowded despite the early hour, were immaculate, with not a piece of trash or beggar in sight. It would be impressive had it not been bought with the lives of innocent people.

No, Bonnie told herself. It was second nature for her to revert to her rebel way of thinking. *There's no evidence that Oll and Gwendolyn told the truth*, she repeated. *The rebels are alive and well in Treehaven.*

Well-dressed people made their way through the streets, bundled against the chill. The sun had melted the layer of frost, but Bonnie knew that the first snowfall of the season wasn't far off.

While she kept her head forward, Bonnie's eyes constantly scanned the area to see if anyone was paying particular attention to their traveling party. Most ignored them; the sight of nobles on beautiful horses was not uncommon here. She didn't recognize anyone from the rebellion, and the few people who looked at her curiously looked away when she caught them staring. Bonnie didn't relax, though. There were dozens of places a spy could hide.

She jumped when Freddie's voice sounded in her ear. "See anyone you recognize?"

"No."

He squeezed his arms around her in response.

She grumbled at the contact. It was distracting. And she couldn't afford distractions.

He chuckled, and it annoyed her how relaxed he was. Could he be serious at least once? Her life was on the line. Her brother's life was on the line.

"How much further?" All the houses that lined the Main Street looked grand enough to house royalty — which one belonged to the Stonewood family?

"Patience, honeybum. We're almost there."

After coming to a busy crossroads, they turned right, and then turned left at the next one. Their path brought them to the widest street yet.

Bonnie gasped as she beheld the home of the king and his family.

It wasn't the castle — probably better described as a palace, it was so large — that shocked Bonnie to her core.

It was the fact that she *remembered* it.

A series of memories flashed through her mind, almost too quickly to process.

A child's hand, holding onto the hand of a man with hard calluses and a large sapphire ring.

The gruff, deep laugh of someone Bonnie cherished.

A worn tapestry, its colors dull with age.

A half-dozen small animals following her footsteps as she skipped down a long stone corridor.

A woman's laugh, high-pitched and infused with joy.

"Impressive, isn't it?" Freddie said, misinterpreting her stunned silence.

She only stared forward dumbly, at a complete loss for words. Freddie led Captain down a few more side streets, finally coming to a stop in front of a large white stone mansion, its roof gilded in gold.

Metal gates swung open to reveal a large courtyard that was

surrounded by the gargantuan house. Servants rushed out, converging on the four horses as they entered.

"My lords!" a harried-looking man exclaimed as he stopped in front of Jasper's horse. He bowed deeply, and the top of his bald head shone in the sunlight. "What a surprise!"

Jasper grinned. "A *good* surprise, right, Smithy?"

The man frowned. "I wouldn't say that, milord. A little warning would have been appreciated."

Jasper smiled as he dismounted, handing his reins to a nearby stableboy. "But where's the fun in that?"

Freddie snorted as he dismounted. "Sorry, Smith," he said diplomatically. "We're only here to bathe and change — we have to go to the castle immediately."

He turned and raised his hands to Bonnie, who had only been half-listening to the interaction. She was still stunned from the onslaught of her half-remembered memories.

Freddie looked at her and his brow furrowed. "Bonnie? What's wrong?"

The others turned to look at her. "I'm fine," she mumbled.

She allowed him to help her down. To avoid looking at him, she turned to Captain's face and rubbed his head. "Thank you, friend," she whispered. He blew a huff of steam at her before he was led away.

Bonnie saw Freddie conversing with the man Jasper called Smithy. His brow was still furrowed when he looked her way.

She must look bad, she thought, if he still looked this concerned. Forcing a smile to her face, she walked over to the two men.

"Smith, this is my . . . Bonnie," Freddie said lamely, gesturing from one to the other. His cheeks turned pink. "Bonnie, this is Smith, our steward."

The bald man inclined his head, looking her over with shrewd focus and undisguised curiosity.

"A pleasure," she said crisply.

"Let me know if you need anything at all," the man said politely.

"Let's go inside," Freddie said. "I think we're all in need of a bath and food."

Smith nodded and led the way. Bonnie kept a step behind Freddie.

"What's going on?" he asked quietly.

"Later," she whispered as she entered the house.

Even the sight of the beautifully decorated foyer wasn't enough to rouse her from her thoughts. The walls, which stretched high overhead, were a lovely blue color, detailed with golden accents. All the furniture and decorations matched the same color scheme — a subtle nod to the king's colors. The Stonewoods were loyal to the bone, after all.

Dressed in a dirty cloak, Bonnie felt out of place. She doubted she was fit to step inside the stables, never mind the main house. She fought the impulse to sniff under her arms.

A servant girl dressed in a black uniform bowed before them. She held out her hand. "Yer cloaks, milord? Lady? I'll get them laundered first thing."

Bonnie was too shaken to laugh at the misplaced title — she was no *lady* — and took her cloak off, keeping hold of the velvet bag she had stashed in its inner pocket.

"We need a change of clothes for myself and the lady here," Freddie told her. "Something fit for the castle, please."

The servant girl scrutinized Bonnie and then gave a quick nod. "I'll see to it right away, milord."

Smith gave Freddie a bow and said something about preparing the kitchen for a quick meal before hurrying down one of the many corridors that were an offshoot of the entry-way. Freddie led her down a different route.

Bonnie lost track of how many rooms they passed. Freddie walked briskly, eventually stopping in an open doorway. She peered inside and saw a room fit for royalty, with a giant four-poster bed and private bathing chamber.

"This will be your room," he said. "Right across from me."

"Afraid I'll run away?"

"No," he said. "But I worry about you." He took her by the elbow and led her inside.

She jerked her arm away.

"What's going on?" he asked. "You're as white as a ghost. Did you see someone you know?"

Bonnie shook her head. "Not someone. Some*thing*. I . . . I remember."

His eyes widened. "Remember? Remember what?"

"This place . . . the castle. Seeing it when we arrived . . . I had a flashback. A memory. At least, I think it was a memory . . ." she said, and then told him what she'd seen.

"Oh gods," he said when she finished.

She threw herself onto a fancy-looking chaise and stared at the ceiling, dirt be damned. "I know." There really wasn't anything else to say.

"I wonder what else will trigger your memories," he said. "And what was it about the castle specifically?"

"No idea. Maybe my parents were servants there or something."

"That could explain how you know multiple languages," he mused. "Higher-ranking servants need to know how to communicate with foreign visitors."

That didn't sit right with her. "I'm *fluent* in these languages, though. I can read and write and speak them. Not just pass-ingly. It's like I was taught." She rubbed the scar on her temple. "I wish I could remember!"

Freddie sighed from where he still stood by the doorway. "I know, Bon. I know. You'll figure it out."

She groaned in frustration. "There's more. Last night I had a dream . . . A nightmare. There was a dead woman in a servant's uniform. Her throat was cut. There was so much blood . . . " she trailed off.

"It was just a nightmare, though, right? You're safe here."

Bonnie shook her head. "I thought so, but I don't know anymore. It felt the same as when I saw the castle."

"What else happened in the dream?"

"I think it was Vale Magicae. I was with my . . . my mother." Her voice broke on the word. "My real mother. Not Gwendolyn. I was young — probably the same age as when I was attacked. We heard screaming, and my mom told me to flee, to go hide, and I tried to, but. . ." she shook her head. "There was a dead woman. I went back to my bedchamber and the door was open, and there was a stranger in there. In a cloak. I didn't see who it was."

Freddie looked thoughtful. "That sounds like it could be a repressed memory that came back to you."

"But why now? Why am I suddenly starting to remember?"

She hated it, this feeling. The uncertainty. She hated feeling weak.

"The attack in Thornwick gave you back your ability to understand other languages. Maybe it unlocked your lost memories as well. You haven't been back in Midverd in twelve years — it makes sense that being here would trigger flashbacks."

"I suppose so," she grumbled. "I hate it."

He looked at her with pity, and she hated that even more. She resisted the urge to scratch the look off his face.

"Did you recognize where you were? Where you lived?"

She shook her head. "No. It seemed overly large, though — maybe the castle? Although this place is pretty big. Could be one of the mansions in the city."

"Maybe you were part of the nobility."

Bonnie nodded. "I think I definitely could have been. My mother wasn't dressed like a servant, and our clothes looked of fine make. I would guess that we were wealthy." She took a deep breath and let it out.

"I can look into records of the noble families who were slaughtered on Vale Magicae," he offered. "Maybe you belong to one of them."

She sat up. "That can wait for later. We need to rescue Felix."

"We need to bathe first, and wait for your new clothes to arrive. If we go to the castle right now they would think we were beggars."

"So? You're a lord. They'd recognize you even if you were covered in muck."

Freddie backed toward the door. "Take a bath, Bonnie. You stink. I told Smith to send food here. We'll leave as soon as we're all properly outfitted." He turned and left, closing the door behind him with a soft *click*.

Exhaustion settled over her. She wasn't even insulted that he told her she smelled — after lifting an armpit to check, she recoiled. He was right. She was in no state to rescue anyone.

She took a quick bath, scrubbing hard to remove all the dirt and grime from the past few days. From the past few weeks, really.

And then she sat on the bed and waited to rescue her brother. Or kill her father. She wasn't really bothered which came first.

CHAPTER THIRTY-FIVE

"PROBLEM?" FREDDIE ASKED UNDER HIS BREATH. DRESSED IN blue, he exuded casual elegance, and Bonnie saw more than one person admire him as they traveled down the main thoroughfare.

She adjusted the collar of her borrowed servant's uniform. After seeing the horrible dress options — she did *not* enjoy the latest fashion trends, she decided — they felt Bonnie would be better off entering the castle as a member of staff. As proven in Navian, people ignored the hired help. She would be invisible.

This uniform was a much better fit than the stolen one she had worn when she snuck into Freddie's bedchamber the night she met him. "I didn't think I'd be wearing one of these anytime soon," she grumbled. She discreetly checked to make sure that her braid covered her scar, paranoid that someone would see it and pay more attention to her.

He huffed a laugh. "You look pretty, you know. I don't think I told you that when we first met."

"You didn't think it would be a good idea to flirt with the rebel who wanted to assassinate you?"

"I did not."

"Smart man. Not smart enough to avoid getting tangled up with me in the end, though."

Bonnie didn't hear his response; her mouth had suddenly gone dry at the sight of the castle looming ahead. She stopped in her tracks, and it took Freddie a few seconds to realize she hadn't followed him.

He walked back to where she stood, frowning. "You don't have to come. We can figure out another plan."

Bonnie shook her head and continued walking. "But who would play your new, loyal servant?" she teased, forcing a smile onto her face. "Bronwyn?"

"Bronwyn isn't allowed within a mile of the castle, for her safety," he said. "Plus, there's the whole blind thing. People know Jasper, and Simon wouldn't be caught dead in a servant uniform. You're the best option, honeybum."

"Lucky me."

Guards stood at the entryway to the castle gates, backs straight, hands on swords. Their keen eyes constantly moved over the group of people gathered before them.

About two dozen people lobbied to get inside the castle. A few were let in — servants with the correct paperwork, low-ranking members of the nobility, couriers of the king. The others grumbled their displeasure, annoyed at the inconvenience.

"They're on alert," Freddie murmured as they pushed their way past displeased civilians. "Looks like only those with high-level clearance are being allowed in right now."

Bonnie hid her smirk as a well-dressed young woman in a ridiculous feathered hat glared at one of the guards.

"What do you mean I'm not allowed in?!" she gasped. "I'm here every day. Let me in!" When the guard refused to give her entry, the woman said something nasty.

"Good afternoon, Lord Stonewood," a different guard said,

his lips twitching as he watched the woman shriek at his counterpart. "Meeting with the king today?"

"Gods, no," Freddie said with a laugh. "Not today, at least. I need to see my father. How are you doing, Givens? How is your family?"

The older guard smiled. "I'm doing well, milord, as is my family. I thank you for inquiring after them." The guard jerked his head toward the entrance to the castle. "Please go in, milord, before Lady Fiona sees you. She's been trying to enter all morning."

Freddie smiled and clapped Givens on the shoulder goodnaturedly. "Thank you, my friend." He hesitated before lowering his voice. "Why is there an increase in security? Something I should know about?"

Givens coughed and then shook his head. "Increase in rebel activity. We're just being careful, milord. Nothing to worry about."

Freddie nodded and moved past, Bonnie trailing behind. She could feel Givens' eyes travel over her. Not creepily, but in a way that told her he wouldn't forget who she was anytime soon. She aimed a polite smile at the ground as she passed through the gate.

"Are you on a first name basis with all of the King's Guards?" she hissed when they were out of earshot.

"Only a few. Why do you think I was adamant we waited until now to come?"

He *had* been pushy about their timing, Bonnie thought. "How do you know him so well?"

"He used to work the night shift. Helped me sort out . . . *issues* involving Jas a few times. We bonded over books — he used to read to keep himself awake during his shift. I helped him secure a morning shift for his discretion."

Bonnie snorted. "It figures that the Lord of Libraries would bond with a seasoned member of the King's Guard."

"It pays to have friends in different places."

Bonnie wondered who else Freddie had befriended. And if she needed to watch out for them.

Looking at the castle before them, she gasped.

It wasn't the sight of the stone entryway that led into the castle, or the grand statue of the king, face turned towards the sun, that triggered the first flashback.

It was a chip in one of the stone bricks that lined the corridor.

A childish shriek of joy, followed by the sense of something heavy flying through the air. A thud when the object hit the wall, and then the ground, breaking off part of the stone brick with it.

Bonnie gripped Freddie's arm, cloaks hiding the movement, to let him know she wasn't entirely present. They had prepared for this. Talked through what to do if she remembered something.

"Almost there," he said.

She blinked a few times and shook her head to clear the sensation. Bonnie couldn't afford to be distracted. Not today.

Freddie kept near. If anyone thought it was strange that Lord Stonewood was walking close to his servant, no one said. He probably wasn't the only noble in the castle who was a little too familiar with the young female help.

They didn't run into many others. The castle really must be on lockdown, Bonnie thought, as they passed another set of guards patrolling the corridor. The courtiers they passed seemed wary. Distant. Almost as if they were nervous to be seen talking to anyone.

Bonnie was only startled by one additional flashback — an old, woven tapestry conjured feelings of joy — before they made it to their destination: the set of rooms dedicated to the King's Advisor. They would use those rooms as their base of operations while they figured out how to free Felix.

Freddie entered his father's chambers without knocking, nodding at the guards stationed at the door.

And then stopped abruptly, too fast for Bonnie. Bumping into Freddie felt like bumping into a brick wall.

"Wha—?" she exclaimed. She peered around his broad back, trying to see what had caused his sudden stop.

"Father?"

"Frederick? What are you doing here?"

Duke Alistair Stonewood stood from his seat in an over-sized armchair, putting down a sheath of papers on a nearby table. They were in an entry room, and several doors led to other parts of the suite. He was alone.

"I could ask you the same thing," Freddie said, striding over. He gave the older man a hug. "I thought you were staying in Navian now that the weather was turning."

"I thought so, too, but then —" Duke Alistair broke off, his honey-colored eyes widening when he looked at Bonnie. His face — so similar to his younger son's, except with the same hair color as Jasper — turned white as the blood drained from his face.

Freddie felt him freeze. He took a step back, hands still on his shoulders. "Father? What's wrong?" Freddie turned his head, following his father's gaze. "Bonnie?"

Bonnie stood frozen. She blinked rapidly, trying to figure out what was happening. She wasn't having a specific flashback, although she understood, deep down, that she knew this man. Had spent time with him — a lot of time — before she lost her memory.

Seeing this man, seeing Freddie's father, had overloaded her senses completely.

"You . . ." Duke Alistair whispered, and the sound sent chills down Bonnie's arms. "You were *dead*." His voice cracked on the last word. "We couldn't find your body, but things were so chaotic after . . . after . . ." He trailed off.

"Father? How do you know Bonnie?" Freddie took a step back, settling himself in between the two of them.

Duke Alistair shook his head. "That's not her name." His eyes searched Bonnie's face, taking in every detail.

"What's my name?" Bonnie whispered. Was this how she was going to find out who she was? After twelve years of wondering, was this the moment she would learn her true identity?

"Where have you been?" His face looked pained, and he seemed to sway on the spot. Just as Freddie reached over to brace him, the man bolted.

"Father!" Freddie yelled, as Duke Alistair ran past Bonnie and out the door.

Bonnie and Freddie only had time to lock eyes before they turned and followed him.

"Father, wait!" Freddie yelled as he trailed the elder Stonewood.

Freddie's father ran as though a demon possessed him.

Bonnie didn't have time to register any of the memories that flooded back, even as they threatened to overwhelm her. This wasn't the first time she had run this route, she was sure of it.

How did Duke Alistair know her? And why did he look as though he had seen a ghost?

"We're going to . . . the throne room?" Freddie huffed as they ran.

Freddie's father was nearing the end of the corridor, and had to choose whether to go left or right. Right led to the throne room, where King Aborn held dinners, feasts, and other events for his court. A memory of sitting in an uncomfortable dress, forced to sit off to the side in immense boredom, flashed through Bonnie.

"No," Bonnie said, surprising herself. "To the receiving room."

Freddie shot her a look as they turned the corner. Bonnie was right — Duke Alistair was heading towards the king's private meeting room.

There were several guards standing in front of the receiving room doors, but they moved out of the way at the sight of Duke Alistair flying down the hallway. They must have recognized Freddie, too, for they made no move to stop him either.

Bonnie was an unknown entity — they jumped into action right before she crossed the threshold, grabbing her by the arms to stop her from entering.

"No!" she cried out as she jerked backwards. "Please!"

Freddie stumbled to a halt. "Let her in," he ordered.

By the time Bonnie shrugged them off, she saw Duke Alistair across the room, panting as he whispered into someone's ear.

Bonnie gasped when she locked eyes with the burly man who sat in an ornate golden chair.

The King of Hallordis looked at Bonnie Blackthorn with wide eyes.

Eyes that were almost as familiar to Bonnie as her own.

She watched his face drain of color, and she imagined her own looked the same.

"Charlotte?" he whispered, his voice hoarse.

Then King Rupert Aborn, the man Bonnie was taught to hate and fear, lurched to his feet, stumbled to the side, and threw up onto the stone floor.

CHAPTER THIRTY-SIX

CHARLOTTE.

A sense of rightness washed over her, followed by a wave of dizziness.

Memories started falling into place. It was as if her name — her true name, her rightful name — was the missing piece of the puzzle.

She stumbled backward, throwing out her arms for balance. Freddie was by her side in an instant, his powerful arm bracing her. She leaned on him, mind spinning with what the king just told her.

What her *father* just told her.

Charlotte. Princess Charlotte Aborn.

She was a princess?

Freddie's mouth was open, his eyes wide, as he looked between Bonnie and the king. His keen eyes were no doubt trying to spot the similarities between them, the familial characteristics that should have told him who he had been traveling with.

How could he have missed it?

But Charlotte — Charlie, to her close friends and family — had always favored her mother.

Her rich brown hair and strong nose were the only features she shared with her father. Separate, it would've been almost impossible to connect the two.

But in the same room for the first time in over a decade?

Only a blind man would deny the fact that these two were blood kin.

It explained so much.

It explained why she could understand other languages — her childhood was spent with scores of tutors from all over the continent.

And it explained why depictions of the royal family had been ripped out of the books in the rebel library. It wasn't to hide the connection between Gwendolyn and the king.

It was to make sure that nobody figured out that *the heir to the kingdom was living among them the entire time.*

Who knew? Surely others had to know.

Felix knew. Or had figured it out. Right before she left, he tried to tell her something — tried to warn her back at Stoneforge. What was that book he was reading? *The History of Hallordis.* Bonnie had been too focused on the fact she could read the title to consider *why* he had been reading such a book.

If it had contained pictures of what King Aborn looked like, what his late wife looked like, his late daughter . . . would he have put the pieces together? He was smart enough to figure it out, she was sure of it.

The king wiped his mouth with the back of his broad hand and walked over to her. Gone were the wide eyes, though he still regarded her warily. The color had returned to his cheeks, at least.

He reached out a hand that shook, and on his ring finger was a large sapphire ring. Bonnie flinched, and he stopped short of touching her. He shook his head as if to clear it. "Charlie . . . is that really you?"

Bonnie blinked. She *knew* that voice. Knew its warmth, its love. She had spent years hearing it, cherishing it.

Still . . .

"I don't know," she whispered. "I don't remember."

"You don't remember? Where have you been all this time?"

"I —"

A knock at the door. A slim man stuck his head in the room. "Pardon me, Your Majesty. I have news."

Just wait until he finds out about what's going on in here, Bonnie thought.

At the king's nod, the man went to him. He whispered something in his ear, and Bonnie saw a look of confusion flash across the king's face. He dismissed the man — likely his steward — with a nod.

The king turned back to her, as if in a trance, unable to take his eyes off her. "Alistair," he addressed the Duke without looking at him. "I need your help."

"Anything, Rupert. You name it."

"Take Charlotte and Frederick — take them somewhere safe. I need them far away from the meeting. I'll join you as soon as I am able."

"Of course, Your Majesty." Duke Alistair moved forward toward where Bonnie and Freddie stood.

"Wait," Freddie said. "Your Majesty — are you talking about the meeting with Oll Blackthorn?"

"Good gods," the king sighed, rolling his eyes towards the ceiling in what Bonnie thought was a very unking-like gesture. "Does everyone know about this godsdamned meeting?"

"By design, Rupert," the Duke said. "The rebels want people to know about it as a layer of protection. If you agreed to a meeting in good faith and then something happened, it would cause an uproar."

The way he said it made Bonnie feel as though they had discussed this many times.

"It's not just Oll meeting with me this time," the king said, eyes thoughtful. "He's bringing his wife to the meeting."

Bonnie's eyes widened in shock.

"*Both* of them?" Freddie asked. He looked at Bonnie in concern.

Back in Crown Harbor she overheard the guards talking about Oll meeting with the king. But not *her*. How could she come here, of all places, considering who she truly was?

Aborn looked at Bonnie, eyebrow raised, before leveling a look at Freddie. "Yes, both of them. They arrived separately, and she demanded to be put in a different room. Lover's spat, I guess. Why? What's wrong?"

Bonnie finally found her voice. "Blackthorn. The name I was given is Bonnie Blackthorn. Oll Blackthorn and Gwendolyn Hatherall adopted me and raised me as their own."

The Duke's mouth dropped open, followed by the king's.

"Did you say . . . *Gwendolyn Hatherall*?"

"Yes."

"Gwendolyn is dead — has been dead for years," Duke Alistair said, shaking his head. "I saw her body after the attack . . . what are you saying? That she's alive? I don't understand."

"It appears the dead don't stay dead, Father," Freddie said drily. "It's a long story, and we'd be happy to tell you about it, but it doesn't seem like we have time right now."

The king stared at Bonnie. "You were raised by Gwendolyn Hatherall? In the Amlucen? You were raised by your aunt?"

Bonnie stilled, blinking a few times. She was still reeling from the revelation that she was Charlotte Aborn; she hadn't thought about what it meant about her relationship with her adopted mother.

Through the stolen letters, she had known that Gwendolyn

had killed Queen Annabeth with poison. And that Gwendolyn had killed Bonnie's mother as well.

Bonnie just hadn't realized that the two women — the queen and Bonnie's mother — were one and the same.

If Bonnie thought Gwendolyn was fucked up before, it was nothing compared to reality.

They shared the same green eyes, Bonnie realized. The one facial feature Gwendolyn hadn't disfigured. People had found it uncanny but reasoned that it was a random coincidence. They weren't the only people in the country with green eyes.

But it wasn't a coincidence, because Gwendolyn was Bonnie's aunt by blood.

Numbly, Bonnie nodded. "I — I didn't know who she was. Until recently, that is. I . . ." she trailed off and reached a shaking hand to brush the scar on her temple.

"She lost all her memories prior to Vale Magicae," Freddie explained. "They're only starting to come back now."

"She killed my mother," Bonnie blurted. "Poisoned her, and then took me when she realized I was still alive. We have letters of correspondence confirming it."

"Annabeth?" the king whispered.

He took a step back and looked like he was about to crumple to the ground. Had the Duke not stepped forward to put a hand on his shoulder, supporting him like Freddie was supporting Bonnie, he may have fallen. "We never knew . . . *She's* the one who killed my wife?"

Bonnie nodded and felt tears spring to her eyes.

She hadn't expected to mourn the loss of her mother — until her dream last night, she hadn't remembered anything about her. But seeing the love and anguish on his face brought forward a rush of emotions she had trouble ignoring.

For the first time, Bonnie saw him not as the king, but as her father.

The Duke squeezed his shoulder. "Easy, Rupert. There will

be a time to process this — to mourn and grieve again. To talk things through and get the full story. But right now you need to be king."

Aborn blinked a few times, and Bonnie saw him shove the emotions down to a place where they wouldn't overwhelm him.

Maybe it wasn't a skill she had learned from the Amlucen after all, she thought. Maybe she had learned it at her father's knee.

"I've met with Oll Blackthorn throughout the years, but never with *her*," he said. "My spies told me that his wife ran the rebellion as an equal partner, but this is the first time she's been in Midverd. I always thought they didn't want to risk both of their leaders meeting with me . . . now I'm guessing they didn't want me to figure out who she really was."

"Why risk it now, though?" Freddie asked. "Surely she knew that you'd recognize her, even disfigured. *I* recognized her, and I only met her when she had visited Navian the one time."

Her father shook his head. "I don't know. Maybe she thinks I've forgotten her. Or maybe she wants to unsettle me."

Either option sounded plausible to Bonnie. Still, though, the risk . . .

"Felix," she said, an idea forming. "You have Felix Blackthorn in your dungeons, correct? Maybe he has something to do with why she's risking revelation. Maybe she wants you to release him."

Freddie shook his head. "She tried to murder Felix the last time she saw him. I can't imagine she's trying to reunite the family now."

"I think Felix figured out who I was," she pushed. "Maybe she realized that, too. Maybe she came here to silence him."

Because if Felix knew the truth — not only that Bonnie was the dead Princess Charlotte, but that Gwyneth was in fact Gwendolyn Hatherall, it would mean the end of the rebellion.

Something nagged at her, though.

Bonnie would've thought that Gwendolyn would be long gone by now, shoring up her defenses against the king and his armies. *Especially* if she thought he had found out who had been leading the rebellion all these years. The last thing Bonnie would do was waltz back to the scene of the crime.

If Bonnie was Gwendolyn, she would get as far away as she could from King Rupert Aborn.

So why was she here?

Freddie's father looked at the king. "We're running out of time — the meeting is soon. Should we reschedule?"

Her father shook his head. "No — it would show weakness. We keep the meeting as scheduled."

"At least now we won't be caught unaware. If — *when* — Gwendolyn reveals herself, you'll be prepared."

"Small mercies," the king said under his breath.

"Can we sit in on the meeting?" Bonnie asked. "I want to see what Oll has to say. I can let you know if he's lying or not."

Half a dozen emotions crossed the king's face, and Bonnie was sure he was going to say no. She wouldn't blame him if he did.

But he surprised her when he turned to the Duke. "Outfit them in guard's gear. Empty the throne room and move the meeting there. Keep her out of sight. Frederick, too."

The Duke nodded and, with a parting look, left the room by a side door.

Her father raised a shaky hand and ran his fingers through his hair. "We have a lot to talk about," he said, looking at Bonnie. "I can't imagine what you've been through. What they told you about me. I hope . . . I hope when this is over, you'll spend some time here. Get to know me and your siblings."

"Oh. Right. We'll see."

She'd forgotten that he remarried and had two more children — he needed to continue the royal family line, after all.

Thinking about them was the last thing she felt like doing at the moment.

He looked crestfallen, but schooled his face into a mask of calm. A moment later, a knock sounded at the door, and two servants carrying armfuls of gear entered the room.

"Two sets of armor, Your Majesty," his steward announced from his place in the doorway. "Hopefully they should fit your . . . visitors." He looked pointedly at Bonnie and Freddie, obviously displeased he'd been kept out of the loop.

"Thank you, Stiles. I'll fill you in later. Is the throne room prepared?"

The man sniffed, but nodded in affirmation. Freddie and Bonnie began strapping on various pieces of equipment.

"Good, good. Thank you. How are our guests?"

"Surrounded by guards and agitated at being kept waiting, Your Majesty."

"Perfect. Give it five more minutes and then bring him to the throne room. I'll meet them there. Frederick and Char — *Bonnie* will get in position now."

Bonnie straightened, moving her shoulders to adjust to the weight of the armor. It was too big, but she didn't think she would look out of place as long as she stayed out of their line of sight. She made sure the knife in her pocket was within easy reach, as well as the one strapped to her ankle.

She looked over at Freddie and blinked. The shoulder plates sat snug on his broad shoulders, and the forearm vambraces were, if anything, too small.

It wasn't a crime to appreciate the view, she decided, as she tried to ignore the stirring in her lower belly. Apparently, she had a thing for a man in a uniform.

"Hmm?" he asked, looking over at her. He grinned when he realized she was staring. "Like what you see, princess?" he teased, and flexed his bicep.

Bonnie swallowed hard and shook her head. "Didn't know if you were smart enough to put it on correctly, is all."

"I'm sure, princess." He winked.

"Stop calling me that," she snapped.

The king's steward coughed from the doorway. "Ready, Lord Stonewood? Lady . . . ?" he trailed off.

Bonnie jumped. Freddie smirked as he nodded, gesturing for Bonnie to take the lead.

She tried to emulate a guard's swagger as she followed the steward out of the room but felt foolish. The armor wasn't comfortable, and it was hard to see out of the visor. But if it was hard for her to see out of it, she figured, it would be hard to see into it, too.

Hopefully they wouldn't recognize her. This was the last place in Hallordis they would expect to find her.

She doubted Oll and Gwendolyn would be foolish enough to pull any tricks — it would be suicide. Then again, it was suicidal to meet with the king in the first place.

Gwendolyn had been practically foaming at the mouth the last time Bonnie had seen her . . . maybe she wasn't in her right mind anymore. Maybe losing Bonnie had been what finally sent her over the edge.

Especially because Bonnie now knew all of her secrets.

She stumbled when she crossed the threshold into the large ornate room. It had hardly changed in the twelve years she had been gone — the same throne sat at the end of the long, rectangular room, and the same gold and blue window hangings brightened the space. Memories of courtiers in their finery, of string quartets and endless hours of waltzing, flashed through her mind. And the feeling of boredom that she often felt, stuck in the corner on her best behavior.

She blinked away memories of her aunt standing near her, dressed in finery but completely out of place. Even at a young age Bonnie wondered why Gwendolyn always frowned when Bonnie's mother was near.

Now she knew; her aunt was *jealous*.

"Easy, princess," Freddie murmured. She jabbed him with her elbow.

She followed his lead, and they situated themselves about halfway down the room. Freddie positioned her next to one of the columns that lined the space, telling her to duck behind it if she thought that Oll or Gwendolyn noticed her.

The king entered through a door behind the throne, eyes searching for Bonnie. Their eyes locked, and he looked away. Two guards flanked him, hands on their swords.

She heard the door open and turned her head.

And then watched as her adopted father entered the throne room of her birth father.

OLL SWAGGERED FORWARD WITH THE ARROGANCE OF A MAN WHO believed he owned the entire world.

He was dressed in the same outfit he wore whenever he was trying to impress, but the horrible fur coat looked worse for wear. She could tell he was hurting — there were dark circles under his eyes, and he walked with a pronounced limp. And he was pale — far paler than normal.

Something was wrong.

Bonnie held her breath, waiting for Gwendolyn to walk in behind him. Of *course* she delayed her entrance. Probably an attempt to increase the shock factor of her reveal.

Little did she know the king was already up to speed. Somewhat, at least. Bonnie wondered how he would feel once he learned the true extent of Gwendolyn's treachery, both in the royal family and in the rebellion.

Her heart thumped wildly as Oll passed by, and it took all of her willpower not to lunge forward and stab him for every-thing he had done.

But he didn't give her a second of his attention. All of his focus was on the king in front of him. The rightful king, not the one that Oll pretended to be.

Oll stopped about ten feet before the throne. He probably would've gone farther if the guards hadn't taken a step towards him, hands on swords.

Stopping short, Oll gave the king a deep nod.

Bonnie had to hold back a snort at the sheer gall and arro-gance, even though she wasn't the least bit surprised. She glanced towards the double doors, which servants were now closing.

Where was Gwendolyn?

The doors closed with a soft *click*. The king looked between Oll and the door several times, his thoughts in sync with Bonnie's.

"Oll Blackthorn," he boomed, and Bonnie almost jumped at the authority in his voice.

There was no doubt who commanded all the power here. Oll never commanded even half as much, even when giving entire speeches.

And the king only said *two words*.

"Where is your wife?"

Bonnie couldn't see Oll's face, but she heard his confusion. "Gwyneth? No idea. The bitch stabbed me and ran off. I hope she's rotting in the ground somewhere."

Bonnie inhaled sharply. She knew Gwendolyn hated Oll — despised him, even. But why had she stabbed him?

The king's eyebrows raised a fraction, the only expression of surprise he allowed.

"I was told she was going to be here today," he said slowly. "Are you saying she's not here?"

Bonnie blinked, and realized why he had asked the same question in two different ways.

His steward had said that Oll and Gwendolyn arrived separately. But the steward didn't know who she really was — he hadn't been told that the dead queen's sister had finally returned home.

If Gwendolyn and Oll weren't speaking . . . why was she here?

And more importantly — where was she now?

"I —" Oll stumbled, and Bonnie knew how much it irked him not to be in charge. "I never sent word that she would be joining me. Your Majesty," he added as an afterthought.

The king's eyes snapped to hers. His gaze lingered only a moment, but it was long enough for Bonnie to know that he was thinking the same thing.

Bonnie squeezed Freddie's arm and walked to one of the side doors. He followed behind, and the door closed with a soft *click* behind him.

In an empty corridor, Bonnie blew out a breath. "I don't think Oll noticed us."

"Me neither. But Bonnie — why did we leave? He just got there."

"We need to find Gwendolyn. I think she's loose in the castle."

CHAPTER THIRTY-SEVEN

THEY RAN.

"Where do we start?" Freddie asked as they neared the end of the corridor.

"The steward. He said he put them in different rooms — he'll know where she is."

She hoped. It was as good a place as any to begin their search.

They doubled back to the receiving room and found it empty. The same guards were posted outside, though, and looked at them with wary expressions.

"Do you know where Stiles is?" Freddie asked.

Bonnie panted, hands on her knees. The armor was *heavy*. She took it off.

"No, my lord," one of the guards responded. "We haven't seen him since he left."

"Do you have any idea where he would put someone who was waiting for a meeting with the king? Which room?"

"That Oll Blackthorn scum was put in the Blue Room." Bonnie blinked away memories of a room decorated only in blue colors.

"Yes, we know," Freddie interjected. "Where else would Stiles put someone?"

"Try the White Room," said the other guard. "I've been stationed there before."

Bonnie and Freddie thanked them, and then bolted.

"You lead," she told Freddie, as they started running once more.

"Are any more of your memories coming back?"

"Constantly," she confirmed. "Not memories, exactly. Just a nagging feeling that I've been here before."

He huffed, probably saving his breath as he led her up one stone staircase and down another. After a few more turns they jolted to a stop outside of one of the many rooms that lined a wide corridor.

Freddie went to open the door.

"Wait," Bonnie said, reaching out to stop him. She pointed to a smear of blood, almost too small to notice, under the handle. Drawing her knife, she held it with a practiced hand. Breathing deeply in, out, in, out, she entered into her killing calm.

Freddie took out his own knife. He jerked his chin toward the door and stepped back.

Opening the door as quietly as she could, she crept forward and peered inside.

There was blood everywhere.

It stained the ornate white rug, the gold-patterned couch, the white-cream wallpaper. Pillows were slashed and vases were smashed, their broken pieces littering the floor like fallen leaves in autumn.

Three guards had fallen, all covered in blood. Their eyes stared sightlessly at the ceiling, chests unmoving. The king's steward lay sprawled against the couch.

"Shit," Bonnie said, running towards him.

Blood leaked from wounds on his chest, and his eyes were

wild with pain and fear. She crouched next to him, and Freddie swore as he joined her.

"What happened?" she asked, checking his wounds.

He inhaled sharply, obviously in pain. "Gwyneth Black-thorn," he wheezed. "Killed the others. Thought she killed me. Ran off."

"How long ago?"

"Not sure. Ten minutes, maybe."

Freddie lay his hands on Stiles's chest. He closed his eyes, grunting in frustration. "I can't heal him."

"The wounds seem shallow. There may be hope for him yet." She turned to the steward. "Did she say anything before she left? Where she was going?" The castle was enormous — blindly searching would take hours, and the possibility of Gwendolyn escaping increased every minute.

"Magic," he wheezed. "She said something about . . . magic."

Magic?

Bonnie looked at Freddie, who took his eyes off of Stiles long enough to give her a helpless look.

Think, Bonnie, think.

She grew up with the madwoman — knew her better than most. Even though her confidence in that relationship was shattered, Bonnie still *knew* her. Where did her adopted mother and magic intersect?

Vale Magicae.

Vale Magicae was the last day that Gwendolyn was in the castle — the day that she killed Bonnie's mother. And almost killed Bonnie, only to spare her.

Could that be the connection?

"I know where she is," Bonnie whispered.

"Where?"

"My childhood bedchamber."

"What? How do you know that?"

Her mind raced. "The last time she was here was on Vale

Magicae. Hear me out — back at the cottage, Bronwyn said she believed the Amlucen attack was the reason magic disappeared. What if she was right?"

"What? Bonnie, that doesn't —"

She cut him off. "All these years, my — my *father* could've put a stop to the Amlucen," she said. "Oll and Gwendolyn knew it. *I* knew it. They did their best to hide it, but I knew our numbers were low. We were weak. My father could've stopped the Amlucen, but chose to meet with Oll in secret an untold number of times instead. Why?"

"I don't know, Bonnie," Freddie said. "Maybe Oll had something the king wanted. Leverage of some sort."

"Oll is a psychotic imbecile. The smartest thing he's ever done was align himself with Gwendolyn."

"Maybe Oll was her puppet, then. Gwendolyn knew she couldn't face the king herself for fear of being discovered. Maybe she sent Oll in her place."

It tracked with what Bonnie knew about the woman who raised her. Gwendolyn always let the others do her dirty work while she did who-knows-what on her frequent trips to Suverd.

"Why do you think she's in your childhood bedchamber?"

"It's where it all began. She knows her days as a free woman are numbered, with Felix captured and Oll on the loose. Because if my father finally found out who was responsible for the murder of his wife and, well, *me* . . . " she trailed off. "It didn't matter what leverage she had. There was no way he'd let her live."

"So . . . what?" Freddie still looked confused. "That still doesn't explain why she'd come here. Why risk it, after all this time?"

Bonnie knew what she said next would sound crazy, but it made sense to her in a strange, distorted way. "Because I think Gwendolyn is the reason magic fled. Think about it —" she said, holding up a hand to stop Freddie from interrupting. "In the letters we decoded, there were missives about discoveries made around the continent. It doesn't say *what* those discoveries were, but what if they figured out how to stop the king and his armies from using magic against the Amlucen?"

"Then those with magic would no longer be in power," Freddie said, catching on. "The rebels could take over if they were on equal playing ground."

"Exactly. No more hierarchy, just like they wanted. Except my father was able to hold on to the throne, despite the loss. Oll and Gwendolyn should've pressed their advantage, but they were drunk on power and relied on weak leaders."

"But why does she want to restore power now? Wouldn't that give the king control over the lands once more? Everyone would get their magic back, not just the rebels."

"I don't know . . . maybe she's hoping that she can slip away in the chaos. She's not exactly sane, is she? She may not have a logical reason for any of this."

"Still . . ."

Bonnie froze as she recalled something that had been bothering her for some time. "Oh, no."

"What?"

"Those rebels . . . the ones in Stoneforge. The ones locked away, hidden. The strange ones."

Freddie sucked in a breath. "You don't think . . . ?"

"They spoke in Suverian. It might be a coincidence, but . . . Suverd is one of the last countries with magic. What if . . . what if those people can wield magic? They were at Stoneforge for a reason. I saw those strange devices . . . What if they're some sort of magic weapon? What if Oll and Gwendolyn are raising a magical army against the king?"

Freddie sucked in a breath. "That would mean she'd know that magic could return to Hallordis. Unless she was trying to launch an attack on Suverd —"

"Highly unlikely," Bonnie broke in. The woman spent almost half her time in that country.

"Yes, highly unlikely. But how would she know how to stop magic in the first place? Or how to bring it back?"

"Does it matter how? I need to go find her. Now."

"Wait — what do you plan on doing? You can't go alone."

"I don't know. Subdue her? Kill her? She's a monster."

"You can't go alone," he repeated, and then looked helplessly at Stiles. While the bleeding from his chest had slowed, blood still leaked sluggishly from under Freddie's fingers. He couldn't leave, not without killing the man.

"You need to stay here — he'll die without you. I'll be fine. Trained killer, remember?"

"She's your mother," he reminded her, his voice gentle. "It may not be as easy as you think."

"*Adopted* mother," Bonnie corrected, but gave him a nod to acknowledge what he was saying. His concern was valid, yes. But the bitch who raised her had a lot coming to her.

"I'll be fine." She had to be.

He said nothing. Stiles gave a shuddering gasp, and Freddie turned back to him. "Go. I'll be there as soon as I can."

"If I see anyone else I'll send them to get a physician," she said, as she went to the door.

"Bonnie?"

She stopped at the threshold, turning back to look at him.

"Be careful," he said, his voice deep and eyes full of concern.

Swallowing, she nodded and made her way out of the room.

It was time to kill her mother.

CHAPTER THIRTY-EIGHT

SHE RAN AS IF SHE WAS IN A DREAM.

It took Bonnie no time at all to recall the way back to her bedchamber. It was strange, running down the same corridors she knew little Charlotte Aborn would've used thousands of times.

Things had changed since those days of peace and innocence. Charlotte Aborn was dead, murdered the night of Vale Magicae.

Bonnie Blackthorn was a survivor. She could never go back to the life of a pampered princess.

Bonnie slowed as she neared the last corridor, all senses on alert. The only sound was her own labored breathing. She was alone.

Entering her killing calm, Bonnie breathed in and out, in and out. Palming one of her knives, she rounded the corner.

And stopped in her tracks.

A sense of déjà vu washed over her as she faced the door of her childhood bedchamber. It felt like she was reliving her nightmare all over again.

This time, though, she was much better prepared.

Heart pounding, she neared the door on silent feet. The door was cracked open, and she shook her head to clear the wave of dizziness that washed over her.

A woman's voice floated through the doorway, and Bonnie felt goosebumps rise on her forearms.

Gwendolyn.

The older woman was chanting in some sort of tongue, one that Bonnie couldn't understand. No one responded, and Bonnie knew instinctively that Gwendolyn was alone.

Creeping forward, she peered around the heavy wooden door. A cloaked figure stood in the middle of the room, back turned to her. There were strange markings on the floor, written in dark red ink. The same ones from Bonnie's dream.

Bonnie glanced around the room, taking in every detail.

It looked exactly as she had remembered, as if her father had ordered the room completely untouched. The bookcase in the corner, filled to the brim with books and papers? The same. The toy chest by the oversized wardrobe? The same. Even the food and water bowls that Bonnie left out for her little animal friends were still there, now empty and pristine.

Gwendolyn, cloaked in black, hadn't noticed Bonnie standing in the doorway. She leaned over, hand outstretched, and made another strange mark on the floor. The red ink she used stained the ground. Light from the nearby torch danced off it, and Bonnie realized in horror that it wasn't ink.

It was blood.

Bonnie swallowed hard. Who did she kill this time to get the blood for this rite? It hadn't been her mother's blood all those years ago — she had been poisoned.

Had Gwendolyn used Bonnie's blood the first time? Was that the blood Gwendolyn had kept in her bag? Bile rose in her throat.

Gwendolyn turned, eyes widening when she saw Bonnie. As fast as a snake, she threw a dagger towards the doorway.

Bonnie ducked, and the blade embedded itself in the door right where her head had been moments before.

"*You*," Gwendolyn hissed. She fumbled in the inner pocket of her cloak, no doubt searching for another knife.

Bonnie dove to the side as a dagger flew through the air. It clattered to the ground somewhere behind her.

A third one flew too fast to dodge, and Bonnie hissed as it sliced open her forearm. Her blood raced down her arm, creating a small puddle on the floor.

Hopefully it wasn't laced with poison.

"Hello, Aunt," Bonnie purred, sliding into a fighting stance as she ignored the pain. The hand that grasped her knife held steady. "It's been, what? Twelve years since we stood here last? Look at us. Full circle."

Gwendolyn's scarred face twisted into a sneer. "So you finally figured it out, huh? I wondered if you'd ever be able to regain your memories."

"The head wound at Thornwick did it," Bonnie said as she circled around the older woman. "It seemed to realign everything inside my brain. Want to know what I remember?"

Gwendolyn didn't respond, but Bonnie could tell by the glint in her eyes that she was interested. Still, the older woman palmed another knife while she pivoted to follow Bonnie.

"I remember things in bits and pieces," she continued. "Sometimes I remember events. Sometimes I remember feelings — joy, pain, fear, things like that. I remember *you*."

"What about me?"

"I remember feeling unsettled by you. Wary. You always lingered on the side, close to the action but separate. A lurker. Out of place."

"I was not out of place. I was watchful. I was regal," Gwendolyn countered, a flush rising to her cheeks. "I belonged in the seat of power."

"You were *jealous*," Bonnie spat. "Power hungry. You wanted what my mother had — you wanted to be *queen*. And when my father didn't choose you it hurt, didn't it? Did it hurt that he chose your baby sister over you?"

Gwendolyn's lip curled, and the knuckles holding the knife turned white. "Your mother was weak. Soft. She didn't deserve the power she wielded. She didn't deserve to be queen."

"But you did? You think mighty highly of yourself."

Gwendolyn didn't rise to the bait, but kept her mouth shut. Bonnie could tell by the way her mutilated face reddened that she was close to losing her temper.

Angry opponents made mistakes. Gwendolyn taught her that.

"So you joined the Amlucen," Bonnie continued. "Thought you'd try your hand at being queen some other way. Gwendolyn Hatherall, Queen of the Rebels. Maybe you'd end up being queen of all of Hallordis, too, if you killed the king."

Gwendolyn said nothing, though the hand holding her knife twitched.

"Why did you kill Oren? Why turn on the man you loved?"

"Oh, please. I never loved Oren. That man was just like my sister. Too soft to do what needed to be done."

The older woman said this so confidently, so sure of herself, that Bonnie blinked. She didn't think she was lying.

Was it true? Gwendolyn hated Oll; she only put up with him because he was the face of the Amlucen. His notoriety allowed her to stay behind the scenes, away from the watchful eyes of her former brother-in-law.

"I read your letters — it seemed like you were in love with him. Obsessive, even." Lie — Bonnie only had access to Oren's letters. Hopefully Gwendolyn fell for it.

Gwendolyn raised an eyebrow, the movement disturbing her scars. "No. I could never love someone like Oren. Or Oll. Not when I lo—" she broke off, and shook her head. "I used them. Both of them."

Bonnie blinked. "To do what? The Amlucen never took over. My father still holds all the power. What good was any of it?"

"You fail to see the big picture, *Charlotte*. Maybe I didn't want Aborn to lose power."

Bonnie cocked an eyebrow. "No? So are you officially admitting the rebellion is a lie, then? You want him in power?"

"Yes, you fool. Tell me, what happens when daddy dearest takes over another land?"

"What is this, a history lesson?"

A sneer. "Humor me."

"That country loses its magic."

"Exactly. Tell me, my dear niece, if he knows this, why does he continue to conquer other territories?"

"You taught us that it was because he was power hungry. That he was angry at the others for holding onto their magic. He wanted to seek justice for what he had lost." Bonnie cackled. "You taught us — you taught *me* — that he hated magic because his wife and daughter were killed on the night magic disappeared. When all along, *I was right there, staring back at you.*"

"You lived. Thrived, even. Don't be ungrateful — I could've killed you. Or left you for dead."

Bonnie was rendered speechless, her mouth open in shock. Did she . . . did she want Bonnie to *thank* her for what she did?

Gwendolyn smirked at Bonnie's outrage. "The king conquers other countries so he can find a way to restore magic." She snorted. "As if that was the way to do it."

"Then who told him that was how he'd free it?"

A small, secret smile. "That doesn't matter. What matters, my dear, is that he believed it. He believed he needed to conquer others to restore what was lost. Which left almost the entire continent devoid of magic."

Bonnie had a feeling she knew what Gwendolyn was getting at but asked anyway. "Your point?"

"My point? My point is *this*."

And with a flourish, Gwendolyn reached her hand down and plunged it in the puddle of Bonnie's blood. She leaned forward so quickly that Bonnie had no time to react, only watch as she made several markings with Bonnie's blood.

Nothing happened. It was very anticlimactic, really.

And then the writing on the floor turned white and almost seemed to pulse with heat.

A gust of wind shot outwards from the symbols, shattering the glass window panes.

And Bonnie fell to her knees as the entire world shook.

BONNIE BARELY REGISTERED THE PAIN OF HER KNEES HITTING THE stone floor.

That pain was *nothing* compared to the shock that reverberated throughout her entire body.

All of her nerve endings were on fire. She opened her mouth in a silent scream, convinced she was about to die from the agony of it all.

Gwendolyn's scarred face contorted into a look of pure ecstasy as she cackled towards the ceiling. She wasn't in pain, which Bonnie had trouble comprehending.

How was she immune to this torture?

The floor was covered with shards of sparkling glass. Screams could be heard inside and outside the castle, eerily similar to the screaming Bonnie had heard from this room twelve years ago.

The world was about to end. There was no way she could endure any more of this and live.

. . .

AND JUST LIKE THE PAIN STARTED, IT STOPPED.

Bonnie couldn't move from her spot on the floor. Her muscles felt like jelly, and she wasn't sure she could stand.

Gwendolyn didn't seem to notice. She was too busy celebrating.

Anger coursed through Bonnie at the sight of the woman who simultaneously ruined and spared her life. Her fingers twitched as she regained feeling in them. She wasn't entirely sure what had just happened, but she focused on one thought:

Gwendolyn needed to die.

Movement. A flock of dark-colored sparrows soared through the window, flying straight towards Gwendolyn. She screamed and slashed blindly at them with her knife, widely missing their little bodies.

Something bolted through the open door. A black cat jumped on Gwendolyn's back, digging its claws into her sensitive flesh before it was thrown towards the wall by the force of the older woman's flailing.

Dogs barked and horses screamed down below. People shouted in pain and fear.

What was happening?

Gritting her teeth, Bonnie stumbled to her feet. It was time to end this.

It took only seven steps to reach Gwendolyn, who was still trying to fight off the birds.

"Enough," Bonnie barked, not sure if they would understand her. But they did, somehow, and flew back outside through the shattered window.

Gwendolyn only had a moment to catch her breath before Bonnie stabbed a knife into her heart.

Eyes wide, face covered in marks left by little beaks, Gwendolyn's mouth opened in shock.

Bonnie grabbed her by the shoulders and laid her down,

right over the symbols now burned into the stone. And then she removed the knife.

"You'll regret this," Gwendolyn whispered, as blood started flowing out of her chest.

"Why did you do this? Why did you do any of this?" Bonnie whispered as she memorized Gwendolyn's scarred face.

Gwendolyn only snarled, and Bonnie knew she would get no more answers from her.

"Goodbye, mother dear," she said, as she sank to the floor. She intended to watch the light leave Gwendolyn's eyes. Only then would she be sure that she was dead.

Too many people had died and come back to life here, Bonnie thought, a little maniacally. Herself included.

She thought watching the life drain out of her adopted mother would give her a sense of pleasure or satisfaction. It did neither. She just felt exhausted.

Still, Bonnie watched. The blood started to drip out of the side of Gwendolyn's mouth, and she heard her raspy inhales. Saw Gwendolyn's fingers twitch toward her side.

Gwendolyn said something too faint to hear.

"What?" Bonnie lurched forward, too exhausted to be graceful about it.

"I should've done this twelve years ago," Gwendolyn said, and plunged her knife into Bonnie's chest.

CHAPTER THIRTY-NINE

Pain.
Muffled sounds.
Extreme pressure.
Choking.
More pain.
Blissful oblivion.

Bonnie woke to the sound of snoring.

She kept her breathing even, unwilling to let her captors know she was awake. Maybe she'd be able to startle them enough to incapacitate them somehow.

She seemed to be in a bed of some sort, inclined at the waist, and covered with a blanket that felt soft to her limited touch. The air smelled clean; not the same stench she woke up to after Thornwick.

Maybe she could use the blanket to tie up her captor, she thought desperately. Use it as a noose if she had to.

She wiggled her fingers, and then her toes. Searched for her constant headache. No pain anywhere.

Was she dead? She hadn't been pain free in over a decade.

The sound of snoring shifted, as if the other person was starting to wake. She cracked one eye open to get a glimpse. Her mouth dropped open.

King Rupert Aborn sat in a chair by her bedside. Dressed casually, he was regal even slumped over. His hair was in disarray, as if he had repeatedly run his hands through it.

How easy it would be to kill him right now.

The man who ruled the continent, asleep at her bedside. Had anyone informed him what she did for a living?

Would he be disappointed to learn what she had become?

He startled awake, eyes wide. Rising halfway out of his chair, his hand moved to his hip, ready to grab the sword strapped there.

"It's just me," she said. It came out as a strangled whisper, and she raised a hand to her throat.

He reached out a shaking hand but stopped before he touched her, probably noting her flinch. He withdrew his hand.

"You were screaming," he said. "Your throat may feel tender."

She nodded, swallowing hard. It was strange to see him hovering there, only a foot away.

Her father.

The king she was taught to hate.

Her heart beat wildly as she shoved all of her programmed feelings down, down, down.

To bide time, she looked around. She wore a cotton shirt, plain but comfortable. She moved the fabric aside to assess the damage from Gwendolyn's attack.

Where she expected to see a fatal stab wound, she saw . . . nothing.

Well, almost nothing. A thin white scar now marred her skin, a few inches above her heart. She ran a finger across it and was amazed to find that it was completely smooth.

She looked at him with wide eyes. "How did I survive?"

"Magic."

Bonnie stilled. "What?"

But even as she questioned it, she realized it was the truth.

The glowing symbols.

The pain as the released magic overloaded her senses.

The rush of air that shattered the windows.

Magic had returned to Hallordis.

It was a miracle. Gwendolyn had been the one to banish magic — and the one who brought it back.

"Did she live?" She didn't need to say who she was referring to.

He shook his head, mouth set in a frown. He cleared his throat. "I, uh, know she raised you, so, I'd understand if you're upset she didn't make it —"

"No," Bonnie interrupted, her voice firm. "She deserved to die a thousand deaths for what she did. Not only to us, but to the rest of the continent as well."

He nodded, and Bonnie swore she saw a look of relief cross his face. He sighed, sitting down.

"Where are we?" she asked.

"Castle infirmary," he said. "In one of the private rooms." He chuckled sadly. "You used to spend quite a fair bit of time here when you were younger, you know," he said. "How are you feeling?"

"Alive. Great, actually. Who healed me?"

"I did," said a familiar voice from across the room.

Bonnie couldn't stop her smile at the sight of Freddie standing in the doorway.

He looked worse for wear. There were dark circles under his eyes, and his hair was disheveled. His shirt was covered in blood, though she didn't think it was his.

The smile that lit up his face took Bonnie's breath away.

"About time you woke up, honeybum," he said, as he strode

into the room. He winced when he locked eyes with the king. "Apologies, Your Majesty."

Bonnie laughed, the sound foreign to her ears. When was the last time she had something to laugh about?

Freddie grinned as he took the seat on the other side of the bed.

"How long was I unconscious?" she asked, looking between the two of them. She was half convinced this was an elaborate dream.

"Just overnight," Freddie said. "But you lost a lot of blood." A shadow crossed his face. "We weren't sure if you were going to make it."

She swallowed. "Thank you," was all she could think of to say.

"He didn't do it alone, girl," another familiar voice said from just beyond the door.

Bronwyn hobbled in on the arm of an amused guard. He deposited her in a bedside chair, bowed to the king and to Bonnie, and left the room.

"Bronwyn," Bonnie said. She reached out and took one of the old woman's gnarled hands in hers. "What are you doing here? I thought you were supposed to stay at Freddie's house."

"Bah," Bronwyn said, squeezing Bonnie's hand before letting go. "The boys were concerned about my safety and tried to keep me there. But I had a feeling I would be needed at the castle before the day was done."

"Well, then. Thank you."

Bronwyn nodded in acceptance. "Now tell us what happened."

Bonnie looked at the three people surrounding her bedside and took a deep breath. She began her tale, starting from when she had left Freddie's side. While she was relieved to hear that Stiles lived, her relief was short-lived when she recalled the conclusions she had made about Gwendolyn's reasons for returning to Midverd.

The magical soldiers. The magical weapons.

"The city has been secured," the king assured her. "I've already sent men to Stoneforge to lock it down and to confiscate any weapons, magical or otherwise."

Bonnie hoped it would be enough.

She continued her tale, hoping she remembered correctly. Everything happened so fast, though, and she worried she would forget something.

She told them about confronting Gwendolyn, and the blood marks on the floor. About what Gwendolyn said about the king's incessant quest for more power.

"Oll Blackthorn told me the only way I could bring magic back was by gaining complete control over the continent," her father said, his brow furrowed. "He showed me documentation from elder mages that supported his claims. I sent my own people to confirm the information he shared with me, of course . . . Why do you think I met with him all these years? It wasn't for the company, I assure you. I knew he was withholding information, though, which is why I kept meeting with him."

"So it's true?" Bonnie asked, eyes wide. "You really met with him regularly?"

Her father nodded. "I need to think about what this all means," he said when he saw that Bonnie and Freddie looked ready to ask more questions. "Please continue."

She told them about how Gwendolyn never loved Oren or Oll, and had only used them in her quest to become queen. And about how the Amlucen wanted her father to remain in power, despite their efforts to remove him from the throne.

"If that was the case, I don't understand why the Amlucen existed in the first place," Bonnie said. "Why create a rebellion intent on destroying the monarchy when you want the monarchy to remain in power?"

"I told you they were a bunch of crazy fanatics," Bronwyn muttered.

Bonnie snorted and continued. She paused when she remembered the animals who attacked on her behalf. "I don't understand what happened. It's like they all went crazy."

Her father gave her a strange look. "You don't . . . you don't remember?"

Bronwyn cackled. "Of course she doesn't remember, Rupert. She lost all her memories."

" . . . Remember what?" Bonnie cut in as the king opened his mouth to argue with the old witch.

His eyes widened. "You can wield magic, Char — Bonnie."

"What?" Surely he was lying. She couldn't wield magic.

"We discovered you could communicate with animals from a very young age."

Communicate with animals?

No. She couldn't talk to animals.

Maybe this *was* an elaborate dream. That was the only explanation.

Bonnie looked at Freddie for support, but saw a slow smile cross his face instead.

"I knew it!" he said, pumping his fist in the air. "It makes sense. Your animal friends joined you wherever we went, but were far more active outside of Bronwyn's cottage. You acted like it was an everyday occurrence — and maybe for you it was. But the behavior was certainly not normal."

Her father smiled. "Do they still follow you around? The littlest creatures loved you the most. We had to keep a water bowl in your bedchamber for all the animals that found their way into your bed." His smile turned down as a look of longing crossed his face. "Your mother loved it. She was happy you had friends wherever you went."

Bonnie swallowed hard and nodded.

Bronwyn reached over and pat the king's arm gently, an awfully intimate gesture for a member of royalty. Bonnie supposed the witch was old enough to get away with flaunting the rules of propriety.

Communicate with animals. The more she thought about it, the more it seemed right. A warm feeling spread through her chest, and another puzzle piece fell into place.

It was true animals followed her wherever she went — Gwendolyn hated it, and tried to forbid the little creatures from the rebel hideouts. Bonnie had snuck them in anyway.

Maybe it wasn't because the dead woman actually hated animals, Bonnie thought. Maybe she forbade them because she feared that Bonnie would suddenly remember her ability to communicate with them.

She shook her head to clear those thoughts. She had a lot to think about when she had a moment to herself.

"The magic," Bronwyn whispered. "I should have known it was you." The old woman's hands were shaking in her lap, her eyes brimming with unshed tears.

Bonnie looked at her curiously. "What?"

Bronwyn's head swiveled towards her. Before she could speak, Bonnie watched as the king took Bronwyn's hand in his larger one.

"Mother, it's alright. Why would you have any reason to think the rebel you were harboring was our Charlotte?"

"Mother?" Bonnie gasped.

She looked at Freddie for confirmation. He nodded, his face impassive as he looked between the three of them.

"You — you're not —" Bonnie trailed off, at a loss for words.

The king looked at his mother, one eyebrow raised. "You didn't tell her I was your son?"

"She most certainly did not," Bonnie muttered.

Bronwyn was her grandmother?

Bronwyn sniffed. "Of course I didn't. She was a rebel fugitive, Rupert. Oh, you should've heard the fights we got into about you. The bloody Amlucen did a number on her. It wouldn't have been safe to tell her."

That's for sure. Bonnie most definitely would've done something to win an advantage for the rebellion had she known. Hold the old woman for ransom, maybe. Threaten to kill her unless the king abdicated his throne.

Now it made sense why Bronwyn said that both King Aborn and King Thorstan allowed her to live on the border of Hallordis and Suverd; she was their mother.

And a former queen, Bonnie remembered. King Thorstan took over rule of Suverd once his parents abdicated. Bonnie would've never guessed that she had been in the company of royalty all this time.

The king looked at Bonnie with concern. Maybe it was finally dawning on him that the daughter before him was a far different person than he remembered.

"You said that Bonnie felt familiar to you," Freddie said from his side of the bed. His eyes were on Bonnie, assessing.

"You said that, too," Bonnie said to him. "Did we meet . . . before?"

Freddie shook his head. "No. Father kept Jasper and I in Navian for most of our childhood. I met your lovely aunt, but not you. I think you seemed familiar to me because of your likeness to the king."

Bonnie stared down at her hands. She felt a headache coming on and knew it wasn't from her temple scar. She couldn't even begin to sort through everything she had learned over the past day.

Everything was different. And she didn't know how she fit in anymore.

"I think it's time we let Bonnie rest," the king said, rising to his feet with a groan. "Healing takes a lot out of someone."

Bonnie nodded in thanks, swallowing past the tightness in her throat. She watched as her father escorted Bronwyn out of the room, leaving her with Freddie.

"How are you doing?" he asked as soon as the door shut.

"Overwhelmed," she admitted, playing with the soft fabric of her blanket.

Understatement of the year.

He reached forward, taking her hand. She felt his calluses scrape against hers as she rotated her palm, interlacing their fingers.

If he was surprised by the gesture, he didn't show it. Together they sat there, fingers entwined, and said nothing for a very long time.

CHAPTER FORTY

Bonnie woke to the sound of a commotion outside of her room.

She had slept in the infirmary, unsure of where else to go. She certainly wasn't going to return to her old bedchamber.

She jumped to her feet and cursed her lack of weapons. Ear to the door, she heard low curses and stomping feet. When the sounds faded, she opened it and peered out.

Four soldiers moved down the corridor toward one of the other private rooms. Judging by their stooped forms and halting steps, she guessed they carried something heavy between them.

Footsteps behind her. She turned to see another soldier. Fighting the urge to attack — until yesterday they had been her enemy, after all — she locked eyes with him.

He stopped, bowing low.

Interesting, she thought. Word must have spread about the sudden reappearance of the long-lost princess.

"What's going on?" she asked.

The soldier's eyes widened, and she saw his throat bob as he swallowed. "Oll Blackthorn, Princess," he said. "Wait!" he cried, as she turned and ran down the corridor.

Bonnie caught up to the guards quickly, telling them to stop. They did as they were told, no doubt hearing the panic in her voice. They were carrying someone on a litter, and a white cloth covered the body.

She peeled back the cloth covering and couldn't hold back her gasp.

Oll Blackthorn, feared leader of the Amlucen, was dead.

His eyes stared sightlessly at the ceiling, and Bonnie could tell from his haunted expression that he died in pain.

She ignored the guard's protest as she carefully peeled the cloth away.

Dozens of stab wounds covered his body — it looked like he had been stabbed and sliced and stabbed again. There was no way he could've done this to himself — there were far too many deep wounds for it to be self-inflicted. He would've bled out.

It was fitting, Bonnie thought, that Oll Blackthorn died by the knives he loved so much.

"Who did this?" she asked, her voice eerily calm.

"We don't know, Princess. We found him this morning."

The king had told her that Oll had been housed in the high-security wing of the dungeons. How could he have been murdered?

She reached out and stroked Oll's face with a finger.

Cold. And judging by his position, he looked stiff. He must've been dead for hours.

She withdrew her finger when she realized how odd she must look. She nodded to the soldier and returned to her room.

Bonnie changed out of her nightclothes and into a fussy, itchy dress that had been left for her, making a mental note to visit the castle seamstress to find something more comfortable to wear. She was an assassin, damn it. She needed more practical clothes.

There was only one person she wanted to speak to about Oll, and she knew just where to find him.

TWENTY MINUTES LATER SHE KNOCKED ON THE HEAVY WOODEN door that led into one of the castle's many turrets. Two burly guards stood outside, the only sign that this room housed someone of importance.

"Go away," a familiar voice called down. She let out the breath she hadn't realized she'd been holding.

She smirked as she climbed the stairs up to Felix's tower room. He sat at a table by one of the windows, his fingers stained with ink as he wrote into a journal of some sorts. He appeared to be healthy, though he had the haggard look of someone who had a rough go. Not tortured, like she half expected.

The room was large. Clean. A comfortable-looking bed sat near one corner, and there was a private bathing chamber. Not a typical prison cell.

"Should I go?" she asked.

He stood, a look of relief crossing his face, and she was glad to see that his movement was smooth, unhindered by his wounds from Stoneforge.

"Bonnie." He gave her a mocking bow. "Or should I say, Princess Charlotte? Nice dress."

"'Your highness' will do quite nicely, I think," she said, and grinned. "This dress is horrible, but it does conceal knives pretty well." She lifted one of the many layers of fabric, showing him a knife she pilfered from the kitchens on the way here.

She stopped a foot away, unsure of what to do next. Hug him? Punch him? Sit at the table and pretend they were civilized adults?

He took a step forward and threw his arms around her. She melted into him, and all the tears that she had held inside cascaded down her face.

"I'm sorry," he said, shuddering with a sob of his own.

"For what?" she asked, holding him tighter.

"Everything."

She leaned back, still holding onto his neck. "What do you mean?" she sniffed.

He squeezed her arms gently and released her, motioning for her to sit at the table. "For being a shit brother. For not protecting you from Oll and Gwyneth. For abandoning you." He wiped his face. "I was jealous — you were always going off and fighting others and being important." He chuckled darkly. "Now that I've had a taste of adventure I can finally say I no longer wish to be you."

She gave him a watery smile. "Let's blame the misunderstanding on our upbringing." She cleared her throat. "I killed mother."

"I know." He held his hand up. "I wish I had been there to see it."

"You're not mad?" she asked as she gave him a high-five.

"Mad? The bitch got what she deserved."

Bonnie agreed. Her only regret was not forcing Gwendolyn to answer *why* she did what she did. Why attack Bonnie all those years ago only to heal her and then raise her?

Now she'd never know.

"I'm sorry about your father," she said instead.

She wasn't. Not really. But she figured she had to say it. Oll was Felix's only living parent, after all. Now he had no one.

Felix's face grew somber. "I heard the news. I take it that's why you're here?"

"Yes and no. I meant to come yesterday, but I couldn't leave my room."

"Being stabbed by dear old Gwyneth does that to a person."

Bonnie laughed. "It does, doesn't it?" She frowned. "How did you find out about Oll?"

"Your father, actually," Felix said. "I believe I was his first stop after he examined the body. I think he wanted to see if I'd been murdered as well."

Bonnie swallowed. The thought had occurred to her, too, but she hadn't wanted to admit how worried she'd been for his safety.

"King Rupert Aborn." He whistled. "You act like him, you know. Some of your mannerisms are the same. It's a bit unnerving."

She was getting tired of hearing that. "Did you know who I was? Did you know who your father brought into the family?"

"Not until Stoneforge. I had always accepted your back-story — who was I to think it was anything but the truth? I was only nine when you joined us. Only recently did I start to question everything."

"Why?"

"Something changed with Gwyneth — *Gwendolyn*," he corrected himself. "You weren't around much, but things got bad. She muttered to herself all the time. Constantly traveled to Suverd. Froze Father out more than normal. I started asking questions, and she started getting angry. In Stoneforge I found a book — one of the few that hadn't been censored. There was a picture of the royal family and I recognized you immediately."

Bonnie had figured as much. "But it's been *twelve years* since I started my life as Bonnie Blackthorn. Oll and Gwendolyn kept me away from pictures and written things — easy to do, considering I couldn't read or write. But you're a bookworm. How have you never seen a picture of the royal family?"

His mouth turned down, and his eyes looked sad as he cleared his throat. "I didn't want to go against their teachings. The few times they sent me on missions I could've learned more about how things really worked. But I was scared. I didn't want to believe they were lying."

Bonnie understood that. She didn't hold it against him — he spent his entire life under their thumbs. "Did you know who Gwyneth really was?"

He shook his head. "There were no pictures of her in that book; it only mentioned that the late queen had a sister. She would've resembled the queen — your mother, I suppose — but with her scars it was hard to make the connection. How are *you* feeling about everything?"

"I'm not sure," she admitted. "I don't think I've processed it all, to be honest. I'm not sure I'll ever be able to process it." She'd take time to reflect later, when things weren't so crazy.

Or she would shove everything down and deal with it in the distant future. Maybe.

She changed the subject. "How do you feel now that he's gone? Now that they're both gone?"

"Relieved. Mother dearest and I didn't exactly part on good terms. And Oll wasn't the best father in the world."

A snort. "That's an understatement. What happened after Stoneforge?"

"I nearly bled to death stumbling through Golwich. I managed to hide from the rebels she sent after me, but it was a close call. Then the strangest thing happened — a horse found me. A gray one, wearing rebel tack. What's wrong?" he asked, when Bonnie's mouth opened in shock.

"A gray horse, you said?" She barked out a laugh. "That was the horse that I took from the stables when I fled."

"No kidding. Well, then, I suppose a thank you is in order."

She gave him a mocking bow.

"Your horse," he mused, sitting back with a chuckle. "I thought it was too good to be true."

"What happened after?"

"Rode to Thornwick, where I finally lost consciousness. I was patched up by the King's Guard and promptly arrested." He snorted. "They took an interest in me once they figured out who I was. I was brought here shortly after."

"Here? To this room?"

Was this really where prisoners were kept?

"No, I was housed in the dungeons for a bit. Hey, don't be upset — it wasn't bad. I wasn't mistreated. The food could use some seasoning, but it was nowhere near as bad as father said it would be."

"When did you move to this room?"

"Yesterday."

Freddie probably told the king to move his accommodations, Bonnie thought.

He clapped twice. "No more delay. I told you my story — now it's time to tell me yours."

So Bonnie did.

Felix kept quiet through most of it, although he exclaimed loudly when she recalled the part about going through Gwendolyn's velvet bag. Otherwise, he held his tongue, which Bonnie appreciated.

Once she was done, they sat in silence. She gestured to the notebook he had been writing in. "What are you writing? Your memoir?"

He snorted. "No. The king asked if I had any thoughts on who killed my father." He sighed. "The list is quite long, unfortunately."

Bonnie's lips quirked. Oll certainly had no shortage of enemies. She sighed, putting her head in her hands. "I'm exhausted, Felix. I'm so godsdamn tired."

"I know," he said. "I know."

"I should find the king," she said, standing up wearily. "See if he knows anything about what happened to Oll. Do you want to come?"

"No, I'm quite content here, thank you."

She nodded and turned to go.

"I'm an orphan now," Felix said with a dramatic sigh.

She turned. "We may not be related by blood, but you'll always be my brother."

He gave her a sad smile.

She paused in the doorway and looked back. "Hold on. Were you the one who told Claire and Stefan to keep me away from Stoneforge?"

Felix swallowed and then nodded.

"Why?"

"It was the only way I could think of to get you out of there. Things weren't good with us, but . . . I've always loved you, little sister. You deserved a better life."

Bonnie had given up on trying to find her father.

She searched high and low, dodging courtiers who looked at her with interest, King's Guard members who looked at her with suspicion, and palace servants who weren't sure *how* to look at her. No one would tell her where he was, and she supposed she couldn't blame them.

Even *she* didn't know how she fit in here.

She made her way back to the infirmary, wondering where he could be. Two guards stood outside of her door. How annoying. Although she supposed it was time that someone stopped her adventuring around the castle. They probably forgot to assign her a guard.

Saluting them cheekily, she entered her room. And stopped short.

The king sat in the bedside chair, and he did not look pleased.

"Oh, hello," she said awkwardly. She sat down in one of the other chairs.

"Good afternoon, Char — Bonnie," he said. Bonnie could see a vein in his temple throb. "Where have you been?"

"Looking for you," she said carefully. "I spoke to Felix."

"You heard about Oll." A statement, not a question.

Bonnie nodded.

He glared at her. "Last night, a man was murdered in our high-security dungeons — the man who raised you. Imagine my surprise and horror when I came here, and *you were gone.*" His voice, so careful and measured, fractured as his chest started to rise and fall rapidly.

Bonnie swallowed.

"You could've been hurt, you could've been taken. You could've been killed —"

"I am perfectly capable of handling myself —"

"I will not lose you again, Charlotte Robin Aborn! It nearly broke me the first time."

Oh.

Oh.

For the first time in twelve years, Bonnie reached out and touched her father's hand. It was large, and warm, and a flood of memories washed over her.

The two of them running through the corridors, laughing.

Sparring with wooden swords, a ring of soldiers laughing merrily at the concentration on her eight-year-old face.

Cozy dinners in his rooms, Bonnie's mother watching them as she worked on needlepoint by the light of the fire.

The king stilled when her hand touched his; she wasn't sure he was breathing. He turned his hand slowly, clutching hers tightly.

Tears streamed down his face.

The mighty Rupert Aborn, conqueror of the continent, brought to tears by a single touch.

Slowly, cautiously — as though she were a wounded animal — he pulled her into his arms. And Bonnie, who lacked love and affection for so many years, found herself crying again for the second time that day.

CHAPTER FORTY-ONE

THE NEXT FEW DAYS WERE CHAOTIC.

No one could figure out who murdered Oll; it was as if the assassin had disappeared without a trace.

The king had more pressing issues to deal with than figuring out who murdered the leader of the Amlucen, even if the circumstances were strange.

Magic was now free in the kingdom.

Magic-wielders had their abilities once more. Children who had never even *seen* magic found that they, too, were now blessed with magical abilities.

It was wondrous.

It was as if the land had come alive. The sky was bluer, the grass greener. Even the winter's chill didn't seem as foreboding as it normally did this time of year.

Water-wielders created intricate works of art that quickly froze in the winter's chill. Flowers, normally dormant, were now seen in window boxes, brightening up the drab city streets. Beautiful music, unheard in over a decade, was now easily played by magically gifted musicians.

Dying people were healed. Sick people were cured.

But it was also dangerous.

A fire-wielding child accidentally set a city block on fire. A teenager, gifted with supernatural climbing ability, had the sudden urge to start stealing from unsuspecting neighbors. Criminals used their newly returned abilities to break out of the local prison, leaving chaos and destruction in their wake.

The king sent scribes and soldiers throughout Hallordis to count the magically gifted. Not to round them up to control them, as Bonnie first feared, but to figure out what resources needed to be recreated to educate the magical population. There had been a magical infrastructure in place before Vale Magicae — Bonnie was sure it would only be a matter of time before things settled down again. She, too, was excited to learn more about her own newfound powers.

And then there was the rebellion to deal with.

To say the rebels were incensed would be an understatement. Crime increased tenfold, and the number of fights between members of the King's Guard and the Rebel Guard put everyone on edge. A curfew was instated throughout Midverd and beyond, and hordes of the king's soldiers patrolled constantly to keep the peace.

Amlucenites had been trained to ignore directives from the king — Bonnie knew it would be futile for her father to simply announce that the leaders of the rebellion were corrupt, or that the rebellion itself was based on falsehoods. *Especially* considering both of their leaders were murdered in the castle. Bonnie knew they would have to convince the rebels to stand down another way.

Felix thought of it first.

The Treehaven rebels.

Freddie had been right — captured rebels were sent to Treehaven to work for food and shelter, not murdered in cold blood like Bonnie had been led to believe. It was a desensitization of sorts, a safe place where the rebels could unlearn the Amlucen ways of life.

Who better to convince the angry rebels that the king wasn't evil than their former comrades?

Felix left the castle to journey to Treehaven. Traveling with a contingent of King's Guards, his mission was to bring a few converted rebels back to Midverd to help spread the word to stand down.

It was worth a shot. Bonnie just wished she could help — she didn't want to see a single rebel die because of the mess created by her former parents. That desire, at least, didn't change. Even if her life looked completely different now.

She couldn't calm the rebels, as Oll and Gwendolyn had declared a bounty on her head after the events in Stoneforge. And her identity as the long-lost princess was being kept secret until the unrest died down.

So where did she fit in now?

She moved from the hospital infirmary to her own private suite of rooms, far enough away from her old bedchamber that she could avoid it entirely if she wished.

And although she groaned about it, she eventually accepted the rotating group of guards that stood watch outside her room. She found she could easily sneak past them if the need arose.

Which it didn't. She couldn't resist checking, though. And late night trips to the kitchens for sweet treats tasted better when no one else knew about it.

Bonnie was stretching in her new room when there was a knock at the door. She looked up to see Freddie standing in the doorway.

"Getting limber?" he asked as he strode in. "Going to assassinate someone today, Princess?"

She smiled and then groaned as she kneaded a sore spot on her calf. "Just finished running with the King's Guard," she said. "I'm out of shape."

"I doubt that," he said as he took a seat by the open window. He sat in the comfortable armchair she had put there after noticing he favored a similar one in the library.

"What's on your agenda today, princess?"

"You really don't have to call me that," she grumbled. It was bad enough that the guards did.

"Fine. What's on your agenda today, honeybum?"

She snorted. "I don't know. Spy on members of the court. Mentally map out the layout of the castle. Eavesdrop on the kitchen staff." Amlucen habits died hard. She swallowed. "Meet my new family."

His honey-brown eyes lit up. "Ah, so the rumors *are* true. I heard that Queen Celeste and her merry brood were returning today. How do you feel about meeting them?"

Bonnie dug her thumb deeper into the knot on her calf. "I'm not sure. It's been nice to pretend that I haven't been replaced."

Bonnie's half-siblings, Rosamund and Jameson, were a few years younger. King Thorstan of Suverd — Bonnie's uncle, which was strange to think about — had also traveled to Midverd to lend his support.

"Bonnie, my dear, you weren't *replaced*."

"I know, I know," she flapped her hand at him. "I just . . . I don't know where I belong anymore. And now I have to deal with family members I didn't know existed. Who didn't know *I* existed. What will they think of me? That I'm the king's half-feral daughter raised by anarchists?"

That's what members of the kitchen staff thought, anyway. They hadn't realized she'd been listening from one of the alcoves in the servant's staircase.

They weren't the only ones displeased by her reappearance. Other courtiers mumbled about the sudden influx of animals.

"This castle is turning into a menagerie," one stiff-lipped nobleman had said when he thought Bonnie wasn't listening. And while she was usually accompanied by at least one animal, at least *they* behaved themselves.

Freddie kneeled next to where she sat on the floor, taking her hand. "Everything will be fine. And if it's not, we'll weather it. Together. You couldn't get rid of me the first day you met me and you're not getting rid of me now."

Bonnie felt tension leave her body. She didn't want him to go, but wasn't sure how to ask him to stay. What if he was needed back in Navian?

Jasper and Simon had both returned to the northern country, and while they were shocked when they learned her true identity, she could tell that Simon would never fully trust her.

Good. She liked his consistency.

Bronwyn didn't treat her differently, either, even if she had somewhat softened toward the former rebel. The old witch had no qualms about arguing with her granddaughter, princess or not. Or her son, which Bonnie was glad to see. She was staying in the castle for the winter, and she and Freddie spent most of their days training new healers.

Bonnie and her father were still figuring things out. They'd been separated for twelve years, Bonnie kept reminding herself; they wouldn't be able to establish a new normal overnight. For now they treaded carefully, their conversations limited to an abundance of pleasantries and neutral topics.

With a final squeeze, Freddie released her hand and returned to his chair. He sprawled out, closing his eyes with a yawn. "Wake me in a few hours."

"Rough night?" she asked, trying not to stare.

He grinned at the ceiling, his eyes still closed. "Good book," he said. "Couldn't put it down."

Minutes later, he was snoring. Very undignified, for a lord — especially for the son of the king's advisor.

He looked peaceful as he slept. Beautiful, even. Dark brown hair curled over his forehead, stirred by the gentle breeze coming from the open window.

Bonnie smiled as she went to her bathing chamber. Things had certainly changed, she thought as she stared at herself in the mirror. But at least she still had Freddie.

She was a princess, yes.

But she would always be a rebel, too.

She would always bear the scars of her history.

And, she thought, as she undid the braid that covered up the scar on her temple, maybe that wasn't such a bad thing.

THE END

THANK YOU

Thank you for reading Bonnie's journey!

The best way to support an indie author is to rate, review, and share your thoughts — don't forget to rate and review BLACKTHORN!

WANT MORE BONNIE & FREDDIE?

Subscribe to my newsletter for sneak peeks, bonus content, writing updates on the currently untitled sequel, and more!

Check out my website for more information: emilyevewrites.com

Follow me on:
- Instagram: @authoremilyeve
- Threads: @authoremilyeve

ACKNOWLEDGMENTS

How do I even begin to thank all of the amazing friends and family who helped me publish this book?

First off I want to thank my amazing family for being an incredible support system. Mom and Dad, JD, Kevin, and Lillie — I love you all to pieces and thank you for supporting me in everything I do.

Mom — thank you for instilling a love of reading in me from a young age 🖤 I love you!

Dad — thank you for championing my story (even though I'm pretty sure this is the first fantasy book you've ever read). I love you! 🖤

To Julie and Krista — thank you for not only accepting me into your family, but also for loving my kiddos. You two are the best in-laws I could've ever hoped for.

To my AMAZING Alpha/Beta readers — Katie A., Melissa B., Olivia B., Jacqui C., Jacqui C., Anna D., Ariah D., Erica F., Kristin F., JD H., Katie O., Meghan P., Kaelie S., Abigail S., — this book would be nowhere near as polished without your feedback, optimism, and — most importantly — your love. Endlessly thankful for all of you (and my sincerest apologies if I forgot anyone!)

To Meghan, my first reader and cheerleader — THANK YOU FOREVER. To Jacqui, the person I go to for all of my marketing questions — THANK YOU FOREVER. To Lindsay, for being on my cheer squad since sixth grade — THANK YOU FOREVER.

To Anna — thank you for writing *The Witches Ball* with me so long ago. You're my best friend and your support means the world.

To Melissa B. & Jacqui C. & Katie O. — you three were some of my first hype women and I LOVE you for it! Thanks for being such a big part of my journey!

To Robin Dykema — ROBIN! You, my dear friend, have been one of my biggest supporters when writing this book, and I miss our in-person writing sessions in Austin. I love and miss you!

To Julia — this novel would've looked COMPLETELY different without your input at the start of my writing process. Thank you for your suggestions — HALLORDIS FOREVER.

To my Austin Mom Gang <3 (Anna, Brianne, Brittany, Eden, Emily, Hayley, Kaelie, Melissa, and Sky) — thank you for being the best support system a mama could have. I wouldn't have survived the newborn/toddler stage without you guys! I love you and I miss you and y'all are the best.

To the Austin Creative Fiction Writing group — our time together may have been short, but the insight I got from joining your ranks for those two years helped bolster my confidence enough to release this story. Thank you to everyone who helped me get back into the creative writing groove!

To Jessica Julien aka my amazing editor from Desert Ink Editorial — you are a goddess and a wonderful human and I cannot thank you enough for helping me polish this story!

To Michelle, the YA librarian at the Peabody Institute Library of Danvers — thank you for welcoming me into your little corner of the library when I was a teen and handing me a copy of *The Hunger Games*. I know it's been a long time since I've seen you, but I'll never forget the impact you had on me as a teen. Thank you.

And finally, to Luke and Lucy and Amelia and Teddy —

thank you. I love you all so, so much. I couldn't ask for a better, more supportive husband or three more perfect gremlins to call my own. Mama loves you, always and forever.

Thank you to the readers who gave Blackthorn a chance. You rock, don't ever change, HAGS <3

ABOUT THE AUTHOR

Emily Eve was born and raised on the north shore of Massachusetts, where she lived for the first twenty-five years of her life. After briefly relocating to Austin, Texas, she moved back home and now resides in southern New Hampshire with her husband, three kiddos, two dogs (Bonnie and Clyde), and two cats (Rio and Pippa). Follow her on social media or join her newsletter for more updates.

Instagram/Threads: @authoremilyeve

Website: emilyevewrites.com